Nefertiti, Immortal Queen

Second edition, Talespinner Press, June, 2010

Nefertiti, Immortal Queen

A Novel
by
Cheryl L. Fluty

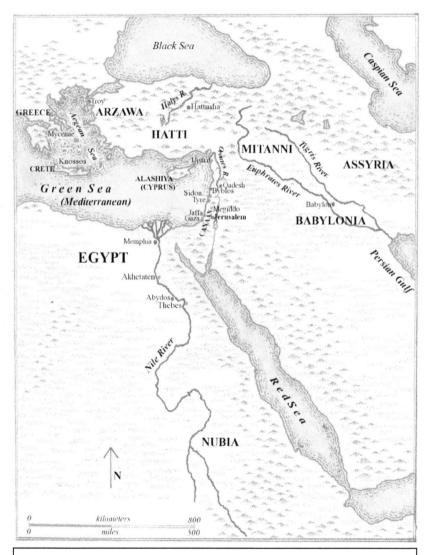

Egypt and the Middle East c. 1350 BC

Prologue

Inscription on the wall of a tomb in the mountains above the Valley of the Kings, Egypt - 1325 BC

I, Thutmose, son of Ahhotep the potter, record these lines here on the wall of my tomb to preserve the memory of my beloved lady, Queen Nefertiti – may she be justified! Her enemies killed her and tried to erase her from history, but my hands have preserved her name and image for eternity, that she may reign immortal.

I am an artist, and for many years, was Chief of Works to His Majesty, Akhenaten - may he be justified! He was my king, my benefactor and my friend. I loved him and served him, and only after his death did I betray his trust.

During my Lord Pharaoh's reign, I served him and his god, the Aten. If it be that this sun deity's power does not extend to the darkness of the underworld after one's ka has left the body, I pray that the ancient gods of the Two Lands will forgive me and justify me before the Forty-two Assessors. May my life balance in the scales against the divine Feather of Ma'at!

I pray, above all, for my beloved Lady, Queen Nefertiti, may she be justified! During her life on earth, I served her with all my heart and hands and body. After her departure from this life, I served her with my paintbrush, my chisel and my pen, to preserve her image and her name in ink, paint and stone. If you regard her image in the works of my hands, O Lover of Beauty, you will see my love for her in every stroke of my brush, every strike of my chisel. And if, O Pilgrim, you stand here reading these lines in my tomb, and you see the scenes painted on these walls, you will know the fullness of my love, the depth of my devotion, and the extent of my treason. May the Aten grant Eternal Life to my Beloved Nefertiti! And may we be united at last in that eternal afterlife, as we could not be on this earth!

Chapter 1: Advent

Thutmose froze when ne neara voices approacning beyond the tall reeds. Looking around, he realized with a sense of rising panic that he had penetrated much farther than he had intended to, well beyond the boundaries of the royal estate. Flattening himself into the mud at the edge of the royal pleasure lake, he peered cautiously through the reeds.

A group of girls dressed in airy linen gowns, many of them with the shaven head and sidelock denoting children of the royal family, trooped down to the dock where the royal barge awaited, chattering like a flock of white-feathered ibises. They were shepherded by several ladies clad in elegant gowns, fine wigs and colorful, jeweled broad collars, and guarded by several armed soldiers. The girls scampered aboard the elaborately carved and gilded barge, with its high pillars topped with the hawk of Horus fore and aft, followed at a more decorous pace by their attendants and guards. At the captain's command, two sailors cast off the ship's moorings and the oarsmen began to warp it away from the dock.

As it pulled away, Thutmose edged further back among the reeds to avoid being seen by the ship's occupants. When he looked back up, however, his eyes met those of a particularly beautiful girl gazing directly at him. He held his breath in horror, sure that she would give him away at any moment. To his astonishment, she merely covered her mouth with one hand, as though to hide a laugh, then lowered one eyelid in a conspiratorial wink before turning back to her companions.

Thutmose breathed a sigh of relief, grateful for this surprising reprieve. His father, the potter, had sent him out in search of a particularly fine type of clay, which he needed in order to complete a set of elegant serving dishes ordered by the Grand Vizier, Lord Yuya, the most powerful man in Egypt, after Pharaoh himself. As the eldest son, it was young Thutmose's job to keep his father supplied with materials for his craft. He knew that the most readily available supply of this particular clay was along the banks of the channel leading from the nearby Bubastite branch of the Nile to the recently dug royal lake, which it supplied with water. The levees along the banks of the lake and canal were a potter's mother lode, the recently turned earth rich with the fine red clay used to make the finest pots.

Once the barge was out of sight, Thutmose cautiously raised his head and checked to see that the coast was clear. Seeing no one, he carefully crept back down to the water's edge and resumed scooping the wet clay into the rough cloth bags he carried. All he wanted now was to finish filling them and get out of the grounds of the royal estate before the guards could catch him. He was filling the very last bag – but even

as he was closing the flap over it, he heard voices approaching once more. He flattened himself on his stomach in the mud and waited for the voices to pass on by, as before. This time, however, they stopped nearby and continued their conversation. He could hear a woman and a boy. Perhaps they were only servants... He raised his head and peered cautiously through the reeds – and froze again, horrified.

There, only a short distance away, strolled the queen, herself, with a boy of about his own age who could only be her younger son, Prince Amenhotep. A number of servants followed at a polite distance and a dozen guards fanned out to patrol the perimeter. Thutmose feared they must hear the wild beating of his heart, so loud it seemed.

"Oh, ye gods of the Two Lands," he prayed fervently, "hide me here and let them not find me! Oh, Hapy, God of the Inundation, let the lake's waters rise and cover me. Amun Re, I beseech thee, let not thy sun's rays reveal me, lest the queen's guards kill me!"

For a time, it seemed his prayers were answered, as the guards remained at their posts and the queen and her son were seated on comfortable chairs on a terrace at the water's edge, while attentive servitors set food and drink before them on small tables. Scarcely daring to breathe, Thutmose could hear them quite clearly.

"I know you think it is *ma'at*, mother," said the boy, "that Thutmosis should get more attention because he is the first-born and the heir, the Horus in the Nest. Sometimes I wish that *I* could be the Horus in the Nest!"

"For shame, my son!" the Queen exclaimed. "The only way you could be the Horus in the Nest would be for your brother to die! You don't want Thutmosis to die, do you?"

"No," sighed the prince. "But did the gods have to give him more of everything?" he complained. "He is taller and stronger than me. He runs faster, shoots a bow straighter and throws a spear farther than I can. He is handsome, everything a prince should be. I am ugly."

"You are not ugly! How can you think such a thing?" exclaimed the queen indignantly.

"It's all right, Mother. I know the truth. I have seen my image in your silver mirror. More than that, I have seen it in the eyes of the courtiers and heard it from their lips when they did not know I was nearby. I know I am no beauty. If any of them says as much, I know he only speaks the truth."

"You are a strange child, my son" commented the Queen, shaking her head. "In many ways, you are wise beyond your tender years. Your brother may be bigger and stronger, and maybe even better looking, but you are a lot smarter than he is. And you have a warm heart. I think you take after your grandfather," mused the Queen.

"What, you mean I'm a dreamer like my grandfather Thutmosis the Fourth?" asked the boy.

Thutmosis the Fourth had put such great stock in his dreams that he had carved one of them on a stone slab and set it between the paws of the Great Sphinx. The stele told how, when Thutmosis was a young prince not in line for the succession, he had one day taken a nap in the shadow of the Sphinx while he was out hunting. He dreamt that the Sphinx told him that, if he cleared away the sand that buried the colossus up to its neck, he would become Pharaoh. Thutmosis had done as the Sphinx had bade him, and as it foretold, he had, indeed, become Pharaoh. He had therefore gained quite a reputation as a prophetic dreamer. The episode had not hurt the Sphinx's oracular reputation, either.

The Queen smiled ruefully. "While it's true that you are a bit of a dreamer, that wasn't what I meant. I meant you take after *my* father, Lord Yuya. You have his brains and his big heart. He had problems with his older brothers, too."

"He did?"

"Yes, indeed - and he didn't have just one. He had eleven of them, and they were all jealous of him," replied the queen.

"Why were they jealous?" asked the boy. "Was he the heir?"

"No," she replied, "he was actually the second youngest – but even so, he was his father's favorite and they hated him for it. They hated him so much that some of them actually wanted to kill him."

"That's awful! Did they gang up on him, all eleven of them?"

"Yes, they did – well, not the littlest one, but the oldest ten did. One day, when they were way out in the desert herding their sheep – "

"*Sheep?!*" cried the boy in horror. "Grandfather Yuya herded *sheep?*"

"Yes, he did," replied his mother, somewhat reluctantly.

Sheep – and shepherds – had been anathema to Egyptians ever since Lower Egypt had been taken over by the Hyksos, Asiatic sheep-herding people, two and a half centuries earlier. Ever since, herding sheep had been regarded as a sign of the worst sort of people. The thought that his own grandfather, the powerful and distinguished Vizier, Lord Yuya, had started life as a shepherd was deeply shocking to the young prince.

"Your grandfather belonged to a wandering, nomadic tribe of herders who were part of the Habiru, who ranged over Canaan and the Sinai desert," the queen told him.

"They weren't any of the Hyksos, were they? The shepherd-kings?" the prince asked.

"No! Don't ever make that mistake," replied the queen emphatically. "They were Asiatics, like the Hyksos, and they did live by herding cattle and sheep - but they were no relation to that loathsome horde of sheep-herding eastern invaders!"

The prince sat silently for a moment, digesting this news, then asked, "So, what did Grandfather's brothers do to him?"

"One of the brothers argued that they should kill him, but another argued that they shouldn't. Instead, they sold him to a caravan of slave-traders - and so he came to Egypt as a slave!"

"Grandfather Yuya was a slave?" The prince found it hard to believe that anyone as powerful, wise and dignified as Grandfather Yuya could ever have been either a sheepherder or a slave.

"Yes, indeed," she replied. "Not only was he a slave, he spent time in prison. But just when things seemed darkest for him, he got a chance to interpret the dreams of your royal grandfather, Thutmosis IV. The king was so impressed, he took him out of prison and made him his Grand Vizier, the second most powerful man in Egypt! So you see, by using his brains, and with the help of his god, your grandfather went from the depths of shame and poverty to the height of riches, power and fame. He went from being a slave and a prisoner to being the most powerful man in Egypt, save only Pharaoh himself. If he was able to do that, starting from such a lowly beginning, then surely you, born a prince, can overcome any slight disadvantages of appearance or athletic prowess and become a truly great man!"

Thutmose lay there in the mud, enrapt by this story of the humble origins of the great Lord Yuya. Suddenly, he heard rustling in the nearby reeds, followed by the appearance of two pairs of sandal-shod feet.

"Oho! What have we here?" growled a man's voice.

Thutmose's eyes traveled from one set of sandaled feet up a pair of hairy legs to the kilt and spear of a soldier.

"What are you doing here, hiding in the rushes, boy? Spying on your betters?" asked the guard, prodding Thutmose with his spear.

"Oh, no, sir," protested Thutmose, scrambling to his knees and bowing low to the soldier. "I wasn't spying!"

"Then what are you doing here?" the soldier demanded.

Thutmose rose up on his knees and grabbed his bags of clay.

"I was gathering clay for my father, the potter," he protested, showing the soldier the bags. "See, here are my bags of clay."

The soldier withdrew his spearpoint from the vicinity of Thutmose's ribs and took one of the bags. He opened it, took some of the clay and rubbed it between his fingers, then handed the bag to his partner, who repeated the process.

"Hmph," the second soldier said. "Looks like clay to me. Feels like it. Even smells – phooey, it stinks like it!"

"The question remains: why are you gathering clay – or doing anything else, for that matter – on royal property, boy?" demanded the first soldier.

"My father is making a set of dishes for the Grand Vizier. For that, he needed the very finest grade of clay, which is found along the banks of the new canal. I guess I lost track of where I was. I was only looking for the finest clay!" the boy explained.

"All right, come along, boy. Let's see what Her Majesty wants us to do with you. But first, wash some of that mud off. You can't go before Her Majesty like that."

Thutmose looked down at the front of his kilt, plastered with mud, and blushed bright red – albeit the mud on his face hid his fiery cheeks from the soldiers' sight. With the guard's spear prodding him, he waded out waist deep into the water, then submerged himself, coming up dripping but relatively free of mud.

"All right, that'll do. Come along, boy," said the guard.

Thutmose clambered out, streaming water. The guard grabbed his arm and hauled him out of the reeds, over to the terrace where young Amenhotep sat with his mother, the queen. The guard shoved the boy, who landed on his face before the queen. Thutmose pulled his knees under him into a more proper obeisance, keeping his face to the ground.

"A thousand pardons for disturbing you, Your Majesty. We found this boy spying in the reeds," said the guard, bowing low.

Thutmose turned his head to the side and protested, "I wasn't spying! I was gathering clay!"

"Quiet, boy!" snarled the guard. "Don't speak unless you're asked!"

The queen eyed the boy speculatively, then asked, "Well, boy? What were you doing on my property? What do you have to say for yourself?"

Thutmose cautiously raised his head and answered, "I was gathering clay for my father, the potter, Your Majesty. He's making pots for the Grand Vizier and wanted only the finest clay. He said the Grand Vizier has very re-, re-, refined - yes, that's it - very *refined* taste and should have only the very best. I was following the deposits of the finest clay and, well, they led me here!"

"I see," said the queen, hiding a smile of amusement behind her hand. "Well, you are right, boy: my father does have very refined taste, very fine taste, indeed. All right, boy, I will pardon you this time, since it's your first offense and your father is making things for my father. However, in the future, you must check with my guards before collecting clay on my estate. I will give you a pass to show them. Bring me a small piece of that clay."

"Yes, Your Majesty!" agreed Thutmose, scrambling to his feet. He reached for one of the bags of clay, which the guards had dropped nearby, and drew out a small gob of clay. He held it out to the queen, who gestured to a small table nearby.

"Now, pat it out flat for me. Good. Put it here on this small table."

Thutmose did as instructed, then stood by expectantly. The queen pulled a gold signet ring off one finger and rolled it firmly across the clay.

"Take that with you - carefully! - and show it to the guards any time you want to collect clay here in the future," the queen said to Thutmose. She turned to the guards and continued, "See to it that the other guards know about this boy. From now on, he shall be allowed to collect clay here on my estate, just as long as you keep track of his whereabouts. He can go back to his father now."

She waved to dismiss them. "You may all go."

The guards and Thutmose bowed low, then backed away from the royal presence. At the gate to the estate, they released Thutmose and sent him on his way back to the village.

Back home, Thutmose's father didn't know whether to be angry, impressed or relieved at his son's escapade. He was, however, delighted with the fine supply of high-quality clay, and pleased to know that there would be more where that came from.

Chapter 2: Meeting Nefertiti

Just a few months after my unintentional visit to the royal villa, I heard that young Prince Thutmosis had been killed in a hunting accident, leaving Prince Amenhotep heir to the Double Crown. All the Two Lands mourned with Pharaoh Amenhotep and Great Wife Tiye. When I heard the news, I couldn't help thinking that now the younger prince had his wish, to be Horus in the Nest. Thus does the fate of nations hang on the fragile life of a child!

My own family's fortunes, however, continued to rise, as it had ever since the building of the royal lake and villa nearby, so much so that my father was able to enlarge our house, from its former single room to several rooms around a courtyard, all having a flat roof with sleeping areas for the family to use in warm weather and a firepit for cooking. The original room was now entirely used as my father's workshop. He had so much business that he had taken on several apprentices, in addition to myself and my two younger brothers. While I was still the most experienced and skillful among them, I turned out fewer pots because I preferred to devote my energy to sculpting figurines. My father was quite exasperated with me until he realized that these miniature vignettes of daily life were very popular with all the people passing by, many of whom stopped to admire, and sometimes, buy them. Most customers purchased them for their tombs, as magical servants to assist them in the afterlife. It was certainly a custom preferable to the earlier practice of interring a person's actual servants with him!

Some customers, however - especially the younger ones - purchased these miniature scenarios as toys, or as artwork to decorate their homes. Thus it was with the young Lady Nefertiti.

One late spring day, when Thutmose was about ten years old, Ahhotep and his apprentices were hard at work making pots. The road to the villa hummed with traffic going to and fro, as the royal family was in residence.

At mid-morning, work ground to a halt when a huge delegation of Mitanni emissaries appeared, the men in their deep-dyed robes bordered with spiraling fringes, with tall caps topping their bearded faces, riding in chariots drawn by magnificent horses. Following them was an entire entourage of women, over three hundred in all, several of them veiled and borne on curtained litters, flanked by armed soldiers. In the middle of this small army was a larger, more elaborate, gilded litter. Word quickly ran through the village that this was occupied by the sister of the king of Mitanni, Princess Gilukhipa, arriving to become one of Pharaoh's wives, sealing the treaty of friendship between the two nations.

Thutmose sat in the shade of a tamarisk tree near the front of the house, busily modeling miniatures of this marvelous cavalcade. His nimble fingers created tiny replicas of soldiers, diplomats, ladies and horses with astonishing speed. Several of the chariots had stopped by the village well to water both men and horses, providing the boy with a rare opportunity to study the horses. Curious, Thutmose put down his tools and clay, wiped his hands on his tunic and casually strolled over to the well, where he could inspect the handsome animals more closely.

While horses had been known in Egypt for more than three hundred years, they were still in relatively short supply and not a common sight. By far the majority belonged to Pharaoh's military. It was said that Pharaoh had over a thousand chariots at his command. The majority of these, however, were stationed at the frontier, or in the twin capitals of Thebes and Memphis. Thutmose had rarely had the chance to study them close up.

He made himself useful to the visitors, eagerly drawing water in the leather bucket and sloshing it into the stone trough for the animals. The bearded strangers smiled and clapped him on the shoulder, thanking him in their strange foreign speech. When he gestured questioningly toward the horses, they amiably agreed to let him approach them. One of them held out a bag of grain and gestured towards Thutmose, then the horse. Thutmose tentatively reached into the bag and pulled out a handful of grain. He cautiously approached one of the horses, holding out his handful of grain.

The horse tossed its head and pricked up its ears, making a soft whickering noise. It approached him with almost equal caution, then dropped its head to his hand and snuffled up the grain with its soft lips. When the grain was gone, it allowed the boy to stroke its soft, velvety nose. He patted its neck, then slowly stroked its side, noting the structure of the muscles and bones beneath its gleaming coat.

By the time the cavalcade moved on, Thutmose had a much better understanding of how horses were built. He proceeded to apply this new-found knowledge to sculpting an even dozen miniature equines, which he then equipped with delicately modeled chariots, complete with their tiny drivers and passengers. He re-created the litters of the ladies, including a grand one painted deep yellow to emulate the gilded palanquin of the foreign princess, accompanied by a full score of exotically arrayed miniature ladies in waiting and dozens of tiny soldiers.·

These joined a display of Egyptian soldiers on a shelf in the front of the shop, where they could catch the eye of passersby. To even up the numbers, Thutmose sculpted a round dozen of Pharaoh's chariots, based on his trips with his father, making deliveries to the garrison at the great border fortress of Tjaru, combined with his newly acquired knowledge of equine anatomy.

"Keep that up, lad, and Pharaoh will call on you when he needs to build up his army," said his father, inspecting the miniature troops. "I just hope somebody likes them enough to pay for them."

"Sorry, father. I know I should be making water pots, and not spending my time building armies," Thutmose apologized.

"It's all right, son. Your little vignettes are beginning to bring in a whole other set of customers. Just see that you make at least a half dozen pots a week, as well."

"I promise I will, father. In fact, I'll work on them right now."

"Good lad," said the potter. "I think that last lot are ready to go into the kiln. I'll start stacking the first layer in, while you fetch some of that dried dung to build the fire. We still have some of the acacia wood charcoal to make it burn hotter."

"Yes, father," Thutmose agreed, putting away the small soldiers.

Ahhotep and his son surrounded the whole assemblage with a lattice-work of acacia wood, careful not to put any weight on the delicate dried greenware. Thutmose fetched several basket loads of dried donkey dung, which he loaded into the tall mud brick kiln, interspersed with layers of charcoal, around the acacia wood lattice surrounding the dried pottery. When the heat of the day began to fade, Ahhotep carefully lit the kiln with hot coals from the cooking fire. For the next several hours, Thutmose and the other apprentices took turns stoking the fire with a foot-pumped bellows. Once the fuel had burned down to glowing embers, they stacked more mud bricks around the kiln to hold the heat in, then left it to burn itself out and cool slowly over the next day.

Important nobles and officials continued to arrive for several days after the arrival of the Mitannian delegation. The dust churned up from the road by the feet of people and animals sometimes made it difficult to work. Just as there was a break and the dust began to settle, another group appeared, led by an impressive nobleman in a fine chariot drawn by two white horses with plumes on their heads. The occupant was a muscular man of middle years with a military bearing, wearing a short Nubian wig and a fine linen tunic, topped with a gold collar of office, with a leopard skin over his shoulder. He was surrounded by a score of guards and followed by an elegant curtained litter, followed in turn by household servants. Thutmose's feet stopped turning the potter's wheel and he dropped his hands from the pot he had been working on as he watched the horses prance by.

The chariot had passed and the litter was almost past the shop when a slender hand pulled the curtain back and an imperious voice called, "Stop!"

The litter bearers came to an immediate halt, the servants and half the soldiers stopping with them. The chariot and its guards had gone on a short distance before the lord in the leopard skin realized that half his entourage was no longer with him. He reluctantly slowed his chariot and gave the order for his troops to about face, while he turned his horses back.

Drawing up beside the palanquin, he asked, with a deep sigh, "What is it now, Nefer?"

"I want to look at the figurines in the potter's shop, Father," said the occupant of the litter.

"All right," he replied, with another sigh. "At this rate, Nefertiti, we'll never get to the royal villa."

At his signal, the bearers set the litter down and a servant helped the young lady out.

Both Thutmose and Ahhotep scrambled to their feet and bowed deferentially to the lord and young lady. From his head-down position, Thutmose looked up under his brows and watched the most beautiful girl he had ever seen step out of the litter. Abruptly, he recognized her as the exquisite girl who had looked at him from the royal barge two years earlier.

She was slender, with delicately modeled features. She wore a linen gown so fine it was almost transparent, tied by the red sash that denoted a royal Heiress. Her head was partially shaven, save for the thick side-lock worn by royal children. Thutmose guessed that she was about his age, maybe ten years old. Dropping his eyes, he bowed even lower.

Thutmose and Ahhotep straightened up as the lord and his daughter passed beneath the awning of the shop. Nefertiti headed straight for the shelves holding Thutmose's miniatures. She intently examined scenes of cattle and herdsmen, of farmers harvesting a miniature field of wheat, of a weaver's shop with tiny figures spinning flax and weaving on a horizontal loom, even a precise miniature version of the potter's shop itself, complete with figures of Ahhotep, Thutmose and the three apprentices.

"Oh, look, Father," she laughed, "it's this very shop! The little potter looks just like you," she commented to Ahhotep. "Isn't it adorable?" she asked her father.

"Yes, Nefer, it's adorable," agreed her indulgent parent. "Pick something and let's get on our way."

"Wait, wait! I want to look at them all," she protested. "Oh, look at this! Is this the Mitanni delegation?" she asked the potter.

"Yes, Your Ladyship. They came through here several days ago. We heard that the Mitanni princess was on her way to marry Pharaoh," he replied.

"Is this her litter here in the middle?" she asked.

"I believe so, Your Eminence. But you'll have to ask my son - it's his work," he replied, pulling Thutmose forward.

The girl turned her exquisite dark eyes to Thutmose inquiringly. He swallowed hard and stammered a reply.

"Yes, Your Highness, it is."

"Is she as pretty as they say?" she asked.

"I - I don't know, Your Highness. I never really saw her. She kept the curtains closed," he explained.

"Ah - of course." She moved on to inspect the horses and chariots. "Well, it seems you got a good look at the horses. These are wonderfully lifelike. Look, Father, see how detailed they are. You can see the muscles under the skin, and their fringed harnesses - and look at the costumes of the men!"

Her father peered closely at the tiny horsemen and grudgingly agreed. "You're right, my dear. They are very good, indeed." He turned to the potter. "The lad has a real gift, and a sharp eye for detail."

"Thank you, My Lord," said Ahhotep, pleased.

Nefertiti had now come to the display of Egyptian soldiers, to which Thutmose had recently added the chariots of the Pharaoh and the Grand Vizier.

"Oh, Father, look at this! It's Pharaoh reviewing his troops! He's got all the right clothing and equipment - even the blue war crown. And there's Grandfather in his own chariot! How wonderful! He has really captured Grandfather's likeness. You can tell that it's him, even if it didn't have the insignia of office, which it does. Don't you think it looks like him?"

The nobleman bent down and peered closely at the miniscule Grand Vizier.

"By Amun, you're right, Nefer! It does look like him. An excellent job."

He turned to Thutmose and asked, "Wherever did you see my father, boy? The Grand Vizier?"

Thutmose stammered nervously, "I - we - that is, we've made several deliveries of pots to the fort at Tjaru, sir, and on one of those, Pharaoh and the Grand Vizier were there, inspecting the troops."

The nobleman looked thoughtful for a moment, then said, "As I recall, it's been nearly five years since Pharaoh last made a visit to Tjaru."

The potter spoke up. "I believe that's when it was, sir, just shortly before they began digging the lake."

"And that's the only time your boy saw the Grand Vizier?"

The potter looked inquiringly at Thutmose, who answered, "Yes, Your Eminence."

"Remarkable!" the lord commented. "You saw him once, all those years ago, and yet you remembered him well enough to capture his likeness. You must have been all of, what, five years old?"

"About that, Your Lordship," agreed the potter.

"Father," interjected Nefertiti, "I've decided. I want this whole scene of Pharaoh inspecting his troops."

"Are you sure you wouldn't rather have something a little less warlike? The weaving shop, perhaps, or even the Mitanni princess's delegation?" he asked her.

"Well, of course, I like those, too. But I like Pharaoh and his troops the best, especially Grandfather in his chariot. I want Grandfather to see it."

"All right, my dear. I'll tell you what: we'll take that, and the Mitanni delegation." He turned to the potter. "Pack them up for us, potter."

"I can deliver them to you at the villa, if you prefer, Your Lordship. You wouldn't have to wait," offered the potter.

"That would be good," His Lordship began to reply, when his daughter interrupted him.

"Oh, no, Father! I want to take them with me!" she protested.

"Oh, all right, sweetheart," he conceded. "You'll be the ruin of me yet! I have to admit you have good taste, though. " He commented to the potter, "The little minx knows I can't resist her wiles! Do pack them up quickly, potter. I don't want to keep Pharaoh waiting."

"We will be as quick as possible, My Lord," the potter hastened to assure him. "Why don't you sit here while you wait?" he added pulling over a cushioned stool. "Would you care for some water or some wine?"

"Water would be fine," the nobleman replied, seating himself on the stool. "My steward will pay you," he added, waving a hand toward the man, who was hovering nearby.

Ahhotep called to his wife to bring a pitcher of water and some cups, then turned to join Thutmose, who was already wrapping the tiny figures in scraps of cloth and packing them into two large baskets filled with straw.

While the vignettes were being packed, young Nefertiti walked around the shop, examining the potter's other wares, then turned to where Thutmose's little sister sat by the doorway, playing with her doll. Disregarding her high rank and fine gown, Nefertiti squatted down beside the little girl and introduced herself.

"Hello, there. My name's Nefertiti - what's yours?" she asked.

The child replied shyly, "Merit Ta-sherit." (She was called "Merit the Younger", after her mother, who was Merit the Elder.)

"That's a very pretty name. What's your dolly's name?" the princess asked.

"Nefer," replied the little girl. "It means 'beautiful'."

"I know - it's part of my name, too. And she really is a beautiful dolly. May I see her?"

Merit smiled and handed the doll to the beautiful young lady. Nefertiti examined the doll, whose head, hands and feet were modeled in finely painted ceramic, attached to a stuffed cloth body. The face was beautifully sculpted, with a fine little nose, rosebud lips and almond eyes outlined in black, just like those of the nobility. She was dressed in a little linen gown, with a black wig made of curly goat hair. Her little hands and feet had individually modeled fingers and toes, a refinement not seen even in royal sculpture at that time.

"She's lovely. Did your brother make her for you?" she asked. The girl nodded. "He did? What a lucky girl you are, to have a brother who can make you such a beautiful dolly!"

The child beamed and glanced proudly at her big brother. The princess handed the doll back to her and stood up, brushing the dust from her gown.

Thutmose and Ahhotep finished packing up the figurines and helped a servant strap the boxes to a donkey. After a brief negotiation with the potter, the steward handed him several sacks of grain and agreed to send him a pair of goats to complete the payment when he reached the villa.

A servant helped the princess back into her litter, her father re-mounted his chariot and the cavalcade resumed its progress toward the royal villa.

Thutmose stood in the road looking after them, entranced, until the whole entourage was merely a cloud of dust in the distance. Little Merit came and stood beside him, taking her brother's hand, almost equally enthralled with the beautiful lady who had been so nice to her and who had admired her doll.

Chapter 3: A Doll for Nefertiti

My father, having seen how enchanted I was by the beautiful princess, teased me mercilessly for weeks. For my part, whenever I was not busy helping my father, I was working on a doll for Princess Nefertiti. Having seen how much she liked Merit's doll, I wanted to make an even finer one for her.

I modeled its face on that of Nefertiti herself, delicate fine features above a long, swanlike neck. I modeled the doll's arms, clear to the shoulder, ending in fine, graceful hands, with individually formed fingers; and long, slender legs with dainty feet. Once the pieces had been fired, I painted them to resemble the princess as closely as possible. I attached the pieces to a cloth body shaped and sewn by my mother and stuffed with barley.

A cousin of my mother's had recently turned her hand to wigmaking, hoping to find a clientele among the nobles and bureaucrats passing up and down the road to the royal villa. So far, business was slow, as most of the folk passing by came from elsewhere in the Two Lands and already had favorite vendors of wigs near their homes. I came up with a plan that I believed would help both of us: I proposed that she make a wig for the doll as an example of her finest work, and promised that I would make sure the princess and her family knew whose work it was. She agreed, but we could not at first agree on what style the wig should be. The princess herself, being still a child, wore the mostly-shaven head and princely sidelock, but my kinswoman protested that a mere sidelock would hardly be a worthy showpiece of her work. I had to agree, and recognized that it would also be very difficult to attach it securely to the doll's head. We considered the classical Hathor style, a very long, full hairstyle, but it would have taken too much hair. We agreed that, for a member of the royal household, the wig should be made of real human hair, not the cheaper goat hair worn by lesser classes, but human hair is costly and hard to come by, especially in longer lengths.

Then I had an inspiration: I remembered that Queen Tiye had been wearing the shorter Nubian style wig when I had seen her at the villa. My cousin Neith felt that this would work very well. I volunteered my own hair for the wig. Neith insisted on washing it very thoroughly first, then she trimmed my shoulder-length locks to a three fingers' width length, keeping the cut locks for the wig. I was secretly pleased that a part of myself would remain so close to the princess.

Father and I had recently begun experimenting with adding faience items to our product line, so I was able to provide a plentiful supply of bright turquoise faience beads to add to the wig. The end product was very fine, indeed, and promised to be an excellent showpiece of my kinswoman's work.

I was also able to fashion a beautiful broad collar of faience beads for the doll, in various shades of blue and turquoise and white, both round beads and bottle-shaped "nefer" beads, thereby incorporating an element of the princess's name into the doll's jewelry.

Finding sufficiently fine linen for the doll's dress was an even greater challenge, as flax for superfine "royal linen" is strictly controlled and very hard to come by. My mother, however, had helped nurse one of the weavers attached to the royal estate when she was ill. When my mother explained the project to her, she was happy to donate a small piece of this fine fabric, which my mother sewed into a splendid gown for the doll.

Red dye for the doll's sash was also difficult to find. The usual red pigment, made from kermes insects, was not as deep and rich a color as that used for the sashes that designated royal Heiresses. When we finally learned the source of the right red dye, my father traded a particularly fine pitcher for a small pouch of vermilion powder, ground from a type of crystal found near volcanoes. Since there are no volcanoes within the Two Lands, this rare and costly powder has to be imported from abroad.

At last, with the sash dyed deep red and the addition of a dainty pair of tiny leather sandals, the doll was finally complete and ready for delivery.

I had used the queen's pass a number of times to gather clay, so by now, the guards at the villa's gate were quite familiar with me. However, they had never seen me so clean, nor asking admittance to the royal presence, for which I had to seek permission from the Chamberlain, a very important and dignified official.

One of the guards led Thutmose to a small room to await the arrival of the Lord Chamberlain. When the Chamberlain, a dignified, portly gentleman of middle years, with a gold *shebu* collar and staff of office, appeared, the guard bowed low and explained that the potter's boy had a gift to deliver to the Princess Nefertiti.

"He bears the Queen's seal," finished the guard.

"The Queen's seal?" the Lord Chamberlain asked skeptically.

Thutmose showed him the clay seal and explained, "She gave me permission to gather clay on the banks of the royal lake."

"A gift for Princess Nefertiti? What manner of gift?" asked the Lord Chamberlain.

"A doll, Your Eminence. The princess and her father recently purchased some things from my father's shop in the village, sir, and the princess admired a doll I had made for my little sister, so I made a special one for her," explained the boy.

"Let me see this doll," the Chamberlain ordered, his voice tinged with doubt.

Thutmose placed the package on a small table and carefully unwound the linen wrappings. The Chamberlain examined the doll closely.

Finally, he said, "Well, boy, I have to admit that I'm impressed. You may deliver the doll to Her Highness."

"Thank you, Your Eminence," replied Thutmose, carefully re-wrapping the doll.

"You say your father is the potter in the village?" he asked. The boy nodded. "What is his name?"

"He is called Ahhotep, Your Lordship."

"And what is your name, young man?"

"My name is Thutmose, Sire."

"All right, young Thutmose, follow me."

So saying, the Chamberlain picked up his staff and headed for the back of the villa, with Thutmose trotting obediently behind.

After passing through a bewildering maze of rooms, they arrived at the Queen's audience chamber. A pair of attendants opened the great bronze-clad doors to admit the Lord Chamberlain and his young follower. The room was filled with elegantly dressed ladies fluttering in attendance on the Queen, who was seated on a gilded throne at the far end of the room. A trio of musicians played a tall harp, a double flute and a pair of drums, while several athletic and scantily clad young women danced.

Two ladies were playing Hounds and Jackals, a board game with pieces of ivory and ebony. At the other end of the room was a group of several young girls with their attendants, playing with an assortment of toys. Among them Thutmose saw the royal princesses, Sitamun and Isis, and their cousin Nefertiti, accompanied by a younger girl who he guessed might be her sister. Sitamun, the eldest princess, sat at a table with a distinguished-looking older man, poring over a scroll. Thutmose later learned that this was the famous sage, Amenhotep son of Hapu, a royal advisor who also managed the princess's extensive estates.

The Chamberlain rapped on the floor three times with his staff. The Queen looked up and gestured for him to approach. Signaling Thutmose to accompany him, the Chamberlain approached the Queen and bowed low. Thutmose followed suit.

"Your Majesty, Thutmose, son of Ahhotep the potter, who carries your seal, brings a gift for the Lady Nefertiti," he announced sonorously.

"Approach, boy," ordered the Queen. Thutmose approached the base of the dais and bowed low.

"Rise, boy. Let me see your face. Ah – if it isn't the young clay-gatherer!" she laughed. "I hardly recognized you without a coating of mud!"

Thutmose turned bright red with embarrassment, remembering his previous muddy encounter with the Queen.

"All right, lad, you may deliver your gift to Princess Nefertiti," she agreed, waving a hand to indicate the princess at the other side of the room.

Thutmose bowed again and backed away. He followed the Chamberlain to the group of children at the far side of the room.

"My Lady Nefertiti! " announced the Chamberlain, "Thutmose, son of Ahhotep, brings a gift for you."

Nefertiti looked up from the game she was playing and exclaimed, "A gift? For me? What is it?"

Thutmose approached and bowed to Nefertiti.

"Oh!" she said, "It's the potter's boy!"

"Yes, Your Highness," he replied shyly.

"You have a gift for me?" she asked.

He approached nearer and held out the package. Nefertiti took it from him and set it on a nearby table. She carefully unwound the linen wrappings.

"Oh!" she exclaimed. "What a beautiful doll! You remembered that I admired your sister's doll. How sweet! Thank you!"

With this, she stepped over to his side and kissed him on the cheek. The other girls giggled.

Thutmose bowed low, feeling his face grow warm again, this time with pleasure. The princess liked his gift!

The other girls gathered around and admired the doll.

"She looks just like you, Nefer," commented young Lady Rai, one of Nefertiti's maternal cousins.

"Except for the wig," said Princess Sitamun, who was a few years older than Nefertiti. "That's the Nubian style my mother likes. But Nefer hasn't outgrown her sidelock yet."

"That style looks really good on the doll, Nefer. I bet it would look good on you, when you come of age," added Rai.

"Yes, I think you're right," agreed Nefertiti.

One of the courtiers, Lady Hatnefer, leaned over Nefertiti's shoulder and commented, "Look how beautifully the wig is made! It's just like a real grownup wig!"

Seeing his opportunity, Thutmose interjected, "It's my mother's cousin's handiwork, Your Ladyship - Neith, wife of Rahotep. She's opened a wig-making shop in the village."

"Tell her to come around to my villa. The guards can direct you - tell them Lady Hatnefer orders it," she instructed.

"I will, Your Ladyship. Thank you," Thutmose replied. He was delighted that his plan was working.

The girls continued to examine the doll's outfit with great interest.

"Oh, look at her cute little sandals!" exclaimed one.

"And her beaded collar," commented another.

"Her dress looks like real royal linen," said another, "and she's wearing the red sash of an heiress."

Just then, the younger girl Thutmose had seen earlier with Nefertiti pushed her way through the crowd.

"Let **me** see!" she demanded loudly, reaching for the doll.

Nefertiti snatched the doll up and held it closely. "You can look at her, Mutnodjmet, but don't touch! She's very delicate and I don't want her broken!" she admonished the child.

Mutnodjment began jumping up and down, grabbing for the doll and yelling, "Give me the doll! Give me the doll! I want a doll, too!"

When Nefertiti turned away, protectively clutching the doll to her chest, the child began screaming at the top of her lungs. All of the adults turned toward the source of the noise, aghast at this outburst in the Queen's presence.

The Queen turned to one of her ladies and snapped, "Lady Tey - quiet your daughter immediately, or I will have the guards remove her! You should train her better. I will not tolerate such behavior in my court!"

Lady Tey blanched and hastened over to the screaming child.

"Mutya! Stop that at once!" she ordered. When the order had no effect, she gritted her teeth and slapped the child across the face.

Mutnodjmet, shocked, paused for breath, then began to cry, "I want a doll! I want a doll of my own! It's not fair if Nefer gets a doll and I don't!"

Thutmose was horrified to see his gift becoming the cause of an unpardonable disruption of the Queen's court. He had to do something to stop the child from making a scene.

Stepping forward, he fell to his knees beside the child. "Your Ladyship," he said, "I will make you a doll, too, a doll of your very own."

This got her attention.

"You will?" she asked. "A doll of my very own?"

"Yes, indeed, a special doll just for you," he answered solemnly.

"Like Nefer's doll?" she asked.

"Yes, but your doll will look like you," he assured her. "Nefertiti's doll looks like her."

"Nefer's is a princess doll," she said, slyly. "I want mine to be a queen doll!"

Thutmose was beginning to wonder what he had gotten himself into, but he had to agree, "All right. Yours will be a queen doll."

"Good," Mutnodjmet sniffed. "Make sure that it is," she added imperiously.

"Yes, Your Ladyship," Thutmose assured her, then added cautiously, "But you know, making a queen doll will take time."

"I want her right away!" she yelled. "I want her now! Right now!"

"Well, Your Ladyship, it takes a couple of weeks, you know, to make even an ordinary doll. And a queen doll takes even longer. I have to gather the special clay, model the doll, then it has to dry and be fired in a very hot oven, then painted and fired again. The wig and the clothes have to be made, and the jewelry. You do want her to have jewels, don't you?" Thutmose asked, disingenuously.

Mutnodjmet nodded.

"Well, then, you can't rush it, or it won't be right. You DO want the very finest queen doll, don't you?" he asked, looking her in the eye.

Mutnodjmet looked rebellious, but then reluctantly nodded. Her nurse took her hand and led her away, looking back at Thutmose with an appreciative smile.

Thutmose stood back up.

The Chamberlain leaned over the boy's shoulder and said quietly, "Well done, young man! That was a wise move!"

Thutmose whispered back, "There's just one problem."

"What's that?" the Chamberlain asked.

"I have no idea how a queen doll should look," he said, anxiously.

During this conversation, the queen had approached, unnoticed behind the courtiers. Now she stepped through their ranks.

"I am how a queen should look, young man! You can make the doll look like me," she said.

Thutmose and the chamberlain bowed low.

"Yes, Your Majesty! I am honored. Would - would it be all right if I sketched you, so I can be sure to get it right?" the boy asked her.

The Queen nodded graciously. "You may," she said.

He looked about, patted his tunic, then remembered that he did not have his grubby old bag full of papyrus scraps and charcoal with him. He said apologetically to the Queen, "Uh - I don't have any drawing materials with me, Your Majesty."

The Queen turned to her steward, who was standing nearby.

"Huya - fetch Master Auta to me. And tell him to bring drawing materials with him."

"Yes, Your Majesty," replied the steward, bowing low. He scurried off to fetch the Queen's Master of Works.

The Queen returned to her throne. At the Chamberlain's direction, Thutmose took a seat on the floor near the dais. A servant set a low table before him. At a sign from the Queen, another servant brought him a refreshing cup of beer.

A few minutes later, the steward returned with Master of Works Auta, a small man with powerful arms. He carried a basket filled with rolls of papyrus, pieces of charcoal, sharpened quills, brushes and a palette with cakes of ink. The steward led him to where Thutmose was seated. The boy scrambled hastily to his feet and bowed to the distinguished artist.

"You are the young dollmaker?" asked Master Auta.

"Yes, sir," replied Thutmose. "It is an honor to meet you, sir."

"Give the boy the materials, Auta, and let him get on with it," ordered the Queen.

"Of course, Your Majesty," Auta replied, bowing to his mistress.

He handed the basket to Thutmose, who resumed his seat on the floor. He selected a roll of papyrus and a thin stick of charcoal. Spreading the papyrus on the small table, he began quickly sketching the Queen as everyone resumed their previous activities.

Thutmose became engrossed in his sketching, oblivious of everyone else around him. Master Auta sat quietly to one side, watching the boy work.

The crown prince entered the room and strolled toward his mother. The crowd made way for him, bowing low as he approached. As he neared the dais, he noticed the boy sketching nearby. He signed to Master Auta not to rise as he drew near. Auta nodded. The prince walked quietly up behind the young artist and watched him sketch the queen. Several completed pieces of papyrus lay on the floor. The prince picked these up and looked through them, then passed them to Auta with a raised eyebrow and a nod.

The master artist leafed through the sheaf of sketches. Catching the prince's eye, he nodded back.

A moment later, Thutmose finished his last sketch. He looked up, startled to find the Crown Prince himself looking over his shoulder. He scrambled quickly to his feet and bowed low.

"Your Royal Highness!" he stammered, aghast at his own breach of etiquette. "I most humbly beseech your pardon! I didn't hear you come in."

"You are forgiven," smiled the prince. "We give wide leeway to artists. And it is apparent that you were doing my mother's bidding."

"Yes, Your Highness," agreed Thutmose.

The prince retrieved the drawings from Master Auta and took them to the Queen. She leafed through them, showing no change of expression. Thutmose watched anxiously, praying all the while that he had not offended the Queen with any unflattering likenesses.

The Queen turned to her Chief of Works.

"Well, Master Auta - what do you think?"

He replied, "Most impressive, Your Majesty. He has caught your likeness very well. The boy has a gift."

"I agree," said the Queen.

Thutmose's knees almost collapsed with relief.

The prince said to his mother, "I think we should apprentice him to the royal workshop." He turned to the master artist and asked, "Don't you think so, Auta?"

The master replied, "I think that's a good idea, Your Highness. As always, Your Highness has a fine eye for art."

"If you think he would make a good artist, Master of Works, then make it so," said the Queen.

Thutmose was dumbfounded. To become an artist in service of the royal household was beyond even his wildest dreams! This must have been what the soothsayer meant who had prophesied great things for him at his birth.

...And so it came to pass that I was apprenticed to the workshop of the artist Auta, Chief of Works to Her Majesty, Queen Tiye (may she live forever!). To tell the truth, I have always been grateful to young Mutnodjmet: were it not for her bad temper, I might never have become an artist at the king's court!

Chapter 4: The Royal Artists' School

The Royal Artists' School was located in Thebes, the southern capital, two weeks' journey up the river. My grief at leaving my parents, my brothers and little sister was far outweighed by my excitement at starting a wonderful new life. Being a member of the royal corps of artists was very prestigious, and a guarantee of lifetime employment. It meant being a part, however ancillary, of Pharaoh's glittering court. But above all, it meant I could actually earn a living doing what I loved most: creating works of art.

Thutmose had bidden a tearful farewell to his parents, brothers and little sister before joining Master Auta and his students for the journey south. The neighbor's daughter, Mariamne, who had had a longstanding crush on the boy, came down to the dock on the river with the potter and his wife to see him off. She sobbed loudly as he hurried up the gangplank with the other students, embarrassing Thutmose and amusing his fellow students.

One of the boys, Bek, a student a year older than Thutmose, teased him, "Eh, newcomer! Breaking hearts already, and not even a man yet! Imagine how bad it'll be, boys, when he sprouts a beard! We poor homely fellows won't have a chance!"

"Shut up, Bek," said Menes, one of the older students, thumping Bek on the back of the head. "Can't you see they're both embarrassed? Besides, with that monkey face of yours, you don't stand a chance with the girls, anyway!"

At this, the boys all laughed.

"Yeah, Bek," called one of the others, "they should have named you Bes, not Bek!" he said, referring to the god of entertainment, who took the form of a baboon with an enormous phallus.

Thutmose grinned gamely and added, "Well, at least with Bek along, we'll never want for entertainment!"

"Ouch!" said Bek, clutching his chest dramatically. "You wound me to the heart! I give up - truce!"

He stuck a hand out to Thutmose, who took it in a firm clasp.

"As you probably gathered, my name is Bek," he said.

"I'm Thutmose, son of Ahhotep the potter."

"Welcome aboard."

From this point on, the two became fast friends, despite personalities as different as their backgrounds and artistic styles. Unlike Thutmose's humble origins, Bek came from a family of artists - his father was currently Pharaoh's Chief of Works, the highest artistic position in the country. Bek hoped to follow in his footsteps. Friendly arguments were the boys' most frequent form of interaction on the long voyage. By the time they reached Thebes, four hundred miles up the Nile, they were boon companions.

The city of Thebes sat on the east bank of the Nile, near the southern end of a huge bend in the river. The immense complex of Malkata Palace sprawled across the river from the city proper, served by its own set of docks and wharves on the river. On the west bank of the Nile opposite the city of the living was the necropolis, city of the dead, with its myriad tombs and mortuary temples between the cliffs and the riverbank. The grandest of these was built into a bay in the cliffs by the famous Queen Hatshepsut, who had ruled as Pharaoh a hundred years earlier. It was known that all the pharaohs since Thutmosis I were buried in secret tombs somewhere in the western cliffs beyond Hatshepsut's temple, but their exact whereabouts was a closely guarded secret.

The large, bustling, lively city came as a bit of a shock to Thutmose, who had lived all his life in a tiny village where he knew everyone. He spent much of his free time for the first several weeks roaming the rabbit warren of a town with Bek, who knew every back alley and disreputable tavern in the city. Bek knew everyone, and all their gossip, and they all knew him. Soon Thutmose, too, became a familiar sight, although it could hardly be said that people really *knew* him, since he was as quiet as his friend Bek was garrulous.

In the Royal Artists' School, Thutmose learned to draw and paint, sculpt in clay and stone, make jewelry and furniture, and to read and write both hieroglyphics and the less formal hieratic script.

The Royal Art Workshop was a large building within the vast complex that formed Malkata Palace. It housed scores of artists and skilled craftsmen, including two dozen young artists-in-training, all under the command of Master Auta.

The main studio and classroom of the artists' school and workshop was a large, airy room with a colonnade surrounding an open courtyard. A linen awning stretched over the opening allowed bright but diffuse light to fill the studio. A full score of boys and young men worked at various projects around the room. Some sketched or painted on papyrus or tablets of clay or wood. Others modeled clay into figures of people, animals or gods. Still others shaped statues from stone or wood, using an assortment of chisels and adzes, while others made jewelry from gold, silver, copper, glass and semi-precious stones such as carnelian, turquoise and lapis lazuli. Others created furniture from ebony, ivory, walnut and other fine woods imported from Lebanon or the forests of Punt.

Thutmose sat with a group of boys learning to write hieroglyphics. A scribe wrote each sign with charcoal on a large white-painted board, naming it and pronouncing its sound. The boys repeated the name and sound and copied the glyph on smaller, individual boards. Once they had learned hieroglyphics, which were now mainly used for formal tomb and temple inscriptions, they would learn the less formal hieratic script, used for commonplace transactions. Neither form used signs for vowel sounds, so they would have to memorize the collection of signs for specific words, as they could not be fully sounded out phonetically. So, for example, *Wadjet*, the tutelary cobra goddess of Lower Egypt, might be written the same as *wedjat*, the Eye of Horus often used for protective amulets. They would have to learn to tell from context which was meant.

The royal family often posed for us and the prince visited frequently. He always had a keen interest in the arts, as well as a true artist's eye. I realize now what extraordinary artistic freedom he gave us, and what liberty he gave us to speak freely around him. Bek always said that Akhenaten was his teacher. I didn't really understand what he meant at the time, but now I see that his remarkable vision and open-mindedness helped us break the shackles of convention and cast off the limitations of tradition.

Egypt is an ancient land, steeped in tradition. Examples of traditional art were displayed all around the studio. Copies of wall paintings from tombs and temples were painted on the walls, on scrolls and scraps of papyrus and sketched on wooden practice boards. Samples of traditional statuary scattered around the room showed the students how pharaohs and their families had been portrayed for two thousand years.

On the one hand, this long-established iconography provided a comforting sense of stability and a storehouse of ready-made symbols artists could call upon to convey particular ideas. On the other hand, however, it was very rigid and hidebound, particularly concerning portrayals of Pharaoh and his family, and tolerated little deviation from time-honored standards. This left very little room for creativity or artistic license. This prince, however, saw things differently.

On this day, the prince was posing for a group of students. He was seated in an elegant chair, while a group of musicians and dancers entertained him. Thutmose, Bek and several other boys sketched or painted the scene on strips of papyrus, while Master Auta examined and commented on the boys' work.

"Good, Senmut," he said to one of the older students. "You've caught the line of the dancers' bodies very nicely. Nice composition."

Looking over the next boy's shoulder, he said, "No, no, Khepra. You've got the figures bunched much too closely, in the middle of all this empty space. Use space *between* the figures as part of your composition."

He demonstrated this concept with a few swift strokes of charcoal on a practice board. Thutmose admired the economy of line with which the master could capture the essence of the scene, the way those few strokes could convey a sense of motion.

Master Auta next turned to Thutmose's work, just as the prince took a break from posing and joined him. Amenhotep took a keen interest in all the boys' work, but he considered Thutmose his personal discovery and protégé. Being under such close royal scrutiny was both flattering and frightening. Thutmose was deeply grateful to the prince for recommending him to the royal academy and anxious not to disappoint his young patron.

His sketch of the scene was very realistic, with shadows and shading providing a strong sense of three dimensions. Thutmose was concerned, however, that the prince might find his realistic portrayal of the prince's peculiar physiognomy unflattering. When he was engrossed in sketching, it seemed as if his hand simply rendered what his eye was seeing, without the intervention of a censor transmuting it to a more polite portrayal.

The prince had a long, narrow face, with prominent, heavy-lidded eyes, full lips and a long, jutting chin. Never very athletic, he had narrow shoulders, heavy thighs and the beginnings of a pot belly. Tradition dictated that pharaohs and future pharaohs should be portrayed in an idealized way that "corrected" such flaws, showing the royal one as the perfect god incarnate he was supposed to be. Given time, Thutmose could alter his initial sketch to portray his patron in a more flattering, but less accurate, manner, but for now, it was uncompromising in its realism.

"Interesting," commented Auta, "very interesting. I like the way you've shaded the figures to give them depth, Thutmose, and the way you've used light and shadow in your composition. The result is remarkably life-like."

"I agree," said the prince. "The dancers seem about to twirl off the page, and you can almost hear the music."

"However," admonished the master, "you have violated the canons for portrayal of the royal family. You can get away with it here, but don't use this style in official art unless it's been pre-approved by the king or queen. And don't ever let the priests catch sight of it! It's far too radical for them - they'd never allow it. And you should make the prince's shoulders broader and his face a more ideal oval."

"Why?" demanded the prince. "Why should he do that? His drawing is correct: my shoulders *are* narrow, and my face is far from ideal. Why shouldn't an artist show people as they really are? I **like** this more realistic style! I want my artists to show me as I really am, imperfections and all!"

Even Master Auta, experienced courtier that he was, didn't know what to make of this.

"Your Highness may, of course, have your artists paint you in whatever manner you choose. Be aware, however, that the priesthood is certain to object. To them, art is part of the ritual of worship, which was ordained of old and must not be changed. A new and different style smacks of heresy to them. Even Pharaoh may not be able to move the priesthood to change."

"In that case," commented Thutmose, "the gods only know what they'd make of Bek's style."

Auta moved on to Bek's drawing.

If Thutmose's style was too realistic, Bek's went to the opposite extreme. No one could accuse him of being a realist! Bek seemed determined to magnify the prince's physical peculiarities in a bizarre, yet unique style all his own. He exaggerated the prince's long face, giving him an elongated, egg-shaped head, large lips and forward-jutting chin, atop a spindly body with narrow shoulders and a distended belly. Having established this caricature of the prince, he then applied its characteristics to all other members of the royal family.

Oddly enough, the prince did not seem the least bit offended by this exceedingly unflattering portrayal. He leafed through a pile of Bek's drawings until he came to one showing a group of priests performing a religious ceremony. Bek had applied his same exaggerated style to this group, showing the high priest with a large beak of a nose, skinny arms and a big belly. Master Auta was horrified, but the prince laughed out loud.

"You've caught the essence of the pompous old goat, Bek," chortled the prince.

"You should be more careful, Bek," chided Master Auta. "The high priest may seem like a foolish old man to you, but he's a very powerful old man. It would be very unwise to offend him. Even Pharaoh goes out of his way not to offend him."

"I don't believe in his god, anyway," replied Bek. "If Amun-Re had any real power, he'd have struck me down by now - and look, no lightning!" Bek put his arms out to the side, turned his face to the heavens and twirled around.

"Hush, you foolish boy!" chided Auta. "The high priest has ears everywhere. He doesn't have to rely on the god for his power. The high priest would be a very bad person to make an enemy! Take my advice and be very wary of him."

"Yes, Master," agreed Bek, somewhat subdued. "Whatever you say."

"Have a care, Bek," seconded the prince. "He's trying to warn you for your own good."

"Yes, Your Highness," agreed Bek.

"But tell me," said the prince, "why do you draw in that exaggerated, elongated style? You make people's heads look like strange, drawn-out melons. I know that I have an odd-shaped head, but all of these other people don't," he added, gesturing toward the group of dancers and musicians.

"I show things the way I see them," stated Bek.

Thutmose protested, "You can't mean to tell me you see people's heads egg-shaped like that! If you do, there's something seriously wrong with your eyes!"

"It's not so much my physical eyes that see them this way," explained Bek, "it's my inner eye. Here, I'll show you."

He pulled out a drawing from the pile.

"All of the people in this scene are members of the royal family. There's a certain family resemblance between them, a look about them, that I'm trying to show by exaggerating their common features - begging your pardon, my Lord Prince. If I repeat this often enough and people get used to seeing it, pretty soon it becomes a way of saying, visually, 'this person is a member of the royal family.' I'm also trying to convey a particular feeling by exaggerating certain gestures and expressions."

The prince and Thutmose looked closely at the drawing, then at others of the royal family.

"An interesting idea," observed the prince. "You're creating your own iconography, as it were."

"That's true," Bek agreed.

"All right," conceded Thutmose, "I'll admit that your work captures a certain something about them. But it seems to me that, by showing them all the same distorted, exaggerated way, you miss their individual characters. They're all the same, not unique individuals - and that's what I'm trying to capture. You're looking at what makes them the same, but I want to show what makes them different, what makes each one a unique individual."

"You show one truth," said Bek, "and I show another - but both are truths."

"I see what you mean, Bek," commented the prince, thoughtfully. "Each artist sees the truth differently, so even if they paint the same scene, each one paints it differently. Fascinating! Each artist's interpretation portrays a different understanding of the truth."

"That's exactly what I meant, Your Highness," agreed Bek.

"So, as long as you are all free to paint according to your own individual vision, in your own individual style, the overall result is a richer view of the world," commented the prince.

"As always, Your Highness is perceptive and wise far beyond your years," observed Master Auta.

"When I am Pharaoh," said the prince, "you will be free to create art in your own unique style. The world continues to change, and so must Egypt. The Two Lands are not the same as they were in Menes' time, or Djoser's time, or even my father's time. We must change, too!"

"Hear, hear!" agreed Bek and Thutmose.

"I agree, my prince," said Master Auta. "But I fear the priesthood will not, and many others will stand with them."

"When I am Pharaoh," said the prince, "I will **make** them agree!"

Auta turned aside and muttered to himself, "Then the gods help you, my prince!"

Chapter 5: Royal Companion

The prince took a liking to Bek and me and often took us with him on his jaunts about the city or countryside, sometimes stopping to have us draw scenes that took his fancy.

The prince's gilded chariot moved slowly through the city street as his horses picked their way through the crowds. A score of guards trotted alongside, clearing the way with their shields, while their captain preceded them, shouting, "Make way for His Highness, Amenhotep, Horus in the Nest!"

On this particular day, Bek balanced precariously in the chariot, wedged in behind His Highness and the charioteer, clutching a leather strap attached to the front railing. Thutmose rode in a second chariot behind them, thankful to have more room, if less honor, in this chariot than in the prince's. He had only rarely ridden in a chariot and felt very ill at ease as the skinny wooden wheels jounced over the uneven cobblestones of the city's streets.

The prince enjoyed these unannounced outings, stopping at random locations, as the fancy took him, to enjoy whatever sights, experiences and goods the city offered. On this day, to Thutmose's vast relief, the fancy that seemed to take the prince was a mighty thirst. They stopped at a tavern to wet the royal palate and enjoy the performance of an itinerant group of acrobats. Thutmose and Bek obediently sketched the gyrations of the acrobats, well lubricated by generous libations of beer. The prince seemed to enjoy their quick sketches of lively city life.

At other times, he made forays into the surrounding desert, apparently seeking solitude. More and more, on these occasions, he chose to leave the loquacious Bek behind, preferring the quiet company of Thutmose. He would have liked to leave his guards behind, but his father had strictly forbidden it. There were far too many dangers, both natural and man-made, for a prince to go wandering around the countryside unguarded.

Late one afternoon, Thutmose and the prince rode out into the eastern desert, accompanied by the captain of the guards in a chariot, and a troop of guards on foot, hard-pressed to keep up with the horses. On an open stretch, the prince mischievously whipped his horses into a gallop. The captain lagged a bit behind, while his foot soldiers gamely double-timed behind them. The captain knew very well that this flat stretch would soon come to an end at the cliffs' edge. He was also well aware that this prince knew this, as he had often ridden here before.

Indeed, by the time the foot soldiers arrived, the prince and Thutmose were standing near the cliffs' edge, admiring the view of the river and city below. Their captain was tending both teams of horses, while keeping an eye on his royal master.

The prince and Thutmose seated themselves in the scanty shade of some large rocks. At the prince's request, the soldiers found places in the rocks at least fifty paces away and maintained a respectful silence. The prince sat cross-legged and meditated, eyes closed, for a full half hour, while Thutmose sketched the view.

The silence was as stark as the landscape, harsh shadows lengthening as the sun sank lower in the sky. Thutmose, absorbed in his sketching, was unaware of anything else around him. Suddenly, he heard the captain's sharp intake of breath a few yards away. At the same moment, a flicker of movement at the far edge of vision caught his eye. Turning towards it, he saw, to his horror, a black cobra slithering straight toward the prince, who was still deep in meditation. Further away, Thutmose saw several of the soldiers stirring and picking up their weapons, but their captain held up a forbidding hand, knowing they were too far away to help. Any attempts to approach might only provoke the snake. Thutmose was closest to the prince, but he was unarmed.

As he was debating whether he could possibly throw himself on the snake before it could strike the prince, the snake coiled itself, reared up and flared its hood before the prince. Its head was less than an armslength from the prince's. Amenhotep's eyes opened and looked into those of the snake, almost at his eye level. Otherwise, he moved not a muscle. The men were frozen in horror, watching their future monarch face the deadly snake. If he died, their lives were forfeit, too.

Amenhotep stared unblinking at the snake for what must have been a full two minutes. To the watching men, it seemed like an eternity. Finally, the snake drew in its hood, sank to the ground and slithered away, disappearing into the rocks. The watching guards and their captain nearly collapsed with relief. Thutmose discovered that his hands were shaking too hard to continue drawing.

He packed up his supplies and carried them back to the chariot, waking the charioteer, who had slept in the shade of his vehicle through the whole incident. He could hear a rising buzz of conversation among the guardsmen, commenting in awe on their prince's calm in the face of imminent death.

"He was very cool, facing it down like that," said one soldier.

"Of course," said another. "It was a royal cobra. He knew it would do him no harm. It is a protector of royalty."

"Did you see?" said a third, "He looked it in the eyes and ordered it to leave, and it did."

Thutmose smiled to himself, realizing he had witnessed a legend in the making. He knew the story would grow and become part of the prince's royal mystique. Although, he admitted to himself, it had been pretty remarkable. Who would have thought this prince, hardly a notable physical specimen, would turn out to be so cool in facing down death?

The royal party returned with alacrity to the palace. The guardsmen headed off to their favorite taverns to slake their desert thirst with plentiful beer and tell the story of how the prince had communed with the royal cobra, eye to eye, and ordered it to leave, and it had gone.

Later, when his hands had stopped shaking, Thutmose painted the scene on a large sheet of papyrus and presented it to the prince. The queen was so taken with the scene, she ordered him to paint it on a wall in the audience chamber, replacing several images of lesser gods.

The royal family moved frequently back and forth between the southern capital of Thebes and the northern capital at Memphis, near the point where the mighty Nile split to form the delta. Some of the more advanced students followed them on these peregrinations. So it was that, after two years of study, Thutmose and Bek made the journey north again in one of the numerous boats following in the wake of the royal barque.

Their earlier journey up the river had been made under sail, using the power of the wind to overcome the Nile current. Thutmose had heard that it was Egyptians who had first harnessed the wind this way, although he was not sure whether this was true or merely patriotic boasting. Others he had met - notably, members of the Mitanni delegation - insisted that Mesopotamia had invented the first sailboats. Of course, they were at least equally guilty of patriotic bias. At any rate, on the voyage downriver, they had no need of sails. The boatmen had only to steer the boat as it rode the river toward the sea.

Their boat was quite long, about fifty royal cubits. The royal barque, "Radiance of the Aten", was much longer, almost ninety royal cubits, and gilded from stem to stern. (Thutmose had heard it said that, if a cubit was the length of a man's forearm, a royal cubit was the length of a *tall* man's forearm.) Like the royal barque, the artists' boat had a hull that was curved in an arc, rising to a pillar taller than a man both fore and aft. The hull was crafted of cedar imported from Lebanon, the planks held together by wooden pegs. Its draught was quite shallow and it was narrow of beam. Most of its deck was occupied by a large cabin and an open-sided, shaded area. It had twin steering oars affixed to the sides near the stern, yoked together so that steering one turned them both.

A few days' pleasant cruising brought them to Memphis, the administrative capital of Egypt. The royal family was anxious to escape the clutches of bureaucracy by repairing to the relative privacy of the royal villa on the Queen's pleasure lake.

Thutmose was happy to accompany them, as this allowed him to visit his family for the first time in two years. He had sent a messenger ahead to warn them of his visit, so he was not surprised to find a flock of neighbors' children keeping watch for him on the road. They immediately sent up a shout upon spotting him. Thutmose's mother and little sister came running and threw themselves on him as soon as he came in sight. His father came along behind at a more dignified pace. He greeted them happily and was introduced to a new baby brother.

After he had held the new baby and made appropriate oohing and aahing noises, they led him to the village square. Here, to his surprise, the entire village turned out to greet him. Since he was the only village son ever to enter service at the royal court, he was an object of intense curiosity. Everyone wanted to know what the palace and the royal family were like. They were all agog on learning that the crown prince not only knew him by name, but often took him along as a chosen companion.

The neighbor girl Mariamne was now more smitten with him than ever, since he had acquired such a glamorous aura by association. Thutmose concluded that she had not taken her eyes off of him for more than two minutes during the entire course of his visit. The girl was a couple of years younger than he was, the daughter of a Habiru herdsman who had settled nearby and taken up farming. Quite a few of these Asiatic herdsmen had settled in this region, Goshen, during his grandfather's time. Thutmose had heard that they were all part of the family of the Grand Vizier Yuya, the Queen's father. Pharaoh Thutmosis IV had given them permission to settle in the area, with generous grants of fertile land. Most had become productive, prosperous farmers, craftsmen and traders, intermarrying with local Egyptians.

There was still, however, a residual level of distrust of Asiatic foreigners moving into the area. This was how the Hyksos had started out, two hundred and fifty years before. They had moved in as peaceful traders and settlers, prospered, multiplied, then gradually taken over. It had taken the Theban Pharaohs Seqenenra, Kamose and Ahmose twenty years of fighting to expel them - and this area near the northeastern frontier was precisely the same area the Hyksos had dominated. The memories were still fresh enough to engender a profound distrust of similar nomadic herdsmen moving in from the deserts to the north and east.

This bias had always seemed unreasonable to Thutmose. The Habiru he knew seemed like good people, and they claimed to be completely unrelated to the Hyksos, even to have fought against some of them in Canaan. Certainly, Mariamne's father was a good sort, a kind, good-natured man who often shared his surplus grapes with the potter's family. Like most boys his age, however, he found the adoration of a younger child - especially a girl - to be an embarrassment. While he had enjoyed his visit home, he was happy to escape Mariamne's omnipresent gaze and return to the royal establishment.

A few days after his return to the villa, the prince commanded his company on an expedition into the marshes. When he was in a mood for peace and quiet, the prince often retired to the countryside to contemplate the beauty of nature, which he deeply loved. He said these interludes restored his soul, after days immersed in the artifice and backbiting atmosphere of court. Thutmose had become his favorite companion on these jaunts, as he was happy to sit quietly and draw, whereas his good friend Bek seemed unable to use his eyes and hands without activating his mouth, which strained even the prince's tolerant nature.

This day's outing was ostensibly a fishing and fowling expedition into the marshes between the river and the royal lake. Thutmose knew this was an excuse, however, as the prince was not an avid or accomplished hunter. He had confessed to Thutmose, in strictest confidence, that his eyesight was very poor. He couldn't see the birds well enough to have a chance of hitting them with a throwing stick, and his unavoidable ineptitude was a source of embarrassment. He also admitted that it grieved him to see the beautiful winged creatures bloody and lifeless. He had a great love of nature and of all living things. Such an attitude was almost unheard of, but Thutmose, lover of beauty, understood how his young master felt. It must have been this sense of finding a kindred spirit that led the prince to confide in the artist. It also made Thutmose the prince's favorite companion for these jaunts, since they both admired the beauty of creation and Thutmose could be trusted to keep the prince's secret.

On this day, a party of some ten or twelve small boats set out from the shore of the royal lake. The prince and Thutmose were in the lead skiff, with Thutmose poling the small papyrus boat while the prince, standing in the rear, made a show of hurling throwing sticks into the air after birds flushed from among the reeds. The prince's bodyguard and a scattering of other young courtiers fanned out behind them in other reed boats.

Once they left the lake, they entered the maze of waterways leading to the river, winding through small islands and reeds almost as tall as the standing boatmen. The water was still high from the inundation two months before. When the high water descending from the mountains of Punt far away in the south reached the Nile delta, they fanned out over the nearly flat landscape, turning it into a vast marshy sea. It was a labyrinth of papyrus and water, filled with birds, fish - and crocodiles.

Once they had entered the forest of reeds, the prince rebelliously outdistanced most of his guardians, urging Thutmose to pole faster through the twisting, reedy channels. Once they had lost most of the others, Thutmose brought down a few birds for the prince to claim as his own catch. Much as they both disliked killing them, Thutmose was competent at it, since he had been helping to feed his family by hunting since childhood, and the prince would be embarrassed to come back totally empty-handed.

After a while, they switched roles, the prince poling the skiff while Thutmose sketched the scene. He was so absorbed in perfecting his drawing of birds' wings that he lost track of their location. Suddenly, a movement at the edge of his vision caught his eye. When he looked up, he saw what appeared to be a floating log in the channel ahead. Looking around, he recognized a particularly large old tree and knew exactly where he was.

"Your Highness!" he cried, "Not this way! We must turn back at once! This is the territory of Old Set, a very large, bad-tempered crocodile. The locals regard him as the incarnation of the crocodile god himself. He is reported to have killed at least a dozen people in the last twenty years."

The prince, in confusion, tried to reverse direction, with limited effectiveness. Thutmose picked up his wooden sketching board and began to use it like a paddle, propelling them back into the channel they had just left. The "log" lazily followed, closing the distance at a leisurely pace. Thutmose paddled harder and the prince poled faster.

Just then, half a dozen of the other boats of their party came around a bend in the channel.

"Help!" cried Thutmose to the boatloads of guards. "There's a crocodile closing in on us!" He paddled harder.

The guards' boats moved quickly around either side of the prince's skiff, their occupants with bows and arrows and spears at the ready. Several guardsmen hurled their spears at the beast and a couple of arrows lodged in its back. While it did not appear to be seriously wounded, this was enough to discourage the crocodile. It broke off pursuit, veered and sped off into a side channel, where it disappeared among the reeds.

The prince and Thutmose shuddered with relief.

Maintaining his apparent calm before the guards, the prince said loudly, "Oh, well, the old bugger had probably eaten all the birds, anyway."

Playing along, Thutmose said, "True. Besides, the sun's getting low. It's probably a good time to go home."

"Agreed," said the prince. "Much as I love to watch the sunset, I dislike being eaten alive by hordes of mosquitoes."

They were only too happy to remain with their escort for the rest of the journey back to the villa. Thutmose resisted the temptation to kiss the ground with relief once they were safely ashore. For a time, he had feared that the Horus in the Nest was about to suffer the same fate as his divine "father", Osiris, who had been torn to pieces by his evil brother, Set, the crocodile god. He resolved to make a sacrifice to Hapy, god of the Nile, for protecting them from the river beast that day.

At the door to the villa, the prince turned to him and said quietly, "Thank you for keeping my secret, and for getting me away from the jaws of the crocodile, my friend. I will not forget this."

Chapter 6: As Above, So Below

Soon after our encounter with the crocodile, we returned south to Thebes. By now, Bek and I were among the senior students, so we were often called upon to sketch and record the lives of the royal family. For official occasions, we sometimes accompanied one of the royal scribes. On less formal occasions, two or three of us would go as a group. Eventually, we were trusted to perform this function without supervision. The royal family and members of the court were so used to our presence, they took no more notice of us than of the furniture. Thus, we were often privy to the most important of state secrets and the most intimate details of the royal family's private lives.

We also attended the many religious functions that were a daily part of Pharaoh's life, such as making offerings in the great Temple of Amun. Although the priesthood of Amun kept growing in power, threatening to encroach upon the privileges of the king, Pharaoh Amenhotep kept them mollified with generous offerings. I strongly doubted, however, that the prince would continue to be so generous when he came to power, given what Bek and I had heard him say in private.

On one of these occasions, several of the young artists had gone to the great temple before the royal family, in order to be in position to capture their entry into the temple. Entering the deep shadow of the sanctuary from the brilliant equatorial sunlight was a physical shock, almost like running into a dark, solid wall. Thutmose stumbled on the paving stones and had to catch himself to keep from falling. He hurried after Bek and his comrades. Together, they took up positions seated on the floor near one of the immense columns supporting the distant roof.

Once his eyes had adjusted to the gloom, Thutmose looked around at the interior of the temple. The walls were covered with paintings and friezes of Pharaoh smiting the enemies of the Two Lands, Pharaoh as the living incarnation of Horus, Pharaoh facing Osiris in the Underworld, and, of course, Pharaoh giving homage to the great god Amun. Huge statues of the god (looking remarkably like Pharaoh, the donor of this mighty temple) flanked a raised dais. In front of this, the High Priest, First Prophet Ptahmosis intoned prayers, swinging a censer of burning incense while dedicating offerings to the god. His lieutenants, the Second, Third and Fourth Prophets of Amun, stood behind him, heads reverently bowed. At one side, a group of the Godswives of Amun punctuated each phrase by jingling their sistrums, small instruments consisting of a loop of wire strung with small metal discs, all mounted on a short stick. These produced jingling tones much like a tambourine.

The Godswives of Amun had been founded early in the current dynasty by the great queen Ahmose-Nefertari, wife of Pharaoh Ahmosis. Ahmosis had completed the expulsion of the Hyksos and founded the present dynasty, elevating his capital, Thebes, and its deity, Amun, in the process. Under his sister-wife Ahmose-Nefertari, the Godswives had become a very powerful organization of women. Following in her footsteps, many future queens had served in the order, often as the Great Wife of Amun - essentially, the spiritual Queen of Egypt. However, later royal women typically retired from the post upon becoming an earthly Queen. The organization continued to acquire more wealth with each generation, as the members' property was typically bequeathed to the order. It became the custom for full-fledged members not to marry. Instead, they adopted new members as their "daughters", who assumed their posts in their own turn. They had their own estates and temples, but almost always participated in ceremonies in the Great Temple at Luxor.

The artists sketched the priests and Godswives, taking a break to prostrate themselves before Pharaoh when he entered, accompanied by the Queen and Prince. The high priest acknowledged Pharaoh's arrival with a dignified bow, then swung the censer all around him to sanctify his presence. The priests resumed their chanting, which seemed to go on interminably.

Thutmose looked up from his papyrus just in time to see the Queen surreptitiously elbow Pharaoh when he started to nod off. Thutmose exchanged looks with Bek, who barely restrained a smile. The prince looked bored with the whole affair.

The priest intoned, "O, mighty Amun-Re, who dost ride thy fiery chariot daily through the sky, confer thy blessings on this land and on its lord, Amenhotep, thy living avatar here in this life! Shower thy waters of life upon the Two Lands, causing the mighty Nile to rise and fall in its appointed cycle, bestowing life and fertility upon the land! Bless us with thy's sun's rays, bringing light and life to all here below."

He paused for breath, then concluded, "So be it here, as in the life hereafter!"

The priest sprinkled a golden yellow powder into a brazier burning before the altar. Bright blue light shot up, accompanied by a pungent smell.

"Essence of volcano, with a hint of rotten eggs," decided Thutmose. He sketched in the flame.

His sketch realistically depicted the royal family, the Godswives and the four priests before the altar. He glanced over at Bek's sketch board and saw a caricature of the scene, with exaggerated long heads and bottom-heavy bodies, which Bek quickly hid beneath a stilted, traditional, orthodox drawing. Meeting Bek's glance, Thutmose rolled his eyes and shook his head in mock despair.

Looking back at the altar, he saw that the high priest had stepped aside. Pharaoh now climbed the steps to the altar, followed by his son. At his sign, Ani, the Royal Accounting Scribe for Offerings to All the Gods, stepped up to the base of the dais. He read out a tally of offerings as each item was brought in by a servant. There were endless jars of oil and bags of grain, followed by coffers of gold and trays of dates and grapes; and men leading bullocks and goats and pigs and carrying cages filled with birds. All of these were deposited in a vast heap at one side of the dais. The reins of the animals were handed off to minor temple priests waiting to receive them.

The temple scribes' eyes glittered as they surveyed all this wealth. Thutmose could see them counting on their fingers as they attempted to evaluate it. The four Prophets looked for all the world like a group of cats who had just inherited a lifetime supply of fresh cream.

Pharaoh made a last obeisance to the altar, then dismissed the servants and the Accounting Scribe. He moved back down to rejoin the Queen. The royal retinue then departed with all due pomp and circumstance, leaving the priests to gleefully count their treasure.

The prince, who had stayed behind, walked over to the group of artists and inspected their work. He looked through several of the younger students' sketches, then moved on to Thutmose.

Pausing at a particularly lifelike sketch of his father and himself before the altar, with the Four Prophets, he exclaimed, "Oh, I really like this one. You've caught my father's likeness very well."

Unnoticed by any of them, the high priest had stepped up behind the prince and was looking over his shoulder. Now his face darkened as he said,

"What is this? This is not how the gods and His Divine Majesty are to be shown! Why, in this drawing, His Majesty looks like a tired old man with a sagging belly, not the perfect earthly incarnation of the god, forever young and strong!"

Thutmose froze. His drawing had not been meant for the eyes of the high priest. He was only too aware of Master Auta's warning not to antagonize this powerful old man.

The prince came to his rescue.

"That may be true," he said calmly, "but his artist's vision is also true. My father may be a god incarnate - as, indeed, am I," he said with added emphasis, "but he is also a man, a man who is no longer young. It is the man this artist has drawn."

The First Prophet was not mollified. He sputtered angrily, "This is sacrilege! Pharaoh must always be shown as perfect, and in the approved, traditional manner!"

"Why?" asked the prince, looking at the priest with the pure, innocent gaze of a child asking a simple question - and in the act, questioning the foundation on which the entire mass of religious tradition was built.

"Because it has always been so, since Horus was first conceived by the resurrected Osiris!" he snapped. "Pharaoh is no ordinary mortal - images of His Divine Majesty must show this! He is the father of his country, indeed, the embodiment of its very soul. As such, he must be shown to be physically perfect, immune to the age and illness that beset ordinary mortals!

"The people must be assured of his physical and spiritual power," he continued. "And he must be shown in the traditional poses that say to the people, 'here is a king, a living god', doing what only kings can do! Any man may eat or sleep, but only a king may smite the enemies of the Two Lands, and only a living god can speak to the gods on behalf of his people, and to his people on behalf of the gods. Do you understand this?"

Thutmose nodded meekly. Even Bek mumbled his agreement.

"Yes, Your Eminence," they agreed.

The prince said nothing.

"Good," said the high priest. "Let me see no more of this sacrilegious art!"

"Yes, Your Eminence," they repeated.

The First Prophet stalked off, followed by his entourage, noses in the air.

When they were gone, Bek made a face and commented, "Yes, Your Sanctimoniousness! The gods forbid there should be anything *new* under the sun!"

Prince Amenhotep looked after the priests, then back at the young artists. He looked at Bek and shook his head. Smiling slightly, he raised an eyebrow, then, placing a finger to his lips, said quietly,

"Bide your time, Bek. My day will come, and when it does, then so shall yours. Until then, do not cross him."

Bek bowed to his young master.

"As Your Highness wishes," he agreed.

This was but the opening skirmish in what would prove to be a long war, a war between tradition and innovation, the old and the new, the royal family and the priesthood - indeed, between the very gods themselves.

Not all wars were so abstract, however, as the Two Lands were forever in conflict with surrounding countries. We had enjoyed a long period of relative peace, having made an alliance with our former rivals, the Mitanni, who lived between the upper reaches of two famous rivers, the Tigris and the Euphrates. Now, a new enemy, the Hittites, to the northwest, were growing ever more powerful, whittling away the territory that had been controlled by the Mitanni, in spite of the reinforcements led by Egypt's commanding general, Ramose.

Thutmose was assigned to record the private meetings of Pharaoh and his top advisors, along with the Royal Scribe, Hunefer. Pharaoh and his father-in-law, the Grand Vizier, Yuya, were discussing affairs of state in a small audience chamber adjoining the royal family's private quarters. The prince lounged in a chair nearby, while servants plied the three men with food and drink. The prince did a poor job of concealing his boredom with foreign affairs.

Pharaoh dismissed the servants with a wave of his hand, but smiled at the scribe and artist, indicating that they should stay, after which he ignored them.

Lord Yuya picked up a roll of papyrus from a pile on a nearby table.

"Have you seen this latest dispatch from General Ramose, Your Majesty?" he asked.

"I haven't read it yet," replied the king. "What does he say?"

"He writes from northern Canaan." Yuya read from the scroll, "'We have fought a long battle against the Hittites north of the River Euphrates. We fought them to a standstill, yet can scarcely claim it as a victory, as the casualties were great on both sides.'"

As the Vizier read General Ramose's report, Thutmose could see the battlefield in his mind's eye. Amid the swirling dust, he could see Egyptian and Mitanni soldiers on foot and in chariots battling Hittite warriors in fierce hand-to-hand fighting. He had recently seen a captured Hittite chariot fitted with a new weapon: a sharp scythe affixed to the axle of each wheel, its cubit-long bronze blade cutting a swathe of destruction on either side. He shuddered at the thought of the carnage it conjured.

The General calmly reported the tally of dead and wounded on both sides, but the artist's eye could see the field of battle, littered now with the bodies of dead and wounded men and horses. Egyptian and Mitanni solders carried their wounded off the field, while others rounded up Hittite prisoners. At one side, he could see the General in his tent, dictating to a scribe.

Yuya resumed reading, "'The Hittites continue to expand their territory, at the expense of the Mitanni to the east and the Canaanites to the south. Together with our ally, King Shuttarna of Mitanni, we have stopped their advance, for now, and have negotiated a truce. However, I doubt it will hold for long. These Hittites are an unrelentingly aggressive, warlike people. All signs indicate that they intend to keep expanding their empire.

"'It behooves us to support our allies in this area, especially the Mitanni, so that they may continue to serve as a buffer between the Empire of Hatti and our homeland,'" he continued. "It is signed, 'Your devoted Servant, Ramose, General of the Army of the North.'"

"I agree with him," said the king. "Better to strengthen the Mitanni, so they can keep the Hittites occupied, rather than wake to find them on our doorstep!"

"Wisely said, Your Majesty," agreed Yuya. "I take it, then, that you agree we should send the gold, men and supplies the general requests?"

"I do," agreed Pharaoh. "See that it is done."

"At once, Your Majesty," answered Lord Yuya.

The Vizier picked up a blank papyrus, dipped a quill into a small blue faience inkpot and wrote out the order. When it was finished, he shook fine sand from a dispenser over it to absorb the excess ink. After blowing off the sand, he handed it to Pharaoh, who read it quickly. He passed the scroll to the scribe, who poured a small amount of melted wax onto it from a small copper pot kept warm over a nearby brazier. Pharaoh pressed his signet ring into the soft wax, then handed it to a waiting messenger.

"Send this to General Ramose," he instructed the man.

"At once, Your Majesty," the messenger acknowledged. He bowed crisply, then dashed off.

Lord Yuya picked up another document from the pile. Unrolling it, he said, "The King of Mitanni also writes to you."

"Hah!" said Amenhotep. "I suppose he's asking for still more gold - as always! He seems to think I'm made of gold."

"He does, indeed," agreed Yuya. "Let's see what he has to say."

He scanned the scroll, then paraphrased its contents. "He greets you as a brother monarch, and so on and so forth, and asks after the well-being of his daughter, the Princess Gilukhipa, whom he sent to become your wife nearly five years ago. Shall I write to tell him she is well?"

"Yes, of course," agreed the king. "And ask her if she wishes to add any personal messages to the missive."

"Certainly, Your Majesty," acknowledged the Vizier. He then consulted the scroll again. "Ah! Just as you expected, My Lord: he asks for more gold. And not merely gold - he wants it in statue form! 'Two statues,' he writes, 'of solid gold, each three cubits in height.'"

"Statues?" exclaimed the king. "Aren't ingots good enough for him any more? Statues, indeed!"

He shook his head skeptically, then relented. "Oh, all right, tell him he can have his statues - but warn him that they'll take some time to make. If he's going to be picky, he can just wait a while. Horus only knows, the Hittites will probably relieve him of his statues soon enough, anyway."

"True enough, Your Majesty," agreed Yuya. "And may I suggest, Your Majesty, that the statues should be of yourself?"

At this, the king laughed and said, "Very good, Lord Yuya. I like the way your mind works. Make them statues of myself and Queen Tiye."

"An excellent idea, Your Majesty. It shall be done," agreed Yuya, signaling to the scribe, who wrote it down.

The king turned to the prince, who was gazing glassy-eyed out the window.

"What do you think, my son?" he asked.

"Think of what, father?" asked the prince, startled.

"The King of Mitanni's demand for two gold statues. Do you think he should get them?" asked the king.

The prince frowned and said, "I don't see why you cater to his demands, father. Under the circumstances, it seems to me that he's in no position to be demanding anything. He ought to be down on his knees begging for whatever help we can give him. It seems to me that he's benefiting much more from this arrangement than we are."

"Now, now, my son," admonished the king. "He is a fellow king, and my father-in-law, as well as one of our oldest allies. And as I said earlier, it is in our own best interest to keep him strong enough to go on fighting the Hittites. Better him than us!"

The prince bowed his head to his father. "You are wise, as always, my father," he acknowledged.

"Speaking of wisdom," said the king, changing the subject, "I don't think it too wise on your part to flaunt your unorthodox views before the First Prophet of Amun."

"He told you about our encounter in the temple?" asked the prince.

"Oh, yes," said the king. "At great length. He told me all about your pet artists' deviations from accepted iconic forms."

The king looked pointedly at Thutmose, who kept his head down and continued sketching.

"I have encouraged you to think for yourself," the king continued, "but it would be wise to temper that freedom of thought with a certain restraint of speech. You're a very bright young man. You should realize that it is not smart to pull the leopard's tail! The priesthood of Amun is very powerful. It would be wise to avoid offending them."

"But that's just the problem, father," the prince protested. "The only way to avoid offending them is never to have a thought of one's own. The priesthood of Amun don't want people to think for themselves."

"Of course not," observed the king. "They're no fools. They know their power comes from tradition, from having people continue to believe as the priests have always taught them. And that is good for us, as well," he added.

"It is one thing for you, as crown prince, to believe as you choose," he continued. "It is another thing entirely to spread those beliefs abroad. If everyone believed exactly as he chose, there would be anarchy! After all, do not forget that we, as Pharaohs, depend upon those beliefs, as well. Our major source of power as kings derives from our divine nature as living avatars of Horus, who is an aspect of Amun-Re. If you undermine the traditional gods, you risk undermining your own source of royal power. You forget that at your own peril!"

"Yes, father," the prince agreed meekly.

Pharaoh patted his son on the shoulder. "Good lad," he said, and started to turn away.

"But, father," interrupted the prince. Pharaoh turned back to him, a look of annoyance on his face. The prince continued anyway. "Haven't you always said that the priesthood are too powerful, that we need to keep them in check?"

"Yes, I have. But I do that indirectly, not by flying in the face of established traditions," replied Pharaoh. "That is one reason I have built up the army and carefully cultivated its generals - that, and of course, to keep our external enemies at bay, people like the Nubians and the Hittites and the Mittani."

"I thought the Mittani were our allies," commented the prince, perplexed.

"They are now - but it was not always so. We began the process of converting them to allies by diplomacy; we continued it by intermarriage; but it has been the rise of the Hittites, the western neighbors of Mittani, their greatest enemy and ours, that has cemented the alliance," Pharaoh pointed out.

"Ah, I see," said the prince. "You mean, the enemies of our greatest enemy are our friends."

"That's the idea. And by the same token, we can weaken our enemies by keeping them at each other's throats, instead of ours. If one threatens to overwhelm another, we can shore up the weaker one - "

"Like Mittani," observed the prince.

"Precisely. We shore up the weaker foe to keep the stronger one at bay," said Pharaoh. "We can maintain internal balance in the Two Lands by the same 'divide and conquer' strategy. Hence, we build up the army to counterbalance the priesthood, but we let the priesthood retain much of its power to keep the army in check. Otherwise, if either generals or priests were to become too powerful, they might be tempted to try and seize the throne."

"I see," said the prince, nodding his head thoughtfully. "You are very wise, my father."

"Indeed he is," agreed Lord Yuya. "See that you learn from him, so that you, too, may become a wise king."

"Yes, Grandfather," the prince agreed.

Chapter 7: Renewal

Not long after that, the old king's health began to fail - not all at once, but a long, slow decline. He was less vigorous and energetic than he had been, and less interested in either foreign or domestic policy. He seemed tired much of the time, and his previously erect posture began to sag.

Queen Tiye was deeply concerned for her husband's health and did everything in her power to help him. She prayed daily to all the Egyptian gods reputed to have healing power, making daily visits to temples in and around Thebes, and frequent pilgrimages to shrines up and down the Nile. In private, she prayed to El, the god of her father's and grandfather's people. In public, she did all she could to disguise Pharaoh's failing health, taking over much of the work of correspondence with foreign rulers, as well as with nomarchs and leaders of Egypt's substantial bureaucracy.

Word filtered out, however, and soon allied leaders began inquiring courteously about Pharaoh's health. The King of Mitanni even sent statues of Ishtar and Baal to aid in the improvement of his brother king's health.

It was all to no avail. Nor was His Majesty helped much by the efforts of his many doctors nor the special diet personally overseen by the Queen. She decided that something special was needed.

She called for her father, the Grand Vizier. They met in private in her small audience chamber. She dismissed all her servants, save only her guard and her father's, who took up their posts outside the door.

"I called you here, father, because I'm concerned about my husband's health," Tiye said, mincing no words.

"I suspected as much," replied her father.

"I've done everything I can, but nothing seems to help. I've prayed to every god I can think of, even the statues of Baal and Ishtar sent by the King of Mitanni, but the king's health continues to decline. Can you suggest anything else?"

Yuya looked thoughtful for a moment, then sadly shook his head. "I'm afraid not. El has given me the power to interpret dreams, but sadly, not the power to heal."

"There is one last thing we haven't tried," said the Queen.

"What's that?"

"A *Sed* festival. It was designed to renew and rejuvenate the kings of Egypt."

Yuya thought about it.

"That's true. It might help," he agreed. "However, he did just have a *Sed* festival three years ago, according to tradition, on the thirtieth anniversary of his reign."

"I know," agreed Queen Tiye. "But it's not uncommon for rulers of the Two Lands to have additional *Sed* festivals after that, often at three-year intervals."

"Hmmm. True enough," agreed Yuya. "It's worth a try. Of course, there is one other thing that often accompanies such a renewal."

"Yes?" asked the Queen.

"In order to completely 'renew' the reign, there should also be a new queen," the old man observed, watching her closely. He knew Tiye to be very attached to her power and her prerogatives. She would not be inclined to relinquish any of them.

"Another wife? Who would you suggest?" she asked cautiously.

"Perhaps a Hittite princess?" suggested Yuya. "We could begin to create an alliance with them, instead of confronting them with brute force."

"Never!" exclaimed the Queen. "I will not take such a serpent into my household! Someone with such powerful backing could be a serious threat to my position. The sisters and daughters of the King of Mitanni are one thing - Mitanni's far weaker than we are, and totally dependent on our gold and our army for their survival. Mitanni women are no threat to me. Not so a Hittite princess. If she were offended, her country's armies could do serious harm to Egypt - which means that she would have a great deal of power in Egypt's court. And that means she would be a serious threat to me!"

Yuya was not surprised. He had suspected that would be her reaction.

"There is one other possibility," he said.

"Which is?"

"According to tradition, he could marry one of his daughters. Sitamun is now old enough."

"Sitamun?" she repeated. "Sitamun... Yes, that might work."

He had expected that the notion would appeal to her. It would be a marriage in name only, to fulfill the requirement for a "new" queen. Sitamun, who was now fifteen, would pose no threat to her powerful mother, who dominated her daughters as she did the rest of Egypt. There was no requirement that the marriage actually be consummated - such formal father-daughter pharaonic marriages

seldom were. Sitamun would benefit by an improvement in her status at
court and would acquire the additional title of Queen, although
everyone would be perfectly clear that the only real Queen in Egypt
was Tiye. Nevertheless, Sitamun would be called a queen, and since she
was also a Pharaoh's Daughter, she would outrank every woman in
Egypt other than her own mother. Besides, royal princesses were
seldom allowed to marry anyone other than their own fathers or
brothers, since the husband of a Pharaoh's Daughter would have a
powerful claim to the throne. It was a neat solution for Sitamun as well
as for Queen Tiye.

So it came about that a new *Sed* festival was arranged. It was
carried out with all due ceremony. Under the careful supervision of his
doctors, Pharaoh practiced running, shooting arrows and various other
martial skills, so that he could run the footrace and perform the other
traditional demonstrations of fitness the ceremony required. Indeed, his
health seemed to improve as a result of all these preparations.

When the day came, Pharaoh performed his feats admirably, to
the great reassurance of the people. He also proclaimed his marriage to
his daughter Sitamun, who was presented to the court and the people in
her finest attire. The Queen and the Two Lands breathed a great sigh of
relief, feeling that the festival had indeed succeeded in renewing the
strength and health of the king.

Once the festival was over, life at court went back to "business
as usual". For Sitamun, very little had changed. True, she had a new
title and a better set of apartments in the palace, and some new clothes
and jewelry. Her grandparents, Lord Yuya and Lady Tuya, presented
her with a new chair carved with her new titles, the third in a series of
chairs. They had given her the first one when she was little more than a
toddler, followed by a larger one several years later. The new chair was
fully adult size, in recognition of her *entrée* into both adulthood and
queenship. Other than that, life went on much as before.

Chapter 8: The Trials of Uncommonly Good-Looking Fellows

"You are growing up, my son," Pharaoh said. "Soon, I will have you crowned as my co-regent. You must learn to rule while I still live to teach and guide you. I believe you are almost ready to assume your throne beside me."

The prince's face lit up at this announcement.

"Thank you, father!" he exclaimed. "You know best, of course."

"There must be an appropriate celebration, of course," said the king. "It will take a while to prepare. I think, perhaps, in the spring: the time of renewal and rebirth. What think you, Lord Yuya?"

"An excellent choice, Sire," agreed the Vizier.

"And we must find you a wife," added the king. "You must marry an Heiress to legitimate your rule."

While it was not strictly required that a Pharaoh should marry a woman of his own family - often his own sister - in order to legitimate his reign, it was a time-honored tradition, one that strengthened a new king's claim to the throne. This was especially important now, since the prince's mother came of non-royal stock.

After a few minutes' deliberation, Pharaoh said, "You shall marry your sister, Isis. She has the purest royal blood."

"But, father," protested the prince, "Isis is only ten years old. It will be years before she can bear children!"

"No matter. You can have children by other wives while you are waiting for Isis to grow up."

"I'll marry Isis if I have to, but she will never be my Great Wife!" exclaimed the prince. "I have chosen the lady I want as my queen."

"And who might that be?" asked the king, shocked.

"The Princess Nefertiti! I will have her, and none other, to be my Great Wife!" said the prince.

The king thought about this.

"Nefertiti, eh? What do you think, Vizier?" he asked.

"It's not a bad idea," replied Lord Yuya thoughtfully. "I know I'm biased, since she is my granddaughter - my favorite granddaughter, I might add. While that means she has some foreign blood, like my daughter the Queen, she also has royal blood. And she is a well-mannered, quiet, dignified girl - good qualities for a queen."

Nefertiti's mother, Tintamun, had been the child of Pharaoh Thutmosis IV by Mutemwiya, his Queen. She had married Yuya's son, Aye, while still quite young, and had died giving birth to Nefertiti. Aye had later married Nefertiti's nurse, Lady Tey. While Tey was of noble birth, she was not of nearly as high a class as Princess Tintamun.

"She might not be your first choice, my king," continued Yuya, "but she *is*, technically, an Heiress. It could work."

The king considered this.

"All right," he said to the prince, "I will consider it." He smiled slyly and added, "I certainly can't fault your taste, my son. The girl is a real beauty. She's well-named! 'A beautiful woman comes', indeed!"

Thus it was that I was among the first to learn that my first patroness, the beautiful Nefertiti, might be chosen to marry my master, Prince Amenhotep. I schooled my face to reveal nothing of my feelings, but I could not escape the pang in my heart. I had always known that the lovely princess was as far above me as I was above a gnat, as unobtainable as the sky. Nevertheless, the budding man in me could not deny a deep, abiding yearning for some miracle to bring us together. As long as she belonged to no other, I could still dream. But I knew that, if she married my master, I must banish her image from my very dreams.

From the first moment I saw Nefertiti in her gilded litter before my father's shop, she drew me like a helpless moth to a shining flame. Even as a child, she was beautiful. Now, as she matured into young womanhood, she was breathtaking. It is fortunate, indeed, that, as an artist, I had an excuse for staring at her, for I could not have taken my eyes from her to save my very life. I treasured every moment spent in her presence and, away from prying eyes, I used up many cubits of costly papyrus secretly drawing and painting images of her, which I hid inside the pallet where I slept. Then, and for all the years to come, Nefertiti was my sun, my moon, the shining beacon of my life. I knew she was always and forever hopelessly beyond me, but I was profoundly grateful to the gods for allowing me to spend my life close to her, serving her.

However, not all the young ladies of the court were as well-mannered and restrained as Nefertiti.

As the students became more skillful, they were often allowed to sketch the royal family in the course of their daily activities, at first in small groups in the charge of an older student or scribe. In time, two or three young artists would go as a group. Eventually, the senior students were trusted to perform this function without supervision. The royal family and members of the court were so used to their quiet presence, they took no more notice of the artists than the furniture. The older students were even allowed to sketch and paint the Queen and her ladies in their own apartments. Often, the princesses and young ladies were present, as well, including Thutmose's original patroness, the lovely Nefertiti, now blossoming into womanhood.

One fine day in late fall, Thutmose and Bek were sketching the Queen and a group of her ladies in one of the audience chambers. A group of young princesses and their companions were gathered in one corner of the room. Several of them were playing hounds and jackals or sennet, both favorite board games, while a group of musicians played nearby. One played a great, curved harp nearly as tall as herself, resembling an exaggerated, many-stringed bow, from which it was said to be descended. Another strummed a three-stringed, guitar-like instrument with a sound box made from a large gourd, while a third girl kept time with a tambourine.

The royal daughters and their noble companions were no longer children, but young ladies on the brink of womanhood. Several of them were already promised in marriage to various young nobles of the court. Even so, their eyes wandered from time to time to the only men in the room, the two young artists. There was much whispering and giggling among the girls. The two young men had the very uncomfortable feeling they were being talked about, but the only thing they could do was to ignore it and go on with their work.

There was a sharp rap at the door. The Queen signaled to a servant, who opened the door to admit the Lord Chamberlain and the Grand Vizier. They bowed to the Queen, who motioned them to approach. The three spent some time in private conference, occasionally glancing at the group of girls on the other side of the room. After some discussion, the Queen nodded and called Nefertiti to her. With a wave of her hand, she dismissed everyone else.

Thutmose and Bek packed up their drawing materials and followed the ladies out into the hall. Lord Yuya and the Chamberlain left the audience chamber, as well, and headed down the hall in opposite directions. As Thutmose and Bek passed the group of girls, several pairs of kohl-painted eyes swiveled to follow Thutmose. One of the older girls ordered him to stop, and he obeyed. Bek stopped as well, watching.

The girl looked Thutmose up and down boldly.

"What is your name, artist?" she asked.

"Thutmose, Your Ladyship," he answered, staring fixedly at a spot on the wall. He could feel his cheeks burning and his ears turning bright red.

"Well, Thutmose," she demanded, "which of us do you think is the most beautiful? In your artist's opinion, that is."

"Amun help me!" he thought desperately. *"There is no way I can answer that question! I'll be in trouble, no matter what I say!"*

Just then, the door to Lord Yuya's office opened. The Vizier appeared in the doorway, a stern look on his face.

"There is too much chattering going on out here," he growled. "You girls go on back to your quarters now. As for you, young artist - Thutmose, is it? - you come with me."

With this, he stepped back into his office, leaving the door open for Thutmose.

Thutmose looked at Bek and shrugged, then followed the Vizier into his office, his heart pounding with trepidation. The old man had a reputation as a stern taskmaster.

Once he entered the office, the Vizier said, "Close the door, young man, and take a seat." He indicated one of a pair of chairs near a window.

Thutmose, who was accustomed to sitting on the floor, was surprised at being offered a chair. He obediently sat. The Vizier took the chair opposite him.

"How old are you, young man?" he asked.

"I - I'm not sure, sir. I think about fifteen, Your Lordship," Thutmose replied.

"Almost a grown man," Lord Yuya commented, surprising Thutmose with a warm smile. "And, I think, an uncommonly good-looking young fellow - good-looking enough to catch the eyes of those silly young girls."

"I'm sorry, Your Lordship," stammered Thutmose. "I didn't mean to cause a disturbance and distract Your Eminence."

"No, no, that's all right," the Vizier assured him. "It's not your fault. Girls will be girls, especially around good-looking young men. That's what I wanted to warn you about."

"Oh, Your Lordship, I would never - " Thutmose began.

"You misunderstand me, lad. It's not *your* behavior I'm worrying about. I wanted to warn you to watch out for those girls. They're a spoiled lot, used to getting their way. A young fellow like you is vulnerable to their machinations, a canary in a roomful of cats. They would think nothing of your life or your career, only of what they want. Believe me, I know," he added, with a wry smile.

"You do?" asked Thutmose, confused.

"I do," the Vizier told him. "Believe it or not, I was once an uncommonly good-looking young fellow, myself."

"Oh, I can well believe it," said Thutmose earnestly. "Your Eminence has excellent bones. I mean, that is - I do a lot of courtiers' portraits, and many of them ask me to - how shall I put it? - remove a few years from their faces."

The old man chuckled. "I'll bet they do!" he agreed. "So, as an artist, you are skilled at seeing the young face behind the old one."

Thutmose nodded.

"Well, then, it won't surprise you to know that, in my youth, I, too, drew many female eyes."

"I can well believe that, My Lord," Thutmose agreed.

"Including those of ladies above my station," Yuya added. "I was Steward to an important official in those days, Potiphar, Master of Horse to His Majesty King Amenhotep II. He trusted me to run his entire estate and rewarded me generously. Unfortunately, my master was often away on the king's business, leaving his pretty wife alone for long stretches. I had the misfortune to catch the lady's eye. One day, she cornered me and insisted that I make love to her. I replied that I could never so betray my master's trust, and I ran away. She clutched at my cloak as I ran, tearing it from my shoulders. Then she called loudly to the servants, claiming that I had attacked her."

"What did you do then?" asked Thutmose.

"There is an old saying, 'The demons of the underworld have no fury like a woman scorned.' It is true. When my master returned, his wife showed him my garment and claimed that I had tried to rape her. I insisted I was innocent, but of course, he believed her. He had me thrown in prison, and there I stayed for three long years," he said.

"That's terrible!" Thutmose said.

"Yes, but strangely enough, it worked out to my advantage," the old man commented. "There was a new pharaoh on the throne by then, Thutmosis IV. He had thrown two of his servants into jail, and they both asked me to interpret their dreams. I predicted that one would be hanged and one would be pardoned - and so it came to pass. Eventually, when pharaoh had persistent nightmares no one could interpret, the servant who was pardoned remembered me - finally! - and recommended me to pharaoh. He called for me, I interpreted his dreams, and the rest, as it is said, is history."

"Ah, yes," exclaimed Thutmose. "I have heard that story: the seven good years and seven lean years. Pharaoh Thutmosis put you in charge of all the granaries and you saw to it that the country survived the seven years of famine."

"That is true," said the Vizier. "But the point I was trying to make is that we uncommonly good-looking fellows have to be wary of

lustful young women of higher station. I, myself, am past having to
worry about it – one of the few advantages of old age! You, on the
other hand, are vulnerable. I suggest that, whenever you are called to
duty among the young ladies, you insist on having one or more of your
fellow artists along."

"I will, My Lord."

"And if that is not sufficient protection, you let me know, and I
will see to it that Master Auta gives you a different assignment. I would
hate to see a talent like yours wasted in His Majesty's prison just
because some silly snippet of a girl took a fancy to you!"

"Thank you, Your Eminence. I am deeply grateful for your
advice and your concern," said Thutmose, rising from his chair and
bowing low. "I will remember what you have told me."

"Good. And send Master Auta to see me," said the Vizier,
dismissing him.

"Yes, Your Eminence," said Thutmose, bowing his way out the
door.

As he closed the door behind him, Bek, who had been waiting
in the hallway, seized his arm.

"What did the old dragon want?" asked Bek. "Are you in
trouble?"

"No," said Thutmose, marveling at his good fortune. "He just
wanted to warn me to watch out for young ladies getting me in trouble.
It seems he had girl trouble, himself, in his youth."

"He did?" asked Bek. "Well, I'll be damned. It's hard to picture
that ferocious, powerful old man being pursued by women. I should get
so lucky!"

"Yes, well, let's just hope we're lucky enough to live to
become old men, ourselves, Bek!" said Thutmose, putting his arm over
his friend's shoulder.

"But then, again," commented Bek, "if the girls would only
chase me, instead of you, I might die young, but happy!"

"Did anyone ever tell you you're a randy young goat?" asked
Thutmose, thumping him in the ribs.

"I've heard a rumor to that effect," replied Bek, as the two of
them sauntered back to their quarters.

Chapter 9: An Irrational Number of Gods

In spite of his father's warning, my master continued to question traditional religion. The prince had a keen and penetrating mind, when he chose to apply it. He was probably the deepest and most brilliant thinker I ever met - but only on those topics that interested him, religion foremost among them. Other topics, such as war or foreign relations, held no interest for him. I have often thought he would have been happier as a priest than a king. The traditional priesthood, on the other hand, would have been happier had he never been born.

On a bright fall morning after the annual Inundation had almost completely subsided, the Children of the Harem (that is, the royal offspring and other noble children studying with them) were attending a class on religion and ritual led by the High Priest, Ptahmosis, himself. The classroom lay off a courtyard at a junction between the women's wing and the labyrinthine administrative section of the palace. Airy linen curtains had been drawn across the colonnaded opening to the courtyard to discourage the pupils from being distracted by the scurry of priests, officials, servants and visitors to the warren of offices beyond.

Thutmose, Bek and several of the other senior art students were in a corner of the room with one of the palace scribes, practicing recording the lesson in hieratic script. Hieratic, a flowing, abstract form of writing derived from hieroglyphics, was used for less formal, more mundane documents, while hieroglyphics were generally reserved for state and religious documents and inscriptions. The young artists were required to be proficient in both forms of script.

"So," the High Priest summarized, "while Amun is the chief sun deity worshipped here in Thebes, he is worshipped as Re in Memphis, the northern capital. Hence, the two deities may be regarded as one and the same; therefore, we now refer to this most powerful god as 'Amun-Re', acknowledging him as one god known by two names. Now, who can tell me the correct name for this deity when he is setting or rising?"

Nefertiti raised her hand.

The priest acknowledged her. "Nefertiti."

"Re-Horakhti," she responded. "Re of the Horizon."

"Thank you, Princess Nefertiti. That is correct," agreed the priest, smiling. He looked around and asked, "And what deity represents the deadly aspect of the noonday sun?"

Several students waved their hands. The priest pointed to a young noble. "Hapu."

"Sekhmet, the lion-headed goddess of Memphis," replied Hapu.

"And what does she symbolize?" asked the priest.

"Destructive power."

Ptahmosis smiled and nodded. "Very good, Hapu. Now, Princess Nefertiti correctly identified Horakhti as being associated with Re of the Horizon. What other deity is Horakhti identified with?" He glanced around the room. "Nebseny?"

"Horus," answered the boy.

"Good," said the priest. "Horus, of course, is seen as bearing the sun disk on his head as he rides his solar chariot across the sky, making him also a solar deity. Now – who can tell me who is both the earliest and the most aged form of the sun god? Ankh-Hor, what do you say?"

Ankh-Hor, the pimple-faced son of a southern nomarch, who had been nodding off at the back of the class, was jolted awake by the priest's question.

"Uh…I'm not sure," he mumbled sleepily. The flush of embarrassment did nothing to improve his complexion.

"Your Highness?" asked the High Priest, turning to the Crown Prince. "What says the Horus in the Nest?"

"I believe the earliest, and thus the oldest, form of the sun god would have to be Atum, or Aten, the primeval creator worshipped at Heliopolis, who represents the aged sun as it is setting," replied the prince coolly.

The High Priest beamed his approval. "Excellent, My Prince!"

"What I want to know," continued the prince, seizing the opportunity, "is why we need so many sun deities. Rising, setting, or at its zenith, we have only one sun. How can one sun be so many different gods? And these are only the best known. There are also Tjekem and Wenti and at least half a dozen other 'sun gods'. Are they separate gods, somehow subdividing one sun between them, or are they all just different names for the same god?"

The High Priest was taken aback by this unorthodox line of questioning, but was forced to recognize it as a legitimate question. "A very…profound…question, Your Highness." He thought a moment, then continued, "I think it would be most correct to regard all these gods as embodying aspects of one Being, with Amun chief among them."

"If Atum was the primeval creator," said the prince, "wouldn't it be most logical to acknowledge him as the source of all the other sun deities?"

"Maybe," agreed the High Priest reluctantly.

"In fact, if he's the *creator*, wouldn't he be the source of everything, including all the gods?"

"You could look at it that way," agreed the priest.

"And if Atum is the creator of all the other gods, doesn't that make **him** the chief god, more powerful than all the rest?" insisted the prince.

"That's one way of looking at it," conceded the priest, looking less and less pleased with the direction of the conversation.

"And surely, if Atum is the creator," continued the prince, pressing his advantage, "and all the other gods are aspects of one Divine Being, why don't we just worship the One Divine Being, considering that it incorporates all the other gods? Why do we need hundreds of separate deities, each with their own temples and priesthoods, if they are all part of One Divine Being?"

By now, the High Priest was looking thunderous. Thutmose, watching from the far side of the room, wondered if the old man wasn't in danger of suffering an apoplexy at any moment.

Suppressing the powerful urge to make some scathing retort to this suspiciously heretical line of questioning, Ptahmosis took a deep breath and replied with forced politeness to his future sovereign, "Your Highness has clearly given this a great deal of thought. But while Your Highness's interest in theology is commendable, there are still certain mysteries that can only be understood by initiates of the highest order, after a lifetime of study. Such high-level initiates may be able to perceive the deep unity among all the gods; for everyone else, these various aspects are still best understood as separate deities."

Thutmose knew his prince well enough to recognize the glint of annoyance in the young man's eyes at the priest's patronizing answer. He could not help feeling that it boded ill for the future of relations between them. Looking from the prince to the priest, and back, he felt a shadow of foreboding pass over him.

With a strained smile, the High Priest looked out at the class. "Well, I think that's enough for today," he said. "Class dismissed."

With that, he made the briefest of bows to the prince, then turned on his heel and left the room.

Nefertiti rose gracefully and made her way over to the prince, who was gathering up his writing implements and several papyrus scrolls and stuffing them into a linen bag, an irritated scowl on his long face. She spoke quietly to him.

"Do you really think it's wise to bait the old man like that? He **is** the High Priest, after all," she commented. "He has a lot of power."

"Not over me," retorted the prince. "If I believed in his god, I might be worried, but I don't. I will soon be Pharaoh and a living god, myself. I don't fear one dried up old man."

"Perhaps you should," she admonished him. "That dried up old man commands thousands of priests and scribes and temple guards, and the loyalty of hundreds of thousands of followers of Amun, not to mention the wealth of hundreds of temples and thousands of *arouras* of land."

"And I will soon command the wealth of the Two Lands, the tribute of dozens of vassal states and the most powerful army in the world. As you know, that army and the priesthood have long been opponents. And without Pharaoh's lavish support, we will see just how much wealth the priesthood will continue to receive. No, I do not fear one ill-tempered old man or his followers," he concluded. "What can he do to me? Call down lightning to strike me dead? Cast a plague upon me? If he could do that, he would have done it just now."

"Maybe he can't smite you with lightning, cousin, but that doesn't mean he can't cause you trouble. I fear for you," she said urgently, laying a hand on his arm. "And strangely enough, I feel fear for myself every time I see that old man." She shivered, then shook it off. "I seem to sense a…darkness around him. I feel almost as though someone had desecrated my tomb." She shivered again.

Amenhotep put a reassuring arm around her shoulders and said, "You're too sensitive, Nefer. Don't let that old hyena get under your skin. You will soon be more powerful than he is. Of this, I can assure you."

"All right. If you say so," she agreed, with a sigh.

"I do," he said. Releasing her, he added, "I must go now. But you cheer up – that's an order!"

"Yes, my Lord Horus in the Nest," she agreed, with a smile and mock bow.

He smiled back, gestured to a servant to pick up his bag, then swept out of the room.

Nefertiti stood in the nearly-empty room, shaking her head in concern. She turned back to where she had been sitting and bent to gather up her things.

Thutmose scrambled to his feet and rushed over to assist her. He put the small cake of solid ink back in its pouch and emptied the remaining bit of liquefied ink from its well in her palette, shaking the dark drops into the dirt of the courtyard outside. He wiped her reed pens on a rag, put them back into their own pouch, together with the small point-sharpening knife, and handed it to her. She put them into a larger bag, together with her wooden palette, the bag with the ink cake, a pouch of charcoal sticks and several loose pieces of papyrus.

"Thank you, Thutmose," she said, smiling at him.

His heart swelled, his cheeks grew warm, and he could have sworn he felt his feet leave the floor. Then she was gone, with a soft swish of fine linen, leaving behind a delicate aura of lotus blossom perfume. Thutmose inhaled deeply and closed his eyes.

"Come on, lover boy," said Bek, elbowing him in the ribs. "Get your stuff and let's go. Master Auta will be waiting for us."

"You are an irredeemable barbarian, Bek," grumbled Thutmose as he bent to pick up his writing paraphernalia. "Your mother must have been descended from the Hyksos."

"Yeah, and your mother was a donkey and your father was a camel-trader of the Shemsu-Hor," Bek retorted.

Thutmose slung his bag over his shoulder and punched Bek playfully in the arm. The two of them left the room, still trading increasingly elaborate insults to each other's parentage.

Across the courtyard, they saw the prince enter the main section of the palace, while Nefertiti and her ladies turned toward the women's quarters.

Chapter 10: God of Our Fathers

The two footmen who had opened the large gilded doors for the prince closed them again behind him, while he strode purposefully toward the great hall.

Seeing him, his father's steward called out, "Your Highness! Your grandfather is looking for you. He asked me to tell you to meet him in his office."

"Thank you, Ipy," replied the prince, turning towards the administrative wing of the palace. "Let my mother know I will be with Lord Yuya."

He made his way quickly through the maze of rooms leading to his grandfather's private office. The imposing bronze-plated door was guarded by a pair of soldiers attired in fine linen kilts with gold collars and bronze-tipped spears befitting the personal guards of the Supreme Commander of All the Armies of the Two Lands. Their sergeant knocked on the door with the butt of his mace.

"The Horus in the Nest requests entrance!" he called.

On receiving permission for the prince to enter, the two soldiers opened the heavy door and stood to attention on either side. The prince entered and they closed the door behind him, crossing their spears before it.

Inside, he found his father and grandfather leaning over a table on which a large parchment map of the lands of Naharin, to the north and east of the Two Lands, was spread out. Small clay soldiers, specially made for the purpose by Thutmose, marked the positions of Egyptian, Mitanni and Hittite forces.

As the prince entered, Pharaoh turned to him and said, "Ah, there you are, my son. I hear that you have been troubling the High Priest again."

"So he's complained to you already, has he?" asked the prince contemptuously.

"Yes, he has," replied Pharaoh. "He is concerned that you are heading toward heresy."

"All I did was to point out to him that it is irrational to divide one sun into a dozen or more deities, all of them styled 'sun gods' of one sort or another."

"It may be irrational, but he has the weight of thousands of years of tradition behind him. Besides, it's religion. That's never rational," Pharaoh pointed out. "It's a matter of faith, not logic. Besides that, the old man's powerful. He's got a lot of followers."

"But you, yourself, have always said the priesthood has grown too powerful, that we need to keep them in check somehow," the prince objected. "You always said that was one more reason for maintaining a standing army, besides defending against foreign powers."

"In spite of that standing army, I've always deemed it wise to stay on the good side of the priesthood," Pharaoh responded. "And you should, too."

"You've been much too good to them, Father. You've built up and expanded their temples and given them huge amounts of tribute. Instead of appreciating your generosity, they have grown arrogant, assuming it is their due. We should remind them of their place!"

Pharaoh glanced out the window, then at a water clock on a nearby table.

"I don't have time to argue religion and politics with you now, my son. I'm scheduled to review the guard, and they'll be waiting for me in the hot sun." Turning to his father-in-law, he said, "See if you can persuade my son to be more cautious around the high priest, Lord Yuya. You were able to talk sense into me when I was young and foolish!"

"You may have been young, Your Majesty, but you were never foolish, " replied the older man.

Pharaoh signaled to a servant, who put the *kepresh*, the blue war crown, on his head, then handed him the Crook and Flail to complete his royal regalia. He already wore the pharaonic kilt with its stiffened front panel and a massive collar of gold studded with carnelian, lapis and turquoise stones clustered around an image of Montu, the God of War.

"Hah! Don't tell anyone else, but you and I know better!" retorted Pharaoh. He rapped on the door with the Crook. It was opened by the soldiers standing guard. They saluted as he passed, then closed the door and resumed their posts.

Lord Yuya turned to his grandson. "He's right, you know. It is dangerous for even a Pharaoh to offend the priesthood, especially the priesthood of Amun."

"But surely you, of all people, don't believe in the power of their god!" protested the prince. "It is well known that you worship only the one god of your people."

"I don't believe in their gods, or their spiritual power, but I do believe in the very real earthly power of the priesthood," he replied. "They have a great deal of material wealth and they have tremendous influence over the people. That's a huge amount of political, economic and emotional power. Don't ever underestimate it."

"All right, all right," conceded the prince. "But leaving earthly power aside, what about spiritual power? Haven't you always said that there is only one true god, the god of your people?"

"For me, and for my people, that is true," agreed the Vizier.

"And haven't you always said that that God protected you and raised you up from slavery to the highest post in the land?" the prince asked.

"Yes," agreed Yuya.

"Well, then, you should understand when I say that I am unmoved by this horde of traditional gods and goddesses!" exclaimed the prince.

"Yes, I do understand. I have paid lip service to them for years, when I couldn't avoid them altogether, and have prayed to El in private to forgive me for doing what I had to do in order to accomplish what I believed He wanted of me."

"I thought as much," said the prince. "You have said very little about your god, but my mother has told me a bit. I would like to hear more."

"Why this sudden interest in the god of my fathers?" asked Yuya.

"Because I had a vision," said the prince hesitantly, "while I was meditating in the desert. A strange god appeared to me, and I believe it is the same god who appeared to your forefathers. I want you to tell me more of this god of yours."

The old man eyed him critically. The prince seemed to be sincere. "I have kept silent on the subject of religion out of respect for your father, and for his and your position as spiritual heads of this great nation. I did not wish to create conflict within you or make it more difficult for you to carry out your traditional role. And while I believe in one god, El Shaddai, the Lord of Hosts, he is the god of *my* people, the children of Israel, not the god of the Egyptians."

"Yet, am I not your grandson?" asked the prince.

"Yes, certainly, you are," agreed the old man.

"Am I not, therefore, also a child of Israel?"

The old man considered this for a moment. "Yes, I suppose you are. My father, Yacub, was called 'Israel', so all of his descendants are 'Children of Israel'. I guess that makes you a Child of Israel, as well."

"So, is not your god - the god of Israel - my god as well?" the prince asked.

"Indeed, it must be so," agreed Yuya.

"And don't the children of Israel believe that there is only one true god," argued the prince, "that all the rest are false gods?"

"That is true."

"So, no matter what my father says or believes," said the prince, "I, too, should worship only the one god."

"You have me there, my boy," agreed the old man ruefully. "I cannot refute your logic - but your father will be furious with me. He is, after all, the living incarnation of the god Horus - as you shall be after him. I should be teaching you to uphold that ancient tradition, which helps you as Pharaoh by giving you the divine right to rule. If you reject Horus and all the other old gods of Egypt, you risk undermining your own authority as Pharaoh."

"But on the other hand," argued the prince, "if there is only one true god, shouldn't we worship Him, and Him alone? If there is only one true God, then any authority based on other gods is useless. Worse - it might offend the one real god if we were to continue worshipping other gods. Shouldn't everybody worship the one, true God? Not just the Israelites, but everyone, everywhere?"

The old man looked troubled.

"I don't know," he said. "The god of my people made a covenant with my great-grandfather, Abraham, then renewed it with each generation: my grandfather, Yitzhak, and my father, Yacub, and then with me. But that covenant was strictly for the tribe of Abraham, not for other peoples or other nations - not even for this nation, where I have been honored and raised above all men. I don't know whether El-Shaddai *wishes* to be the god of other peoples, whether He is willing to hear their prayers, as well as those of Israel. After all," he added ruefully, "I can tell you from experience, receiving the petitions of all the people of Egypt is a very great burden."

"Yet, if there is only one god," reasoned the prince, "it surely follows that He is the only god who should be worshipped by all people. It seems to me that you must either see the divine realm as being divided into many petty kingdoms with their multitude of deities, or you must believe that there is only one God, one divine power over all things. You can't have it both ways."

"I don't know, my child," said the old man. "Men have accounted me wise, but this thing is beyond me. El-Shaddai has sometimes spoken to me, as He did to my forefathers, yet it always concerned *my* behavior, my fate, or that of my tribe. I do not know whether He meant His word to extend beyond the tribe of Israel."

"Yet He sent my grandfather, Pharaoh Thutmosis, several prophetic dreams that came true, one directing him to repair the Sphinx, and two that you, yourself, interpreted, warning him of a famine to come. Those three dreams, at least, affected the whole nation of Egypt, not simply your tribe," the prince pointed out.

"I don't know the whole of what God's intention was," said Yuya. "Perhaps He only sent those dreams to Pharaoh in order to insure the survival of the tribe of Israel - maybe the benefit to Egypt was just a side effect. I simply do not know. God did not see fit to tell me that."

"Be that as it may, I believe there must be only one god," declared the prince, "and that He's the God of everyone. When I am Pharaoh, I shall deliver that message to my people. I will tell them God has revealed that truth to me and make it the official religion."

The old man shook his head doubtfully. "I don't think it will work, my son. You can't change people's beliefs that easily. Even within the one small tribe of Israel, people have persistently fallen back into worshipping other gods, despite El's recurrent miraculous intervention in their lives. I don't think you can convert an entire nation such as Egypt, just because you, as Pharaoh, order it to be so."

"Perhaps if this god wears a familiar face," mused the prince, thinking aloud, "He will be easier for people to accept. Among all the many gods of Egypt, there is one deity with many forms who ranks above all others: the sun god. Egyptians worship different aspects of the sun as different gods: Re, the sun at its zenith; Re-Harakhti, the sun at the horizon; the burning aspect of the sun as the lion goddess, Sekhmet; Horus, embodied as Pharaoh, who bears the sun upon his head. It is overwhelmingly obvious that the sun rules every aspect life in the Two Lands. If I can bring all these many aspects together into one divine being, perhaps I can persuade them. What physical form does your god, El, assume? How is He pictured?"

"None," Yuya replied. "El has forbidden us to make graven images."

"Maybe that is part of the reason your people have had trouble remaining faithful to the worship of El," observed the prince. "He is too abstract. The people need some kind of symbol to focus on, something tangible. Yet, perhaps it is time for them to outgrow the concept of the deity as a person, made in our human image, instead of the other way around. Perhaps I can offer them a middle ground, an abstract form that is neither animal nor human, yet a symbol people can grasp..."

"The people will never accept it," commented the old man, shaking his head.

"I will order them to. My new religion will become the state religion, the only legal religion!"

"I don't know, my son," said Yuya. "I don't think you can just invent a new religion and order people to accept it, even by royal decree. And I don't know that El would take kindly to being represented by some arbitrary symbol chosen by you, or being called by some other name."

"Yet you have said that 'El Shaddai' is not even a name," commented the prince.

"True. It simply means 'Lord of Hosts'".

"So, does El-Shaddai have an actual *name*?" asked the prince.

"It is said among my people that the real name of God is unpronounceable by mere mortals. 'El' or 'El Shaddai' or 'Elohim' are merely ways of referring to that which cannot be spoken," said the old man.

"You see?" said the young man. "It shouldn't really matter, then, by what name I call Him. If I use the old symbol of the sun disk and refer to it by the old name, 'Aten', it should be as valid a name for the Nameless One as any other."

"Perhaps. But I still fear for you, my son. Even if you do not incur the wrath of God for such presumption, you will certainly incur the wrath of the priesthood of Amun - and that could be almost as disastrous," observed the old man.

"I know you mean well, Grandfather, and that you fear my plan might be blasphemous - but I assure you, I have prayed long and hard about this, and my heart compels me to proceed."

"If so, my son," said the old man, mournfully, "then God protect you, for certainly no man will be able to."

Chapter 11: So Near and Yet So Far

Several months had passed since I had heard Pharaoh's plan for the marriage and ascension to the throne of his son, Prince Amenhotep. I had managed to push it to the back of my mind by concentrating on my work, recording palace life around me. Life, however, would not let me forget it for long.

One morning, Thutmose and Bek and two of the other senior art students sat around a courtyard in the ladies' wing of the palace where a number of the women of the royal family and their ladies were gathered. Lady Senusret, governess of Nefertiti and her half-sister Mutnodjmet, was overseeing the completion of their toilette. Sitamun - now her father's second "Great Wife" - sat to one side with her ladies, no longer a part of the group of young, unmarried girls, yet not really a member of the older group.

The heat was oppressive, despite the presence of several servants swinging large fans mounted on long poles. Nefertiti's maid had finished shaving her young mistress's head, a practice the princess had sensibly adopted for the sake of comfort in the hot climate. She was now choosing a wig from among several styles on stands carried by a group of attendants. One of these servant girls presented her now with a long, full wig parted at the center, with a mass of dark, straight hair that would fall almost halfway to the wearer's waist. Nefertiti waved it away.

"No, no," she said, "not the Hathor - not in this weather. I'd die of the heat. That great mass of hair - it's like wearing a lion's mane!"

She rejected several more long, classic styles.

Finally, she instructed her maid, "Bring me the Nubian wig, the one with the lapis beads."

Thutmose smiled to himself, recognizing that this was the same style as the wig his kinswoman had created for Nefertiti's doll, all those years ago.

The maid brought over a stand with a wig featuring the multi-layered short hairstyle first introduced by soldiers from Nubia, popularized by Queen Tiye a few years ago. The maid set the stand on a small table, then lifted the wig off and fitted it onto her mistress's head. She adjusted it carefully, then handed the princess a polished silver mirror with an ivory handle carved in the shape of a swimming woman. Nefertiti inspected herself in the mirror.

"Yes," she said, smiling, "that's much better."

Meanwhile, her stepmother, Lady Tey, had been supervising the toilette of her daughter, Mutnodjmet, Nefertiti's half-sister.

Mutnodjmet, now twelve, was as strident and demanding as ever. When her mother attempted to choose a short wig for her, the girl flung it away.

"No, I will not wear that one!" she snapped. "I am not a child any more. I have outgrown the sidelock. I want long hair," she complained petulantly.

The royal children always wore their heads shaved, except for a long sidelock on one side of the head. The shaved head was cool and practical for children, and the sidelock identified them as royalty. One sign that a royal son or daughter had come of age was the cutting of the sidelock and its replacement by an adult hairstyle. Mutnodjmet had recently abandoned the sidelock and begun growing out her own hair, which had reached a length about as long as the last joint of her index finger, standing out in dark fuzz all over her head.

"The queen has long hair," she pointed out. "Even though she often wears a short wig, she still has long hair underneath it."

While Queen Tiye often chose the Nubian wig, she sometimes wore more traditional styles, and sometimes even her own natural hair, a remarkable mass of auburn curls falling well below her shoulders, still lush and colorful even though she was no longer young. Its coppery color was quite striking among all the black-haired Egyptians, a reminder of her foreign parentage.

"I want the Hathor wig," demanded Mutnodjmet, choosing the long, full style. "Hathor is 'the Beautiful One'. I want to be beautiful, too!"

"But, sweetheart," protested her mother weakly, "the Hathor wig is too big for your small face."

"No, it's not!" insisted Mutnodjmet, stamping her foot. "I'm a young woman now. I'm big enough to wear the Hathor wig!"

Since the girl's courses had recently begun flowing, she was now officially considered a woman, and was determined to exercise all the prerogatives of her new adult status.

"Oh, all right," said Lady Tey, giving up the struggle. She signaled to the maid. "Let her have the Hathor wig."

The girl's maid servant brought over the huge wig and adjusted it on her head. Mutnodjmet snatched up her hand mirror and inspected the result, turning this way and that to admire her grownup reflection.

Several of the other young noblewomen present hid smiles behind raised hands. On the far side of the room, one of them said to her companion, "It looks like the wig is wearing her!" The companion shushed her lest the younger princess should hear. Mutnodjmet's temper tantrums were infamous and almost anything could set her off. And as she matured, the girl was becoming increasingly vindictive.

Thutmose had been focused on painting Nefertiti, always his favorite subject. Hearing this remark, however, he couldn't resist making a quick sketch of Mutnodjmet, his least favorite subject, looking like a caricature of her mother, with her eyes in their heavy kohl eye liner peering out from beneath the enormous wig, like a mouse taking refuge under an enormously furry cat. When she glanced his way, he quickly slipped the sketch beneath a pile of drawings, mindful of her notorious temper. Fortunately, she took no notice of him, being focused on her own reflection in the mirror.

Lady Senusret turned away from the younger girl, rolling her eyes. She turned back to Nefertiti and smiled.

"Splendid, Your Highness! You look radiant. I believe you are, indeed, fit to greet your royal suitor! Are you ready?"

Thutmose's heart skipped a beat.

"Soon, Senusret, soon," replied Nefertiti. "I need to prepare my mind and spirit first, to greet my lord properly. And I must thank the gods for my good fortune."

"A very proper attitude, my lady!" Senusret commended her. "The gods have smiled on you, indeed, that you should be chosen to be Great Wife of the next Pharaoh!"

So, Thutmose realized, Pharaoh had indeed accepted the match proposed by the Crown Prince all those months ago.

"Indeed they have," replied Nefertiti. "I am the most fortunate of women, not only to be chosen as queen, but to wed a kind and loving lord, as well."

Mutnodjmet, scowling, entered the conversation uninvited. "I'd love to be queen, but I wouldn't want to have to marry Prince Amenhotep to do it! I don't see how you can stand him! He looks like some strange bird, with that long face, those puny shoulders and that big belly! He's not my idea of a proper prince, at all!"

The twitter of conversation around the room died abruptly. The other ladies were aghast at this characterization of the Crown Prince, soon to be the next Pharaoh of Egypt. At the same time, knowing this unflattering description to be accurate, they found it hard to contradict. The result was a deafening silence, which the courtiers strained to break with half-hearted protestations in the prince's defense. Only Nefertiti spoke out vehemently in his behalf.

"Mutya! Shame on you! The prince may not be handsome, but he's kind and caring, and the smartest man I know. He's full of new and fascinating ideas, and what's more, he's interested in **my** ideas. I like him!"

"'Like him,'" Thutmose thought, snatching at straws, "not 'love him'."

"I still don't see how you can stand to let him touch you," said Mutnodjmet. "I wouldn't want to marry him, even if he is the Horus in the Nest!"

"Women of the royal family have no choice who they marry, Mutya," Nefertiti told her. "When it comes to marriage, a poor peasant woman grubbing in the dirt has more freedom of choice than a princess. Even the greatest queens of the past, queens like Ahmose Nefertari or Tetisheri, or even the powerful Hatshepsut, have had no choice of who they would marry."

Tetisheri had been the grandmother of Kamose and Ahmose, the royal brothers who had driven out the Hyksos and founded the present dynasty. She had been a powerful queen, staunchly holding her family together after her son, Pharaoh Seqenenra, had been slain in battle against the evil Hyksos king, Apophis. Ahmose-Nefertari was the sister-wife of Ahmose and had helped lead troops into battle after his elder brother Kamose had been slain. Hatshepsut, of course, was the most famous queen of the Eighteenth Dynasty, having reigned as Pharaoh in her own right, wearing masculine attire and a false pharaonic beard, all the while somehow keeping her nephew, Thutmosis, in check for over twenty years. This was a truly remarkable feat in itself, as Thutmosis III turned out to be Egypt's most powerful military leader ever, who conquered several other nations and expanded the empire to its greatest extent. Yet even these powerful queens had had to marry a prince of their own blood and had no say in the matter.

"I consider myself very fortunate to be marrying a man I **like**," continued Nefertiti, "a good man, a man I consider to be my friend. Do not let me hear you speak ill of him again!"

"Yes, Nefer," muttered Mutnodjmet, still sullen. "Whatever you say."

I sat as still as the pillars of the courtyard, turned to stone like them. Listening to this exchange, my heart was torn within me. The prince was my kind and generous benefactor - I might even say, my friend - and I called daily upon the gods to shower him with blessings, as he had showered me. A part of me rejoiced that he should have a consort as kind and caring, as generous of spirit, as she was beautiful. Pharaoh, after all, is a living god - he deserves the best.

Another part of me, however, the part that was just becoming a man, burned with jealousy and ached to know that this exquisite creature, so near and yet so far beyond my reach, was destined to wed

another man. I wanted to spend every moment basking in the sunlight of
her presence, yet it was agony to be so near, and to know I could never
so much as touch the hem of her gown.

Her toilette completed, Nefertiti crossed the room and invited
Great Wife Sitamun to play a game of Hounds and Jackals with her.
Sitamun gladly accepted, happy to relieve the boredom of her haughty
isolation. Thutmose followed. Seating himself on the floor nearby, he
began sketching the two royal ladies, an activity that allowed him to
linger near his adored Nefertiti.

"I'm afraid Mutnodjmet is going to be severely disappointed
with her lot in life," commented Sitamun, advancing one of her Hounds
across the board. "Even if she ever gets to be a queen, as she so
obviously wants, she's almost certainly going to find it a lot less fun
than she thinks it will be. A royal daughter, even one thrice-removed
like Mutnodjmet, has so few choices in life - and almost none in who
she marries."

"That's why I consider myself so fortunate," agreed Nefertiti.
"The Prince may not be as fine a physical specimen as one might
desire, but he's a good, kind young man."

"And he clearly adores you," added Sitamun. "Plus, he's only
your cousin - "

"Not my brother!" said Nefertiti.

"Or worse yet, your father," whispered Sitamun, leaning across
the board so the other ladies couldn't hear.

Nefertiti reached across the board and squeezed the older girl's
hand sympathetically. Sitamun's eyes glittered with unshed tears. She
bit her lip and sniffed surreptitiously. She glanced around to confirm
that no one else could overhear. She looked sharply at Thutmose, but he
kept on sketching intently, as though he had only eyes and hands, but
no ears.

Reassured, Sitamun continued in a conspiratorial whisper,
"Hopefully, since Amenhotep is only your cousin, you may escape any
breeding problems."

"What do you mean?" Nefertiti whispered back. "What kind of
breeding problems?"

Sitamun glanced around again, then continued. "My chariot
driver once told me about how they breed horses and other animals for
desired traits. He said that they might breed a mare back to her sire to
increase the likelihood of continuing a certain trait like coat color or
smoothness of gait in the line - but then he said they could only do this
a limited number of times before problems began to develop."

"What kind of problems?" asked Nefertiti.

"I asked the same thing," replied Sitamun. "He said that if there was too much inbreeding between siblings or parents and children, the offspring began to be born sickly, or worse yet, deformed."

"Do you think that happens to people?" asked Nefertiti.

"That's what I wondered, so I asked Pentu, the King's Physician."

"What did he say?"

"He looked uncomfortable and tried to dodge the question," said Sitamun. "Of course, that made me even more suspicious, so I insisted on an answer. He finally admitted, reluctantly, that there seemed to be a greater number of stillbirths and deformities among the children of royal women married to their own brothers or fathers. Then there are my two other sisters, Nebetiah and Hennutaneb."

"Your sisters?" asked Nefertiti, puzzled. "I thought Isis was your only living sister, that the other two died in infancy."

"That's what they want everyone to think," Sitamun whispered. "But I know the truth. They're still alive, hidden away on a royal estate in the north, where no one ever sees them."

"But, why?" asked Nefertiti.

"Because they're deformed," replied Sitamun, "severely deformed. Both of them have crooked backs and twisted feet. They can't even walk on those feet – they have to be carried around in special chairs."

"By the Great Mother Isis!" exclaimed Nefertiti. "That's terrible! Yet you and Isis and Amenhotep are all right, aren't you?"

"Isis and I seem to have been lucky," replied Sitamun, "although Isis does have a slight curvature of the back, which she says pains her. And Amenhotep, your future husband, has some difficulty with his speech, although it is subtle, and his health is poor."

"Yes, I have always known that his speech is a little difficult to understand," commented Nefertiti, "but I never realized it might be something he was born with. If that's the worst of it, perhaps our children will be all right, especially as we are only cousins."

"True," agreed Sitamun, "but you did have all the same grandparents, since your maternal grandparents, Thutmosis and Mutemwiya, are our paternal grandparents; and your father's parents, Yuya and Thuya, are our mother's parents. And even though Amenhotep doesn't appear to have any actual deformities, he has never been very robust. He's not much of an athlete, you know – not like our brother Thutmosis was. He gets winded easily, and when his military instructors forced him to run as a boy, he fainted so often, they gave up, for fear he might drop dead and they would be blamed. I fear for him yet. I don't think he's very strong. When you become his Queen, you will have to protect him from over-exerting himself."

"I will," Nefertiti agreed. "I'm glad you told me. I will take care to see that he doesn't overtax himself. And I promise, I won't tell a soul."

"I knew I could trust you," said Sitamun.

"Always," Nefertiti assured her. "You're my closest friend, as well as my cousin."

At this, Sitamun's composure slipped and a tear slid silently down her cheek, quickly dabbed away with a fold of her linen gown. "And I will always be your friend. You can count on me - you, and your children, and your children's children - especially as I am unlikely to have any of my own. Given what I have just told you, it is as well that my marriage to my father did not produce any children; and as a Pharaoh's Daughter, I will probably never be allowed to marry anyone else, even after my father dies - may he live!" she added hastily.

At this, she looked so sad, Nefertiti said to her, "When I have children, you can be a second mother to them, and they will love you second only to their father and me!"

"I promise I will love them like they were my own!" Sitamun replied. "I wish you and my brother every happiness, and many healthy children!"

I felt again the knife in my heart, at the thought of Nefertiti and the Prince producing many children. Yet it is only right and proper, I scolded myself, for the King and Queen, who represent the land itself, to be fertile and productive.

I prayed to the gods for release from this pain in my heart and these wicked thoughts, and I forced myself to pray for the health, happiness and long life of the Horus in the Nest and his bride-to-be, and for their many healthy children. I think my prayers confused the gods, for on the one hand, I beseeched them to take this painful love away, to pull the knife blade out of my heart; and on the other hand, I begged them to let me remain near her, to serve her all my life in any way I could. The second request they granted, yet showed me no mercy with regard to the first. She was destined to marry a king, and I, to serve her all my life, in this world and the next. I would gladly have lain down my life for her. Little did I know that I would soon have the opportunity to do just that.

Chapter 12: Old Set

A couple of months later, Thutmose traveled north again with the royal family. The Queen and her ladies, Pharaoh and the Crown Prince all stayed at the royal villa. They spent many of their days on board the royal barge, "Radiance of the Aten", enjoying the cool waters of the pleasure lake, often accompanied by many smaller boats bearing lesser nobles and their entourages. The royal barge carried its own musicians, cooks and entertainers. Before long, enterprising locals set out in their own small boats, supplying food, drink and local wares to the lesser vessels in the colorful flotilla.

When the Queen complained that the traffic on the water was becoming a nuisance, the Prince suggested that it be limited by requiring all vessels to have a royal license. Those desiring admittance to the lake must apply to an outpost of the royal guard, where an official would issue a limited number of permits to nobles and commercial licenses to would-be purveyors of food and merchandise. An appropriate fee was charged for each type of license, so many head of livestock or bags of grain, which helped to diminish traffic and augment royal income.

Thutmose was able to visit his home village and see his family and childhood friends again. He was amazed to see how much the village had grown since his last visit, due mainly to its proximity to the royal villa, but also due in part to the increased demand for his father's pottery. He played with his younger brothers and sisters and bounced the latest addition, another little sister, on his knee. He had brought his mother several lengths of fine linen and a stack of drawings of the royal family and nobles of the court, illustrating the palace, the great temples and daily life at court. What most fascinated his mother and sisters, however, were the latest fashions in clothing, jewelry and hairstyles. With Thutmose as their exclusive source of inside information, they enjoyed a decided fashion advantage over their neighbors, which greatly enhanced their status in the region. He also brought a necklace for his mother, bracelets for his sisters and a pair of lapis and turquoise earrings for his neighbor, Mariamne, still his ardent admirer. He gave his father a fine collar of many colorful beads, suitable to his status as one of the area's leading artisans.

Some days, the younger members of the royal family and their nobles went hunting in the marshes surrounding the villa and its lake. Thutmose often went along to draw and paint the young hunters and the wildlife of the marshes. One day, he accompanied the Princess Nefertiti and several young noblemen and women on one of these expeditions. Each noble had his or her reed boat, poled along by a servant, while the young hunter stood in the prow to launch throwsticks at birds or to spear fish. Several boatloads of guards accompanied them, as well.

Thutmose sat cross-legged in his own reed boat, poled by his own
boatman, sketching the scene. He made numerous ink drawings of the
princess throwing the curved hunting sticks at waterfowl or kneeling in
the prow, spearing fish. Throwing sticks were considered an obsolete
hunting tool by the general populace, but they were still used by nobles,
as prowess with the throwstick was considered a cultured accomplish-
ment among the upper classes.

Thutmose had been so intent on his drawing - and on watching
the princess - for hours that he had been unaware of his surroundings,
beyond whatever he was drawing. Finishing one sketch, he stopped to
stretch his cramped fingers and stood up to relieve the kinks in his
knees. He shifted his shoulders and stretched his arms and looked
around him at the water channel, islands of reeds and trees on the
higher shore. With a sudden shock, he recognized the outline of a large
tree nearby. This was Old Set's territory! He anxiously scanned the
nearby shore, but saw no sign of the old bull crocodile. He craned his
neck and looked behind him to where several boatloads of guards idled
along, but saw nothing suspicious. He glanced across to where the princess stood in the prow of her boat, taking aim at a flight of ducks.

Then, to his horror, he saw it: a huge, dark shape nearly ten
cubits long masquerading as a log, apparently drifting aimlessly right
toward the princess's boat! A pair of beady eyes on one end and a
twitch of movement at the other betrayed the true identity of the massive crocodile. The huge beast cut between his boat and that of the princess, who was still unaware of her danger.

"Your Highness," Thutmose yelled, "get down! Crocodile!"

Nefertiti glanced around and saw the crocodile, headed straight
for her. She dropped to her knees, snatched up a spear and crouched
low in the boat. Thutmose looked around frantically for help.

"Guards!" he yelled. "Help the Princess! Crocodile!"

Several boatmen began poling their craft toward the princess, as
the guards raised bows and spears - but it was apparent to Thutmose
that they were too far away. They would never get close enough to the
crocodile before it reached the princess's boat.

Thutmose snatched up the knife he used to sharpen his quill
pens, clamped it in his teeth and dived headlong into the water, headed
straight for the crocodile. Swimming with all his might, he reached it
while it was still several yards away from the princess. Without pausing
to think, he launched himself at the beast and pulled himself onto its
back. Wrapping his legs around its body, he circled its neck with his left
arm and pulled its head back as hard as he could, slashing its throat with
the knife in his right hand.

As the water turned bloody, the giant crocodile thrashed and rolled, trying to throw its attacker off. Thutmose held on with all his strength. The crocodile dived for the bottom, determined to drown its annoying rider. Thutmose knew he couldn't hold his breath for long - and if he let go, the crocodile's huge jaws would have him. To weaken the crocodile and encourage it to leave the bottom, Thutmose stabbed its throat repeatedly with his knife. Finally, just when his lungs were about to burst and he was growing dizzy from lack of air, the crocodile lunged to the surface again.

As the huge beast surfaced, several of the guards fired their arrows at it. However, most of them dared not fire, for fear of hitting the princess in her boat nearby. Most of the arrows that were fired missed, falling in the water all around Thutmose, who was still astride the creature's back.

"Stop!" cried the Princess. "You'll hit the artist!"

The crocodile turned toward the sound of her voice. Seeing his original target, he headed towards it, full speed. Before the reptilian juggernaut could ram the boat, Thutmose hauled up on its head with all his remaining strength. He was nearly spent, but determined to protect the princess to the very end.

Fighting the encircling arm and the pain in its throat, the crocodile reared out of the water just before it reached Nefertiti's boat. As its chest rose out of the water, Nefertiti jammed her spear into it as hard as she could. The crocodile thrashed violently, rolling over and over, finally throwing the exhausted Thutmose off its back. The boats of the guards closed around it in the bloody waters, but its struggles were becoming feebler as blood loss drained its strength.

Nefertiti scanned the water anxiously, looking for the artist. Finally, his dark head bobbed to the surface near her.

"Thutmose! Over here!" she called to him.

Thutmose turned at the sound of her voice. He was so exhausted, he could barely stay afloat. His arms shook with the effort of swimming through the water. By the time he reached her boat, he was too weak to pull himself over the side. Nefertiti reached down to him.

"Here, take my hand," she said.

He reached up and took her hand. Leaning back, she pulled with all her might and heaved him into the boat. The flimsy craft rocked violently, toppling her backwards. Thutmose landed on top of her in the bottom of the tiny boat.

For a time, he was too exhausted to understand where he was. After a minute, however, he felt her body warm and soft beneath him. He was suddenly acutely aware that he was lying on top of the princess.

"Your Highness," he stammered, attempting to roll off of her, "I'm so sorry! I didn't mean to…"

"That's all right," she laughed. "You saved my life. You were incredibly brave! That's the bravest thing I've ever seen, you tackling that crocodile like that. I owe you my life."

The boat being very small, his efforts to roll off of her had succeeded only in leaving them both side by side in the bottom of the boat. He was very aware of the length of her body, warm and pliant against the whole cold, wet length of his own, and her lovely face nose to nose just inches from his.

"And I owe *you* my life," he replied. "If you hadn't speared him when you did, he would have had me. That was a mighty spear thrust, Your Highness, well-aimed and well-timed!"

"Well," she said, looking deep into his eyes, "I couldn't let him kill my favorite artist, now, could I?"

"You couldn't?" he asked stupidly. He couldn't look away from her eyes, whose gaze left him weaker than the struggle with the crocodile.

"No, I couldn't," she answered, and kissed him gently on the forehead.

She rose to her elbow just as a great cheer went up from the circle of boats surrounding the now-still body of the crocodile. The boat of the captain of the guards broke away from the group and headed toward hers.

"Your Highness," called the captain, "are you all right?"

"Yes, Captain Paramessu," she replied, "I'm fine. Is the crocodile dead?"

"Yes, Your Highness. What would you like us to do with him?" called the captain.

"Bring him back to the villa. I want to have him stuffed as a trophy. I think perhaps I'll have him mounted as a guardian at the gateway of the palace!"

"Very good, Your Highness," replied the captain. Then, looking about him at the still red-stained waters, he asked, "What happened to the artist? Did he drown?"

Thutmose decided the moment was ripe for his reappearance. He sat up in the bottom of the boat just as Nefertiti said,

"No, he survived. I fished him out after the crocodile threw him off. He saved my life. After all that, I couldn't very well let the crocodile have him."

The captain looked back and forth between them, then replied diplomatically, "Your Highness is too modest. I am sure Your Highness's spear thrust was the fatal one, the blow that really finished the beast. His carcass will make a fine trophy for a mighty huntress."

"Thank you, Captain," Nefertiti replied. "I'll see you ashore." She turned to her boatman, still trembling in the prow after such a close call. "Boatman, take us home."

The boatman hastily complied, only too happy to head for the safety of the villa's shore. The flotilla of small boats closed in behind her like a flock of goslings following their mother. A clump of guardsmen's boats towed the body of the crocodile along behind.

Several days later, Thutmose was feted at a banquet at the royal villa. Pharaoh himself awarded him the gold *shebu* collar of honor. Thutmose, in turn, thanked the princess for saving his own humble life and led a toast in her honor.

When the royal entourage returned to Thebes the next month, the stuffed body of the crocodile accompanied them, mounted on a boom at the prow of the boat. The body of the huge beast occasioned endless comment at every village they passed on the journey south, with the story of Thutmose's daring attack and the princess's mighty spear-thrust re-told at every stop, the magnitude of their exploits growing with each re-telling. In the way of gossip everywhere, the story somehow raced ahead and reached Thebes before them, so that a huge crowd gathered to meet them at the dock, all wanting to see the infamous crocodile for themselves.

The admiring crowd cheered the princess and showered her with flowers. An even larger cheer went up when the artists' boat docked and Thutmose came ashore. To his acute embarrassment, his admirers lifted him up and carried him to the palace on their shoulders.

Bek, who had stayed behind in Thebes, was there to greet him when they finally let him down.

"To hear the people tell it," he said disgustedly, "one would think you'd single-handedly slain a regiment of crocodiles."

"Pay no attention to the tales," Thutmose assured him. "The rumors of my prowess are greatly exaggerated. It was only *half* a regiment of crocodiles!"

However, after he had a chance to inspect the gigantic stuffed carcass, Bek grudgingly conceded, "I have to admit, it's impressive. It's amazing, what a man will do to win the favor of a beautiful woman!"

Nefertiti requested that he paint scenes of the hunt on the walls of her apartment in the palace, and insisted that he include a picture of himself on the back of the beast. When he objected that he couldn't see himself and didn't know what he looked like, she had her servants bring him a large silver mirror. Out of excuses, he reluctantly complied. The mural was much admired and he was well paid for his art work.

Back in his small room in the artists' quarters, Thutmose reflected on the episode and concluded that his greatest reward had not been gold or public acclaim, but Nefertiti's soft kiss on his forehead.

"I will treasure that kiss as long as I live," he thought to himself.

Chapter 13: End of an Era

During the winter, plans began to be laid for the crowning of a new pharaoh, when young Amenhotep would assume a throne beside his father. But as fate would have it, before a new power could arise, an old one would pass away.

One day in late winter, the Grand Vizier called for Thutmose to attend him in his office. The young man was instructed to practice his hieratic by recording the proceedings transacted between Lord Yuya and a long procession of supplicants, courtiers and foreign diplomats.

Late in the day, Thutmose sketched the Vizier as he sat in private conversation with a visitor from Mitanni who had come to discuss the marriage of yet another Mitanni princess to the Crown Prince. As he sketched, he noted the lines of strain around the old man's mouth and across his brow.

"He must be nearly seventy," the young man thought, "and he still works longer hours than anyone else in the palace."

After the Mitanni ambassador left, Lord Yuya signaled his steward that the day's business was ended. The steward dismissed other waiting supplicants, telling them to return the next morning. He instructed servants to bring refreshments, which they set on small tables near the Vizier's chair.

Thutmose was gathering up his papyrus, quills and ink, preparing to leave, when the old man stopped him.

"Stay, Thutmose," he said. "Have some food and drink. You've worked tirelessly all day."

"Thank you, my lord," the young man replied, helping himself to fresh dates, figs, bread and beer.

Although he, himself, was famished, he noticed that the old man scarcely touched the food, taking only sips of his beer. Now that his visitors were gone, the Vizier's shoulders sagged. He looked exhausted.

Nevertheless, he looked up and said, "Let me see your sketches, young man."

Thutmose brought over the pile of papyrus drawings he had made that day, plus some he had done recently of the Queen, the Prince, and Princesses Nefertiti and Mutnodjmet. The Vizier examined the drawings one by one.

Despite the risk of disapproval, Thutmose continued to draw the deeper truth of what he saw around him. Some of these drawings he wisely concealed from most other people, but he had long ago discovered that Lord Yuya, who had a keen but well-disguised sense of humor, particularly enjoyed these irreverent artistic observations. Thutmose had made a practice of bringing the Vizier a variety of his sketches of palace and city life. He had observed that many of these made the old man smile, and occasionally even laugh out loud, which seemed to provide him with some relief from the many cares of his day.

The Vizier chuckled as he inspected a sketch of the pompous, self-important Mitanni ambassador.

"Ah, yes," he said, "you've captured his air of superiority and boredom perfectly! I can almost hear his breathy voice and that execrable Egyptian he speaks."

He paged through the rest of the pictures, lingering over a fine portrait of his daughter, Queen Tiye.

"A very fine portrait of the Queen, my boy, very fine. You've not only captured her power and hauteur, you've managed to suggest a bit of the little girl behind her eyes. I'd like you to do a portable version of this one on animal skin, the way you did my portrait for her."

"Certainly, my Lord," Thutmose replied.

He had recently created an innovative portrait of the Grand Vizier as a gift for the Queen. It was painted on lambskin stretched over a wooden framework, durable yet light weight, so that it could be carried about. The Queen was greatly taken with it and delighted that she could take it with her on her travels, and need not be dependent on whatever decoration was painted on the walls wherever she went.

The Vizier continued leafing through the drawings until he came to the last one, a sketch of Nefertiti and her younger sister, Mutnodjmet. It was a study in contrasts. Nefertiti was as calm, dignified and lovely as ever, while Mutnodjmet, wearing the oversized Hathor wig and an enormous jeweled collar, stamped her foot and scowled, pointing an imperious, demanding finger at something. Lord Yuya smiled ruefully and shook his head.

"Ah, my granddaughters! You've captured both of them accurately, too. Nefertiti will make a fine queen - everything a grandfather could want. But Mutnodjmet! May the God of my fathers help us if that child ever becomes Queen! Fortunately, that isn't terribly likely. Hopefully, Amenhotep and Nefertiti will give Egypt so many heirs that Mutnodjmet will never get nearer the throne than she is today."

"Yes, my Lord," murmured Thutmose, with mixed feelings.

"And yet," continued the old man softly, "I have the most ominous feeling…"

As the Vizier continued to inspect the drawings, Thutmose took the opportunity to stretch his cramped limbs and relieve his tired backside, sore from sitting cross-legged for hours on the stone floor. He stepped out on the balcony, stretched his arms and back and moved them about.

Suddenly, he heard a strange noise in the room behind him, a brief cry followed by a dull thud. Concerned, he stepped back into the room. Lord Yuya sat slumped over his desk, his right hand clutching his chest. Thutmose rushed over to him.

"My Lord! Are you in pain?" he cried.

The old man nodded and gasped, "Call my physician!"

Thutmose rushed to the door and called out to the servants, "The Vizier is ill! Call his physician, quickly!"

The steward jumped to his feet and sent a messenger off post-haste to fetch the doctor. Thutmose dashed back over to the Vizier's side.

"Help me to the bed," the old man wheezed.

Thutmose slid an arm beneath the old man's and raised him from his chair. It was clear that the Vizier could not stand on his own, so Thutmose lifted him in his arms and carried him to his bed. After depositing him carefully on the bed, the young man arranged a woven coverlet over him just as the steward rushed in.

"I've sent for the physician, my Lord," he said. "He should be here in a few minutes. What else can I do for you, my Lord?"

Seeing that the old man seemed to be shivering, Thutmose turned to the steward and said, "Bring him some more blankets. He's cold."

The steward rushed off, apparently relieved to have something to do.

"Thutmose," the old man's voice rasped weakly.

Thutmose leaned down so that his ear was close to the old man's lips.

"Before the others arrive, there's something I want to ask of you."

"Anything, my Lord," Thutmose replied.

"I know that you love my granddaughter, Nefertiti," he wheezed.

Shocked, Thutmose stammered, "My Lord! I would never..."

The old man waved a hand feebly. "I know you are a loyal and honorable young man and would never presume beyond your place. But I know you love her - I have seen it in your eyes." His old eyes, growing dim, but still fierce, held Thutmose's.

Not daring to break that gaze, Thutmose replied, "Yes, my Lord. What would you have of me?"

"Protect her, and stand by her and my grandson. I fear for them. If he proceeds with his religious reforms, they will both need all the intelligent and loyal friends they can find. Will you do that?"

"Of course, my Lord!" Thutmose assured him, grasping the thin old hand atop the coverlet. "I will stand by them both as long as I live!"

"That's a good lad," the old man rasped, squeezing his hand.

Just then, the steward rushed in with more blankets, followed shortly by the royal physician.

The physician, a short, pudgy man with a shaven head and a snowy linen robe, set his leather bag on a nearby table. Thutmose stepped back and the physician stepped up to the bedside. He took the old man's wrist and closed his eyes, feeling the pulse. He felt the pulse at his patient's neck and checked the upper and lower lids of his eyes. Peeling back the upper edge of the covers, he felt the patient's chest with his hands. Then he reached into his bag and took out a hollow reed tube. He placed one end on the old man's chest and bent his ear to the other end. He moved the tube about the patient's chest and listened to his breathing and heartbeat.

After a few minutes, he straightened up and stepped over to where the steward stood anxiously wringing his hands.

"How is he, doctor?" asked the steward.

The physician gravely shook his head. "Not good, I'm afraid. I fear his heart is giving out. His pulse is weak and thready, his breathing labored, and his heartbeat is weak and irregular. You had better notify the king and queen. He doesn't have much time left."

The steward appeared ready to cry, himself. He had served the Vizier most of his life and could not imagine Egypt without his powerful guiding hand. He nodded dumbly to the physician, then turned and left to notify the royal family.

A short time later, the Queen arrived, clearly distraught, and took a seat at her father's side.

After relinquishing his bedside post to the Queen, Thutmose gathered up his things, thinking he should leave, but the old man stopped him.

"Thutmose," he rasped.

"Yes, my Lord?"

"Stay, and record the proceedings," he ordered, still a power to be reckoned with, even as he lay dying.

"Yes, my Lord," the artist agreed. He set his things back down and took out his quill and ink.

The Queen was soon followed by the king, the Crown Prince and Princess Nefertiti. A couple of hours later, the Vizier's son Aye, Nefertiti's father, arrived, clearly travel-stained; and was joined several hours later by his elder brother, Anen, a priest of Min who had been officiating at a temple in a town downriver.

The old man opened his eyes and looked at his family, gathered at his bedside. "My children," he said, looking at his two sons and his daughter, including the king as well in his gaze. "I think my time has come to bid you all farewell."

The Queen sobbed loudly and pleaded, "Don't leave us, father! How can we manage without you?"

The old man smiled weakly at her and said, "Very well, I think. I have taught you well, all of you. I know that the Two Lands will be safe in your capable hands. And I know that the God of my Fathers will watch over you, as he has watched over me, and will keep you safe." Turning his eyes heavenwards, he continued, "Truly, El has watched over me and blessed me all my life. I came into this land a slave, friendless and alone, but the Lord of Hosts raised me up to the highest post in the land. He has made me the father and grandfather of kings. Praise be to the God of my Fathers!"

"Praise be to the God of Our Fathers!" echoed the Queen and her brother Aye. After a moment's hesitation, they were joined by their elder brother, Anen.

The two men knelt by their father's bedside. The Queen slipped an arm behind the old man's shoulders and helped him sit up. Crossing his hands one over the other, he placed his right hand on the head of Aye, the younger son, and his left hand on the head of Anen, the older son. He spoke to them in the Habiru tongue, using the Habiru version of their names.

"I bless you both, but recall the blessing of my own father, Yacub, on his deathbed. You will both be great, but Efraim, though younger, will be the greater. You, Manasseh," he said to Anen, "my firstborn son, belong wholly to Egypt, serving an Egyptian god. You, Efraim," he said to Aye, "will rise still further. The day is coming when you will lead Egypt. Yet your children's children will someday leave this land and return to the land promised to our Fathers. When they do, tell them they must carry my bones back to be buried with those of my ancestors, in the cave with Abraham and Sarah, Yitzhak and Rebekah, where I buried my father Yacub, the cave that Abraham purchased from Ephron the Hittite. Promise me you will do this."

"Yes, father," agreed Anen and Aye.

The old man turned his eyes to where Pharaoh stood at the other side of the bed and spoke in Egyptian. "And to you, Amenhotep, my son by marriage, may the gods of Egypt continue to smile on you, as they have all your life. Egypt has endured long, and will endure longer yet. Thousands of years from now, men of many lands will look back upon your reign as the pinnacle of greatness, the richest reign in Egypt's long history, my son, and they will remember the glory of Amenhotep, Third of the Name."

Tears stood in the king's eyes. He resolutely choked back a sob and knelt at the old man's bedside.

"If Egypt has been great in my reign or my father's," said the king, "it has been thanks to you, O Godsfather. You have been my strong right arm, my wise advisor, all my life. I will be lost without you!"

"Nay, my son," the old man replied. "You, and Egypt, will go on without me. I leave you my daughter, Tiye, to love, help and guide you, and my son, Aye, to take my place as Grand Vizier and Supreme Commander of the Army. My son, Anen, will continue to serve you before the gods of the Two Lands. I leave my granddaughter, Nefertiti," he continued, looking at the girl standing at the foot of the bed with the Crown Prince, "as the helpmeet to my grandson, Amenhotep, the next pharaoh of the Two Lands. I can go in peace now, knowing that I am leaving my country and my loved ones in good hands."

He looked between the prince and princess to where Thutmose stood against the wall. The artist met his gaze and nodded solemnly. The Vizier smiled and sank back against the cushions. His eyes closed and he drifted off.

A short time later, the old man's face went slack and his head slipped to the side. The physician bent over him, listened to his chest, then held a polished metal mirror under his nose. Looking up, the doctor shook his head and pronounced him dead.

The family gathered around the bed tore their clothes and raised their hands and voices in lamentation.

Thutmose gathered up his materials and slipped away, tears sliding unnoticed down his face as he went.

I couldn't help thinking it was the end of an era. Egypt's wisest guardian was gone, the man who had guided the Two Lands for nearly forty years. Who knew what folly her leaders might commit in the coming years, without that fine mind and steady hand to guide them!

Chapter 14: Stranger in the Valley of the Kings

Plans for the coronation and marriage of the Horus in the Nest were delayed to allow the traditional seventy days for the funeral rites of Lord Yuya. First, his body was to be turned over to the *wab* priests for "Beautification", the mummification process that would preserve it for eternity.

There was some dispute over this among members of Yuya's extended family, since embalming was not a normal Habiru practice. Tradition among the wild nomads required burial of the body within 24 hours, a practice that made imminent good sense among wandering desert tribes. Yuya, however, had long since ceased to be a desert nomad. Besides, his sons pointed out to their kinsmen, Yuya himself had had the body of his father, Yacub, the clan patriarch, embalmed in the Egyptian fashion before returning it to Canaan for burial with his ancestors. If Yuya had felt that this was right for his own father, who was very much a desert nomad, then surely it was right for the son, who had become a thoroughgoing Egyptian in most of his ways. Besides, they added, the king, who was also his kinsman by marriage, insisted; and all of Egyptian society would be shocked if the second most important man in the country was not given the proper treatment after his death. The clansmen reluctantly agreed to the mummification.

This family dispute settled, the mortuary priests took possession of the body and began the elaborate embalming process. First, the liver, stomach and entrails were removed and the body cavity packed with linen soaked in natron, a naturally occurring mixture of sodium bicarbonate and salt, which would draw out all the moisture from the tissues. The brain was carefully removed through the nose, using a special hook designed for the purpose. The internal organs were preserved separately and packed in four alabaster canopic jars. The jars were stored in a beautiful wooden chest with inscriptions all around, sealed with golden bands, which would be buried with the body.

Once the tissues were thoroughly desiccated, the body was repacked with linen soaked in costly preservative spices. More spice-soaked linen was wrapped around the body, with every finger and toe wrapped separately. The royal embalmers of the Eighteenth Dynasty were justly proud of their craft, which had now reached the very pinnacle of perfection. The exact details of the process were a closely kept secret, especially the precise mixture of spices, unguents and herbs used to combat putrescence and preserve the body for posterity.

The complete process of beautification took forty days. An additional 30 days was devoted to prayers and rituals for the spirit of the dead, to assist him in his journey into the afterlife. The time was also needed to complete the preparation of the dead man's tomb.

Every Egyptian who could afford a proper burial spent many years and a large portion of his resources preparing his tomb, his home for eternity. Originally, pre-dynastic Egyptians had buried their dead in shallow graves in the sand. The bodies were buried in the fetal position, with their heads toward the West, the horizon where the sun set daily, beyond which the dead were thought to journey after death. Sometimes jackals or hyenas dug up these shallow graves, revealing bodies naturally desiccated and preserved by the dry desert sands.

Over the centuries, as Egyptian society became more complex and elaborate, the wealthier members of society were buried in underground chambers lined with mud brick, and later, in more elaborate rock-cut or rock-lined tombs. Unfortunately, once the body of the deceased was no longer in direct contact with the sand, the natural mummification process could no longer occur, and bodies began to putrefy. At the same time, Egyptian religion developed the belief that the body was needed, intact, together with all its parts, after death in order for the deceased to be able to "live" in the afterlife. Eventually, an increasingly elaborate and sophisticated process of mummification was developed to replace nature's original process.

Tombs had continued to become more extensive and elaborate over the millennia. The tombs of kings became, first, larger and more elaborate underground chambers, topped with a *mastaba*, a bench-shaped rectangular mound. The burial chambers were filled with a variety of increasingly rich grave goods, including everything the deceased might need or want in the afterlife: dishes, food, clothing, jewelry, weapons and later, whole chariots.

During the Third Dynasty, Pharaoh Djoser kept demanding that his mastaba tomb be made larger and larger. His architect, the famous architect/physician/philosopher Imhotep, first enlarged the mastaba several times, then stacked another, smaller mastaba atop the bottom one. Pharaoh continued to demand more, so Imhotep eventually erected five layers, each smaller than the last, to create the famous Step Pyramid, the world's first monumental stone building. In addition to his elaborate burial chambers beneath the pyramid, Djoser built a large mortuary temple decorated with beautiful turquoise tiles, all enclosed within a splendid wall.

The Step Pyramid was such a hit that pharaohs of the next two dynasties kept building larger and more perfect versions. However, pyramids had several distinct disadvantages as tombs. First of all, they required an immense expenditure of labor, materials and other resources, which put a strain on the economy. Second, they required an inordinate amount of time to build, running the risk that a pharaoh's tomb might not be completed by the time of his death. But worst of all, after the inevitable series of tomb robberies, succeeding pharaohs realized that a putting a massive pyramid atop one's burial chamber was tantamount to lighting an enormous beacon fire proclaiming, "Here lies treasure - come and get it!" So, after little more than a century, they abandoned the practice of pyramid building in favor of tombs cut into the rock.

When the 18th Dynasty came to power, moving the center of political power to Thebes, they began building secret tombs hidden away up a set of dry canyons in the mountains to the west of Thebes, an area that eventually came to be called "The Valley of the Kings." Many 18th Dynasty queens were buried in their husbands' tombs, although some later began to create their own tombs in a parallel Valley of the Queens. These tombs were dug by a specialized set of workmen, decorated by a dedicated group of artists, all living in their own village in a nearby valley. Location of the tombs was a closely-guarded secret. After a pharaoh's burial, the entrance to his tomb was sealed and covered over, and a guard was set over the whole valley, in the hope of protecting the pharaohs' eternal rest from tomb robbers. Even with all these safeguards, tomb robbers occasionally broke in. The incredible wealth buried with these pharaohs of Egypt's Golden Age would continue to lure tomb raiders for thousands of years.

Most pharaohs began building their tombs as soon as they came to the throne, each generation building larger, more intricate and elaborate passageways, stairs, burial chambers and storerooms. Since each tomb was supposed to be secret, there was no "master plan" of the whole valley, so it was not uncommon for workers on one pharaoh's tomb to break through into an older tomb. The whole mountain was eventually honeycombed with passageways.

Pharaoh Amenhotep's tomb was well along, having been under construction for nearly thirty years by the time his father-in-law died. Pharaoh was also paying for construction of a tomb for the Grand Vizier in the valley, not too far from his own. Yuya's wife, Lady Tuya, had been buried here a few years earlier, with only the king and her immediate family, along with the priests, in attendance. Now Pharaoh gave orders that Yuya's body would be buried there, alongside his wife - a singular honor, as theirs was the only non-royal burial in the Valley of the Kings.

When news of the planned quasi-royal burial reached Yuya's Habiru kinsmen in the delta, there was a renewed outcry. Several leaders of the tribe hurried upriver to Thebes to protest the plan, pointing out that Yuya had given deathbed instructions that, when his descendants eventually left Egypt, they should carry his bones back to Canaan to be buried with his forefathers. He had said nothing about being buried in a secret rock-cut tomb in the Valley of the Kings. How, they asked, would they be able to carry his bones away if they were buried in a closely-guarded tomb in the Valley of the Kings?

Pharaoh listened politely to their protests, then firmly overruled them. He pointed out that he, too, was Lord Yuya's kinsman, as were his father and his children. It was simply unthinkable, he said, that the second most important man in the greatest empire on earth should be buried with anything less than full honors - and that included a tomb amongst the kings he had served in life. If ever his descendants should leave Egypt - which Pharaoh doubted - they could petition the current king for permission to remove his bones in order to bury them with his ancestors in Canaan.

The Israelite clansmen were distraught and disappointed, but there was nothing more they could do, in the face of Pharaoh's refusal.

Realizing their distress, Queen Tiye requested that Thutmose sculpt a life-size statue of Lord Yuya to stand in for his mummified body. It was common Egyptian practice to place one or more replicas of the deceased in his tomb as "backups", so that if the body decayed or was damaged, the deceased could use the statue as an alternative body. Thutmose was happy to do this service for the Queen and the old Vizier, of whom he had grown surprisingly fond.

At the Queen's behest, he was able to acquire a piece of fine Lebanese cedar originally destined for the ship-building trade. From this, he carved a life-size portrait in his own realistic style. The statue was painted to resemble the original, and was dressed in a fine linen robe with a massive gold, lapis and carnelian collar of office. Like the mummy, the statue's hands were in an unusual position, held together in front of his chest in a position of prayer. The statue was placed in a set of three nested coffins, identical to those in which the mummified body was to be buried. These were presented to Yuya's three surviving brothers and their sons, who solemnly returned to Goshen with them.

On the trip downriver, the three brothers agreed that they would not tell their clansmen that the coffins held only a statue, not their kinsman's bones. They swore their sons to secrecy, making them vow to pass the secret on, but tell no one else until the day came to leave Egypt, at which time they could petition Pharaoh for the release of Yuya's mummy, as Pharaoh Amenhotep had indicated. Until that day, they concluded, there was no point in upsetting the tribe over something they could do nothing about.

At the end of the seventy day period of mourning, the mummy of the Grand Vizier was transported by sledge, with great ceremony, to the great temple at Karnak, where Amun heard the petitions of the royal family for the safe passage of his spirit through the hazards of the *Duat* (the underworld). From there, it was drawn onward to Lord Yuya's small mortuary temple near the mouth of the Valley of the Kings, where Yuya's son, Aye, performed the ceremony of the Opening of the Mouth so that his father could live again in the afterlife. Using a special instrument similar to the type of adze used by sculptors, Aye touched each opening of the dead man's head, so that his spirit might freely come and go to and from his "beautified" body and use all of its faculties.

After this, a small, select entourage consisting of the immediate family and several mortuary priests accompanied the body on its final journey to the tomb prepared for it in the Valley of the Kings. The procession halted at the mouth of the tomb while it was unsealed by the priests. All the larger pieces of funerary equipment had already been installed in the tomb, alongside the shrine containing the double coffins of Yuya's wife, Thuya, who had died three years previously. The equipment included three successively larger chairs belonging to the deceased couple's granddaughter, Sitamun, daughter of Pharaoh Amenhotep. She had spent a lot of time with her grandparents while she was growing up and was devoted to them. They had had the chairs carved for her, first, when she was a toddler, then a young girl, and finally, an adult; so she had given the chairs back to them as mementoes through eternity. Also included in the tomb were two fine chariots, one of them elaborately decorated and gilded: Pharaoh's second-best chariot, given to Yuya in recognition of his distinguished service to the Two Lands.

As he looked about the tomb, Pharaoh frowned a bit. The decorations and equipment were elegant, all of first quality workmanship, but not as grand or extensive as Pharaoh had wanted. Yuya had insisted that in death, as in life, he preferred more austere surroundings. He had never been a pretentious man, despite his great power, and he continued to favor simplicity throughout his life, and now, in his death.

The triple coffins containing the mummy were carried in and installed in the burial shrine. Wreaths of flowers and strings of garlic were laid on the outer coffin by the Queen and her brothers, followed by Prince Amenhotep and Princess Nefertiti. Nefertiti also placed a scroll of prayers from the Book of the Dead on the coffin. This scroll, over twenty cubits in length, had been prepared by Thutmose and Bek and several of the other senior artists to assist the soul of the dead man in his journey through the afterlife.

It was believed that the soul of the deceased journeyed beyond the western horizon into the underworld, where it faced a number of hazards. Chief among these was the weighing of his heart against the Feather of Ma'at. If they balanced, as judged by Osiris and a group of deities known as the Forty-Two Assessors, the deceased could continue his journey. If, however, his heart outweighed the Feather of Truth, he would be fed to Ammit, a terrible monster with the head of a crocodile and the body of a lion, and he would die forever.

The scroll prepared by the artists contained maps of the Duat, drawings of the trials faced by the deceased and spells to assist him in getting through them. These included the spell for the Judgement of the Dead, which begins,

"O my heart which I had from my mother! O my heart of my different ages! Do not stand up as a witness against me, do not be opposed to me in the tribunal, do not be hostile to me in the presence of the Keeper of the Balance, for you are my *ka* which was in my body, the protector who made my members hale. Go forth to the happy place whereto we speed; do not make my name stink to the Entourage who make men. Do not tell lies about me in the presence of the god; it is indeed well that you should hear!

"Thus says Thoth, judge of truth, to the Great Ennead [a group of nine major gods] which is in the presence of Osiris: Hear this word of very truth. I have judged the heart of the deceased, and his soul stands as a witness for him. His deeds are righteous in the great balance, and no sin has been found in him. He did not diminish the offerings in the temples, he did not destroy what had been made, he did not go about with deceitful speech while he was on earth."

This was followed by the Negative Confession, a prayer reciting all the specific sins of which the deceased was innocent.

After the scroll had been placed on the outer coffin, the chest of canopic jars was brought in and deposited nearby, then the doors of the shrine were closed and sealed. Other small gifts of jewelry, cosmetics, jars of rare perfumes and unguents, food and statuary were brought in. There were also plentiful numbers of *shabti*, small statues designed to do the work of the dead person. Finally, the mourners, with ashes on their heads, tearing their clothes and lamenting the loss of the great man, left the tomb, followed by the *wab* priests. The workmen then bricked up the entrance and plastered it over, and the chief priest sealed it with the mortuary seal. Later, workmen would fill in the steps down to the doorway with rubble, hiding its location from tomb robbers.

The prayers of the mourners must have been powerful, indeed, for except for some minor pilfering of unguent jars soon after burial, the tomb of Yuya and Thuya would lie undisturbed for over 3300 years, the only non-royal persons buried in the Valley of the Kings.

Chapter 15: Two Coronations and a Wedding

Lord Yuya was buried in the spring, which in Egypt is the time of the harvest. Not long after the harvest, but before the full heat of summer set in, the Prince was crowned co-pharaoh with his father.

The coronation was celebrated throughout the Two Lands. Invitations had been sent out half a year in advance to the rulers of all the known lands. Many sent emissaries with gifts to the two rulers of the greatest empire of the age. Thebes was a vast fairground, decorated throughout with colorful flags and garlands of flowers. Beer and wine flowed freely in homes and taverns throughout the city, and the smoke of incense and sacrifices rose from its many temples.

In the great temple of Amun, before the statue of the god in the Holy of Holies, Pharaoh Amenhotep the Third set the double crown of the Two Lands on the head of his son, crowning him Pharaoh Amenhotep the Fourth, in the presence of the Four Prophets of Amun.

"By the power of Amun, vested in me," cried the old pharaoh, setting the double crown on his son's head, "I crown you King of the Two Lands, with the white crown of Lower Egypt and the red crown of Upper Egypt. Oh ye gods of the Two Lands, behold the living incarnation of Horus, ruling this land as King Amenhotep the Fourth, known as Neferkheperure-Waenre!"

The Four Prophets raised up their arms and cried, "Hail, Amenhotep Neferkheperure-Waenre, beloved child of Amun!"

After the crowning, the two pharaohs were carried out of the temple in gilded sedan chairs, each borne by a dozen muscular bearers. A contingent of charioteers rode in front to clear the way, followed by trumpeters and bands of priests and priestesses, singing and chanting and swinging censers burning precious incense. A group of the God's Wives of Amun scattered rose petals before the litters of the kings. Guards flanked either side of the sedan chairs. They were carried through the streets of Thebes, both kings solemn as statues, while cheering throngs strewed their path with flowers. Behind the king came more priests, priestesses and soldiers, followed by handlers parading live lions and leopards on leashes. These were followed by a phalanx of chariots, then corps of foot soldiers, interspersed with musicians, dancers and tumblers. After the royal procession passed by, jovial merrymakers danced in the streets, bought food and drink from passing hawkers, or crowded into the taverns and villas of the city to celebrate the crowning of a new pharaoh who would uphold tradition and continue to maintain *ma'at* and the health and harmony of the land.

At the palace, the two pharaohs were carried into the vast, colonnaded throne room through a gathering of bowing courtiers, to a dais at the front of the room where a pair of gilded thrones awaited them.

Queen Tiye took her place on a smaller throne at the left hand of her husband, the senior Pharaoh. The newly crowned Pharaoh, Amenhotep the Fourth, sat to the elder king's right. Behind and to his right sat the Princess Nefertiti. The older Pharaoh's daughters sat on the lower steps, with young Mutnodjmet on the bottom step. Aye, now Grand Vizier, stood behind and between the two sovereigns, wearing the leopard skin and golden collar of office, carrying the staff of office. The Four Prophets of Amun stood at the right of the dais, while priests of several other deities stood on the other side. Master Auta, Thutmose and Bek sat near them, sketching the brilliant assemblage.

Aye pounded his staff on the floor, calling the assembly to attention. Four trumpeters blew rams' horns, announcing the first of a long series of foreign emissaries.

Aye called out in a loud voice, "Let the representatives of many lands enter with gifts for the Kings of the Two Lands!" He rapped his staff three times on the floor.

The Lord Chamberlain announced each group as they entered.

"The King of Nubia sends you greetings and gifts of gold, ivory and exotic beasts!" he cried.

A delegation of black men and women in colorful robes, short wigs and plentiful gold jewelry entered, bearing stacks of gold rings the size of saucers, whole elephant tusks and objects of carved ivory. Two men led in a black panther on a chain, while others carried monkeys and colorful exotic birds. A number of courtiers in the front row drew back nervously as the black cat padded by, snarling quietly as it passed. Next came eight men pounding out a pulsing, intricate rhythm on drums of various sizes, followed by a gyrating troupe of sinuous black dancers and a group of leaping, bounding acrobats who performed somersaults, backbends and splits around the room.

The Nubians proceeded by the foot of the dais, depositing their gifts in a pile at one side. They then paraded, leaped and pirouetted to a space at one side of the room.

The horns sounded again and the Lord Chamberlain cried out, "The King of Philistia sends you fine linen dyed with rare Tyrian purple, fetched from the bottom of the sea by divers, at great risk to their lives."
A delegation of bearded men wearing multilayered, close-fitting robes entered, bearing armloads of purple fabric, some of it embroidered with gold. These they deposited ceremoniously next to the gifts of the Nubians.

"The King of Mitanni sends you alabaster lamps to light your way," cried out the Chamberlain, "and a splendid pair of matched white horses and a gilded chariot."

Another delegation of bearded men in part armor of leather and bronze entered, bearing lighted alabaster lamps, while another came behind, bearing a small model of a gilded chariot drawn by two horses. He whispered something to the Chamberlain.

"Ah," said the Chamberlain, nodding. "This model represents the horses and chariot, Your Majesty, which await you in the royal stables." He added as an aside, "They thought it best to leave the horses outside."

The king laughed and the court followed suit.

"The King of Babylon sends you statues of the god Marduk, blessed by the deity himself, and his consort, Ishtar, renowned for healing..."

Two sets of bearers entered, bearing heavy stone statues of the two Babylonian deities.

"...and a fine suit of armor," continued the Chamberlain, "made by the king's personal armorer."

Another man with black hair and beard worn in ringlets, in a robe with fringe spiralling around it, entered bearing a staff with a crossbar from which hung a leather and bronze corselet, with greaves, arm braces and gauntlets and a gold-trimmed bronze helmet.

And so on it went, for hours, as all the rulers of the known world (and some unknown, as well) paid tribute to the greatest among them, the King of Egypt.

The next day, the marriage of Pharaoh Amenhotep the Fourth to Princess Nefertiti was celebrated, with almost equal pomp and cere-mony. Once again, the great throne room was packed with courtiers and foreign dignitaries, all sumptuously dressed and bejeweled. The Egyp-tian courtiers were elaborately bewigged and made up, their eyes out-lined in kohl, lips and palms stained red with henna. Cones of perfumed nard were fastened atop their wigs, melting over the course of the day and evening, releasing a continuous stream of perfume over their wearers.

Musicians played at one side of the room, while dancers enter-tained the waiting courtiers. Priests of the various temples stood at the sides of the royal dais, while a dwarf dressed as Bes, the prodigiously endowed god of entertainment and fertility, capered about in front of it. Artists from the royal workshop were scattered around the sides of the room, with the senior artists and Master Auta at the front. The master artist looked about with a frown, looking for Thutmose, who finally staggered in unsteadily from a side door, hauled along by Bek.

I had tried to beg off, pleading illness, but Auta would have none of it, insisting that nothing short of a severe case of leprosy could excuse me from such an event. With courage drawn from a full skin of wine, I took my place near the front of the court.

They took their place in front of a column just as a trumpeter blew a horn and the Chamberlain rapped on the floor with his staff.

"All bow down to their Majesties, Pharaoh Amenhotep the Third and his Great Wife, Queen Tiye!" he cried.

Like a field of wheat before a mighty wind, the assembled crowd bowed low as the king and queen entered and proceeded to their thrones on the dais.

Next, the Chamberlain announced the younger Pharaoh, who entered and took his place.

Finally, another fanfare announced the arrival of the bride and her father.

"Make way for the Grand Vizier, Aye, son of Yuya - may he be justified! And for his daughter, Princess Nefer-neferuaten Nefertiti, betrothed of Pharaoh Amenhotep the Fourth!" cried the Chamberlain.

The doors opened to admit Aye, resplendent in his robes of office, leading his daughter Nefertiti by the hand. The members of the royal family rose to greet them, while the assembled courtiers bowed low.

For this occasion, Nefertiti wore a gown of linen so fine it floated about her in the breeze from the fans wielded by servants all around the room. It was spangled all over with tiny gold stars that glittered in the sunlight filtering down from the high clerestory windows. She wore a low, flat-topped gilded cap with two red ribbons trailing down her back. At her waist she wore the red girdle of a Royal Heiress.

Aye led his daughter up the stairs of the dais to where the young Pharaoh stood awaiting her. Placing her hand in Amenhotep's, Aye announced,

"My Lord Pharaoh, I present to you my daughter, Neferneferuaten Nefertiti, to be your Royal Wife."

The elder Pharaoh stepped to his son's side and asked, "Pharaoh Amenhotep Neferkheperure-Waenre, do you take this woman, Neferneferuaten Nefertiti, to be your Queen and Great Wife from this day forth?"

"I do," agreed the younger Pharaoh, looking steadily into Nefertiti's eyes.

"And do you, Neferneferuaten Nefertiti, pledge your faith to this man, Amenhotep Neferkheperure-Waenre, as your Lord and Husband, from this day forward?"

"I do," agreed Nefertiti, meeting her new husband's gaze.

The elder Pharaoh placed his hand over their clasped hands and said in a loud voice, "All hail Pharaoh Amenhotep Neferkheperure-Waenre and his Great Wife, Queen Neferneferuaten Nefertiti!"

The assembled crowd repeated, "Long live Pharaoh Amenhotep Neferkheperure-Waenre and his Great Wife, Queen Neferneferuaten Nefertiti!" followed by a great cheer.

The old Pharaoh returned to his throne, while his son led Nefertiti to a new throne beside his own. He stepped behind her throne, while she removed her cap and handed it to Princess Sitamun. Aye came forward from the back of the dais, carrying a cushion bearing a tall crown topped with two long feathers. The young Pharaoh took the crown from the cushion and placed it on Nefertiti's head, saying,

"I crown you Queen Neferneferuaten Nefertiti!"

The crowd cheered again as the younger Pharaoh returned to his throne.

The older Pharaoh clapped his hands and called out, "Let the feast begin!"

The side doors opened to admit scores of servants carrying stools and small tables, enough for all the guests to be seated, as the musicians struck up a merry song. More servants entered bearing copious platters of fresh bread, steaming meats, stewed grains and fresh fruits, accompanied by generous pitchers of beer and fine wine. As the guests feasted, the musicians played on, accompanying lithe dancers and limber acrobats.

Although a feast had also been prepared for the artists in a nearby chamber, Thutmose felt he could not bear even this proximity to the royal couple on their wedding night.

Bek eyed him knowingly. "Ah, so that's how it is with you, my friend. Not a good thing, that, not good at all."

Thutmose looked away, refusing to meet Bek's gaze.

Bek sighed, shook his head, then took a firm grasp of his comrade's arm and hauled him away from the banqueting guests.

"Come, my friend, this is no place for you. I know a nice dark, friendly tavern where you can drown your sorrows."

Chapter 16: A Night on the Town

Bek led Thutmose out of the vast warren of Malkata Palace, across the river, then through torch-lit streets thronged with merry-makers. They threaded their way through streets crowded with visitors from all corners of the known world: Bedu tribesmen from the Sinai desert; Nubians from the south; Keftiu traders from Crete; soldiers who had accompanied Canaanite petty kings, vassals of Pharoah; Mitanni noblemen; even a sprinkling of Hittites, here under banners of peace for the coronation and wedding. They worked their way past jugglers, min-strels and dancers, and itinerant sellers of meats, bread, beer and wine, as well as vendors of figurines of various deities. Most popular among them were Hathor, the Great Mother; Bes, god of merriment and enter-tainment; and Taueret, the hippopotamus goddess of fertility and child-birth. At last, Bek pulled Thutmose into the doorway of a tavern, which proved to be even more crowded than the street.

Thutmose followed him blindly through the jovial crowd. The lamplit interior of the tavern was dim after the torchlit streets. As their eyes grew accustomed to the dim light, Bek called out greetings to familiar regulars among the throng of strangers.

"Userhat! How are you, you old dog?" he called out to a scribe Thutmose recognized from the palace. "And who's this ravishing crea-ture with you?" he continued, putting an arm around the scribe's ma-tronly companion. "Does your wife know about her? Oh, she **is** your wife?!" he exclaimed, in feigned surprise.

The lady in question tried to frown, but the effect was spoiled by a fit of giggles.

"Bek, you are an incorrigible liar!" she exclaimed, waggling a finger at him. "But keep it up – Hathor knows, I need the compli-ments!"

Bek attempted to sweep her a lavish bow, but was brought up short when his backside collided with a Mitanni soldier's knife scab-bard.

"Ow!" Rubbing his behind, Bek turned to the scowling soldier. "I beg your pardon, your lordship, I was unaware you were so... well equipped!"

The soldier grumbled something, then turned back to his com-panions.

Turning back to the scribe and his wife, Bek seized the lady's hand and planted a noisy kiss on it.

"Madam, your servant! If you ever tire of this old reprobate, just look me up!"

The lady laughed and waved him off. "Look who's calling who a reprobate!"

Bek and Thutmose nodded farewell to the couple and continued toward the back of the tavern, where several musicians played, almost inaudible over the din.

Bek pinched a passing serving girl, who turned to him with a glare, then broke into a smile when she saw who it was. He asked her something Thutmose couldn't hear, and she replied with a gesture of her head. Following her movement, Bek saw the owner of the tavern carrying several ceramic pitchers of beer through the crowd.

Pulling Thutmose in his wake, Bek threaded his way to the back of the tavern, where he greeted the harried owner.

"Nebseny!"

Hearing his name, the owner turned. Seeing Bek, he smiled broadly. "Master Bek! We missed you."

"Is there any room left upstairs, Nebseny?"

"Oh, I think we could find a bit of space for my best customer, Master Bek – and for your friend," he added, eyeing Thutmose. "You know the way – go on up."

"Great. And send a girl up with plenty of beer, and your best meat and bread. On second thought, make that *two* girls, and some musicians. My friend, here, could use a little company this evening."

"Ah, yes," said the tavern owner, winking broadly. "It wouldn't do to let such a fine young man be lonely on a night such as this."

Bek led Thutmose up a stair at the back of the room to a second story. Finding this story crowded, as well, they continued up to the roof. Here there were only a few customers, most of them couples amorously occupied. Bek led the way to a corner largely screened off by a jog in the parapet wall. There was a spectacular view of the city from this vantage point. Sounds of revelry drifted up from the streets below, while the major thoroughfares were picked out in flickering torchlight. The many temples were also brilliantly lit, and the torchlight revealed gaily colored banners floating over temples, palaces and battlements. The light of stars above and torches below was reflected in the waters of the mighty Nile surging past the city walls.

By the time they had settled themselves on cushions on the floor, the tavern owner appeared with tall jugs of wine and wide ceramic drinking bowls.

"In honor of this auspicious occasion, Master Bek," said the innkeeper, "I have brought you two bottles of my best wine."

The innkeeper set the two ceramic wine jars on the floor, then carefully removed the plug of wax sealing the first jar. He poured wine into the painted ceramic cups and handed them to the young men.

He was followed by two young women bearing platters of steaming meats, bread and fruit. They were soon joined by three musicians: a drummer, a harpist and a girl who played a three-stringed lute-like instrument. Nebseny introduced the two girls as Mut-hepti and Ta-Amen, then bowed his way out. While Mut-hepti served the two artists, Ta-Amen began to sway and twirl to the music, wrist and ankle bracelets jingling.

Before long, Thutmose relaxed under the influence of the music, the wine, the soft warm night and the even softer, warmer girls. In time, the fumes of the wine began to blur the image of Nefertiti beside the young king, Great Wife to the new Pharaoh. Under the influence of wine and caresses, the sharp ache in his heart became a dull throb.

Bek spoke to the girls aside, telling them, "My friend, here, is very sad because his lady love has married another man. I'm counting on you girls to cheer him up." He reached into a bag he carried at his waist and pulled out two exquisite bracelets, one studded with turquoise and carnelian, the other with lapis lazuli, both fine examples of his own workmanship. "I have a fine bracelet as a gift for whoever cheers him up - and another for whoever cheers me up!"

"I would be only too happy to share the bed of such a fine young man," said Ta-Amen, admiring Thutmose's finely molded features and well-muscled physique.

"So would I," agreed Mut-hepti. "His lady must be mad, to wed another when she could have such a man as this!"

"Indeed," concurred Ta-Amen, shaking her head. "Loving such a man as this would be reward enough, in itself."

"True," nodded Mut-hepti. "It is seldom such a man comes our way."

"Ah, then, if my friend is such a prize," drawled Bek, reaching for the bracelets, "you won't be needing these."

"Now, now," said Mut-hepti quickly, snatching up the bracelets, "don't be hasty, my lord. You said that these were *gifts*, did you not? A gift's a gift, after all – it would be most ungracious of you to take it back."

"Ah, so it would, ladies," agreed Bek, "so it would. I fear you have me there."

Mut-hepti extended her hands, a bracelet in each, and let Ta-Amen make her choice. She chose the lapis lazuli. Mut-hepti extended her hand to Bek, holding out the turquoise and carnelian bracelet.

"If you please, my lord," she said coyly, "fasten it for me."

Bek obliged her, then pulled her, giggling, onto his lap.

Ta-Amen danced her way over to Thutmose, her hips swaying in time to the rhythmic beat of the drums. He waved a chicken drumstick along with the beat, periodically washing the meat down with wine. Ta-Amen plucked a bunch of grapes from a platter of fruit and began feeding them to him as she danced past.

Bek and Mut-hepti were wrapped in a friendly libidinous embrace. Mut-hepti later assured her friend that, while Bek might have a mug like the dwarf god, Bes, he was also as erotically well-endowed as that priapic fertility god.

"And in the dark," she said with a lascivious wink, "that counts for far more than looks!"

And so the evening continued. It soon blurred into a whirl of food, music and girls as Thutmose and Bek worked their way through first one, then the other, jug of wine.

Before dawn, Thutmose awoke briefly, entangled in warm female limbs. He staggered unsteadily to his feet and relieved himself into a piss-pot the host had placed conveniently nearby. Stumbling his way back to the nest of cushions, he settled in next to Ta-Amen. He groggily concluded that he must not have been too badly impaired by the wine when he heard her whisper, "Ah, Thutmose, I have had many men, but never one like you!"

So, despite its inauspicious beginning for me, the night wound up being most memorable for its pleasurable ending.

I had spent the last ten years in the Royal Artists' Workshop, sleeping in a small cell with several other boys. Despite the usual rutting and imaginings of pubescent boys, and the openness of Egyptian society, this setting afforded little opportunity for sexual exploration. Oh, I had experienced the usual fumblings with palace maidservants in dark corners, but nothing like the sheer sensuality of this night's adventure. Now I knew why Bek was so fond of this tavern!

Chapter 17: The New Broom

When the festivities were finally over and the foreign delegations had departed for their far-off homes, life began to settle into a new
routine, with the two pharaohs ruling side by side: Amenhotep III as the
Senior King, his son, Amenhotep IV, as the Junior King. Nefertiti took
her new place, quietly, behind her husband.

While the old pharaoh was still the senior King, with the right
to overrule his son, he seldom did so. The truth was that he was growing old and tired, and seemed glad to let the reins of power slip slowly
from his grasp into his son's.

Queen Tiye, on the other hand, was as vigorous, energetic and
tireless as ever, shoring up her weakening husband with one hand while
guiding her naïve, impractical son with the other. She grew increasingly
alarmed at his campaign to institute a new interpretation of Egypt's traditional religion so radical it edged ever closer to becoming an entirely
new religion - so radical it verged on heresy.

Tiye had grown up in a family that straddled two cultures and
two religions, and knew from personal experience that Egypt's multifa-
rious polytheism allowed it to be very tolerant of other beliefs, having
already absorbed the variant beliefs of many regions. But she had also
seen that her father's more insular tribal belief system was far less tolerant of any of his own people straying to follow other people's gods.
She knew that, while Yuya had wisely acknowledged, respected and
paid lip service to the gods of his adopted land, he had privately adhered to the religion of his forefathers, worshipping El in the privacy of
his own home. Although he had been entirely willing to let other people
worship as they chose, he had struggled with his King's role as a living
god to his people, and with his own role as "god's father" to that King.
While Tiye had not been privy to most of her father's discussions of
religion with her son, she suspected that the powerful old man's beliefs
had had a marked influence on the boy. She feared that her son's beliefs
could easily become even less tolerant than her father's. And indeed,
the first project he undertook as a new King was the building of a temple for his newly reinterpreted version of the god Aten.

For this purpose, he called together the Master Builder, Master
Mason, and his chief artists: Bek, newly designated Chief of Works,
and Thutmose, now Chief Artist and Sculptor.

From the day after his coronation, the young King had begun
his "new broom" campaign, sweeping away old office-holders and ap-
pointing new ones. While his favorite artists were among the first of the
new appointees, the appointment of these talented young men who had
been trained in the royal workshop was no surprise. The same could not
be said, however, of some of his other appointments, many of whom

were complete newcomers who replaced incumbents whose families
had held their posts for generations. The new King's iconoclasm was
already causing uproar and resentment among Egypt's highest-ranking
families.

Amenhotep IV orderered his artists and builders to create a new
temple, the *Gem pa'Aten*, to his deity within the vast Luxor temple precinct. It was to be of a new and radical design, suitable to the omnipresent solar nature of its deity, the Aten.

"Through long consideration and deep contemplation,"
anounced the young King, "I have come to recognize that Aten - or
Atum, as he has sometimes been called - being the Creator God, is also
the supreme God, having created all the rest. All the other deities are
but aspects of this one Supreme Being, whose principal manifestation is
the sun: the life-giving, omnipresent sun. Therefore, the inner sanctum
of his temple must be open to the sun; and since the sun sheds its rays
on all men, this inner courtyard must be open to all, not only to his
priests. And around this central courtyard, I want colossal statues of
myself and my Great Wife, Nefertiti, the principal worshippers and
conduits between Aten and our subjects."

"Yes, my King," agreed the builders and artists.

But the builders, with their heads still bowed, glanced at each
other in surprise. Bek and Thutmose, having known the young king so
long, were less surprised.

It was small wonder the builders should be surprised by their
new king's request. All traditional Egyptian temples were built on the
same model, which had originated thousands of years earlier as a simple reed building on a higher piece of ground rising above the Nile's
flood, representing the original *benben*, the primordial Mound of Creation, the first piece of dry ground to appear out of the Waters of Chaos.
Therefore, every temple, however grand and massive, followed a plan
that included a floor that rose gradually from the forecourt, accessible
to the public, through the shadowed inner hall, to its highest point in the
darkened, private Inner Sanctum, home of the god and accessible only
to the King and the priests. The traditional Egyptian temple was not
conceived of as a place where worshippers gathered or came to pray,
but as the earthly home of its god or goddess. The public was no more
welcome there than in the private apartments of the King himself.

Therefore, the temple plan the new King had requested came as
a complete surprise to the builders, who were accustomed to building
traditional Egyptian temples. This new design stood all the traditional
precepts on their heads: an Inner Sanctum not dark and enclosed, but
open to the sun; a light-filled inner court open to all comers, to be filled
with individual offering tables where all might make their own personal
offering to the god; and mighty statues and carvings representing both

the Pharaoh and his wife. Further, there was to be no statue of the god. With the god himself shining down from above, said Pharaoh, what need was there for an image of mere stone or metal to represent the glorious presence of the deity?

Others, however, argued that the temple should contain **some** kind of symbol representing the deity for whom it was built. The King resisted, protesting that the deity was invisible, abstract and ineffable - how could one picture the invisible?

By now, the old King had nodded off, since his Queen was not there that day to prod him awake, and no one else dared.

At this point, Nefertiti leaned forward and tapped her husband on the shoulder.

"May I say something, my Lord Husband?" she asked demurely.

"Of course, my dear. My ears are always open to you," replied the younger Amenhotep, smiling.

"It seems to me, my husband, that while your point is very logical, that a god whose rays are all around us needs no representation, nevertheless, his human subjects may need some tangible symbol on which to focus their prayers. While the god himself is limitless, the minds of his subjects, alas, are not. We poor mortals can do with a little symbolic help."

The young King thought this over.

"Your point is well taken, my Queen. Very well," he said, turning to the artists, "we need a symbol of this new, old deity. You artists, this falls in your area of expertise. Any ideas?"

Thutmose and Bek glanced at each other, startled to be asked to create a new symbol for a reinterpreted old god.

Finally, Thutmose hesitantly ventured a proposal.

"Well, Your Majesty," he said, "since the Aten manifests as the sun, perhaps a simple solar disk would be an appropriate symbol. It's still very abstract - just a circle - but it's the closest thing to an image of the god, especially if it's covered with gold. Then, in the open courtyard, it will reflect the rays of the sun itself. The effect should be quite dazzling."

"A fine idea!" agreed the King. "I like it. Make it so."

Thutmose was rewarded by a brilliant smile from the Queen, as well as by the King's approval.

Over the next several weeks, Bek and Thutmose worked closely with the King to develop a plan for the new Gem pa'Aten temple, to be built within the precinct of the vast Temple of Amun at Luxor. At its heart was the great open courtyard specified by the King, to be surrounded by colossal statues and an open colonnade. Over Thutmose's protest, Bek proposed a startling design for the huge royal statues. He resurrected the strange, distorted style he had experimented with in his youth, to the horror of the High Priest of Amun. The priests were sure to be even more horrified when they saw that the ten-cubit high statues were to be hermaphroditic composites of both the King and Queen, neither fully male nor fully female, wearing the masculine royal kilt, but clearly lacking male genitalia and sporting distinct breasts. Thutmose was appalled, but the King accepted Bek's argument that his orders had specified that the statues be of "the king and the queen", and that, just as the Aten embodied all the gods, so these colossi embodied both the male and female aspects of the royal pair who formed the earthly link with the god.

As if the indeterminate sexual nature of the colossi were not startling enough, Bek also utilized a distorted perspective, more elongated towards the top, pointing out that human visitors would see the statues only from below, since even the tallest man would come no higher than their knees. From this viewpoint, the figures were more normally proportioned, if still disturbingly androgynous.

In a further surprising move, the King specified that the large square columns making up the colonnade behind the colossi should all feature images of Nefertiti conducting rituals and sacrificing to the Aten. Thus, on the columns, the Queen appears alone conducting rituals, a role traditionally performed only by the King.

In addition to the temple, the young King also ordered that a new palace be built to house his family, the Queen having quickly become pregnant with their first child. Like the temple, the new palace also had some unusual features. Foremost among these was a large window with a balcony overlooking an interior courtyard.

Inspecting the plans, the Master Builder asked, "What is this window with the balcony, Your Majesty?"

"Ah," said the King, "I'm glad you asked. That is another feature you had better get used to. That is my Window of Appearances. Henceforth, every palace shall have at least one."

"But what is its function, Your Majesty?" asked the Master Builder.

"That is where I will appear to my loyal subjects. From this window, I will reward them for their good service with the Gold of Distinction."

"Ah, I see," said the Master Builder.

The Gold of Distinction generally took the form of golden *shebu* collars, which were traditionally awarded for acts of valor in war or distinguished service in peacetime. These cleverly-designed collars could be worn singly or hooked together to form larger designs, for those who had received multiple awards.

"It is where I will reward you, Master Builder, when my new temple is done."

"Ah!" said the Master Builder with a smile, "That I can understand!"

However, the weeks flew by, then the months, and very little progress had been made on the temple. The King once again called together the artists and the builders. From his thunderous countenance, it was apparent that he was not pleased.

"Why is it taking so long to build my new temple?" the King demanded.

The Master Builder reluctantly spoke up. "Well, Your Majesty," he said, "there are a great many stones needed for the temple, of many sizes and shapes, and they must all be cut at Aswan and transported down the Nile to the building site. Once they arrive, they must all be placed in a specific order and location. Many of the stones are quite large, requiring teams of many men to move and raise them."

"Yet the palace progresses much more quickly," observed the King, "even though it was started much later. Why is this?"

"Well, Your Majesty, the palace is a different kind of building. It is built of adobe brick covered with plaster. It is much easier, hence faster, to build."

"Why?" asked the King.

The Master Builder was taken aback by this simple, direct question, so like a child's perennial "why".

"Why, because it's made of *bricks*, Your Majesty, not stone," he answered.

"What difference does that make?" asked the King.

The Master Mason stepped forward. "I can answer that, Your Majesty. There are many differences. First of all, bricks can be made right here, at the building site. Bricks are simply mud and water and straw, all of which are available here in ample amounts. With enough manpower and a little patience, we can create an endless supply.

"Stone, on the other hand, is another matter. You have to use the proper kind of stone for a given type of building. In the case of

Your Majesty's temple, the nearest source for the proper kind of stone is several days' journey upriver, at Aswan. Many stones are required, of various sizes and shapes. These must be laboriously cut, detached, shaped and hauled to the river, then loaded onto barges for transport down the river. Each of these jobs requires many men, doing work which is slow and difficult. Bricks are all one size, and several can be carried at one time by one man. Building stones come in many sizes, and almost all are far too large and heavy for one man to carry. And once they arrive here, it once again requires many men to drag each stone to the site and raise it into place."

"So, let me get this straight," said the King. "Are you telling me, that if I were to build two walls, each the same height and length, one of brick and one of stone, that the stone wall would take much longer and require more men to build?"

"That's absolutely right, Your Majesty," said the Master Mason. "You have got it exactly!"

"And the main reason for that," continued the King, "is that stones are usually bigger and heavier and come in different sizes, while bricks are smaller, lighter and come in only one size?"

"That's correct, Your Majesty," agreed both the Master Mason and the Master Builder.

At this point, Nefertiti spoke up.

"Is there any particular reason why stones need to be bigger than bricks and to come in different sizes?" she asked.

"Not really, Your Majesty," replied the Master Mason. "That's just what the Master Builder orders from us."

The Master Builder was quick to point out, "I only order what the building plans call for."

The King turned to Bek and Thutmose.

"Is there any reason," he asked, "why the temple couldn't be built with smaller stones, all the same size?"

The two artists, who had jointly designed the temple, looked at each other. They conferred aside for a minute, then Bek answered the King.

"I suppose not, Your Majesty," he admitted. "I confess, we followed the traditional method of designing a stone building, requiring blocks to be cut to different sizes for different parts of the building."

The King gave a short laugh. "What, you, Bek, following tradition? That's a switch!"

Bek gave a rueful smile and raised his shoulders in a self-deprecating shrug.

"I admit, it's a bit out of character," agreed Bek. "Leave it to Your Majesty to see where we have been blinded by tradition! Shall we re-design the temple, then, to use smaller, uniform blocks?"

"Definitely," replied the King.

The Master Mason raised a hand. "If I may ask, Your Majesty - what size blocks?"

The builders and artists all looked at each other and shrugged.

Nefertiti spoke up again. "Husband - I think we should specify that they be no larger than can be carried by one man, and an *average* man at that."

"Excellent idea, my dear," agreed the King. "Let it be so."

Bek turned to the Master Mason. "How large a block can be carried by one man?"

"I'm not entirely sure," he answered. "It would depend some- what on the type of stone, but I would think, generally, not more than a cubit in length, and maybe half that in height and depth."

"But remember," said the Master Builder, "the men have to be able to keep carrying them all day. We have to allow for that."

"Why don't we test different size blocks?" suggested Thut- mose. "We can have several teams of men carry different size blocks back and forth for several hours, and see what size works best. Then Bek and I can re-design the temple to use that size block."

"Good idea," said the King. "Make it so."

So the King cut to the heart of the problem and conceived of the standard stone blocks that came to be known as talatat *blocks. Bek and I re-designed the temple and sent the order for the new blocks to the Master Mason. He informed us that the work went much faster at the quarry, and we soon had an ample supply of stone to work with. From that point on, the temple grew quickly, much to the pleasure of the King - and the displeasure of the priests.*

Chapter 18: To Catch an Artist...

Meanwhile, the new palace also progressed quickly. The main mud-brick walls were soon completed and a dazzlingly white lime plaster applied to the exterior. Unfortunately, this shining white canvas soon attracted another, less welcome crew of artists: every night, street urchins with charcoal and crude paints decorated its walls with less-than-flattering images of the King and his family and a variety of unpopular public officials. Bek and I were thoroughly annoyed with this demeaning amateur embellishment of our handiwork, and the King was irate at this desecration of his home. We set guards to watch for the vandals at night, which diminished the attacks, but did not altogether stop them. My trained eye told me that the majority of the continuing drawings were the work of one hand - one with a surprising amount of raw talent. I was determined to catch this talented vandal in the act.

Thutmose discussed his suspicions with the sergeant of the guards.

"Oh, aye," agreed the sergeant, "I reckon I knows this miscreant. 'Tis one young hellion named Ipy. If'n I catch that young bugger one more time, it's the copper mines o' the Sinai fer him! He's been floutin' Theban law long enough - the local magistrate is no fonder of 'im than meself. 'E's promised t'send 'im t'the mines f'r twenty years if'n the barstard turns up in 'is court agin!"

"I want to catch him, too," commented Thutmose, "but I think I might have a more constructive, local use for the lad. And I think I know how to catch this particular rat."

In order to catch the persistent graffiti artist, Thutmose set guards to patrol the perimeter of the palace. These patrols covered the exterior at fairly frequent, regular intervals. The master artist, however, set a trap for the canny vandal by insuring that the entryway to a newly completed, freshly lime-washed courtyard was poorly lighted and fell midway between the most widely-spaced patrol posts. To further bait the trap, he began having servants deliver hot food for the crew an hour before dawn each day, figuring that this would be sure to attract the attention of hungry street urchins. What was less apparent was that he, himself, quietly preceded the arrival of the food each day and took up a post behind a decorative wall with pierced air vents through which he could watch the full sweep of the courtyard. Two more guards were stationed at hidden posts outside the courtyard. Once they saw the boy enter, they had orders to advance quietly and take up posts just outside the gateway, hidden by the entry pylons.

The first two nights, Thutmose and the guards watched in vain for the artistic intruder. The third night, however, was more successful.

While the sky was still dark, Thutmose arrived silently, threading his way through the darkened palace to arrive unseen at his post behind the courtyard wall. He had been there only a few minutes when he was alerted by faint noises within the courtyard. Peering through the vents, he could make out a slight figure moving along the blank back wall of the courtyard, clearly visible in the light of a nearly-full moon. While he could not make out the images from this distance, Thutmose knew from the scratching sounds and the figure's swooping and dipping movements that the boy was sketching something in charcoal on the invitingly blank wall. Some time later, as the sky was just beginning to pale, Thutmose could hear the approach of the servant. He smelled the inviting aroma of hot, fresh-baked bread and thick, yeasty beer. The young graffiti artist stopped, sniffed the air, then disappeared behind a column with his charcoal and paints.

The servant, appearing oblivious to anything untoward happening in the courtyard, filled a brazier with hot coals he had brought in a pot with a handle. He added fuel to the brazier, then tucked the covered basket of bread nearby, where it would stay warm. The servant had no sooner left the courtyard than the boy reappeared from his hiding place. Abandoning his drawing tools, he dashed over to the basket of bread, all the while glancing suspiciously around the quiet courtyard. Seeing no one, he lifted the cover and pulled out a flat loaf of bread, still steaming in the cool dawn air. He wolfed this down, then pulled out another loaf, washing it down with long draughts of the thick, foamy beer. Thutmose let him eat and drink, partly out of sympathy for his whip-thin body, its rib cage clearly visible in the moonlight, and partly figuring a full belly and some beer might slow the vandal down.

As the boy ate and drank, Thutmose quietly pulled on a cord that ran over the wall and was attached to a red cloth on the outside. This was his signal to the guards outside, who had been instructed to be prepared to block the entryway when the cloth flapped. After several silent tugs, he released the cord and worked his way around the back side of the vent wall to where a back entrance opened onto the courtyard. From there, he quietly took up a position at the back of a column, only a few feet away from where the starving boy was hungrily gobbling the bread and beer. When the boy tilted up the pitcher to wash down the last of the bread, Thutmose darted out and grabbed him.

The sound of the pitcher shattering, followed by the noise of a scuffle, alerted the guards poised just outside the gate, who rushed to block the narrow entrance with their bodies. It was fortunate they were there, for tight as Thutmose's grip was, the boy was slippery and agile as an eel, made frantic by fear and desperation. Despite the master artist's best efforts, the wiry boy twisted free and bolted for the exit - but the two guards brought him down and wrestled him to the ground.

As the sun peered over the horizon, the two guards bound the boy's hands behind him and hobbled his feet, then stood him upright for the artist's inspection.

"Well, well, well," commented Thutmose, walking around the boy. "What have we here? A would-be artist, is it?"

He signaled the guards to bring the boy over by the wall he had been defacing. Thutmose examined the sketches in the growing light. To his private amusement, the centerpiece was a remarkably good - if exaggerated - drawing of the High Priest and his three cronies.

"Ah!" he continued, trying not to laugh, "The Four Prophets of Amun! A fitting subject! I daresay the King will want to see this."

Turning to the two guards, he instructed them to bring the boy to his workroom and guard him there. As they left with the boy, workmen began arriving to finish the wall, and artists, to decorate it. He instructed them to leave the graffiti for the moment, but to begin painting the other walls with their intended design of gardens, flowers and wildfowl. Other workmen began tiling a lotus pool which would occupy the center of the courtyard.

Once the work was underway, Thutmose returned to his workroom to deal with the young vandal.

Instructing the guards to stand outside the door, he turned to the boy.

"So, young man," he said, severely, "you think you're qualified to decorate the King's palace, do you?"

The boy said nothing, but held up his head defiantly.

"Do you have a name?" asked Thutmose.

The boy hesitated a moment, then spat out, "I am Ipy, son of Hapuseneb."

"And what does Hapuseneb do?" asked Thutmose.

"He feeds worms," replied the boy. "He's dead. He used to be a drover, but he died two years ago."

"And your mother?" asked Thutmose. "Does she yet live?"

"No," replied the boy. "She's dead, too - died when I was little."

"So, then, you have no family?" asked Thutmose. "No aunts or uncles or cousins?"

"None," said the boy, holding his head up as if to belie his shameful lack of status.

"So...you've just been scavenging a living on the streets since your father died?" Thutmose asked gently.

"More or less," the boy admitted, with a shrug. "I get by."

"I have a proposition for you," said Thutmose. "How would you like a chance to earn your living as a real artist?"

The boy looked skeptical, his eyes narrowed in distrust. "What kind of an artist? I don't see how I could ever become an artist."

"You could, if I recommend you," said Thutmose. "In fact, you might have a chance to become an artist in the Royal Workshop."

"And who are you, that you can offer me this?" challenged the boy.

"Ah, I see that I forgot to introduce myself," Thutmose laughed. "I am Thutmose, Chief Artist and Sculptor to His Majesty, Pharaoh Amenhotep IV, at your service."

He made a mock bow to the boy, who tried - but failed - not to look impressed.

"Chief Artist, eh?" he sneered. "But I'll bet you were born to it."

"No," observed Thutmose, "I wasn't. My father was a potter in a village in the delta."

"A potter? You were a potter's son?" exclaimed the boy. "How did you come to be an artist for the King?"

"One day when I was about your age, the Princess Nefertiti stopped at my father's shop to buy some figurines I had made. She admired my sister's doll, so I made one just for her. When I delivered it to her, the prince asked me to draw some sketches. He liked them, and decided I should be enrolled in the Royal Artists' School. I did well in the school, and here I am today, Pharaoh's Chief Artist. I am offering you the same chance. If you work hard, and have as much talent as I think, perhaps you can do as well."

The boy pondered this for a while, then said hesitantly, "You think I actually have talent?"

Thutmose grinned, then leaned close and said conspiratorially, "Don't ever tell anyone I said this, but your portrait of the Four Prophets was very good. Irreverent - but very true to life."

At this, the boy broke into a smile and whispered back, "I rather thought so, myself!"

"Mind you," said Thutmose, "if you tell anyone else, I will deny I ever said it!"

"Don't worry," agreed the boy. "I can't tell anyone else without admitting that I drew it."

"True enough!" laughed Thutmose. "So, what do you say? Do you want to become an artist?"

"Shades of *Am Duat* [the Underworld], of course I do!" he exclaimed. "What do I have to do to be admitted to this school?"

"Well, the first thing you're going to have to do," said Thutmose, cutting the rope that bound the boy's hands, "is to clean the graffiti off the palace walls." He leaned down and cut the rope that hobbled the boy's legs. "However, I want the King to see the Four Prophets first. I think it'll give him a laugh - he's not too fond of them, either!"

"He's not?" asked the boy, surprised.

"No," confirmed Thutmose, "and I don't think they like him very much, either."

"Boy," said Ipy, shaking off the last of his bonds, "this day is full of surprises. What's next?"

"Next, we need to get you cleaned up and properly clothed, and find you a place to sleep," replied Thutmose.

He stuck his head out the door and instructed one of the guards to call the steward. When the man appeared, Thutmose told him,

"Pinhasy, this is Ipy, son of Hapuseneb. He is a new student for the art school. Please see to it that he is given a bath, a haircut and a new kilt, and find him a place to sleep. Then see that he is introduced to Master Auta and enrolled in the school."

Pinhasy looked down his long and very proper nose at the boy and sniffed doubtfully.

"If you say so, m'lord," he agreed reluctantly. "I'll do my best to see that the servants scrub the dirt off him, but I can't promise they'll succeed. Come along, boy."

So saying, he turned on his heel and marched down the hall, the boy half-running to keep up with him.

Later that day, I invited the young Pharaoh to inspect the progress on the palace, making sure he saw the courtyard in which I had caught the young miscreant. As we entered it, I explained how I had caught the graffiti artist that morning, in the act of drawing a most irreverent portrait of the Four Prophets, gesturing toward the drawing as I spoke. The King took one look and burst out laughing.

"By Set's teeth!" he exclaimed, examining the image of the High Priest. "He has captured the likeness of the old buzzard, to the life! The little demon has a talent!"

"That's what I thought, Your Majesty," Thutmose agreed, "so I took the liberty of enrolling him in the Royal Artists' School."

"Good idea," agreed the young Pharaoh, "We might as well put his talent to good use!"

"Your Majesty is very wise. Better by far to raise up an artist than continue to do battle with a vandal!" said Thutmose, bowing to the King.

Over the next couple of weeks, I kept young Ipy busy whitewashing over all the graffiti he and his friends had drawn on the palace walls. A couple of the other boys came forward and agreed to help, hopeful that they, too, might land a place in the art school. However, none of them showed the kind of talent Ipy displayed, so I had to dash their hopes of artistic careers. I did, nonetheless, manage to find places for them as servitors in the royal household or stables - not as glamorous as being an artist, but at least well-fed, dressed and securely housed - a substantial improvement over life on the streets.

In time, my unlikely protégé developed into a fine young artist, with a keen eye for his subject, and a deft touch with pen and brush. He showed little aptitude for the three-dimensionality of sculpture, but he had a great gift for color. I took great interest in his progress, and in time, became quite fond of the boy, almost like an adopted son. He, in turn, was devoted to me, and followed me anywhere I allowed him to go. Pinhasy never fully accepted the boy, suspecting him of mischief any time something went missing, but even he eventually mellowed into reluctant tolerance of the boy's presence in the school and in my household.

Chapter 19: A New House

Soon, enough of the new palace was completed for the young Pharaoh and his wife to take up residence. Work continued on other portions of the palace, as well as on the Gem Pa'aten temple. The remaining mud-brick walls of the palace were in the process of being plastered over and decorated. Before long, vivid paintings of Egyptian life began to adorn the interior, while the bright white lime coating on the exterior (now free of graffiti) glistened in the brilliant Egyptian sun. The interiors, whose decoration was supervised by Thutmose, featured scenes of the river, marshes and fields, with birds and flowers, grapes and grain, and scenes of the king and queen, many in the family's private rooms done in Thutmose's new realistic style, while Bek's caricatured style appeared in many of the public rooms. To everyone's surprise, the king insisted that he and Nefertiti be shown in scenes of daily life, in addition to the traditional poses of the king holding court, receiving foreign tributes and smiting his enemies.

Malicious gossips who had claimed that the new king's unmanly physique meant he would never be able to sire an heir were given the lie when it became clear that the new queen was pregnant. Her happy condition was apparent for all to see, as she went everywhere with her royal husband. She rode with him in her own chariot in royal processions, travelled with him in the royal barge and appeared beside him in the new Window of Appearances, helping him award the Gold of Distinction to citizens who rendered meritorious service to the crown. The citizenry prayed for a male heir to secure the throne for another generation.

When her time came, however, Nefertiti delivered a daughter, who was named Meritaten, "Beloved of Aten", in honor of her father's favored deity. While the citizenry and his parents may have been mildly disappointed, the young Pharaoh himself appeared delighted with the new baby. In yet another break with tradition, both Nefertiti and the infant princess soon joined the king in public appearances.

At first, Nefertiti had been very shy about appearing in public, standing behind her husband, wearing traditional queenly garb. Over time, however, with his encouragement, she became bolder, standing beside instead of behind him. She largely abandoned the traditional long wig, preferring the short Nubian wig or her own unique, tall flat-topped crown, unlike any worn by previous queens. While this crown became her signature headgear, it was soon joined by an extensive wardrobe of other crowns, a feminine version to match all the myriad crowns worn by Pharaoh, in addition to others worn by previous queens. She had her own version of the tall Osiris crown, with its two flanking feathers; the traditional war crown, the blue leather *khepresh*, sewn with metal rings; even the extravagant, elaborate *atef* crown, topped with a wide circle of royal cobras, each bearing a sun disk. With each new crown, Nefertiti seemed to become more sure of herself and her role in this brave new Egypt, rapidly being overhauled by her husband.

Amenhotep surrounded himself with new appointees to traditional posts, blithely deaf to the disgruntled muttering of displaced nobles. This new in-group were quick to adopt the young queen's styles of dress and coiffure, and even expressed admiration for Bek's peculiar new style of art, which adorned many surfaces of the new Gem Pa'aten temple, now nearing completion.

Thutmose himself was less enthusiastic about Bek's style, despite his longer familiarity with it. Bek had applied his strange caricature of the king, with its elongated, egg-shaped head, to other members of the royal family, including Nefertiti. It grieved Thutmose to see his adored Nefertiti portrayed in this distorted fashion. He felt torn, since the iconoclasm of the young pharaoh that allowed Thutmose the freedom to create his own artistic vision also allowed Bek the freedom to produce his odd, distorted, "modernistic" portraits of the royal family. Although Bek was his closest friend, Thutmose had never been fond of his style of portraiture.

The young pharaoh, however, seemed to take great delight in the strange, surreal images - the stranger, the better, it appeared. Their very strangeness seemed to symbolize his radical break with the past.

His even greater religious break with the past was rapidly becoming clear for all to see as the new temple neared completion. Thutmose was already hearing alarmed protests from the old priesthood, especially the priesthood of Amun-Re. The new Gem Pa'aten temple actually occupied a portion of the temple precinct heretofore dedicated to Amun. The priesthood had been unhappy enough when a portion of their territory was claimed for the new temple. Now, its radical design, there for all to see, was generating a storm of protest, particularly among the vast clergy of Amun-Re.

Thutmose was spending much of his time supervising work on the new temple. His hours there increased when Bek, in his role as Chief of Works, went upriver to Aswan to oversee the cutting of stones for the temple. While he was there, Bek cut his name into the stone, along with that of his father, who had also spent time there during his term as Chief of Works. When he finally returned, it wasn't long before he married a young woman from a good family, "starting his house", as was the Egyptian custom. So, while Bek was enjoying time with his new bride, Thutmose again worked long hours, taking up the slack.

When Bek did show up for work, well-fed and smiling from the new joys of marriage, Thutmose teased him good-naturedly.

As they ate their lunch in the shade of the colonnaded portico, Thutmose commented, "Hah, Bek, marriage is making you soft! Look at you, all fat and content! We'll have to send you back to Aswan to toughen you up in the stone quarries again!"

"I can tell you haven't been back to the tavern often enough, my friend. You're as grumpy and dried up as an old man!" replied Bek, thumping his friend on the arm.

Bek's jest hit close to home. Thutmose, being quieter and less gregarious than Bek, was not inclined to frequent the tavern alone - although when he did, Nebseny's girls made sure he didn't remain alone for long. Still, such encounters were not really his style, so they remained infrequent, although pleasant.

Seeing his sober face, Bek continued, "You should get married, Thutmose. It's high time you started your own house. You're getting to be an old bachelor, for an Egyptian!"

It was true. Most Egyptians married soon after puberty, so Thutmose, now in his early twenties, really was an old bachelor.

"Pah! You sound like my mother, Bek," he replied. "She keeps sending me messages, recommending this girl or that as a bride."

"Well? Why don't you take her up on one of them?" Bek asked.

Thutmose hesitated. He could hardly admit, even to Bek, that the only woman he really wanted was married to the king.

"What about that neighbor girl who was so crazy about you?" continued Bek. "The one who always came down to the dock to say goodbye. What was her name?"

"You mean Mariamne?"

"Yes! That's the one. She was pretty enough, and she obviously worshipped you. She'd make a good wife."

"Probably true. However, she gave up on me several years ago and married a farmer favored by her father, one of her Habiru relatives," Thutmose replied.

"Too bad," said Bek. "She would have been a good choice. You'll have to come over to dinner at my house. My wife has several sisters of marriageable age. I'll have her introduce you. It would be nice to have you in the family."

"Who appointed you matchmaker?" asked Thutmose. "When I need your help picking a wife, I'll let you know. I accept the offer of dinner, however - I'm always happy to eat!"

"Good. I'll tell my wife to expect you tomorrow night."

"I'll be there," agreed Thutmose.

After lunch, Thutmose and Bek joined the workers in a siesta, wisely sleeping through the hottest hours of the day. On this day, however, with thoughts of unavailable women on his mind, Thutmose couldn't sleep, so he got up and quietly strolled around the temple precinct. Pausing in the shade of the colonnade surrounding the open central courtyard, he ran a hand thoughtfully over an image of Nefertiti making an offering to Aten carved on the square column. In an extraordinary break with tradition, all of the columns showed the queen, alone or with her young daughter, paying homage to the new sun god, a role traditionally performed only by kings. The huge hermaphroditic royal statues, incorporating traits of both the king and queen, were in the process of being installed around the radical courtyard, open to the sun above and the public below.

Thutmose looked the colossi over with a critical eye, to insure there were no flaws in the workmanship. Although he still felt they were bizarre, he had to admit that the odd perspective was peculiarly impressive, since the statues were always viewed from below. The result was to make them appear to be even taller and more massive than they were. No matter where it was viewed from, however, the effect was shocking to Egyptian eyes, accustomed to the staid, formalized, stilted forms of traditional art. It was certainly guaranteed to make people talk.

As he stood in the deep shade, Thutmose heard voices from nearby. Looking around, he saw that the High Priest and Third Prophet had entered the courtyard. They stopped just inside the entrance, looking around in shock.

"Great Amun's balls!" swore the High Priest. "It's worse than I thought!"

"I told you," commented Third Prophet.

"I know you did," admitted the High Priest, "but I couldn't believe that even this foolish king would go this far! Everything about this place defies tradition. It breaks every standard and convention of what an Egyptian temple should be! All this glaring sunlight! There is no relief from it. Surely even a sun god needs a place of refuge and respite, where he can be refreshed in peace and comfort, away from the importunate pleas of the unwashed masses! And you say he plans for this to be open to the public? Anyone can come in here, anyone at all?"

"So I am told, Your Eminence," Third Prophet replied.

"And these statues!" commented the High Priest in tones dripping disapproval. "They are hardly proper portraits of the king! Even this ill-favored king is not as, as... unmanly as these! Whatever is he thinking?"

"I am told, Your Eminence, that they are supposed to represent a synthesis of both the king and the queen," commented the Third Prophet.

"Synthesis, my ass!" snarled the High Priest. "They're an abomination!"

Thutmose drew back into the shadow as the High Priest strode around the courtyard like an angry lion, Third Prophet trailing in his wake like a neglected cub. Thutmose almost expected to see a tawny, tufted tail lashing the old man's backside.

"We cannot allow this monstrosity to foul the sanctity of this hallowed ground!" expostulated the High Priest. "Its very existence is an insult to the time-honored gods of the Two Lands! We must do something to curb this new religion before it gets entirely out of hand!"

"But what can we do?" wailed Third Prophet.

"We must oppose this. We must put a stop to it now!" said the High Priest, banging his staff on the pavement so hard the tip broke off.

"Uh-oh," thought Thutmose to himself. "I smell trouble."

The High Priest looked at the bottom of his staff in disgust as Third Prophet scrambled to retrieve the broken piece from the ground.

"The omens were right. This king is turning out to be an enemy of the rightful gods of Egypt!" he muttered. "We must expel him! We must turn him out of the sacred enclave of the gods."

"But, Your Eminence," protested the Third Prophet, "how can we do that? After all, he is the King - and the King is a living god!"

"Maybe so," conceded the First Prophet. "But his power is the power of this world - so we must counter it in this world. We are not without power, ourselves. *I* am not without power. Nevertheless," he muttered, more to himself than his companion, "I need to develop a core of followers, men who are loyal to *me*, personally, who will carry out my wishes without question!"

So saying, he turned on his heel and strode wrathfully out of the Gem Pa'aten, Third Prophet bobbing along behind him like a gosling after its mother.

I felt a chill come over me at that moment, as though a great storm cloud had shadowed the brilliant sunshine of the courtyard. Bek and I had been so caught up in the exuberant spirit of change, the renaissance of art and music and literature, the heady ferment of religious, social and political change that filled the court of the young king, we had never considered the danger it might pose. I knew in an abstract way that the old priesthood would be outraged and would oppose any change, but I had been swept up in Pharaoh's belief in his own power and the rightness *of his cause. Now, an ominous foreboding perched heavily on my shoulders, like an evil bird of prey waiting to pounce.*

Not long after this incident, I heard that the High Priest had begun a new charitable program, taking in orphaned children from the streets and training them as temple servants, priests or administrators, according to their abilities. It didn't take me long to realize that he was doing precisely what he had told his colleague was needed: developing a cadre of followers indebted, and personally loyal, to him. While it was not unlike my own acquisition of my protégé, Ipy, it somehow made me uneasy, knowing that my young master's powerful opponent was building a corps of fanatically devoted followers.

Chapter 20: Marriage

The young Pharaoh often had me paint him and his family in
scenes of daily life - something no Pharaoh before him had ever done. I
painted the royal family, or sculpted them in bas relief, eating together,
distributing the gold shebu collars of honor from the Window of Ap-
pearances, riding together in the royal chariot, and holding their two
baby daughters on their laps. At first, the Queen appeared behind her
husband, smaller in size, in the traditional manner, but she soon began
to appear beside him, or with an arm draped affectionately over the
back of his chair, or even sitting on his lap. The royal couple delighted
in dashing about in their chariot together - how they loved speed! -
often with the eldest little princess along. I drew them together in the
chariot, the Queen turned affectionately to her husband as he managed
the spirited horses, the ribbons on her crown streaming in the breeze,
with little Meritaten reaching over the chariot railing toward the arrow
case attached to the side. I showed the horses in mid-stride, with the
nearer horse's face looking straight out at the beholder, a novel view
that very much pleased the king.

"Look, Nefer," said the young Pharaoh. "See how alive the
horses look, and how Thutmose has caught the feeling of speed."

The Queen looked over his shoulder at the papyrus drawing.

"He certainly has!" she agreed. "I can almost feel the wind on
my face!"

She looked up and smiled at Thutmose, who bowed low in
acknowledgement, which allowed him to hide his flushed cheeks.

The king continued to browse through the papyri, choosing
sketches to be sculpted on the walls of the palace or around the courtyard of the Gem Pa'aten. He gestured at one pile.

"I want these family sketches for the walls of our apartments in
the new palace," he said.

Thutmose gathered them up, looking to see which ones the king
had chosen.

"And these," continued the king, indicating another pile,
"should go in the courtyard of Nefertiti's chapel in the temple. The
rest," he said, indicating a third pile, "can be used in other public
buildings around town."

The images for Nefertiti's temple were also groundbreaking.
Many of them showed the Queen performing acts of worship that were
traditionally performed only by the King. Several others showed her
performing other ritual acts normally reserved for Pharaoh, such as receiving the tribute of foreign emissaries, or the traditional pose of
"smiting the enemies", with the symbolic mace raised on high. Thut-

mose had been surprised when he was asked to sketch these unorthodox queenly poses.

He was also surprised to see that the king had included several of the intimate family poses among those to be used on the walls of public buildings. In the past, Pharaoh was rarely shown with any family members. On those rare occurrences where the Great Royal Wife was also shown, such portraits were always rigidly formal, with the Queen portrayed much smaller than Pharaoh, seldom reaching above his knee. By contrast, these affectionate, informal portraits of the royal family, with all members shown in the same scale, were likely to cause almost as great a stir as the new Aten temple itself.

They occasioned a stir of a different kind in the artist's heart. Every affectionate royal caress was like a knife cutting his flesh. He would have welcomed a sojourn in the quarries of Aswan in Bek's place, as a relief from the pain of drawing the King's arm around Nefertiti, her hand caressing Pharaoh's cheek, her face turned to his in the chariot; or the Queen sitting on the King's lap. He loved and was loyal to them both and consciously wished them happiness and long life, but his heart ached secretly at every affectionate caress they exchanged.

Now, Thutmose kept his face turned toward the stacks of drawings as an excuse to look away from the King's arm circling Nefertiti's waist.

The young Pharaoh smiled fondly at his wife, then commented to the artist, "Marriage is a wonderful thing, Thutmose. You should try it. Shouldn't he, my dear?" he asked his wife.

"Very true," she agreed. "You should get married, Thutmose. It's high time for you to start your own house."

"Begging your pardon, Your Majesties, but you both sound like my mother!" Thutmose replied with a wry smile.

The royal couple laughed.

"Your mother is right, Thutmose," commented the King. "You should listen to her."

Just then, the senior Queen, Tiye, entered the room, just in time to hear her son's last comment.

"Of course he should listen to his mother!" agreed Queen Tiye. "What is she advising him to do?"

"Get married," answered her son.

"Ah! An excellent idea!" she agreed.

"Alas," lamented Thutmose, with mock drama, "I have never met the right woman, and I fear that I never shall. After all, what poor mortal woman can measure up to the standards set for me here? When I have two such divine examples of feminine perfection before me, all other women fade into dull insignificance!"

This was close enough to the truth, yet it could be construed as mere courtly flattery. The two queens laughed appreciatively.

"You, sir," scolded Queen Tiye, "are a shameless flatterer - even in a court full of flatterers! Nevertheless, I encourage you to continue the practice, as no woman can get too much of such flattery!"

"May all my assignments be so pleasant, Your Majesty!" Thutmose continued, bowing low. "But I must beg to take my leave of Your Majesties. My colleague Bek has asked me to dine at his house. He says he wants to introduce me to his wife's sisters. It appears that he, too, wishes to play matchmaker."

"You have leave to go, then," said Pharaoh, dismissing him with a wave of the hand. "And good luck with Master Bek's sisters!"

Thutmose gathered up his papyri and bowed his way backwards out of the royal presence. As he did, he saw Queen Tiye holding out a clay plaque to her son. He recognized it as a cuneiform tablet such as those used by the courts of Babylonia and Mitanni to communicate with the Egyptian monarchy.

"Really, my son," said Queen Tiye, "you must pay more attention to correspondence with our allies abroad! The King of Mitanni has grown so frustrated with your lack of response, he has written to me, personally, asking me to intercede!"

"You know I find all those foreigners unbearably tiresome and utterly irrelevant," complained the young Pharaoh. "All the King of Mitanni does is ask for more gold and military aid, and all the dozens of Canaanite vassal kings do is complain about each other. I can't keep all the petty kings of tiny two-hectare kingdoms straight. As far as I'm concerned, you're welcome to handle *all* the foreign correspondence. I believe you've been doing most of it, anyway, ever since Father's health began to decline."

"That's true," Queen Tiye agreed.

"Well, I would be quite happy to have you keep doing it," he said.

"Very well, I will," she replied. "But there are a few items you need to attend to."

"Oh, all right. What are they?" he asked reluctantly.

"King Tushratta of Mitanni has written to say--" she began.

"Wait!" he interrupted. "I thought Shuttarna was the King of Mitanni."

"Shuttarna died two years ago," Queen Tiye said. "His son, Tushratta, has succeeded him."

"Oh. All right - go on," the young Pharaoh acknowledged, digesting the information.

"Anyway, King Tushratta has written to inform Pharaoh," she said, scanning the cuneiform tablet she held, " - I don't know whether he meant this for you, or your father - he wishes to inform Pharaoh that he is sending his daughter, the Princess Tadukhipa, to be your wife, thus reaffirming the alliance between our two nations."

"Didn't my father already marry a Mitanni princess?" he asked.

"Yes, he did - Princess Gilukhipa," she replied coolly. "She's still here. She tends to keep to her own section of the palace, with all her own entourage. They're practically a small kingdom to themselves - after all, she brought more than three hundred people with her!"

The young Pharaoh groaned. "If this new princess does the same, their little kingdom may be larger than some of those Canaanite fiefs! We may have to build them a palace of their own!" Turning to his mother, he asked, "I don't suppose we can turn down this marriage, tell her not to come?"

"Too late," she replied. "According to this letter, she's already on her way here."

Just then, the Chamberlain announced the arrival of Pentu, the old king's physician. The physician approached the dais, followed by his two assistants. All three bowed low to the young Pharaoh and the two Queens.

"Rise, Pentu," said the young king. "How is my father's health today?"

The physician straightened up and responded, "Not good, Your Majesty. He is increasingly weak and short of breath. The swelling of his feet and ankles, combined with an irregular heartbeat, indicates that his heart is failing."

Queen Tiye was visibly distressed. "Is there nothing more we can do, Master Pentu? Perhaps another *sed* festival? The last one seemed to revive him for a while."

"I don't know, Your Majesty. I don't think his heart could withstand tests of fitness, like running a footrace, or even the excite-ment of taking a new wife," the doctor opined.

"What if we kept it purely ceremonial?" asked Tiye. "No foot-race - nothing strenuous - and our daughter Isis is twelve, old enough to become Great Wife, yet young enough not to excite too much passion."

"Possibly," conceded the doctor. "Although I must say that I suspect most of the power of the ritual is in the physical conditioning and, ah, marital stimulation. At the risk of sounding heretical, I doubt that the ritual by itself has very much rejuvenating power."

He paused, apparently deep in thought, then continued, "Nevertheless, I think it can't hurt, and it might yet do him some good."

"That settles it, then," said the elder Queen. "We shall hold the *sed* festival in two months' time - providing you agree, my son?"

"Of course, Mother," he agreed. "Let it be so."

Thus it was that Amenhotep III celebrated his third sed festival that spring, in his thirty-sixth regnal year. I, myself, missed it, as I had travelled north to see my own father, who was also ill. Thankfully, by the time I arrived home, my father was on the mend.

Once her concern for my father's health receded, my mother turned her attention back to the matter of finding me a wife. Neither of Bek's sisters-in-law had appealed to me, so I remained as glaringly single as ever.

However, as the gods would have it, our neighbor Mariamne's farmer husband had been bitten by a cobra and died a few months before my visit. His corpse was scarcely cool in its tomb before my mother opened negotiations with the widow through the village marriage broker. I protested to my mother that such haste seemed scarcely respectful of the dead, Mariamne's late husband having been a good man I had known all my life. My mother pointed out that, as I would soon be returning to court, time was of the essence. Also, the widow was not only young and attractive, she had also inherited her late husband's house and land, and she had proven her fertility by producing a son to carry on the dead man's name, all of which made her more desirable as a wife. If I didn't make an offer for her hand soon, said my mother, someone else would surely beat me to it.

At last, I bowed to the inevitable and told the marriage broker to make an offer to Mariamne on my behalf. Even so, there were three other suitors at her door. However, her longstanding affection for me, as well as the good fortune and glamor of my position at court, made me the most desirable suitor of the lot, and Mariamne promptly accepted my proposal.

My mother joyfully applied herself to planning the finest marriage banquet our little village had ever seen, which was attended by guests from throughout the Delta, even some from the northern court at Memphis. In truth, I didn't recognize over half the guests. My mother, however, was in her element. It was the high point of her life, showing off her son, the Chief Artist of Pharaoh's court. It gave her and my father a chance to wear the collars and other finery I had given them over the years, while also demonstrating what fine marriage candidates my remaining brothers and sisters were.

A fine time was had by all, and the wedding night and subsequent two weeks proved that I had acquired a supportive, affectionate - indeed, passionate - wife, one well-supplied with all the requisite domestic accomplishments. Indeed, she was all any reasonable man could ask for. As far as I was concerned, she had only one shortcoming: she wasn't Nefertiti.

At the end of two weeks, I took ship for Thebes, leaving Mariamne behind me. I explained that I must first find a house for us, as my small apartment at the palace – more of a monastic cell, really - was hardly suitable for a family. I assured her that I would send for her as soon as I had secured a place for us to live. Though clearly disappointed, she accepted my rationale.

Chapter 21: Recruiting

The old Pharaoh was less fortunate in his health than my father. The ritual of the sed festival and marriage with his younger daughter did little to improve his health, which continued to decline.

And while young Isis had passed the required night in her father's chamber, everyone in the palace doubted that the marriage had, in fact, been consummated. Other than the addition of a new title, the Princess's life remained essentially unchanged – as did her father's health.

Not long after the sed festival, heralds arrived to announce the imminent arrival of the promised Mitanni princess, Tadukhipa. The young pharaoh was notified that his foreign bride and her entourage had taken ship at Tanis and were on their way upriver. They were expected to arrive in about two weeks time.

I sent a messenger downriver to my own recent bride, warning her that the arrival of the Mitanni princess and subsequent marriage festivities would require my attention, and were likely to prevent me from finding an appropriate house for her in the near future. I could not quite admit to myself that I was stalling, putting off the inevitable introduction of my wife to the woman I secretly loved. I knew it was a mad notion, but I felt that, by capitulating to the social pressure to marry, I had somehow been unfaithful to Nefertiti, even though none but I knew of my hopeless attachment to her.

Or did I perhaps fear that that attachment would be all too obvious to my sharp-eyed new wife...? I knew that Mariamne was no fool. When she arrived, would I be able to keep my true feelings from her?

For the next two weeks, the palace bustled with preparations for the reception of the Mitanni princess. The younger Pharaoh expressed his annoyance with such distractions, so Queen Tiye oversaw the activities, with occasional assistance from Nefertiti. The elder Pharaoh, whose health continued to decline, kept mostly to his rooms except for periodic attendance at the temple of Amun. On the rare occasions when the younger Amenhotep accompanied his father, the High Priest looked daggers at him throughout the ceremony. In one of his irreverent sketches, Bek portrayed him with a dark thundercloud hovering over his head. The young pharaoh was greatly amused by the portrait, but far less amused by First Prophet's increasingly vehement objections to the worship of Aten within the precincts heretofore sacred to Amun. It was clear to Thutmose that the two deities and their earthly proponents were on a collision course.

He and Bek discussed the situation over lunch one day at the nearly finished Gem Pa'aten temple, as the crew rested in the shade.

"I don't know what the end result of all this will be, Bek," Thutmose said, gesturing at the temple around them. "It is clear that the High Priest and his followers oppose our young Pharaoh's religious reformation."

"Reformation?" snorted Bek. "More of a revolution, don't you think? He is standing every tenet of traditional religion on its head!"

"It may well look that way to you and me – and to the High Priest – but I think Pharaoh sincerely believes he is reforming a religion that had strayed very far from its roots. Just the other day, he cited a scroll from the 4th Dynasty he had found in the archives, from the time of Pharaoh Sneferu, father of Khufu the Great…"

"Yes, yes, I know – I've heard it straight from him, how the Aten is the oldest of all the gods," Bek protested, "the Creator, and hence the only *real* god. But I think he's the only one who actually *believes* it! All that talk's done nothing but aggravate the priesthood of every other god in Egypt – but most especially the priesthood of Amun, who are daily confronted by the temple of a competing deity within their own sacred precinct! I'm not surprised they're up in arms. I'm just worried about what they may choose to do about it."

"I am, too," Thutmose agreed, and confided what he had over-heard that day when First and Third Prophets had visited the new temple. "I'm concerned," he concluded, "that it could lead to violence."

"You don't think they'd be foolish enough to make an attempt on Pharaoh's life, do you?" Bek wondered aloud.

"You never know," replied Thutmose. "There's nothing like religious fervor for making people think any action is justified, no matter how drastic. I think maybe we should speak to the Captain of the Royal Guards."

"Perhaps we should wait until the Mitanni delegation gets here. I have heard that General Ramose is accompanying them south. I think we should bring the matter to his attention," cautioned Bek.

"That's a good idea," agreed Thutmose.

Just then, his young protégé, Ipy, arrived. Strapped to his back was a large basket, like those the workers used to carry loose materials – but the tantalizing aromas wafting from this basket spoke of contents very different from the workmen's loose stones, dirt and mortar. Thutmose waved and rose from his seat on a pile of *talatat* blocks, brushing the stone dust from his tunic.

"Ah, Ipy, there you are! Did you get everything I asked for?" he asked the boy.

"Yes, I've got everything: bread, fruit, beer – although it wasn't easy persuading cook to part with them!" the boy replied.

"All right – let's go, then!" said Thutmose.

"Where are you off to?" Bek asked, puzzled.

"Ah, that's a secret! But you'll soon see," Thutmose assured him. With a parting wave, he followed the boy out of the temple court-yard.

A few days previously, at the end of a sketching session, Queen Nefertiti had asked Thutmose about his new protegé – who he was and where he had come from. Thutmose told her the story of his campaign to stop vandalism at the new palace and how it had resulted in his cap-turing and recruiting young Ipy.

"You mean the boy had no family at all, and no place to live?" she asked.

"That's right, Your Majesty. And it appears that he is only one of many homeless children on the streets," he replied.

"That's awful!" she exclaimed. "It never occurred to me that there might be children wandering our streets, with nowhere to go and no one to care for them! Although, to be honest, I have to admit I never thought about it at all. I feel ashamed. As Queen, I am the mother to my people. I feel that I have personally failed to care for these homeless young ones!"

The Vizier of Lower Egypt interjected, "Your Majesty can hardly be expected to wander the poorest streets of your kingdom, searching for homeless children!"

"Yet, perhaps I should," she replied thoughtfully. "Thutmose!" she said, turning to the artist.

"Yes, Your Majesty?"

"Do you think your young apprentice could locate more of these children of the streets?"

"I'm fairly sure that he could, Your Majesty," Thutmose replied.

"Good," she said, then turned to her husband, who was re-viewing some recent diplomatic correspondence. "My Lord Husband, I would like to bring some of these homeless waifs from the streets to the palace."

"Whatever for?" asked Pharaoh, looking up from a papyrus scroll that held a translation of a cuneiform document from Mitanni.

"Thutmose has set us an example. He has taken a trouble-mak-ing young vandal and turned him into a valuable citizen and is teaching him a useful trade as an artist. I would like to do something similar with other homeless children in the city," she explained.

He frowned doubtfully. "Do you really think it's a good idea to bring them right into the palace with us, though?" he asked.

"I don't contemplate actually having most of them in our immediate surroundings. I'd like to find places on the staff for those who have some useful aptitude, as servants or grooms or messengers. And I'd like to see to it that they all receive training in some kind of useful occupation, so they can grow up to be productive citizens instead of thieves, whores and assassins. That seems to me like a better alternative."

"All right, my dear. I certainly can't argue with your logic – or your soft heart!" Pharaoh replied.

Nefertiti smiled at his approval of her plan. It seemed to the artist that the room lit up. She turned to him.

"Thutmose, I leave it to you and your apprentice to locate these neglected children and bring them here to the palace. Take food with you, to alleviate their hunger and show that we mean them well. Steward – tell the cooks to supply them with ample food and drink for the purpose."

"Aye, Your Majesty," replied Thutmose and the Steward together.

I was deeply touched, though not surprised, by this evidence of my beloved queen's caring nature and generosity of spirit towards even the lowliest of her people. It but confirmed the kindness and open-mindedness that had brought me to her attention, and so to court, so many years before. I gladly took on this additional assignment, which was not only beneficent in and of itself, but also a chance to further endear myself to my adored lady.

So it was that Thutmose and Ipy set out into the streets of Thebes to recruit some more of Ipy's former peers.

As they wound their way through the streets heading toward the river, they passed through knots of people speculating excitedly about when the Mitanni delegation would arrive. Once they neared the dock area, however, young Ipy led the way past the well-kept shops and market stalls into a dark and squalid part of town where suspicious eyes peered out at them from behind wooden-barred windows and piles of trash.

"So where are all these children you told me about?" Thutmose asked his apprentice.

"Wait, Master," the boy replied, seating himself on a dock piling and taking out a warm loaf of bread. "Most of them are shy, very wary of strangers. Let us just sit quietly for a while and let them see that we mean them no harm – and let the smell of food speak to their bellies!" he said, smiling, as he broke open the bread and let the yeasty aroma waft out into the street. He handed Thutmose a piece and popped another piece into his own mouth.

Soon, heads began to appear hesitantly from behind piles of trash and narrow side alleys. One after another, gaunt, hungry children began to appear, following their noses toward the scent of the bread. Ipy pulled out another loaf and handed it to Thutmose, then took another one for himself and began breaking pieces off and holding them out to the nearest children. Thutmose did the same. Soon, one of the braver boys approached Ipy, snatched a piece of bread and dashed to the mouth of the nearest alleyway, stuffing the bread in his mouth as he went. Seeing his success, other children began approaching the two artists, who soon threatened to be overwhelmed by hungry children.

"Patience, patience!" admonished Thutmose. "There's plenty for everyone! And when we do run out, there is more for you at the palace."

At this last statement, the children stopped pushing forward and looked at him suspiciously.

"Whaddya mean?" asked one of the older boys, scowling.

"He means the Queen has sent you this food," explained Ipy, "and there's more where this came from."

"Why'd she wanna do that?" asked another ragged, dirty lad.

"Because she has a kind heart," said Thutmose, "and she wants to help find homes and work for all of you."

"Since when?" challenged the first boy. "And why should we believe the likes of a couple of fine gentlemen like you?"

At this, Ipy smiled broadly. "Neb-sen-neferu!" he said to the boy, "don't you recognize me? It's me, Ipy, your old partner! Fine gentleman, indeed!"

Neb-sen-neferu came closer and peered intently at Ipy.

"Let me see your back," he challenged. "If'n you're really Ipy, you should have some stripes on your back from the Captain of the Guards' whip."

Ipy turned around and pulled the loose neck of his tunic down from one shoulder. Neb-sen-neferu took hold of the tunic and peered inside doubtfully. After a moment, he released the tunic and turned to the other children.

"Well," he said, "it looks like he's tellin' the truth. "He's got a good set of scars on 'is back." He turned back to Ipy. "So how come y'r in the comp'ny of this here fine gent, handin' out bread?" he asked.

"You remember how we were 'decorating' the walls of the new palace?" Ipy asked him.

"Yeah," agreed Neb-sen-neferu. "But then you ups and disappears. I figgered the Guard 'ad you."

"Close," agreed Ipy. "But it was Master Thutmose, here, who found me, not the Guard. And he made me an offer I couldn't refuse."

"Oh, yeah?" replied Neb-sen-neferu. "And what was that?"

Ipy grinned broadly and said to the gathered boys, "Lads, you are now looking at the newest apprentice in the Royal Artists' School!"

"No way!" said one of the younger boys.

"G'wan!" added Neb-sen-neferu. "You don't expect us t'b'lieve that, do you? What a load of donkey crap!"

"It's true," said Thutmose. "Ipy is now my apprentice."

"And 'oo might you be?" asked Neb-sen-neferu suspiciously.

"This here is Master Thutmose, Chief Sculptor and Painter to His Majesty, Amenhotep the Fourth," proclaimed Ipy proudly, in a creditable imitation of the Lord Chamberlain announcing a new arrival at court. "And if you don't believe it, just look at his insignia of office!" added the boy.

At this, Thutmose threw back the cloak he was wearing, revealing the golden *shebu* collar around his neck. The children oohed and aahed, never having seen so much wealth up close. They did not, of course, recognize the royal insignia, picked out in lapis and carnelian beads, but they were certainly impressed. Some of them sketched a brief bow, others shied away, and still others crowded closer to look at the golden collar.

In the end, most of the children agreed to come with Thutmose and Ipy to the palace, where they were turned over to one of the understewards, who would be responsible for cleaning them up, seeing that any illnesses or injuries were treated, and attempting to sort them out into various groups to be housed and trained, according to their abilities. Some were selected to be trained as servants in the kitchen, some as other house servants, some to the stables, and a couple of the older boys, to become soldiers. All were cleaned, fed, treated, housed and assigned to some form of work or further training. One younger lad was found to have some aptitude for shaping clay and was apprenticed to a potter, and another appeared intelligent enough that he was entered into the school for royal scribes.

Later forays into the streets brought in some girls, as well, rescuing most of them from lives of prostitution or the lowest forms of servitude. Most of them became house servants; one even went on to become one of Nefertiti's own maids.

There came a day, however, when Thutmose and Ipy arrived at the streets near the docks to find someone else there before them, recruiting street urchins: none other than the High Priest, First Prophet himself. Seeing him, the artist and his apprentice drew back behind the corner of a building.

"First Prophet? Whatever is he doing here?" exclaimed Thutmose.

The two of them peered cautiously around the corner. The High Priest, accompanied by Third Prophet, with a couple of guards at a discreet distance, appeared to be luring out children with loaves of fresh bread, just as Thutmose and Ipy had been doing, themselves.

"It looks like they've copied our recruiting program," commented Ipy.

"Yes," agreed Thutmose, "but why? What are they up to? From what I've seen of the Priesthood of Amun, I don't think alms for the poor are a part of the usual largesse of the god."

Just then, a gaunt boy clothed only in a ragged loincloth limped out of an alley and approached the High Priest.

"I know that boy," exclaimed Ipy. "That's Ani, the drover's son. He picks on the smaller boys, but the bigger ones pick on him."

"Looks like somebody picked on him recently," commented Thutmose, observing the boy's limp.

In the end, Ani and several of the other boys went with the priests. Thutmose and Ipy followed at a discreet distance and saw the lot of them disappear into the Temple of Amun.

"I wonder what the High Priest is up to, recruiting ragamuffins like this," Thutmose mused. "Generosity of heart has never been in his character. I think he's got some use for these boys – and whatever it is, I suspect it's not good. I wish we could get a spy into the temple precinct."

"I could do it," volunteered Ipy. "I can get all dirty and go back to my old haunts. Then I can let them recruit me, like they did those others. Once I'm on the inside, I can find out what they're up to."

"It could be dangerous," Thutmose warned. "Especially if they figure out you're a spy."

"No problem," Ipy assured him. "I'll make an obedient and diligent little *sem* priest—"

"Hah! This I'd like to see!" exclaimed Thutmose. "You, obedient?"

"As a lamb! They'll have no reason to suspect me. Once I find out what they're up to, I'll slip out of the temple and over to the Gem Pa'aten and report to you."

"All right, boy – but be careful."

"I will," Ipy assured him.

A few days later, with his hair roughly chopped, wearing a tattered tunic, and with ample dirt smeared on his face and body, Ipy resumed life on the street. It was only a couple more days until the High Priest and his cohorts reappeared, looking for boys to enlist. Ipy pretended to hesitate, then accepted the priests' offer to join the temple. Pretending to dash back to fetch his small bag, he scrawled a sign on a nearby wall, as he had agreed, to notify Thutmose that he had succeeded in the first part of his mission.

Chapter 22: Rivals

Over the next couple of weeks, I kept a nervous watch for any sign of my bold young apprentice. I finally spotted him in the temple precinct, pacing in a stately procession of priests heading toward the sacred lake for ritual cleansing. He marched solemnly along with the other acolytes, wearing a simple white, one-shouldered tunic, shaven head meekly bowed, with every appearance of being absorbed in chanting his prayers. He had, however, managed to position himself on the side of the group nearest to the Aten temple, giving me the best opportunity to observe him.

Seeing in a quick sidelong glance that I was watching, he kept his head bowed, but made a quick series of pre-arranged hand signals to let me know what progress he had made. With his hand down at his side, he first made a fist with the thumb tucked inside, to indicate that he had managed to work his way into the inner circle of recruits. He then straightened his fingers stiffly and made a short downward stab, indicating that he had discovered a conspiracy. Following that, he reached up as though he were swatting a fly and briefly tapped his head – the sign indicating that there was a plot against the king. And finally, he dropped his hand by his side again and closed all but the index finger, thus informing me that the instigator of the plot was none other than the First Prophet of Amun. (The middle finger extended would have indicated Second Prophet; the fourth finger, Third Prophet; and the little finger would have signified Fourth Prophet. The thumb would have meant that the instigator was someone else entirely, not one of the Four Prophets.) Signals completed, he continued calmly on toward the lake with the rest of the priestly contingent.

I was fearful about his safety there in the Temple of Amun, especially if the priests should discover his true identity and his association with me. I feared that some of the other urchins recruited from the streets would recognize him from his previous existence on the waterfront – although I had to admit that I had barely recognized him, myself, with his face and hands scrubbed clean and his head shaved. That, and his meek and self-effacing mien, so unlike his usual saucy, irreverent demeanor, made him almost unrecognizable. Nevertheless, I worried.

I mentioned my concerns to Bek, who was now more convinced than ever that we should take whatever we discovered to General Ramose, who was expected to arrive at any moment with the Mitanni delegation.

At last, after weeks of excited expectation, the sound of horns was heard floating up the river, announcing the arrival of the Mitanni delegation and their princess. Soon, the sails of the lead vessels appeared around the great bend in the river, their masts flying gaily colored pennants, their brightly decorated sails bellying in the breeze. Excited crowds gathered along the riverbank, waving and cheering as the procession of boats sailed into view.

It was clear to Thutmose and Bek that their artists and laborers were getting little work done on the temple, so distracted were they by the crowd and the approaching flotilla. Bowing to the inevitable, they gave the workmen the rest of the day off and headed toward the docks themselves. Attaching themselves to a passing contingent of royal guards, they passed through the crowds and found a place on shore near the foot of the royal dock. To justify their position in the official greeting party, each of them carried his artist's tablet, sheets of papyrus, charcoal, quills and ink pot in a linen bag.

Thutmose had just settled in when he felt a tug at his arm. Looking down, he saw a young street urchin, perhaps seven or eight years old.

"Are you Master Thutmose?" the boy asked.

"Yes, I am," Thutmose answered.

"Well, I have a message for you from…" He screwed his face up in concentration, apparently trying to remember the exact content of the message. "…from one who draws on walls."

"Yes?" Thutmose asked. "What did he have to say?"

"He wants you to meet him," said the boy. "He said you would remember the alley, not far from here, where he left a sign for you."

"I know the place," said Thutmose. "When did he want me to meet him?"

"Now, if you please," the boy replied. "And he said you'd pay me for bringing you the message," he continued, thrusting one grimy hand out, palm up.

"Oh, he did, did he?" said Thutmose, pretending to scowl. "Oh, all right."

He laughed and relented, reaching into his scrip and handing the boy a string of small, brightly colored beads. The boy's eyes lit up. He grabbed the beads and ran off.

Thutmose turned to Bek and asked him to hold his place, telling him he would be back shortly.

"Seems our young spy wants to meet me," he whispered in Bek's ear.

Bek nodded his understanding.

"Be careful," he said. "It could be a trap."

"I'll be on my guard," Thutmose assured him.

Elbowing his way through the crowd, Thutmose headed along the waterfront to the alley where Ipy had scrawled his sign. He watched carefully for any signs of danger, but saw only the backs of cheering crowds. He sauntered casually through the crossroads in front of the alleyway, as though he were just another onlooker trying to catch sight of the foreign princess.

After a moment, he heard a whistle that penetrated the crowd noise. Looking around, he saw what appeared to be an itinerant Habiru trader in a multicolored robe and head cloth. Looking closer, he saw that the man's bushy black beard was looked suspiciously woolly, and recognized above it the impish eyes of his young apprentice.

"Well, well," he said loudly, looking the boy up and down, "if it isn't a wandering herdsman of the desert!"

"My lord," said the phony Habiru, bowing low, "I bring you fine colored pigments from the desert, lapis and turquoise and vermilion, fit to paint a king."

"You do, eh? Well, let us see your wares, trader," Thutmose replied.

Ipy led him over to the ruins of a low wall, where he made a great show of opening up several skin bags full of dirt – his supposed "fine pigments" – and Thutmose made an equal show of examining them, while the boy talked in a low voice.

"First Prophet is recruiting poor boys from the streets and training them to be fanatically loyal to himself. He is teaching them to hate the King and Queen, who he says are heretics. He plans to assassinate the King, and possibly the Queen, as well," the boy told him.

"The Queen!" exclaimed Thutmose. "It's bad enough he should plan to assassinate the King – but why the Queen? What has she done to deserve his wrath?"

"She's a part of the King's new religion," the boy explained. "He holds her to be just as much to blame as the King for what he considers to be sacrilege."

"Have you learned any details of the plot? How, or where, or when?" Thutmose asked.

"Not really," the boy replied, shaking his head. "I gathered that it's to be soon – I'm not sure they've actually settled on an event, yet. As to how, I suspect they'll use one or more of these boys to get in close with a knife, probably at some crowded event."

"Good work, lad. But that's enough. You should come away now, leave the temple," Thutmose admonished the boy.

Ipy shook his head.

"Not yet, Master. If I stay a bit longer, I may be able to learn more about where and how they plan to kill the King."

"It's too dangerous, boy. If they find you out, you'll be the first to die," Thutmose protested.

"Hah! They have no suspicion. I'm a good actor, and a master of disguises. Just look at this one!" he boasted, pivoting about. "Would you have recognized me, if you weren't forewarned?"

"Maybe," Thutmose replied. "It's not bad, provided you don't get too close. Where did you get those clothes – and what poor sheep did you steal that beard from?"

"I nipped the clothes from a Habiru trader's pack, and his black sheep's rump may be sporting a bald patch," the boy replied. "Never fear: I'll slip the robe back in his pack tonight. If he hasn't opened it, he'll never know it was gone. If he did notice the loss, he'll be thankful to his heathen god for its return. The sheep's loss is another matter. I daresay it'll survive a cold spot on its bum."

Thutmose had to smile at the picture thus portrayed. Nevertheless, he was still concerned about the boy.

"What about the priests? Won't they notice that you're gone?"

"Naah," the boy replied. "Not in this mob. The boys are spread out all through the crowd. We've all got orders to start a whispering campaign to spread discontent about the King's new religion. It's supposed to look like a grassroots movement."

"I see," Thutmose observed. "All right, rejoin your priestly cohorts. Just please be very careful. You'll do no one any good dead."

"Not to worry," Ipy assured him. "I'll be the soul of caution."

"That'll be the day!" commented Thutmose wryly.

"You'll see," said the boy, with a grin. "Or rather, you won't see. Just watch me disappear."

And true to his word, he vanished into the crowd. Thutmose strained to see any sign of his colorful robe, but it was lost in the press of people. Shaking his head, he turned back toward the royal dock.

By the time he managed to worm his way through the mob to where Bek stood, the last of the Mitannian rear guard were just disappearing up the street toward the palace, followed by a gaggle of servants. Thutmose shrugged his shoulders and turned back to Bek.

"I guess I missed them."

"We'll have another chance later, when they're received at the palace. The king has already sent a courier, commanding our presence at the reception," Bek informed him. "But where were you all this time?"

"In an alley, meeting with our young apprentice, who appeared today in the guise of a wandering Habiru trader. I've got to hand it to the little imp: he's got courage and imagination, maybe too much for his own good."

"Did he find out anything?" Bek asked.

"Yes. I'll tell you later – too many ears about out here," Thutmose replied.

He bent down to retrieve his wooden tablet and bag of artist's supplies from the ground behind Bek. In doing so, he missed the last of the procession and was disguised from the eyes of its members. Following the last of the servants was a small group of Egyptians from downriver: Mariamne, her son and three servants. As Thutmose was bent over, they also did not recognize him, but followed after the foreign delegation toward the vast rambling bulk of Malkata palace. It was the only place Mariamne knew to search for her errant husband.

After retrieving their drawing materials, Thutmose and Bek turned aside and took a narrow side road, a shortcut to the palace through back streets not suitable for processions of foreign royalty.

Arriving at the palace before the Mitanni delegation, they entered through a side gate and were seated in their usual places below and to the side of the dais long before the procession arrived.

Having been forewarned of the arrival of the foreign party, the King and Queen were already seated on their thrones, close enough together that their arms touched. Nefertiti wore her signature tall, flat-topped crown. Her sheer linen dress revealed that she was noticeably pregnant with her third child. The two little princesses, attended by their nurses, played on the steps of the dais. They presented a formidable picture of domestic solidarity when the long-awaited Mitanni delegation arrived at the door of the throne room.

A fanfare of horns announced the delegation's arrival outside the door. A great gong sounded and two huge Nubian soldiers hauled back the massive pair of doors. With a clash of cymbals, a troupe of gaily clad acrobats tumbled through the doorway, and rolled and leapt their way down the aisle, to end prostrate before the dais.

They were followed by a solemn procession of diplomats, each duly announced by heralds. After making their obeisances to the royal couple, they formed ranks on either side of the central aisle, while the acrobats retired to the back of the crowd.

A pair of trumpeters playing six-foot-long animal horns marched in and positioned themselves on either side of the doors. A Mitanni herald announced the princess's long string of titles, pausing periodically to allow the court herald to repeat them in Egyptian. After this, the trumpeters blew a fanfare on their long *shofars*, and the golden litter of the princess was carried into the room by eight muscular bearers.

The Lord Chamberlain stopped them just inside the door, insisting that the litter could be carried no further, as no one's head could be higher than the King's. The bearers looked questioningly at the princess. Quickly suppressing a frown of annoyance, she signaled them to put the litter down. They complied smartly, then prostrated themselves before her. The lead bearer bowed beside the litter and helped the princess step down, using the prostrate back of another bearer as a step. She stepped daintily onto the intricately tiled floor, a forced smile on her face, her head held high, and moved toward the dais.

Thutmose eyed her, head to foot, even as his nimble fingers captured her image on papyrus. She moved toward the throne with an arrogant grace, utterly assured of her irresistible beauty, hips swinging, head high. Her dark, almond-shaped eyes never left Pharaoh's. She reminded Thutmose of nothing so much as a hunting lioness, stalking its prey.

Resisting the temptation to draw her as a lioness, Thutmose studied the foreign princess, his fingers expressing honestly what his eyes beheld. Although her haughty carriage gave the impression of height, the artist realized she was actually a bit below average height. Her face was a classic oval, with rounded cheeks, a small nose and full lips, her skin pale, her inky black hair curled in myriad ringlets, held back by a golden diadem. She wore an intricate gold necklace studded with lapis, amber and carnelian, with a central pendant that trembled tantalizingly between full, rounded breasts revealed by her low-cut gown. An equally gem-laden girdle cinched her narrow waist, while the fine linen of her gown clung revealingly to her rounded hips and thighs. Her long earrings jingled as she walked, accompanied by the jangle of multiple bracelets on either arm.

"She seems to be wearing the entire contents of a jeweler's shop," whispered Thutmose to Bek.

"I guess that's why her father kept asking for more gold," Bek replied.

Arriving at the foot of the dais, the princess sank gracefully to one knee before the king, her head bowed just enough to appear respectful. The Queen, she ignored completely. Her attitude conveyed the impression that Nefertiti was as invisible to her as any of the servants.

The princess, Thutmose concluded, knew which side of her bread held the honey – and cared not a whit if she offended everyone else.

The senior Mitanni legate stepped forward and said, "Your Majesty, I present the Princess Tadukhipa of Mitanni, daughter of the Most High King Shuttarna of Mitanni. His Majesty sends you his daughter to be your wife, in token of his deep love for his brother, the Lord of the Two Lands, and to seal the alliance between our two nations."

"Our brother, Shuttarna, honors us. Arise, Princess Tadukhipa. You are welcome in our house," Pharaoh declared.

"I thank you, my Lord King," Tadukhipa replied, rising gracefully. "I am here purely to serve you, my king, to bring you pleasure," she said in a breathy voice, with a smoldering glance from beneath dark brows, "and to give you many strong sons to guard your throne." This last was said with a brief but telling glance toward Nefertiti and the two small princesses.

Thutmose was proud to see that the Queen held her composure, apparently unruffled by the veiled insult, implying she could produce only daughters, not a son to inherit the throne. Only because he knew her face so well was he able to observe a slight tightening of her jaw and a glint in her eyes he had never seen there before.

After a final exchange of pleasantries and the presentation of gifts, the princess and her entourage bowed their way out of the audience chamber.

Thutmose was left with an ominous feeling that the peace and tranquility of the royal household would never be quite the same as it had been. The serpent had entered the garden.

Once the Mitanni delegation had departed, the artists began to gather up their things. Then, unexpectedly, the Lord Chamberlain cleared his throat and announced one last set of visitors.

"Your Majesties," he cried, "the wife of the artist Thutmose seeks audience!"

Startled, Thutmose looked toward the entryway. There he saw Mariamne, her son, and her two servants. He exchanged glances with Bek, who looked amused.

"She may approach," stated Pharaoh. He then turned to the group of artists to the left of the dais. "Thutmose – I believe you have a visitor."

Thutmose dropped his bag and stepped forward, just as Mariamne and her small entourage approached the throne. He fell in beside her and offered her his arm. Together, they made obeisance before the King and Queen. The King gestured for them to rise.

"Your Majesties," said Thutmose, "may I present my wife, Mariamne, of the house of Benyamin, of the Habiru of Goshen."

Pharaoh smiled and said, "Welcome to Thebes, wife of Thutmose. May you bring as much happiness to your husband as my Great Wife has brought to me," he added, smiling at Nefertiti and taking her hand.

Nefertiti smiled back at him, then turned a welcoming smile to Mariamne.

"Welcome, my dear," she said, graciously. "We treasure the talent and loyalty of your husband, and wish him every happiness. You are welcome in our house."

Then she turned to Pharaoh and added, "We must give them an appropriate wedding gift."

"Most certainly," he agreed. "Thutmose, is there anything that you and your wife particularly desire?"

Thutmose shrugged and looked questioningly at his wife. She replied to the King, "There is one thing, Your Majesty. I believe my husband has not yet found us a house…" She looked at Thutmose inquiringly. He nodded. "So, we would appreciate it if one of Your Majesty's servants could assist us in this search…"

The Queen leaned over and whispered something to the King, who nodded.

She turned back to Mariamne and smiled. "We will do more than that," she said. Raising her voice, she added, "My Lord Husband and I now give to the artist Thutmose and his wife a house and grounds as our wedding gift. My Lord Chamberlain," she said, signaling the official to approach, "See to it that a suitable house, with a garden, is found and purchased for our much-valued artist, Thutmose, and his wife, and that it is appropriately furnished. I am sure that mistress Mariamne can inform you of what is needed."

Turning back to the couple, she added, "And may your new house be always filled with love and happiness."

"Oh, thank you, thank you, Your Majesties!" cried Mariamne, prostrating herself before the dais. Thutmose quickly joined her, stunned at the sudden turn of events, and his good fortune.

Pharaoh gestured for them to rise.

Thutmose sprang back to his feet, then helped his wife to rise.

"I thank you, Your Majesties," he added. "Your generosity overwhelms me – ah, us," he amended, glancing at his wife.

"In the mean time," added Nefertiti, to the Chamberlain, "They shall be our guests in the palace. See to it that a comfortable set of apartments is made available to them."

"Yes, Your Majesty," acknowledged the Chamberlain, bowing to the Queen. "It shall be done." He turned to Thutmose and Mariamne. "Follow me, please."

With a final obeisance to the King and Queen, the artist and his wife turned and followed the Chamberlain to the door. There they were met by Bek, who handed Thutmose his palette and bag of supplies, then followed them out the door.

Chapter 23: Death of the Old Order

Not long after the arrival of Princess Kiya (as everyone in the palace soon called her), Bek and Thutmose met with General Ramose, who had been promoted to Vizier of Upper Egypt upon his return from Canaan, and told him about the plot.

Young Ipy had continued spying on the priesthood of Amun, but had thus far been unable to discover any further details of the plot against the king. Since nothing specific was known, Ramose felt that the best that could be done was to re-double the guard around the king.

Protection of the king would normally have fallen under the jurisdiction of General Horemheb, who had been promoted to Chief General of the Armies of Pharaoh to replace Ramose. Horemheb, however, was already on his way to Canaan to take command of the army, so the duty was delegated to Paramessu, who had now been named Captain of the Royal Guard, the king's own personal regiment. Vizier Ramose called for the captain to join them. Thutmose recognized him as the young officer who had been in charge of the guard detail during the incident with the crocodile several years earlier. The man apparently remembered him, as well.

"Thutmose…" Captain Paramessu mused. "Aren't you the artist who saved our queen from the great crocodile in the delta many years ago?"

Thutmose, looking a bit embarrassed, admitted to being that very man.

"You were very brave," the captain acknowledged. "I would have been proud to have you as a soldier in my regiment."

"Thank you, Captain," Thutmose said. "I only did my duty in guarding Her Majesty's life."

"Still, it's not the usual duty of an artist to leap onto the back of a giant crocodile! It was well done."

Despite the compliment, Thutmose had the uncomfortable feeling that the young officer was less admiring than his words suggested, that he was even somewhat annoyed, a bit – what? – jealous, perhaps? Thutmose realized that it had been Paramessu's duty, far more than his own, to guard the princess, and that he had fundamentally failed in it. Had it not been for the actions of Thutmose and, indeed, of the princess herself, she would probably have been killed – and Paramessu's career, and possibly his life, would have been ended. So, on the one hand, the young officer owed his life and career to the artist – but on the other hand, Thutmose must be a continual reminder of Paramessu's failure. Thutmose realized he would have to tread softly around this young officer who was apparently the favored second of Horemheb, now the most powerful general in the land. He was careful to be very complimentary and deferential from that point on.

Thutmose and Bek thanked the new Vizier and guard Captain at the end of the meeting and bowed their way out.

Once out of earshot, they agreed that they were not entirely satisfied that enough was being done to safeguard the king and queen. They vowed to continue keeping their own watch whenever possible, especially in the temple precinct, where they could now spare a few workers for the task.

The new Gem Pa'aten temple honoring the young Pharaoh's deity, the Aten, was now nearing completion. It was already in regular use by the royal family, but a grand celebration was planned for its formal inauguration and unprecedented opening to the public. There was already an excited buzz of expectation in the streets, which the king encouraged, as he wanted to feed the people's curiosity about his temple and its deity. He wanted the new religion to become popular and lure people away from the old gods.

Fate, however, did not cooperate. Soon after Princess Kiya's arrival, the old King's health began to deteriorate rapidly, culminating in his passing early in the first month of *Shemu*, the season of harvest. His *khat*, or earthly body, was turned over to the *heb* priests for Beautification and the palace was filled with mourning. The opening of the new temple would have to be delayed until after the seventy days of mourning were completed.

Queen Tiye was deeply grief-stricken, since her marriage to Amenhotep had been a genuine love match, so rare among royal marriages. It was particularly difficult, since she had only recently discovered that she was pregnant again – a great surprise, since the Queen was already in her mid-forties, an advanced age in a time when the average life expectancy was thirty-seven and healthy young women regularly died in childbirth. Nevertheless, she found some comfort in feeling the new life within her womb, knowing that this child would carry on some essence of its father, even though it would never know him.

Queen Nefertiti's pregnancy was advancing, too. She had been very happy during her two earlier pregnancies, knowing that, by bearing children, she was fulfilling her duty, not only as queen and wife, but also as a religious symbol of fertility. In the new religion, she formed an essential part of the Divine Triad, consisting of King, Queen and Aten. In the new iconography developed by Bek and Thutmose, the disk of the Aten had now been extended into rays ending in hands, each offering an *ankh*, the symbol of life, to the king and queen. The concept was that the Aten gave life to the royal couple, and they in turn conveyed it to their people.

While her health remained good and the pregnancy advanced smoothly, it made Nefertiti, the wife, less happy than the previous two pregnancies. Instead of feeling proud of her swelling belly, now Nefertiti felt it put her at a disadvantage versus her rival, Kiya - for rival, indeed, was what Kiya was turning out to be.

The foreign princess was doing everything in her considerable power to ingratiate herself sexually with the young Pharaoh. She was continually around, daring to intrude even on those scenes of domesticity that had always been Nefertiti's exclusive domain. She would show up when the young Pharaoh and his Great Wife were dining with their children. While Nefertiti sat heavily in her gilded chair, weighed down with pregnancy and an infant daughter on her knee, Kiya would appear and offer her husband choice morsels of food, taking care to lean against him while doing so. As she reached for a grape, her round breast would brush his shoulder; as she leaned over to hand it to him, her perfumed hair would brush his cheek.

Nefertiti, made sensitive to smells by her pregnancy, found Kiya's heavy, musky perfume particularly cloying. It nauseated her violently – but it clearly didn't have that effect on Pharaoh. And Kiya's clothes -- !

In a land as hot as Egypt, clothing was usually lightweight and minimal, designed to keep the wearer cool while providing a modicum of protection from the fierce desert sun. Men – even Pharaoh – generally wore a simple kilt of white linen (although Pharaoh's was a bit more elaborate) and women a gown of lightweight linen that clung to the body due to its myriad fine pleats, and which might cover the breasts, or leave one bare. Royal linen, such as that worn by Nefertiti, was especially prized for its softness, and was so fine as to be almost transparent. Under these circumstances, Egyptians were usually quite unself-conscious about their bodies and casual about nudity, in general. Indeed, dancing girls and acrobats typically performed totally nude. The Queen, like most Egyptians, was normally blithely unconcerned about revealing her body.

Kiya, on the other hand, derived from a more northerly country where clothing was typically more concealing, woven of heavier linen or wool. Her gowns were brightly multi-colored, fitted closely to the body and wound about by spirals of fringe. Nevertheless, where her ladies' gowns came up modestly under their armpits and over one shoulder, Kiya's gowns managed to be low-cut, revealing her ample cleavage in an unmistakably sexual fashion. Nefertiti was both baffled and annoyed by how Kiya managed to use partial concealment as a sexual come-on. She was even more annoyed by her husband's obvious reaction to it.

Thutmose, who was present, as usual, drawing the domestic scene, doggedly excluded the Mitanni princess from the picture. He painted the family gathering as he had in the past, the happy royal couple and their children. He would not stoop to commemorating Kiya's blatantly seductive behavior – nor, indeed, her very presence. He wouldn't dignify her presence by recording it. He felt angry that Pharaoh would tolerate such an insult to his queen, and angry at himself when he found himself aroused by Kiya's overt sexuality – and her occasional steamy glances in his direction. After such occasions, he always felt that he needed to bathe.

After one such session, when Kiya had finally withdrawn, only to be followed soon after by the king, Thutmose broached the subject to the Queen.

Putting down his brush, Thutmose commented quietly, "Surely, Your Majesty need not put up with such behavior. The woman has no place intruding on your private family time."

Nefertiti bit her lip and looked away, but Thutmose could see a tear trickling silently down her cheek. It broke his heart not to be able to wipe it away and put his arms around her to comfort her. The best he could offer her was a somewhat clean square of linen from the supply of cloths he kept for wiping off his brushes. She accepted it and dabbed quietly at her eyes and nose.

"I don't know what to do, Thutmose. He's never reacted like this to any of his other wives or concubines."

"None of them has ever dared this kind of behavior. Native Egyptians are too well aware of Your Majesty's position and power, too awed to dare to cross you," he replied. "This foreign woman has grown up believing she has the right to do anything she pleases. You need to put her in her place, remind her who is Great Wife here."

Lady Mutreshti, Nefertiti's chief Lady in Waiting, stepped forward from the shadows.

"He's right, Your Majesty. The foreign woman is a snake in the grass!" she said, and spat on the floor to indicate her contempt. "You should order your servants to forbid her to enter here! You deserve some time with Pharaoh uninterrupted by her wiles!"

"Do you think that would work?" the Queen asked anxiously. "She's used to giving orders. I don't think any servant would dare stop her."

"Perhaps not," said Thutmose thoughtfully, "but I'll bet a couple of soldiers would stop her. Why don't you speak to Captain Paramessu and ask him to assign some guards to safeguard your family time with Pharaoh?"

"Do you think he would?" she asked, uncertainly. "Would he accept the order from me, and not from Pharaoh?"

"He wouldn't dare refuse his Queen!" sputtered Mutreshti.

"I think he might feel he owes it to you," mused Thutmose.

"Owes it to me? How so?" she asked.

"Remember the incident with the crocodile?" he asked her.

"How could I possibly forget it?" she exclaimed.

"Well, Paramessu was the officer in charge of the detachment that was supposed to be guarding you that day on the lake. I think he feels guilty about failing you that time. That may motivate him to do better now – especially if you ask him very nicely," he added, smiling. "You are, after all, still the most beautiful woman in Egypt."

"Darn right, she is!" Lady Mutreshti added vehemently. "He's right, My Lady. You should use your power and your feminine wiles to keep that foreign slut in her place!"

"All right, I will," she said, lifting her chin. "You – boy," she added, calling a servant, "run to the Captain of the Guard's office and tell Captain Paramessu to come here!"

"Yes, Your Majesty!" the boy replied, bowing, then ran out the door.

Once again in possession of her poise, Nefertiti proceeded to charm the guard captain, winning his whole-hearted support. He, in turn, impressed upon his men that they were to guard Her Majesty's peace from disruption by the foreign princess, no matter what wiles she might use on them. He emphasized that only a direct order from the King could supersede that of the Queen.

While Nefertiti met with the guard Captain, Thutmose conferred with Lady Mutreshti. He promised that his artists would do anything they could to help, while Mutreshti agreed to speak with the servants.

As it turned out, both groups were happy to assist, as the Queen had always been kind to them, while the foreign woman was high-handed and demanding. The slightest imperfection was enough to set her off and provoke her into beating them. It soon appeared that the only people who did not dislike her were the people she had brought with her and the King.

The servants felt that, if she was going to beat them anyway, they might as well get in her way whenever they could. After that, she found that her meals were often delayed, the food cold, the fruit wormy, the wine an inferior vintage. Her bath water was too cold in winter and too hot in summer. When she attempted to go to the King, she was led the long way around, and was sometimes lost entirely.

Still, while these ruses and the presence of soldiers served to keep her out of family gatherings, they were not sufficient to keep Pharaoh out of Kiya's bed. Her influence over him continued to grow.

Meanwhile, the seventy days of mourning for the old King passed and the day came when he was ceremoniously interred in his fine tomb in the Valley of the Kings. Thutmose, who had overseen the decoration of the tomb, and even painted some of the murals with his own hand, watched the High Priest seal the tomb. He felt a strange sense of foreboding, a feeling that an era was ending, and uncertainty about what would take its place.

He knew that the reign of Amenhotep III would be remembered as a great one, a time of unparalleled peace and prosperity. There had been no major foreign wars; Egyptian armies patrolling the borders had been sufficient to hold back any would-be invaders without extreme effort. Once the Seven Lean Years foretold by Yuya had ended, the annual Inundation of the Nile had been regular and plentiful. The land had prospered under Amenhotep's rule, and tribute had poured in from abroad. All in all, it had been a good reign, and the old king would be missed. Thutmose had seen it in the tearful faces of the people who had lined the streets and river banks to watch his funeral cortege.

Once the funeral was over, plans for the opening of the new Aten temple could proceed. Thutmose was very concerned about the king and queen's safety during the ceremony. Captain Paramessu agreed that it was likely to be a particularly hazardous occasion. He planned to station guards along the route, as well as in a cordon around the young monarch. Even so, Thutmose feared that it would not be enough.

He waited anxiously for any sign from Ipy, but when the lad appeared, for days on end, he had nothing to report. Nevertheless, Thutmose stationed his artists around the temple, secreting them in locations unknown to outsiders, but familiar to his workmen. He, himself, vowed to stay as close to the king as he could. Since he and Bek were the principal architects and decorators of the temple, they would have the honor of introducing it to the royal party, which enabled them to stay close by.

The day of the ceremony, in the last week of Shemu, dawned bright and clear. It seemed that the Aten himself would be dazzlingly present to celebrate the opening of his temple.

Pharaoh and his Great Wife rose before dawn to complete their ablutions and be dressed in time to greet their god as he rose above the eastern horizon – the most sacred moment of their day. The royal party

made their way through the still-dark streets to the temple complex,
closely guarded by Paramessu's men. Thutmose and Bek waited by the
gates of the temple to welcome the king and queen. They were in position flanking the royal couple in the great courtyard when the sun rose
above the horizon, striking straight down the processional way above
the sacred lake, through the great gates and colonnade of the temple,
touching the king and queen just before lighting the huge golden disk
behind them. It did, indeed, look just like the official portraits, with the
sun sending its life-giving rays first to the king and queen, and then to
the rest of the Two Lands. The nobles and common folk who had
packed the courtyard sank to the ground and prostrated themselves before the Aten and the king and queen, its human incarnation and inter-
mediaries.

Thutmose found himself very touched by the scene, even
though he, himself, had done so much to create it.

Just then, he caught sight of a flutter of white behind a nearby
column. He glanced over and saw Ipy gesturing frantically to him. He
couldn't make out what the boy was pointing to – he seemed to be indicating someone in the crowd, but Thutmose could not tell who.

As the crowd returned to their feet, Thutmose caught sight of a
shaven head in a group near the gate. There was something familiar
about the man. Thutmose glanced back and saw Ipy struggling to work
his way through the crowd in that direction. Thutmose could see that
the shaven-headed stranger was close to where the king would pass on
his way out the gate. Alarmed, he moved closer to Pharaoh's side. He
tried to catch Paramessu's eye, but the young captain was fully occupied with helping his men try to hold back the crowd.

Thutmose could see Ipy elbowing his way around the back of
the crowd, trying to work his way over to the gate. As the royal party
approached it, Thutmose realized that the faces of several of the men
near the gate were familiar to him – he had seen them in processions
every day in the temple complex. Then he recognized them: priests of
Amun, but dressed in nondescript civilian clothes, their shaven heads
covered by wigs or headcloths.

As the royal party approached the gate, the disguised priests on
either side pushed and shoved the other spectators closer and closer to
the king. The soldiers struggled to keep them back, with only partial
success. Suddenly, as the king and queen reached the narrowest point,
the ranks of the crowd opened and expelled the shaven-headed man,
right into the path of the king. A man on the other side struggled to get
through, but was met with a guardsman's shoulder. As the shaven-
headed man lurched toward the king, appearing to be stumbling out of
the crowd, Thutmose caught the gleam of bronze in his hand.

With a cry of "Guard the king!" Thutmose launched himself at the man, catching the wrist of his dagger hand in his own left hand. The man was strong, and struggled to bring the dagger around behind Thutmose, to where the king stood, uncertain what was happening. But Thutmose was all lean muscle from years of working and hauling stone. He drove the man's hand up, where all could see the bronze knife. There it trembled until Ipy, breaking through the crowd, tackled the man's knees from behind. As he went down, several men in the crowd fell upon him.

"Stop!" Thutmose yelled, trying to pull them off. "We need to take him alive! He must be questioned!"

But by the time the over-zealous onlookers were pulled off, the assassin was dead, stabbed with his own blade.

The guards formed a solid wall around the king and queen as the screaming crowd pelted out of the gate. Soon, only the royal party, artists and guards remained. Paramessu ordered the gates closed and chariots to be fetched for the king and queen.

He came up beside Thutmose and bent to examine the body of the assassin.

"Does anyone know who he is?" he asked. The guards all shook their heads.

"I don't know his name," said Thutmose, "but I've seen him before in the temple complex."

"I know who he is," said Ipy, stepping forward. "He's a *sed* priest of Amun, one of First Prophet's men. His name's Ankh-Hap. He wasn't the only one of them here, either."

"That's true," Thutmose agreed. "Just before the attack, I saw several men I recognized as priests of Amun, all disguised as ordinary citizens. They were pushing the crowd forward."

"So," said the king, stepping forward, "this was a plot by the priesthood of Amun! They dare attack their rightful king! Get me home – and bring me First Prophet!"

Once the chariots arrived, the king and queen made straight for the palace, with twenty guards running along at full speed on either side. It was a sight soon to become all too familiar.

Later that day, First Prophet Ptahmose was dragged before the king, under heavy guard. He was wearing his priestly regalia, still attempting to retain his dignity and stand on the untouchability of his position.

"On your knees before your king, villain!" hissed Captain Paramessu, shoving him to the floor.

The king stepped down from his throne and descended the steps of the dais to where the High Priest trembled, his forehead touching the floor.

"Vile false priest," thundered the king, yanking him up by his pectoral of office. "False priest of a false god, that dares to attack his king! I know that the assassin was one of your men!"

At this, there was a startled intake of breath by all the courtiers present.

The king paced back and forth before the cowering priest like an angry lion. The normally good-tempered, easy-going young man was transformed into a figure of towering wrath.

"I have tolerated you and your treacherous, greedy, deceitful brethren long enough! Your priesthood is a den of serpents!" the king shouted. "For this, you deserve to die – to die a slow and painful death."

At this, Grand Vizier Aye dared to come forward and approach the king. Speaking quietly, so that others could not overhear, he said:

"Your Majesty, is that wise? The people still revere his god. He has a huge following. They might riot if you kill the High Priest. Besides, he is your cousin twice removed. It might be a bad precedent, spilling even partly royal blood."

The king considered this a moment.

"All right," he said, turning back toward the priest. "I will be merciful. I will spare your miserable life. Since you saw fit to have your creature attack me in my own temple, you shall labor to build more temples to my god, the Aten – the one true god! I sentence you to hard labor in the stone quarries of Aswan!"

The crowd gasped. It was unheard of, to sentence a High Priest to the stone quarries.

"But, sire," protested the priest, "I am an old man, and not very strong."

"A little honest work will make you stronger," said the king. "You will grow stronger – or you will die. If you grow stronger, you will do useful work. If you die – so be it. It is the will of Aten. You can go to meet your own god in person."

"For, for…how long, sire?"

The king considered this. While the priest was older than most Egyptians, he was not really *old*, being somewhere in his forties. He had a chance of surviving some years in the quarries.

"I will give you a chance, priest – more than you intended to give me. Seven years. If you survive that long, and you don't make any trouble, I will let you retire to a little farm, under house arrest. It is better than you deserve."

"Yes, Your Majesty," mumbled the priest, his forehead to the floor.

"Stand him up," said the king to the soldiers.

They hauled the priest upright.

The king stepped up to him. "I hereby strip you of your priestly office," he said, tearing off the priest's pectoral of office, "and all rights and privileges pertaining to it."

He pulled off the priest's headgear and trampled it underfoot. He then climbed back up the stairs of the dais and looked out at the assembled courtiers. After a moment's silence, he cried out in a stentorian voice:

"Hear your king! I hereby order the temple of Amun to be closed – ALL of the temples of Amun! All its treasures and stores of grain shall be the property of the crown, to be held for the benefit of the state! The priesthood of Amun is herewith disbanded and shall be dispersed!"

There was a collective gasp and murmur around the room.

One courtier ventured to protest. "But, sire, Amun is the state god of the Two Lands, and the tutelary deity of Thebes!"

"Not any more, he isn't!" replied the king. "From this moment forward, the state religion shall be the worship of the Aten! *He* is the state god! He is the one and only god, and his religion shall be the only one in the Two Lands!"

There were more murmurs of shock and protest.

"Hear me well, you people. Aten is the only god! In token of this, I hereby change my name – I am no longer Amenhotep. From this moment forward, I shall be known as Akhenaten: He in Whose Actions Aten is Well Pleased!

"Captain Paramessu," he called.

The soldier stepped forward and saluted.

"Send soldiers throughout the land. The temples of the old gods are to be closed. Their treasuries are henceforth the property of the crown. The name of Amun is to be stricken from every place where it occurs: every inscription, every scroll, every temple, stele and tomb. Every place where it forms even part of a name is to be removed."

"Yes, Your Majesty!" the soldier acknowledged. As an afterthought, he added, "But, Your Majesty, does that include even…your own name – your old name, that is - and your father's?"

"Even my name, Captain – my *former* name – and that of my father. The name of Amun shall be anathema. Let it vanish from the land of Egypt! I, Pharaoh Akhenaten, have spoken! Go and do your duty, Captain!"

The soldier saluted smartly, then turned on his heel, gathered up his men and left.

The Grand Vizier signaled to the courtiers that the audience was ended. They all sank to the floor as their newly renamed Pharaoh stalked out of the room, followed by his immediate family and entourage.

Chapter 24: Birthing Pains

The newly-renamed Pharaoh Akhenaten wasted no time in moving to suppress the old religion. He sent troops out all over the Two Lands with orders to turn out the priests, close the temples and seize their treasuries. Since much of the temples' wealth was held in the form of grain, Pharaoh set civil servants as administrators over all of the granaries, much as his grandfather Yuya had done during the infamous Seven Years' Famine in the time of Thutmosis IV, two generations earlier.

Officers of the army, the traditional opponents of the priesthood, were happy to enforce these edicts. Some of the common soldiers, however, were uneasy about desecrating the temples of a religion they had been brought up to revere. While some were glad of an opportunity for a little personal plunder, others grumbled and moved reluctantly, all the while glancing nervously over their shoulders, as though expecting divine lightning to strike at any moment.

While there was, as yet, no actual rioting in the streets, there was a continual muttering among the people, like the uneasy tide of a turbulent sea. The direct effect on their daily lives was not all that large, since the temples were not places of prayer and ritual for the common people, but rather the private dwelling places of the gods. While the impact on the priesthood was certainly drastic, the effect on the common people was far more subtle. The effect on the nobility fell somewhere in between, as Akhenaten pressed them harder to pay homage to his new god. The nobility were the people who counted, the people who would set the path for others to follow – the common folk counted for little.

For the old nobility, many of whose families Akhenaten had already pushed out of the offices they had held by tradition for generations, the suppression of the old religion was one more straw in the load of resentment they were accumulating against the young king. The *nouveau* nobility, on the other hand, those who had been created by Akhenaten to take the places of the old, were quick to adopt the new religion and enthusiastic in its observance. It was not long before the entire land was divided between those who followed the new religion and those who clung to the old.

The common folk, by and large, continued as they always had, worshipping the everyday deities of common household functions, such as Bes and Taueret.

Eventually, soldiers entered the houses of those nobles who resisted the new religion, smashing their household shrines and statues of Amun and other traditional gods, and reporting their resistance back to Pharaoh. The common folk, on the other hand, went largely unmolested. Members of the dispossessed priesthoods and younger members of old noble families roamed the streets, haranguing the commoners and trying to stir up rebellion against the king and his new religion. While they attracted a modest following among the already-disgruntled, most common people ignored them and went on about their business. However, roving bands of young adherents of the old religion made travel through the streets of the larger cities increasingly hazardous for followers of the new religion –even for the King and his family.

Thutmose and Mariamne, meanwhile, had settled into a pleasant house on the outskirts of the city, safe behind a high wall, in a quiet neighborhood untroubled by the current religious strife. Mariamne bustled happily around the new house, doing everything in her considerable power to make it a real home. For Thutmose, it was a bit strange, living in an individual house of his own. He had lived in a small room in the palace for almost as long as he could remember. He had only hazy memories of living in his parents' modest house as a small child.

Mariamne, of course, had always lived in a small private house in a small village. She had been thrilled and awed by the experience of living in a luxurious apartment within the royal palace for several weeks while the Lord Chamberlain's servants worked to find her and Thutmose a house. She would have a lot to tell her former neighbors whenever she managed to get back to the village for a visit. Thutmose, of course, was accustomed to the palace and took it for granted. Oddly enough, even though, as an artist, he was very sensitive to his surroundings, he had never acquired a personal taste for luxury and preferred to maintain a very simple, almost austere lifestyle. Mariamne's awe at the palatial setting and the company of important people merely amused him. If she didn't get over it soon, however, he feared it would begin to wear on him. But for now, it gave him a certain pleasure to watch her wide-eyed fascination with court life. It gave him a fresh perspective and a new appreciation of his privileged lifestyle.

Meanwhile, the growing tension in the streets was echoed by the tension in the royal palace. Akhenaten was surprised and bewildered by the continued resistance to his new religion. It seemed to him so inherently obvious that there could be only one real god, so utterly logical, that he couldn't understand why people didn't get it and didn't immediately rush to embrace his new monotheistic religion.

Now, he paced up and down in the airy chamber he used as an office, gesticulating as he spoke to his closest advisors.

"How can they not see it?" he asked. "It seems so simple, and so obvious. There is only one universe. There can be only one All-Powerful Being. Any gods more than one are, by definition, not All-

Powerful. There cannot be multiple gods, except as servants or agents of the One All-Powerful Being. Why is this so difficult to grasp?"

"Well, Your Majesty," ventured one of his advisors, "it is a new idea to them. Egypt has always had many gods, for thousands of years now. The Two Lands change but slowly, my king – you need to give them time to assimilate this idea. It is one they have never conceived of before."

"Very few men are as brilliant as Your Majesty, or such deep thinkers," pointed out Aper-El, the newly-appointed Vizier of Lower Egypt, Rahmose's counterpart in the North. "What seems utterly obvious to Your Majesty is a complete mystery to most other men."

Aper-El, a Habiru from the Delta region, was a distant cousin to both the king and queen – and of Mariamne, as well, since they were all descendants of the Habiru patriarch Yacub, the father of Yuya. Aper-El (called Ashbel in the Habiru tongue) was one of the sons of Benyamin, Yuya's youngest brother.

The king demanded solutions from his advisors, ways to promulgate his new religion throughout the land. On their advice, he founded a school for a new priesthood, headquartered in the Gem Pa'aten temple. Once trained, the new priests went throughout the country, teaching the precepts of the new religion to the people. He also called upon the talents of his artists to design new temples to be built in all the major cities, and artwork to carry the message to the masses of people who could not read.

Later, as Thutmose and Mariamne entertained Bek and his wife and several other artists and scribes from the palace, all close friends, at their new house, the men entered into a spirited discussion of the strong and weak points of the new religion, while the ladies retired to the women's quarters to discuss topics closer to feminine hearts. Since this was a trusted group of close friends, all loyal supporters of the young king, they felt free to speak openly among themselves.

"As an artist," said Thutmose, "I find Pharaoh's concept of one over-arching creator god very appealing. When I look around me at this beautiful world, I think its creator must be a very great artist, the greatest of all, to bring such beauty into being. And it seems to me to show the brush strokes of a single hand, the coherent design of a single mind – not the work of a committee of disparate gods, each with his or her own interests to advance."

"Have you heard Pharaoh's new psalm, the Hymn to the Aten?" asked Nebseny, a scribe from the Gem Pa-aten temple. "It is a fine example of the appreciation of the unity and beauty of nature of which our host speaks, and a beautiful piece of poetry."

"I haven't heard it yet," ventured Ipy. "I've spent the last several months immured in the Temple of Amun, pretending to be a priest in training."

"That's right," commented Hapuseneb, a young artist, "our heroic spy! Of course you wouldn't have heard the great Hymn to the Aten! You must be the only person in the palace who hasn't heard it!"

"How does it go?" Ipy asked.

Nebseny obliged him by reciting:

"'Thou arisest fair in the horizon of Heaven, O Living Aten, Beginner of Life. When thou dawnest in the East, thou fillest every land with thy beauty. Thou art indeed comely, great, radiant and high over every land. Thy rays embrace the lands to the full extent of all that thou hast made, for thou art Re and thou attainest their limits and subduest them for thy beloved son' – that would be Akhenaten," he commented aside. *"'Thou art remote, yet thy rays are upon the earth. Thou art in the sight of men, yet thy ways are not known.*

"'When thou settest in the Western horizon,'" he continued, *"'the earth is in darkness after the manner of death. Men spend the night indoors with the head covered, the eye not seeing its fellow. Their possessions might be stolen, even when under their heads, and they would be unaware of it. Every lion comes forth from its lair and all snakes bite. Darkness lurks, and the earth is silent when their Creator rests in his habitation.*

"'The earth brightens when thou arisest in the Eastern horizon and shinest forth as Aten in the daytime. Thou drivest away the night when thou givest forth thy beams. The Two Lands are in festival. They awake and stand upon their feet, for thou hast raised them up.'"

He took a deep breath and paraphrased the next two verses. "It goes on about all the animals and things of nature being ordered by Aten and rejoicing at his rising."

Ipy commented, "Well, so far, it isn't very different from the prayers to Amun that I heard in his temple."

Parennefer, the King's Cupbearer and an ardent adherent of the new religion, broke in, "That may be so, but what's really different is not what's included in it, but what is not: namely, any other gods. No Amun, Re, Isis, Min, or any of the rest them. There's none of Amun is in charge of this, Min in charge of that, and so on – Aten does it all. It makes sense, really – if Aten created everything, He should have power over it all. Thus, the hymn says:

"How manifold are thy works! They are hidden from the sight of men, O Sole God, like unto whom there is no other! Thou didst fashion the earth according to thy desire when thou wast alone – all men,

all cattle great and small, all that are upon the earth that run upon their feet or rise up on high, flying with their wings."

Userhat, a palace scribe, added, "Yes, but it's not only what's left out that is unique – it's also **who** is included." To demonstrate his point, he took up the chant:

"'And the lands of Syria and Kush and Egypt – thou appointest every man to his place and satisfiest his needs. Everyone receives his sustenance and his days are numbered. Their tongues are diverse in speech and their qualities likewise, and their color is differentiated, for thou hast distinguished the nations.'

"'Thou makest the waters under the earth and thou bringest them forth as the Nile to sustain the people of Egypt, even as thou hast made them live for thee, O Divine Lord of them all, toiling for them, the Lord of every land, shining forth for them, the Aten Disk of the day time, great in majesty!'

"'All distant foreign lands also, thou createst their life. Thou hast placed a Nile in heaven to come forth for them and make a flood upon the mountains like the sea in order to water the fields of their villages. How excellent are thy plans, O Lord of Eternity! – a Nile in the sky is thy gift to foreigners and to beasts of their lands; but the true Nile flows from under the earth for Egypt.'"

"You hear that? 'All distant foreign lands.' This god is not only supposed to be the supreme god, the only god – he's also the god of all lands – even 'distant foreign lands'," Userhat pointed out. "That's new. All the old gods were only gods of Egypt. And foreigners have always had their own gods. Our gods were never over, say, the Hittites, and their gods were never over us. But now, along comes Aten, and he's supposed to be the only god over everybody! That's definitely a new idea."

"Well, it is logical," observed Ipy, nibbling at a bunch of grapes. "If Aten is supposed to be the Supreme God, and he's supposed to have created the world, then it makes sense that He would be over everyone and everything – including all of Egypt and all foreign countries."

They continued their lively debate on the merits of the new religion versus the old until well into the night. Nowhere else in the country could they discuss these issues as freely as in this select company. Elsewhere, they risked the wrath of the old priesthood or its adherents, or, sad to say, informants hoping to ingratiate themselves with the new regime by bearing tales against their neighbors, real or invented.

As time went on, disquiet spread throughout the land. Before long, neither Akhenaten nor Nefertiti felt safe abroad in the streets unless accompanied by a substantial bodyguard. Pharaoh finally decided he could no longer tolerate such conditions in his own capital. He decided that he would found a new capital, a city never previously dedicated to any other god. He sent out scouts up and down the Nile to find potential sites where he could build his new city. They returned with varying reports, but no clear-cut recommendation of a building site. Finally, he resolved to make the journey himself, certain that the Aten would reveal to him the perfect site on which to build his capital city.

After the waters of the Inundation receded in the fall, Akhenaten set out in his royal barge, accompanied by several shiploads of soldiers, plus a coterie of royal surveyors. No one was sure beforehand whether he intended to start by traveling up the Nile towards Nubia, or down toward the sea.

But Pharaoh had had a dream the night before. He dreamed of the Two Ladies, the Vulture and the Cobra, symbols of Upper and Lower Egypt, and between and behind them rose a line of cliffs. Before them lay the shining ribbon of the Nile, and through a notch in the cliffs between them could be seen the rays of the rising sun. Akhenaten discerned the meaning of the dream: In the middle of the country, halfway between Upper and Lower Egypt, he would find a place east of the river, where the rising sun could be seen through a notch in the cliffs, and there he would build his capital city. So, since Thebes was south – upriver – of the center of the country, Akhenaten ordered the steersman to turn the boat north, downriver. There, somewhere midway between Thebes and Memphis, he was sure he would find the place he had seen in his dream.

Nefertiti did not travel with him, as her third pregnancy was now well advanced. Of the artists, Bek accompanied Pharaoh, while the newlywed Thutmose remained in Thebes with his wife.

Despite her pregnancy, Nefertiti grew restless confined to the palace and insisted on going out riding in her chariot. At Captain Paramessu's insistence, she was accompanied by a full contingent of bodyguards, running full tilt to keep pace alongside her chariot. She usually rode out in the open space between the city and the hills, passing between the last of the tilled fields, into the arid desert plain. The dry, flat space was ideal for letting the horses run.

On a bright fall day, when the fields were green from the receding waters of the Inundation, Nefertiti insisted on going riding. Captain Paramessu protested that it was dangerous – she was very near term and the crowds in the streets threatened to explode into outright rioting at any moment. Nevertheless, Nefertiti insisted, and she was the

Queen, so Paramessu had to acquiesce. However, he insisted that she let her charioteer drive, so she would have both hands free to hold onto the chariot rail – it wouldn't do for her to be jolted out if the chariot hit a bump. The Queen, fully conscious of the awkwardness of late pregnancy, agreed with this stricture. So they set out, Nefertiti in her gilded chariot driven by her charioteer, Thutmose riding in Captain Paramessu's chariot, followed by that of his lieutenant and a utilitarian cart filled with baskets of food for a picnic lunch; accompanied by twenty soldiers loping along on either side. They left the city through one of the smaller eastern gates and headed toward the hills. (The city was often described in poetry as "many-gated Thebes", due to its many portals.) They picked their way carefully between fields where green shoots poked several inches above rich earth still black with wet new soil deposited by the annual flooding of the Nile.

Eventually, they reached drier ground untouched by the river's flood, where they could let the horses set a faster pace. Soon the three chariots had run well ahead of the foot soldiers, who were straining to catch up. Before long, however, the rocky margin of the foothills forced them to call a halt. The Queen's charioteer pulled his horses to a stop in the shade of a grove of acacia trees surrounding a natural spring in a cleft in the rocks. The captain and his lieutenant pulled up on either side. The Queen's charioteer tied off his reins, jumped down and helped Her Majesty to alight. Moments later, the panting soldiers and jouncing cart of provisions caught up with them. In just a few minutes, servants had set out a comfortable chair for the Queen, with a footstool, surrounded by several small tables piled high with food and drink. There were folding stools for Thutmose, the captain and lieutenant, while all the men sprawled in the shade around the pool of water, quenching their thirst, splashing themselves with water and relaxing, weapons at the ready nearby. Even though there were no people nearby, other than a few peasants in the distant fields, there were always natural hazards to beware of: scorpions, snakes, lions, jackals and hyenas.

Sure enough, they had scarcely finished their lunch when Nefertiti's charioteer let out a howl and leaped up from where he had been seated on the ground. A large black scorpion scuttled away into the rocks. The charioteer hopped about on one leg, holding the other foot off the ground and moaning in pain. The captain ordered him to sit on a large boulder so he could examine the leg. An angry, rapidly swelling red patch on the back of the calf showed where he had been stung. Moments later, he collapsed and would have toppled off the rock but for the quick action of the lieutenant, who caught him. The captain splashed the afflicted leg with water from the spring, sucked out as much of the venom as he could, then turned to the Queen.

"Your Majesty, we must get this man back to the palace immediately, or he is likely to die. The sting of the black scorpion is often
fatal."

"Very well, Captain," she replied. "Send him in the chariot with
Lieutenant Amenemhet. Thutmose can drive me back."

Concerned, the captain turned to Thutmose and asked, "Are
you sure you can handle these horses?"

"Certainly, Captain," Thutmose assured him. "When His Majesty was a young prince, I used to accompany him on his rides about
the city and the countryside. I often drove the chariot."

"Don't worry, Captain," added the Queen. "Thutmose is very
good with horses."

Thutmose felt a private glow of satisfaction at the Queen's confidence in him.

"Very good, Your Majesty," said the captain, saluting. He
turned quickly and directed his men to lift the semi-conscious charioteer into the lieutenant's chariot. The lieutenant jumped into the chariot,
grabbed the reins and wheeled the chariot about, then cracked his whip,
urging the horses to full speed. They galloped toward the city, raising
clouds of dust. If they could reach the palace in time, skilled doctors
might yet be able to save the man's life.

After this incident, no one felt any desire to linger. Everything
was quickly packed up and returned to the baggage cart. Thutmose
brought the Queen's chariot over to her, and Captain Paramessu helped
her up, then hopped into his own chariot, now driven by the lieutenant's
charioteer. They turned and headed back toward the city at a brisk pace,
until they had to slow down to negotiate the narrow paths between the
muddy fields.

They were almost back to the city when the Queen suddenly let
out a cry and bent over, clutching her belly. Thutmose immediately
halted and turned to her.

"What is it, Your Majesty? Is it the baby?" he asked.

She nodded quickly, grimacing and biting back a groan of pain.
As the spasm passed, she gasped, "Get me home quickly, Thutmose! I
don't want to have this baby right here in the fields!"

The captain, who had drawn up close beside them during this
interchange, shouted to one of the men to run ahead to the gate and
have the men on duty there clear the streets on the way to the palace.
The man dashed off toward the gate as the two chariots got under way
again, the Queen now crouching on the floor of her chariot, clutching

the railing with one hand and her belly with the other. Worried, Thutmose glanced down at her from time to time.

Before they could reach the gate, the messenger came tearing back out, signaling frantically to the royal party. Thutmose and the captain reined their horses in and pulled to a halt.

"We can't go this way, Captain," panted the soldier. "The people are rioting. The street is blocked between here and the palace! We have to find another way!"

"By the Aten!" swore the captain. "Now what are we going to do? We've got to get the Queen back to the palace! If we have to go clear around to the south side, she'll never make it!"

As if to punctuate his words, the Queen moaned aloud.

Thutmose thought quickly, then spoke up. "I've got a better idea, Captain. We can take her to my house. It's not far from here, and my wife is an experienced midwife."

"That's a good idea," gasped the Queen between contractions. "Take me there, quickly!"

Thutmose wheeled the chariot about and galloped for another nearby gate, followed closely by the captain's chariot, trailed by the bodyguard struggling to catch up. Due to the trouble in the city, the gate was closed, but opened quickly to admit the Queen's party.

Thutmose threaded the chariot expertly through the narrow streets, the horse's hooves clattering over the cobblestones. He drew up before the closed gate in the wall of his own villa and pounded on it, calling for Mariamne and the servants. The gate was quickly thrown open, admitting the master of the house and his royal patron. He led the horses inside the gate, followed by the captain, who ordered the gate shut behind them. Captain Paramessu assigned half a dozen men to keep guard inside the wall, appointed two to run to the palace and fetch the Queen's doctor, while the rest of the men were posted outside the wall.

In the courtyard, Thutmose told Mariamne, "The Queen is in labor, and the streets to the palace are blocked by rioters. We need to get her inside."

Mariamne nodded. "Put her in our room. I'll get everything ready."

Thutmose picked up the Queen and carried her into the house. He was acutely aware of her warm weight in his arms, her head against his bare chest. He could smell the fragrance of costly myrrh she wore, mingled with the scent of her skin – skin in close contact with his own. How long he had dreamt of holding her, though not in a moment quite like this!

Between contractions, which commanded her attention, Nefertiti relaxed into the security of Thutmose's strong arms. A part of her wished she could just remain there, a wish quickly rejected by a consciousness trained to a lifetime of royal discipline. She knew as well as Thutmose that this was a rare moment of contact, never to be repeated. Still, for these few moments, she let her senses revel in his masculine closeness, soaking in the sensation of his skin warm against hers, the clean lines of his face above her, the reassuring strength of his muscular arms and chest cradling her. She could not help but be aware of the contrast between his handsome face and muscular physique and the softer, less manly frame and odd visage of the king. Try as she might, she could not wholly suppress such disloyal thoughts.

Thutmose carried her into the bedroom and set her carefully on the bed. Mariamne bustled into the room behind him, then shooed him out. He went back out into the courtyard and joined Captain Paramessu. A few minutes later, Mariamne's son, Shemu-El, hurried back in the gate, followed by two women Thutmose recognized as neighbors. The boy led the women into the house.

"Your son?" asked the captain.

Thutmose shook his head. "My wife's son by her former husband," he said, then added, "may he be justified." The standard phrase made it clear the first husband was dead.

"Ah," said the captain. "Any children of your own?"

"Not yet," Thutmose replied. "We've only been married about three months. How about you?"

"Two," replied Paramessu. "A girl, Merit, and two boys, Ramses and Seti. Both bright lads – my pride and joy."

"You're a fortunate man, captain."

"Well, Aten willing, you'll probably soon have sons of your own," he said, clapping Thutmose on the back.

The two men paced back and forth in the courtyard, the quiet occasionally broken by loud cries from the house. After a while, the boy came back out of the house carrying a basket of bread and a pitcher of beer for the two men. The captain, realizing that his men must also be thirsty and hungry, asked the boy to fetch water for them and ordered his sergeant to distribute the food remaining in the baskets of provisions in the baggage cart to the men.

Suddenly, the quiet was split by a baby's loud wail. They all looked toward the house, then the captain said, "Well, it looks as though the Two Lands have a new royal son or daughter. I wonder which?"

A few minutes later, Mariamne came out of the house, smiling.

"The Queen has been safely delivered of a healthy daughter," she announced.

"And the Queen?" asked Thutmose. "How is she?"

"She's doing fine," replied Mariamne.

Just then, there was a commotion at the gate, then a soldier entered, followed by two men Thutmose recognized as royal physicians. Thutmose introduced them to Mariamne, who led them into the bedchamber.

Some time later, the doctors came back out, pronouncing both the Queen and her new daughter strong and healthy. Then they left to return to the palace, saying there was nothing more for them to do.

"Her Majesty appears to be in good hands here," commented the elder physician, Pentu. "Your wife is a fine midwife," he added, to Thutmose.

Shortly thereafter, Mariamne brought the new baby out for them to see.

"She's a fine baby girl," she said. "The Queen says she and Pharaoh had already agreed that, if the baby was a girl, she was to be named Ankhsenpaaten."

"'Life Beloved of Aten'" commented Paramessu. "A fine name."

Thutmose looked at the tiny, wrinkled red face and marveled at the miracle of new life. He reached up and cautiously touched the baby's cheek and looked into her indeterminate-colored newborn eyes. The baby waved her tiny fist, then took hold of Thutmose's index finger and hung on with surprising strength. He smiled down at her, then looked wonderingly at his wife.

"Hah! She's already claimed you as her first subject, Master Thutmose," laughed the captain, clapping Thutmose on the back. "I can see you're in her thrall already."

And, indeed, it was true. I felt that some mysterious bond had been formed between myself and this child born under my roof, a bond that would last as long as either of us lived.

Chapter 25: Birth of a City

Shortly after the birth of Princess Ankhsenpaaten, Pharaoh returned to Thebes. The royal barge, "Radiance of the Aten", was spotted mid-morning, approaching upriver with the aid of a stiff breeze, its colorful striped sail bellied out, pennants flying from the mast. A short time later, it landed at the royal wharf, accompanied by dozens of lesser craft filled with soldiers. A strangely silent, sullen crowd greeted Pharaoh's arrival at the dock and lined the streets leading to the palace.

The palace guard, headed by Captain Paramessu, were drawn up in formation on the shore. As the King stepped ashore, Paramessu saluted him smartly.

"Greetings, Your Majesty," he said. "Welcome home."

"Hah!" replied the King. "This may be where I was born, but Thebes is no longer home to me!"

He strode to his waiting chariot. Taking the charioteer's proferred hand, he stepped into it. Surveying the silent throng, he turned to Paramessu and asked,

"Why are they so quiet? What has been going on here?"

Paramessu stepped into his own chariot and drew up near the King.

"There has been rioting in the streets in your absence, Your Majesty," he said quietly, so only the King could hear. "We should get you to the palace as quickly as possible. I have soldiers stationed all along the way."

"All right," agreed Pharaoh. "Make it so. You lead, Captain."

Paramessu acknowledged the order with a brief nod, then pulled his chariot ahead of Pharaoh's. He urged his horses to a brisk trot, then a gallop, looking back only briefly to be sure Pharaoh's chariot was following closely in his wake. As they neared the palace, Paramessu gave a brief blast on his bugle carved from a bull's horn and edged with silver.

As they approached, the huge main gate of the palace creaked open before them, drawn back by squads of soldiers on either side. Paramessu drew his chariot to one side and allowed the King to enter first, then followed him through the gate. They clattered through a familiar passageway, then drew to a halt in an inner courtyard. As grooms rushed forward to take the reins of their horses, Paramessu jumped to the ground and turned to help the King down.

Akhenaten strode imperiously into the great audience chamber, where many of his lesser wives and courtiers were assembled to greet them. He went directly to his beautiful carved and gilded throne, barely acknowledging the obeisance of his courtiers on every side. He took his seat on the throne, accepting a cup of wine offered by his royal cupbearer as he did. Quickly draining it, he looked about him and asked,

"Where's the Queen? Where is Queen Nefertiti? Why isn't she here to greet me?"

Vizier Aye spoke up.

"Sire, the child...she..."

"The child? Has the child been born?" the King asked, impatiently.

"Yes, Your Majesty. The Queen was delivered of a healthy baby girl three days ago. She said that you had agreed to call the child Ankhsenpaaten."

"Yes, yes – that is so. But the Queen – how fares the Queen? Is she all right? Why is she not here?"

Vizier Aye continued. "She is fine, Your Majesty, but still a bit weak from childbirth. As to why she is not here, well, she is at the house of the artist Thutmose, being tended by his wife."

"Why in the world is she at the artist's house?" asked the King, puzzled.

"Well, you see, Your Majesty, the Queen had gone out riding on the plain three days ago with her guard, when she suddenly went into labor. When the party sought to return to the palace, umm, well, the streets were full of rioters. Since it would have been unsafe to try to bring her through their midst, the artist offered his house, which lies near the Sunrise Gate. She was taken there and placed in the care of the artist's wife, a skilled midwife. There she was safely delivered of the babe, and mother and child are still there, doing well. The royal physicians suggested that she remain there until tomorrow, when it should be safe to bring her and the baby back to the palace."

"Safe? Are the streets still hazardous?" asked the King.

"Oh, heavens, no, Your Majesty!" Aye hastened to say. "The streets have been quiet for the last two days. No, I meant only that the Queen's health and that of the child should permit them to be moved by tomorrow."

"Ah! I see," said Pharaoh, apparently mollified. He reached over and took a bunch of grapes from a tray offered him by a servant. "Well, after I have rested and bathed, I shall visit the Queen at the artist's house. Send to let her know I am coming."

"Yes, Your Majesty," responded Aye. He turned to a scribe and dictated a short note to the Queen, then sent a messenger off to deliver it.

Just then, the great doors opened to admit the Dowager Queen Tiye's steward, who conferred briefly with the Chamberlain, who then anounced:

"Her Majesty, the Queen Mother Tiye!"

Tiye swept into the room, followed by her retinue. Her normally trim figure was distorted by the swelling of a clearly advanced pregnancy, the penultimate bequest of her late husband, Amenhotep III. The young king himself rose to greet her, offering his hand to help her up the steps of the dais, then embracing her warmly.

"Mother! It's so good to see you. How are you?" he said, kissing her cheek.

"Large!" she said, with a rueful chuckle. "I'm getting a bit old for this childbearing business. Now that your father's gone, this should be the last one. Other than that, I'm quite well, thank you. It's nice to see you, too, my son. Did you find a site for your city?"

"I did. I found a splendid site, never before occupied or dedicated to any other god. Just as my dream promised, it sits right in the center of Egypt, halfway between the sea to the north and the fourth cataract to the south. I recognized it the instant I laid eyes on it, a great semicircular plain on the east bank of the Nile, surrounded by cliffs. And there, in the center of the cliffs, was the notch through which the sun rises, just as in my dream!"

Pharaoh's face shone as he described the site.

"That's wonderful, my son!" Tiye congratulated him. "How soon will you start building?"

"As soon as possible," he replied. "The lessons learned in building the new palace and the Gem Pa'aten temple will stand me in good stead. I have already laid out the boundaries of my new city – which I shall call Akhetaten – and ordered stelae to be set up to mark them. All the buildings shall be erected of brick or talatat blocks, so the work should go quickly. I want to move there as soon as possible, even if I have to live in a tent for a while!"

"A tent!" Tiye exclaimed. "Well, you're young. You can stand a few hardships. If you don't mind, though, I think I'll wait until there are some solid walls and a real roof to shelter me before I join you there – especially with this last baby coming."

"Of course, Mother. I understand," he agreed. "How much longer do you think it will be until the baby arrives?"

"It shouldn't be long now," she replied, "maybe two or three more weeks. I've had enough babies to be a pretty good judge of these things. And speaking of babies, I am told you have a new daughter. I haven't seen her yet. Did the doctors say when Nefertiti and the babe are coming back to the palace?"

"Tomorrow, they tell me. I am going to see them at the artist's house as soon as I have eaten and washed off the dirt of travel," he said.

"Ah! Very good," she agreed. "I told Nefertiti she shouldn't leave the palace this late in her pregnancy. Damn fool thing to do, gallivanting around in her chariot when she was due any minute! She's lucky she didn't deliver the child in some peasant's field! It's a good thing young Thutmose's house was nearby, and his wife skilled in midwifery!"

"I guess it's fortunate we gave them that house," Pharaoh observed.

"Yes, it is," his mother agreed.

A couple of hours later, Akhenaten paid a visit to the house of the artist Thutmose, to visit his Great Wife and new daughter. From the moment the messenger had arrived, Mariamne had been frantically cleaning the house and preparing food, aided by several neighbors. Having the Queen as an unexpected guest had been quite exciting, but now, having the King himself pay a visit to her house was the high point of Mariamne's life. She was so excited, and so desperate to have everything perfect for the royal visit, Thutmose feared she would suffer an apoplexy. He kept assuring her that the house was fine and that the King was not going to check to make sure she had dusted everything. He finally forced her to sit down and drink a cup of wine.

In the actual event, the visit went smoothly. Pharaoh graciously accepted a chalice of wine and nibbled on some of the delicacies Mariamne had prepared, praised her cooking and thanked her profusely for her care of his wife and child. Mariamne positively glowed.

He visited Nefertiti, still abed under doctor's orders, kissed her, and happily cuddled the new baby. He seemed genuinely delighted with his new daughter, the third girl in a row, not the least bit disappointed that the child was not a boy. Everyone agreed that this Pharaoh was a real family man, one who truly loved his wife and enjoyed his children, and was happy to let the whole world know it. He was nothing like the formal, cold, distant rulers of the past. Mariamne thought it was very endearing to see the richest, most powerful ruler in the world kissing his wife and cuddling his child like any ordinary man.

Thutmose, on the other hand, felt like an outsider looking in on a scene he could never be part of. He was relieved when Pharaoh turned to him in the courtyard before leaving and told him about the site he had found for his new city.

"I want it built quickly," Pharaoh told him. "And I want you to build it."

"Me?" asked Thutmose, surprised.

"Yes," Pharaoh told him. "I'm making you my new Chief of Works. I want you to get started right away. My surveyors have brought back detailed maps of the terrain, so you can start laying out the town even before you visit the site."

"Yes, Your Majesty," Thutmose agreed, bowing low. "Thank you for your confidence in me. I will do my best to be worthy of it."

"I know you will," said the King, turning to leave.

However, when the happy family man returned to the palace, he "accidentally" encountered the Mitanni princess, Kiya, in the courtyard leading to his private apartments. After his long journey, and given the unavailability of the Queen, the young Pharaoh was unusually susceptible to the charms of the foreign princess. Thutmose, who had returned to the palace with his royal master, witnessed the encounter, which he later recounted to Bek.

"It's amazing how she just *happened* to be there," he said sourly. "The woman has a remarkably efficient network of spies all over the palace."

"Or possibly a house servant keeping company with a stable hand," commented Bek. "They could alert her the moment Pharaoh's chariot appeared."

"Well, however she did it, she managed the catch him at the right time. You should have heard her. Nard[1] wouldn't melt in her mouth! The woman is a serpent, devious and dangerous as an asp!"

"So she snared his company?" Bek asked.

"Aye, she did," Thutmose acknowledged. "They went off to his quarters together, where I saw her again the following morning. At least she had the wisdom to clear out before the Queen returned."

However, Kiya did manage to postpone her exit until just before the Queen's return, so that the two royal wives met in the King's courtyard, right where Kiya had met the King the previous day. It was painfully apparent to Nefertiti just where her rival was returning from.

Seeing Nefertiti, Kiya swept her an exaggerated bow and said with a blatantly false smile, "Your Majesty – congratulations on the

---

[1] Semi-solid cones of scented fat, usually worn on top of the head, which melt and run down, perfuming the wearer.

birth of your new child. Another girl, I hear – I believe that makes three now?"

As she knew it would, Kiya's remark hit on Nefertiti's greatest sore spot, her inability, so far, to produce a male heir to the throne. The Queen forced herself to smile back.

"Yes," she commented, "another Heiress to the throne," a reminder to the foreign princess that it was through the Egyptian royal daughters – who, unlike foreigners, *never* married abroad – that legitimate claim to the throne was passed from one generation to the next.

Ipy, on his way to answers a summons from his master, Thutmose, witnessed this interchange, which he later recounted to his master.

As it happened, Thutmose had summoned the lad to assist him in his latest assignment from Pharaoh, a commission to create a series of portrait busts, paintings and statues of Princess Kiya. Since Thutmose not only disliked the foreign princess, but also had his hands full with designing the King's new city, it was reasonable that his favored protégé should assume the lead on this new assignment. It turned out, however, that there was an added benefit to Ipy's involvement.

After Thutmose, Ipy and several of the more advanced students had spent the morning sketching the princess, Thutmose reviewed their sketches and decided which of them should be the basis for busts and full-length statues to be carved of stone. Throughout their session with the princess, she had repeatedly turned her most seductive wiles on Thutmose, unable to accept that any man might be immune to her charms. Having failed in repeated attempts, she dismissed the artists in an obvious fit of pique, which Thutmose thoroughly enjoyed. He was reminded of Lord Yuya's tale and very glad he had followed the wise old man's advice, which he decided to pass on to his own protégé.

"Ipy, my boy," he said, "I'm turning most of this assignment over to you. It's a great responsibility, and a great opportunity – however, it comes with a warning. Do not trust that woman, and above all, do not fall for her seductive wiles. That could cost you your life. I give you the advice a very wise old man gave me: always take a group of students with you when she is to pose for you."

"Thank you, Master, for both the opportunity and the advice. I had wondered how I could protect myself from her. It is obvious she thinks herself irresistible and does not hesitate to turn her charms on any man," Ipy replied. "I was not sure whether I was authorized to take other apprentices with me."

"Absolutely," Thutmose affirmed. "If she objects, point out that we consider her portraits to be of so much importance that we wanted to assign as much manpower as possible to the project."

"And if she objects that she expected you, yourself, to be her portraitist?" the boy asked.

"Remind her that the King has now appointed me Chief of Works and that I have my hands full with his dearest project, designing his new city," Thutmose replied.

"Very good, sir," Ipy acknowledged.

"I only wish I knew what the witch was up to," observed Thutmose ruefully. "I wish I had someone I could assign who knows her barbarous language. Too bad we haven't any Mitanni students in the school."

"I think I can be of some help there, Sir," Ipy commented. "As it happens, I speak some Hurrian."

Thutmose looked at him, eyes wide in astonishment. "**You** speak Hurrian? How did that happen?"

"Well, sir," said the boy, "after my father died, my mother took up with a Mitanni trader named Jubrael who lived in town during the breaks between caravan trips. We lived with him and his sister Rahab for several years, and I picked the language up from listening to Jubrael and Rahab talk.

"After my mother died, Rahab married a former Mitanni trader who had been lamed when a camel kicked him. He couldn't get around well enough to travel any more, so he'd opened a shop in town selling the goods his brother-in-law imported. But Jubrael the trader never came back from his next caravan and I was soon kicked out of his house.

"I appealed to Rahab, and she and her husband took me in for a while, so I continued to hear Hurrian spoken. But they treated me badly – beat me and kept me on short rations. When Jubrael didn't return, Shemshak – the brother-in-law – soon ran out of imported wares to sell, so he set me to stealing goods from other store keepers around town. It didn't take me long to figure out that I could do that better on my own – and that way, I could insist that Shemshak pay me something reasonable for the goods I brought him. So I started living on the streets and stealing for a living."

"And thus began your life of crime," commented Thutmose, shaking his head.

"Until you caught me, Master," Ipy observed.

"Well, maybe your devious ways can stand us in good stead again. Pay close attention to what the foreign princess and her women talk about, but be careful not to let them know you can understand them."

"Oh, I am very good at that, Master! I never let even Shemshak know I spoke Hurrian!" he said with a grin. "It's amazing what people will say when they don't believe you can understand them!"

The Queen Dowager's baby, another girl, was born a couple of weeks after Nefertiti's return to the palace. The senior Queen named her new daughter Beketaten. It was quickly apparent that she felt a particularly close bond with this posthumous child of her late husband, who she had loved deeply and now greatly mourned. This child was to be the boon companion of the Dowager's remaining years, a substitute for the husband she so sorely missed.

Over the next several weeks, Ipy and his flock of aspiring younger artists danced attendance on Princess Kiya and her entourage. Kiya and her attendants soon took them for granted and chattered freely in their presence. She complained of Thutmose's absence, annoyed that something else merited his attention more than she did, but her annoyance was somewhat mollified by Ipy's fine (and flattering) sketches. Ham that he was, he played the role of sycophant to the hilt, yet adroitly kept the seductive princess at arms' length. Employing his straightest face, he never let slip his understanding of her language.

Every evening, he reported back to Thutmose and Bek the gist of what he had overheard. He heard Kiya's many plans to snare the King's affection and lure him away from Nefertiti, hoping even to displace her as Great Wife. Forewarned, Thutmose, Ipy and Bek were often able to thwart her plots by engaging the King elsewhere before she could get to him. With plans for the new city to discuss, this was seldom difficult to do.

By then, Thutmose had drawn up an overall plan for Akhetaten ("Horizon of the Aten"), with a broad processional way running the length of the city, parallel to the Nile, providing the King and Queen a perfect chariot raceway to indulge their love of speed. The city would be studded with palaces and temples, like a diadem with jewels. An immense central temple would rise near the river, next to a grand palace, its two parts joined by a bridge over the processional way, featuring a Window of Appearances over the roadway. Administrative buildings behind the palace called the King's House, to the east of the great processional way, would house the small army of clerks that served the King and provide storage for official correspondence, copies of every document housed in Thebes and Memphis. Additional palaces for various members of the royal family would be added over time, as well as private villas for the wealthy. The workmen who were already beginning to build the new capital were to be housed in a separate village located in a valley in the hills southeast of the city.

Tombs would be built in the cliffs surrounding the city, with that of Pharaoh built in a cliff above the wadi that formed the eastern notch through which the rising sun appeared. Thus, the holy Aten, the sun disk itself, would be seen to rise out of the tomb of the King. On the plan of the city, Thutmose showed Pharaoh how lines drawn from the tomb would run through the temple, palace and other major buildings on the east bank like the rays of the sun. Where each of these "rays" terminated at the cliffs on the west bank of the river, Akhenaten decreed that stelae should be carved into the cliff faces, marking the boundaries of his new capital city.

Pharaoh was delighted with the emerging plan and authorized Thutmose to proceed with building it, posthaste.

So, for the next several years, I spent much of my time at Akhetaten, building Pharaoh's new capital city, travelling back to Thebes every month or so to report on its progress. I only saw the Queen briefly during these visits and had little time to spend with my wife. These visits were sufficient, however, for her to conceive a child. Just as I finished the first residence for the royal family, I received word that Mariamne had given birth to a son. We had previously discussed names for children; as we had agreed, she named him Senmut, my private tribute to the great architect who had served (and loved) Queen Hatshepsut, who had ruled as Pharaoh in her own right 150 years earlier. What no one realized was that my choice of name for my firstborn was as much in honor of the great architect's relationship with his Queen as for his artistic talent.

Chapter 26: Sisters in Sorrow

As soon as the King received word that the first, temporary royal residence was ready for occupancy, he began the lengthy process of moving the royal family and administrative officials to the new capital. He, himself, was the first to move, accompanied by the Grand Vizier, Aye, and a few of the most essential officers of the court and their staffs. They were soon followed by Queen Nefertiti and her daughters, of whom there were now four. Other nobles of the court made the move as their private villas were completed.

At first, conditions were cramped and a bit primitive, with many officials living in tents like nomads of the desert. But this soon improved, as palaces, temples, gardens, marketplaces, offices and villas were completed. By now, Thutmose commanded a sizable army of laborers. Some of them were permanent, full-time bricklayers, stonemasons, tile layers, painters and other professional builders and decorators. A much larger contingent, however, were seasonal workers, paying their taxes to the crown as their pyramid-building ancestors had, by building public works during periods when they were not needed at home, tilling, planting or harvesting the fields.

Over the next several years, the east bank of the once-empty bowl straddling the river sprouted an exquisite, well-planned city, while irrigation ditches turned the fertile plain on the west bank green with crops to feed the new city. The city's population grew rapidly, with a steady stream of nobles, bureaucrats, clerks, merchants, servants and a small army of newly-sanctified Aten priests arriving daily.

Soon, the Great Temple was completed, an enormous edifice right on the river. Shortly thereafter, Pharaoh and his family were able to move into the Great Palace, a magnificent complex with beautifully tiled floors and walls painted with scenes of gardens, rivers and marshes filled with flowers, birds, fish and other wildlife. There were numerous lovely courtyards with pools of cool, running water, rimmed with low walls to help keep little ones from falling in and to provide pleasant seating for adults. The palaces and private villas were cleverly designed to channel cool air through, making them delightful, cool oases in this hot desert land.

With the major buildings completed or well along, under the supervision of competent overseers, Thutmose was once more able to devote his time to art, creating new sculptures, reliefs and murals to adorn the fine new palaces. Increasingly, his relaxed, natural, "realistic" style came to be favored over both the stilted old styles and Bek's more distorted, stylized images that had been favored earlier in Akhenaten's reign. Indeed, Thutmose's star was riding high, with his artwork the height of fashion and his position as Chief of Works making him one of the most powerful men in the kingdom.

He had been so busy, he had had little time to build a villa for himself, although a prime site near the river had been allotted for it from the very outset. He had, of course, built a workshop on the site, since that was essential to the work of constructing, decorating and furnishing Pharaoh's new city. He had quickly established a corps of artists there, busy creating statuary, furniture and other decorative items for Pharaoh's new temples and palaces. He had created models of statues of the royal family, to be replicated by a kind of artistic assembly line and distributed throughout the kingdom, as well as throughout the new capital city. His workshop was lined with shelves and cupboards filled with plaster casts of various parts of statuary to be copied and assembled into complete statues by his subordinates. There were artists who specialized in hands, or legs, or torsos, while Thutmose himself and his most skilled assistants completed the faces of the royal family. It was a highly organized, efficient factory, cranking out exquisite works of art at an astonishing pace. Indeed, the entire city could be viewed as one vast, integrated work of art, all created by the mind and hand of Thutmose. It was no wonder Pharaoh was pleased, and rewarded his Chief of Works generously.

Using lessons learned from building the Gem Pa'aten temple and Pharaoh's palace in Thebes, the building of an entire new city progressed with amazing speed. Started in Year 5 of Akhenaten's reign, by the end of Year 6, both Pharaoh and his key officials were already in residence, with the court and administrative departments fully functional. By the middle of Year 7, the entire city was functional, from the lowest peasant laboring in the west bank fields, to the merchant plying his trade in the new bazaar, to the priests manning the many new temples and the nobles thronging the colorful courts of the new palaces, all with their own splendid new villas. The entire royal family was in residence, with the exception of Queen Tiye, who had chosen to remain in Malkata Palace, her familiar home in Thebes, and several of Pharaoh's sisters.

Akhenaten's eldest sister, Sitamun, and second sister, Isis, had retired to their estates in the delta after the death of the old Pharaoh, to whom they had both been married. As was common for royal women, they had both joined the Godswives of Amun, the female Adoratrices of the Theban deity, with Sitamun designated to the position of Great Wife of Amun. However, since Akhenaten had outlawed the worship of Amun after its priests had attempted to assassinate him, the cult of the Godswives was left in limbo. Since many of the women had donated all of their property to the organization when they had joined, many of them now had no place to go. While it might eventually be possible for them to recover their property, clarification of its legal status through the courts was likely to take a long time. And while the Godswives were technically part of the worship of Amun, they were obviously innocent of any involvement in the assassination attempt, so Pharaoh chose to simply ignore them. This being the case, most of them chose to remain quietly in their enclave in Thebes or on the order's estates. Sitamun and Isis had settled for quietly running their respective estates, raising flax and grapes for the royal household. By tradition, the royal women had a monopoly on the production of royal linen, the highly prized, ultrafine fabric woven from the long staple core taken from the stems of the specially bred flax grown on their estates in the delta. The abundant supply of water made possible several crops a year of both grapes and flax, so the royal female flax monopoly was a very valuable franchise.

One day shortly before the beginning of the Inundation, the blowing of horns heralded the arrival of an important dignitary. Akhenaten and Nefertiti, holding court in the Audience Chamber of their splendid new palace, looked expectantly toward the Lord Chamberlain, who hurried to the door to greet a herald who had just arrived, breathless in his haste to anounce the new arrival. The Chamberlain hurried to whisper the anouncement in His Majesty's ear.

"Your sister, the Divine Consort Sitamun, is here, Your Majesty," he said.

Smiling, Akhenaten repeated the message to Nefertiti. He had scarce finished when Sitamun's party appeared at the door, heralded with appropriate fanfare.

"Hear ye, hear ye! Make way for the King's Daughter, Royal Consort and Great Wife of A...," cried the Chamberlain, almost forgetting the proscription against mentioning the name of the deity, Amun. He hastily amended it to simply, "the Great Godswife, Sitamun!"

Sitamun swept through the great gilded, bronze-clad doors, trailing diaphanous linen draperies and a cloud of costly scent, and paused dramatically just inside the entrance. She put on a bold front and made a brave show so that none of the courtiers might realize with what trepidation she, the official representative of a forbidden deity, faced her royal brother, the ruler who had proscribed her god.

But to her vast relief, Akhenaten himself rose from his throne, arms outstretched in welcome, quickly followed by his queen.

"Sitamun! Beloved sister! We have missed you. It is so long since we have seen you," cried the King. "Come – sit by us!"

Sitamun fairly flew up the aisle flanked by bowing courtiers, stopping only to kneel at her brother's feet. He pulled her up and embraced her heartily, clearly delighted to see her. Nefertiti hugged her with equal warmth.

"Sitamun!" she cried. "Dearest cousin and royal sister! It is so wonderful to see you again!"

By then, servants had moved an elegant, cushioned chair to a place just behind and between Akhenaten's and Nefertiti's chairs. Sitamun happily took her place there, while servants brought her cool water to bathe her hands and face and a cup of cool wine. As she dried her hands on a fine linen cloth (probably a product of her own royal workshop), Akhenaten instructed his steward to see to the disposition of the princess's retinue, then quickly concluded his official business for the day.

"We shall resume court tomorrow morning. Hold your petitions until then. That is all!" he anounced.

Akhenaten and Nefertiti rose, accompanied by Sitamun. Pharaoh indicated that she should follow them, and the courtiers knelt, heads to the floor, while the three of them exited through a private door behind the dais. The Royal Steward joined them, waiting for his master's further orders.

"Steward – have a luncheon served in our private courtyard," Akhenaten instructed him.

Pharaoh himself led his sister to the royal family's private apartments, proudly pointing out the features of his fine new palace. Sitamun duly admired the elegant design, with its open, airy spaces cleverly channeling cool air, the beautiful frescoed walls and tiled floors, with their lifelike images of flowers, birds and wildlife, and the sparkling, refreshing pools of water gracing open courtyards.

"Oh, Brother, it is beautiful! Your architects and artists have outdone themselves," she exclaimed.

"I owe it all to the creative mind of one man, my Chief of Works, Lord Thutmose," Akhenaten declared. "And, lo, here is the man himself," he remarked, as Thutmose was anounced by the Steward.

Thutmose made his obeisance to the royal party.

"Thutmose!" cried Akhenaten, clapping him on the back, "You remember my sister, Sitamun, don't you?"

"Of course," agreed Thutmose, bowing low to the princess. "How could I possibly forget the lovely Princess Sitamun, Daughter and Royal Consort of His Majesty, Amenhotep, may he be justified!"

"Master Thutmose," she acknowledged. "I believe you did my portrait bust years ago."

"So I did, Your Highness – but that was a long time ago. Clearly, I should do another one. You were but a young girl then – now you are a beautiful woman," he observed.

"Indeed," agreed Akhenaten, "that is an excellent idea. See that it is done, Thutmose."

"It will be my pleasure," acknowledged the artist, bowing again to Pharaoh.

"Now, let us have lunch," ordered Akhenaten, seating himself in a comfortable chair. A servant placed a low, cushioned stool beneath the royal feet.

Nefertiti and Sitamun were seated nearby in similar chairs, with footstools for their feet, as well. A procession of servants brought platters of fruit, bread and meats, flagons of wine and beer, which were set on small individual tables beside each of the diners. The Royal Cupbearer tasted each flagon of beer and wine, then poured a cupful for each of the royal diners.

Thutmose was seated cross-legged on the ground nearby, as was his wont, surrounded by piles of papyrus rolls, his artist's palette and brushes and numerous small pots of pigments, ink and water. A servant set platters of food and a cup of beer on the floor near him. Only a valued follower of high rank was allowed to eat in the royal presence like this, a sure sign of the King's favor toward his Chief of Works. As the royal party dined and reminisced together, Thutmose sketched them, commemorating the King's reunion with his sister.

Sitamun was greatly relieved and genuinely happy at being so warmly received by the royal brother she had not seen in several years. And she had forgotten how much she enjoyed Nefertiti's company. She and the Queen were the closest in age and rank of the royal women, and well matched in temperament. It was not long before they had re-established old bonds and began to forge new ones. They quickly became boon companions and mutual confidants, able to trust in each other as in no one else.

One day, after Akhenaten and Nefertiti had taken Sitamun on a whirlwind chariot tour of their new city, Nefertiti and Sitamun repaired to the Queen's private sitting room, which had a balcony with a magnificent view of the river. As they enjoyed the view and sipped cool wine sweetened with honey, they chatted together like old friends.

"So, what do you think of our city?" asked Nefertiti.

"Magnificent, absolutely magnificent. It's amazing what you have accomplished here in such a short time," commented Sitamun. "However, I think I might prefer my tour at a little slower speed," she continued. "It's all such a blur, going by at a gallop like that! You two move at a much faster pace than I'm used to. I don't know how you do it!"

"We do like speed, both of us," Nefertiti admitted. "Akhenaten got me used to it, and now I love driving fast. I like the feel of the wind rushing by, and the sensation of controlling two big, powerful animals. I adore the freedom of being able to drive my own chariot."

"Well, you're a braver woman than I am, Nefer. I would sooner have some nice, strong, competent man take charge of those horses."

"You'll get used to it," Nefertiti assured her. "You'll see – you'll develop a taste for it. We'll make a chariot driver out of you, yet, dear sister."

Just then, a nursemaid brought in Nefertiti's youngest daughter, Meritaten-Tasherit (Meritaten the Younger), a toddler just beginning to walk. In her wake, the three older princesses bounded into the room, followed by their respective nurses. Meritaten, the eldest, carried a kitten, which the younger girls clamored to play with.

Nefertiti took the baby from her nursemaid and set her on her lap. The little girl promptly took hold of the lapis and turquoise beads dangling from her mother's jeweled collar and began putting them in her mouth. Nefertiti firmly removed the beads from her daughter's mouth, giving her a piece of fruit, instead.

Sitamun wistfully watched this exhibition of maternal affection, and glanced over to where the three older girls were playing with the kitten, coaxing it to follow a piece of string. She looked back at Nefertiti, who was now bouncing the baby on her knee. It was clear Nefertiti was beginning to tire, and that the knee was likely to wear out before the baby did.

"Here, let me hold her," said Sitamun, holding out her arms for the child.

Nefertiti happily turned the baby over to her aunt, who bounced her up and down enthusiastically. Eventually, the child wore out and fell asleep in Sitamun's arms.

"You like children, don't you?" observed Nefertiti, watching Sitamun contentedly cuddling the baby.

"Yes, I do," sighed Sitamun. "And I'm not ever likely to have any of my own. As a King's Daughter and former Royal Consort, there's nobody of my own rank I can marry in Egypt, even supposing the King would let me. And as a Godswife of Amun – even though Amun is proscribed – I'm not supposed to marry. So, that leaves me pretty much an untouchable old maid. And no children."

"But, as a Godswife, can't you adopt children? I thought that was how Godswives chose a successor, was by adopting them."

NEFERTITI, IMMORTAL QUEEN

"Yes," replied Sitamun, "but we usually adopt only daughters, and the girls are usually grown up, or nearly so, so they aren't really *children* – not small children, at any rate."

"But surely you *could* adopt a small child, a baby, even. There isn't anything to stop you, is there?" Nefertiti asked.

Sitamun thought about this for a moment. "No, I guess there isn't, nothing I know of, anyway. The whole business is simply a tradition – there aren't any specific, formal rules about it, and certainly nothing written down."

"For that matter," continued Nefertiti, "is there anything to prevent you from adopting boy children?"

"No-o," replied Sitamun, thoughtfully, "I suppose there isn't. It's just that it's usually done to provide for a successor, who obviously has to be female to be a Godswife. But once that's taken care of, I suppose there isn't any real reason why a Godswife couldn't adopt additional children, and why they couldn't be small children or infants, providing the order was willing to support them."

"Well, in your case, that surely shouldn't be a problem," observed Nefertiti.

"No, I suppose not. I don't know about adopting boys, though. There aren't supposed to be any men in the enclaves of the Godswives."

"But you're not living there at present, anyway," Nefertiti pointed out. "You've already told me you're living on your own estate. And that's a royal property, not the property of the order. Surely you have men there, carrying out all the normal functions of a large estate."

"Of course," agreed Sitamun. "I have dozens, maybe even hundreds, of men there: field hands, cattle drovers, craftsmen, house servants – and of course…" she hesitated, "my Steward, Senmut."

Nefertiti noted the hesitation, thinking it odd. She glanced at her sister in law and was surprised to see that her cheeks seemed unusually rosy. "Interesting," she thought to herself.

"Still," Sitamun continued, shifting the topic, "you are so very, very fortunate, Nefertiti. You have a wonderful family. Your husband adores you – even more than our father adored our mother, and I would not have thought that possible. And you have four beautiful daughters, who you are clearly very close to. You're living in this beautiful new palace, in your fine new city, with your fine chariot and your fast horses – and you have more power and influence than any queen since Hatshepsut. What more could any woman want?"

"Well, there are a couple of things," Nefertiti replied. "A son, for one. A royal heir to the throne. And there is one other fly in the ointment…"

"Oh? What's that?" Sitamun asked.

"The foreign woman, Tadukhipa – 'The Favorite', as she styles herself now."

"Kiya? Is she making trouble?" asked Sitamun.

"She **is** trouble," commented Nefertiti wryly. "She's managed to worm her way into Akhenaten's good graces – and his bedchamber. She's the one real snake in the garden of Akhetaten. And now, to top it all off, I'm told that she's pregnant."

"Well, it may be an annoyance, but such things are to be expected in a royal harem. A king is expected to have many wives, to reflect his position and insure the succession," Sitamun observed with a shrug. "I don't think it has diminished his love for you one bit. And she will never, ever be Great Wife, no matter what she does."

"Yes, but what if her child is a son?" asked Nefertiti. "If she produces a son, and I don't, her son will be heir. And she will be…unbearable."

"That would be a problem," conceded Sitamun. "But even so, I think your position is secure. Not only does Akhenaten adore you, he has built you so thoroughly into his new religion, you are practically a goddess in your own right. I don't think any foreigner could ever undo that."

"No, I suppose not," conceded Nefertiti.

"If she does have a boy, you'll just have to take charge of his upbringing," Sitamun advised. "Make sure he grows up regarding you as his true mother. While she may have given him life, you can determine what kind of life it is. She may have his body, but see to it that you have his heart."

"Yes," agreed Nefertiti, "that is wise."

"That's right," said Sitamun, with a rueful laugh. "You just listen to your wise Auntie Sitamun, who knows so much about raising children! – And about winning men's hearts!"

"Ah, Sitamun, dear royal sister! You would make such a good mother – and a good wife. It's a shame you are denied these things!" exclaimed Nefertiti.

"Well, I shall consider your advice about adopting children," said Sitamun, a bit sadly. "I can at least be a good mother that way, if not a wife. I have to confess that I envy you the joy of having a loving and protective husband, who can keep you from loneliness and keep you safe within his strong arms."

"It is true that Akhenaten loves me, and is a good companion and wonderful father – but I'm not so sure about the strong arms," commented Nefertiti. "His health is not the best. He's never been strong, you know. I worry about him. Sometimes he has difficulty breathing, especially after the Inundation, when there are growing things all about. He was never very athletic as a child – that's why he's avoided the traditional warlike exercises of a king."

"That's true," agreed Sitamun. "He always suffered by comparison to our older brother. Thutmosis was a natural athlete – poor Amenhotep never could keep up. And I remember his bouts of breathlessness. It's been a problem since he was little. I didn't realize he still suffered from it, though."

"He hides it as best he can," said Nefertiti. "The people need to see their king as a strong defender of the realm and upholder of *ma'at*. But sometimes, it costs him a terrible effort to do it. At times, I fear for his life. That is why I have been taking a more and more active role in governing the country. Some people think I'm ambitious, but that's not it. If I can take some of the burden off him, he can get more rest and preserve his health – and no one will see his weakness."

"Ah, so that's why you've been emulating our reviled ancestress, Hatshepsut!" observed Sitamun. "When I first began to hear stories about your growing exercise of power, I was puzzled: knowing you, it seemed out of character. You were always such a quiet child, even rather shy. It just didn't seem like you to be taking over the Pharaoh's regalia and rituals. And when I saw the murals of you smiting the enemy – well, I have to admit, I was dumbfounded."

"Now you know," said Nefertiti. "It is not ambition. It has not come easily. In my heart, I'm still that rather shy, quiet girl. I only wish my husband were a stronger man and could handle all the traditional duties of a king, with only the traditional support from me. But I'm afraid that it would kill him. And then where would we all be?"

"In chaos," replied Sitamun with a shudder. "Ma'at would crumble; Egypt would be in shambles; and our enemies would swarm in on us. No, you are right, my sister. You must do the best you can to support your husband, and the throne, to keep both him and Egypt safe."

Sitamun got up and moved to Nefertiti's side. She put her arms around the queen and held her, like a mother comforting her child.

"I will keep your secret," Sitamun assured her, kneeling beside her chair. "I don't know what I can do to help, but if ever there is anything you need from me, you have only to let me know."

"Thank you, dearest sister," Nefertiti replied, with tears in her eyes. "You have helped me already, more than you know. There has been no one else I could confide in. It helps to be able to talk to someone about it. Bearing it alone has been the worst part."

"Is there no one in your immediate circle you could trust?" asked Sitamun. "No one you could turn to in an emergency?"

"Well, there is one man I would trust my life to, one who has already saved it several times: the artist, Thutmose."

"Isn't he the one who saved you from the crocodile?" Sitamun asked.

"The very same," Nefertiti agreed. "And he and his apprentice saved Akhenaten and me from assassination by those renegade priests. But I mustn't place too much reliance on him – people would think it strange. They would take it wrong, if the queen got too close to any man."

Sitamun looked at her closely.

"Yes, no doubt they would," she agreed. "Especially a man as handsome as that one. I suspect it could be very hard, being close to him – yet not too close," she commented shrewdly.

Nefertiti looked away and replied softly, "Yes, it is – that is, it could be."

"Ah, so that's how it is," said Sitamun. "I suspected as much. I saw how you glanced at him when you thought no one was looking – and how you avoided looking at him at times when it would be normal to do so. Well, I can't say that I blame you. I could hardly keep my own eyes off him. He's a very fine figure of a man!"

"Sitamun!" exclaimed Nefertiti. "I thought you Godswives were supposed to be virginal!"

"I may not be allowed to touch, but I'll be damned if I'm going to allow anyone to tell me I can't look!" Sitamun exclaimed. "Besides, I can't even be a Godswife these days, with my divine 'husband' outlawed! I can see that you know only too well that even a royal princess, or a queen, can hunger for a little passion in her life!"

"I fear you are right," conceded Nefertiti. "I am so fortunate. I know that I am blessed, and I should just be thankful for all that Aten has given me. But something deep within me cries out, 'Is this all there is?' I have a good and loving husband, and he is very dear to me. I should be more than satisfied. Yet, there is a hunger deep inside me that I cannot deny, a longing for a kind of passion I have never known. I struggle with it every day, and wrestle with it, wakefully, every night. I know that this is wrong, and I must resist it with every fiber of my being. I must not betray my husband, my king, my country – yet I cannot help feeling what I feel."

"Ah, my poor dear sister!" said Sitamun, wiping Nefertiti's tears away with a fold of her gown. "I do know how it is. Believe me, I know what you are going through, better than you know!"

"Sitamun! You, too?" Nefertiti cried.

"I'm afraid so," replied Sitamun wryly. "Royal wife or not, Godswife or not, I'm afraid I wasn't cut out for the pious and passionless life. I had no choice in the matter of marriage, no more than you did. We may have rank and wealth and a certain amount of power, we royal women, but we have less freedom in the matter of love than the lowest peasant woman toiling in the fields. Yet, we are every bit as human as they are, and every bit as much in need of love! Why should we be denied it, especially when we have already done our duty and served our royal purpose? I have already outlived one royal husband and been denied one divine one – why should I not find love where I can?"

"I see no reason why you shouldn't," agreed Nefertiti. "Who is – no, I shouldn't ask."

"That's all right – I trust you," said Sitamun. "He's my steward, Senmut."

"Ah, that's why Hatshepsut is so much on your mind!" exclaimed Nefertiti, referring to the great architect, Senmut, who had served Queen Hatshepsut, and who was widely suspected of having been her lover.

"True enough," agreed Sitamun.

"Well, don't worry," Nefertiti assured her, "your secret's safe with me. Just promise me you'll be very careful."

"I always have been," Sitamun replied. "But the same applies even more to you. Hopefully, others who do not know you as well as I do will not see what I have seen. But, dearest Nefer, please be very, very careful."

"I, too, have always been, and will continue to be, extremely careful. I have schooled my heart, and will continue to school my face. It is as well, for me, that royalty are expected to be stone-faced. Still, it is a relief for me that you know, that at least one person shares my secret."

"For me, as well," agreed Sitamun. "So, we shall be sisters in secrecy, sisters in love, as well as in blood."

"So we shall," agreed Nefertiti.

The two of them embraced and patted each other on the back, drawing comfort from their sisterhood of sorrow.

Chapter 27: Of Foreign Lands

It gladdened my heart to see friendship growing between the Lady Sitamun and my beloved queen. As closely as I had watched Nefertiti for years, I had seen how lonely she was, even in the midst of her doting family and adoring courtiers. She was isolated, both by her position as queen and by her own natural reserve. It was clear to me that she desperately needed a confidante – and much as I would have loved to be that person, I knew that could never be. So I was glad to see that she had at last found someone of her own class, age and gender who she could trust and to whom she could unburden herself. It was clear to me that she was much happier since Sitamun arrived.

It was also fortunate that Sitamun was there to cushion the shock of the next major event, the birth of Kiya's son. While it was a cause for rejoicing for Pharaoh and the Two Lands, it was a terrible blow for Nefertiti, for her rival to give birth to the royal heir. It was also bad news for the palace staff and many of the courtiers, as the foreign princess now became totally insufferable. She had always been demanding and overbearing, finding fault with everything, and spiteful toward those she deemed had failed her or crossed her. Now, power made her spite very dangerous.

The staff no longer dared to obstruct and frustrate her, for fear it might cost them their lives. Thus far, at least, Captain Paramessu and his soldiers continued to defend the Queen's privacy, but thus far, the foreign princess had made no further attempt to disrupt the private gatherings of the King's innermost family. Thutmose was not at all sure whether they would hold firm and withstand a direct frontal assault, should she attempt to do so. He hoped she would be content with all the attention the king now lavished on her and her child, whom he had named Tutankhaten – "Life Beloved of Aten".

Akhenaten, of course, was delighted with his new son and heir, and quickly agreed to Kiya's demand to make her title, "The Favorite", official. It would have to do, because even as the mother of the new heir, she still ranked below the queen, the Great Wife, Nefertiti. Nevertheless, Pharaoh was happy enough to indulge most of her other demands. He showered her with gifts: jewelry; clothes; a gilded chariot and fine horses; and her own splendid barge, carved, painted and gilded, with bright red sails and her personal pennant fluttering from the mast.

Thutmose thought the chariot and barge a huge waste of money, as Kiya had always preferred riding in a litter to jouncing along in a chariot – being borne on men's shoulders suited her. And she had complained bitterly of sea sickness every time she had to travel on the Nile. He had, however, forgotten her love of ostentation and her unending need to compete with Nefertiti. Kiya soon developed a habit of being rowed up and down the river in her splendid new boat, showing off her new possessions, the sure signs of her newly acquired power.

And once she was recovered from childbearing, she soon had Pharaoh back in her bed on frequent occasions. While it was clear to Thutmose that this still galled Nefertiti, he noticed that she seemed more resigned to it than in the past – it was almost as if she were a bit relieved. He attributed this to the influence of Sitamun, who appeared to have counseled her not to let the foreign woman upset her. However, he was at a loss to explain why the two of them seemed to look in his direction more often than expected. Had he committed some gaffe, done something to amuse them? He was beginning to feel a bit self-conscious.

After a while, however, Akhenaten's thrill at having a son began to wear off, as did his favor for Kiya. Before long, her demands began to grate on him, and he fled back to Nefertiti, she of the sweet voice and gentle hands of which he had written. Not for nothing had he engraved in stone his praise of her! He returned more and more often to the bosom of his original nuclear family with a feeling of relief and joy, of coming home after a sojourn in a hostile foreign land.

But Kiya was not to be put off so easily. She continued to nag and demand, until poor, patient, long-suffering Akhenaten couldn't stand it any more.

One day, Thutmose sat in the king's private study, conferring with him about the latest building projects, while Akhenaten paced furiously back and forth, like a caged lion.

"What troubles you, Your Majesty?" asked the artist.

"It's Kiya, of course," the king replied, "always Kiya. I don't know what to do about that woman. She has given me a son, the heir I needed, so I must honor her as the mother of the next king. But her endless demands are getting on my nerves. I don't think all the gold of Nubia would be enough to satisfy her. And I used to think her father wanted a lot of gold! Hah! His demands are nothing, next to hers! The woman is a bottomless pit!"

Thutmose was uncertain what to say. He so longed to say exactly what he and all the rest of the staff had always thought of the woman, but feared overstepping his bounds. After all, this was the King, and the foreign woman was still "The Favorite".

"I don't know what to do with her. I am beginning to suspect she has played me for a fool – a silly, male fool – all along, seducing me into thinking she really cared for me," he continued, still pacing.

"Well, Your Majesty," ventured Thutmose, "you would hardly be the first man who's been taken in by a seductive woman. I'm afraid you have lots of company there."

"Yes, but I'm the King," Akhenaten replied. "I have a whole harem of beautiful women, all of them vying to please me, the most beautiful of whom is my Great Wife. I should not get worked up or allow myself to be manipulated by one more woman, no matter how pretty or how seductive she may be!"

"Well, at least now you have seen through her, Your Majesty. That knowledge should help you to withstand the greatest of her wiles," Thutmose pointed out. "You are now that much wiser than before."

"True, true," Pharaoh conceded, somewhat mollified. "That does not bring me peace, however, or restore the tranquility of my home. How am I ever to do that, while still according her the respect due the mother of the heir?"

Thutmose pondered this a moment – then an idea came to him.

"I have a suggestion, Your Majesty," he said.

"Yes?" asked the King.

"Why not build her a palace of her own? There is a very nice plot in the northern part of the city, still unused. It is well situated, catches the prevailing breeze, and has magnificent views of the city. And it has the added advantage of being at some distance from the main palace, and Your Majesty's residence," he added slyly.

"A brilliant idea, Thutmose! I like it. I could both honor her publicly, and put her at a distance, all in one stroke!" cried the King. "By all means, do it! Start today! I shall announce the gift from the Window of Appearances tomorrow."

And so it was that the Northern Palace was built to "honor" Princess Kiya, the so-called "Favorite". The only down side was that I had to spend far more time in her company for a while than I cared for. But it put a definite limit on her access to the King and went a long way toward restoring domestic tranquility.

Meanwhile, the new Crown Prince, the cause of all the excitement, was not doing as well as his mother. He was not a very strong baby to begin with, and was afflicted with colic. The poor child cried and cried and cried, keeping his stable of caregivers up all night, taking turns walking the floor with him.

Princess Kiya was originally determined to keep him by her, intent on insuring that she, and only she, should be the dominant force in his life. She intended to make sure that her position was assured for life by enforcing her will on the child and insuring that he would always do her bidding. She felt that nothing less could possibly compensate her for having had to endure the wretchedness of pregnancy and the whole messy, painful, demeaning process of childbirth. But the baby's incessant crying quickly wore her down, and it was not long before she screamed at her attendants to take the child away, far, far away where she couldn't hear him cry.

When the boy was about two weeks old, Queen Nefertiti came to his nursery to pay her official respects to the new Heir Apparent. She had inquired carefully in advance about Kiya's habits with regard to visits with her son, so as to avoid coming face to face with her rival. She learned that The Favorite was in the habit of visiting at certain hours, apparently those when the child was most likely to be quiet; and that her visits had grown shorter and less frequent by the day. She had also heard about the child's colic and how it was making his nurses frantic. So when she went to visit, she took along an old folk remedy she had found effective with her own children.

When she arrived at the nursery, Nefertiti found it in a state of uproar, with the baby screaming at the top of his little lungs, and the bevy of nurses quarreling with one another over the best way to calm him down. After shaking her head and rolling her eyes at the chaotic scene, Nefertiti swept imperiously into the room and took charge. She ordered one nurse to remove the baby's sopping breechclout, several others to fetch buckets of clean water, one to stoke the fire in a charcoal brazier and another to fill a large pot with water and set it to heat over the coals. Once the water was hot, she had them fill a large basin with hot and cold water mixed so that it was just a bit above skin temperature. She picked up the baby, wrapped in a swaddling cloth, and carried him over to the basin, then immersed him in the warm water. Holding his head up with one hand, she gently washed him all over in the warm water. As she stroked his little body, the Queen sang to him softly, a lullaby her own children had always liked. He gradually stopped crying and relaxed in the warm water, so like the environment he had known in the womb. After a bit, he perked up and began to splash with his arms and legs, apparently enjoying himself. The nurses looked at each other in amazement. This was the first time they had seen the baby appear calm and happy in his entire short life.

After a bit, Nefertiti removed him from the water and dried him with a cloth, then wrapped him in another one. Cuddling him in her arms, with his head on her chest, just over her heart, she walked back and forth with him for a while, until he appeared to be asleep. When he was thoroughly out, she set him in his elaborate cradle and tiptoed out of the room. For the first time, both the baby and his nurses enjoyed several hours of uninterrupted sleep.

The next day, she returned and repeated the process. She also instructed the wet-nurse in how to apply a very small amount of poppy juice to her nipples, which the baby would take in with her milk. This also helped to sooth him, as did rubbing his little tummy.

Princess Kiya was at first pleased when her next visit to the nursery found the little prince blissfully quiet – until she learned the cause of his new-found peace. She was infuriated to find that her arch-rival had the motherly knack of quieting the screaming child, while she, herself, only made him scream the louder.

She tried doing all the things the nursemaids told her the Queen had done, bathing and cuddling the child, but her tension communicated itself to him, and he reacted predictably, screaming every time she touched him. The Favorite stormed out in a fury. There were moments when the nurses feared she might actually harm her own child, she was so obviously angry.

Of course, the story soon made the rounds, telling how the foreign woman was a terrible mother whose mere touch set her child to screaming, while the Queen, by now the experienced mother of five, was able to calm him down almost magically. Hearing the tale, Kiya ground her teeth in frustration and swore to get even, somehow.

"One of these days," she swore, "I will get one of her precious children to betray her! I will prove that they are not perfect children, and she is not a perfect mother!"

Ipy, who was working on yet another statue of The Favorite, overheard this remark (in her native Hurrian, of course), which he duly reported to Thutmose.

"Hmmm," said Thutmose, deliberating what to do about this remark. "I don't think she could actually get at any of the Queen's daughters to do them any harm – but I will speak to Lady Mutreshti and tell her to warn the children's nurses to keep an especially sharp eye out. For now, I think that's all we can do."

Meanwhile, Pharaoh's own mother, the redoubtable Dowager Queen Tiye, had sent a messenger saying she was coming for a visit. The King was delighted to hear that she was coming and couldn't wait to show off his new city to his mother. He wanted to be sure that everything was in order for her visit and immediately began issuing orders to insure that it was. The net result, of course, was to create confusion and slow down the very work he wanted to speed up.

Watching this, Nefertiti shook her head and commented to Sitamun, "Look at him, rushing around like he was ten years old, trying to please his mother! Men! They're such perpetual little boys!"

Finally, unable to stand it, she decided it was time to remind him of who he was.

"Akhenaten! Beloved lord and husband! Let me speak."

"Yes, my love?" he asked, turning to her.

"Remember who you are, my lord! You are the Great King of the Two Lands, the richest and most powerful nation on earth. You have tens of thousands of servants, all ready to fulfill your slightest desire. You need not put yourself out for anyone, not even – dare I say it? – your beloved mother, the illustrious Queen Tiye!" she said gently, with her sweetest smile.

For a moment, Pharaoh, still tense, frowned as though she had overstepped her bounds. Then he relaxed, and said, with a little laugh, "You are right, of course, my dear. As always, you are very wise. I don't know why I always feel I have to measure up to my mother's high expectations."

"I think we all feel that way about our mothers," she said, smiling. "But I don't think you need to worry. Your mother adores you. She worries about you, of course – what mother doesn't? – but that's just because she loves you."

"I guess I still feel in my heart that she's disappointed in me. My brother was the perfect one – the perfect warrior, the perfect athlete, the perfect prince. I was never as good at anything," he replied.

"Yes, and your perfect athlete brother got himself killed trying to be the perfect warrior!" she reminded him. "If he hadn't been trying to shoot a bow while steering a chariot with no hands, he wouldn't have been thrown out and killed! That just proves what I always said – "

"And what was that?" he asked.

"That you were the smarter one! The fact that you're still alive, and he's not, proves that! I've always thought that being less physically strong made you a better person," she added.

"How is that?" he asked.

"It gave you a better idea of what other people were going through, and that has made you kinder and more tolerant," she said, squeezing his arm. "So now, you need to let your people go about their work and prepare everything for your mother. You have appointed good people, capable people – trust them to do their jobs well!"

"You are right, my love. If I look over their shoulders all the time, it will just slow them down," he observed. "But there are still some things that I need to do, things that can only be done by me."

"Tell me what they are," she said. "Perhaps I can help."

"Perhaps you can, at that," he agreed. "The chief thing I need to do is deal with the foreign correspondence, the letters from foreign kings. I've been so preoccupied with my new religion and building my new city, I've let that slide. I know there are many letters I haven't answered, and foreign messengers we've been playing host to for several years. Now that the new administrative offices are finished and the archives transferred here, I have no excuse to put it off any longer – and I know it's one of the first things my mother will ask about!"

"I believe you're right," agreed Nefertiti. "Replying to foreign kings, at least, is something I can help you with!"

"Yes, you always did have a diplomatic way with words," he said. "I'm afraid I have sometimes lost my temper with these foreigners, these so-called 'brother' kings, with their unending complaints and their perpetual requests for gold! I think it's a mistake to send them so much gold: the more we send, the more convinced they are that gold is as plentiful as dirt in the Two Lands! If I hear that one more time, I think I will scream!"

"Yes, I know," she agreed, with a sigh. "But if you don't send it, they are insulted, and convinced you are being stingy with them! Well, let us gird up our loins and go deal with them. Perhaps, if we do it together, we can laugh about it instead of screaming!"

"Excellent idea, my dear. When do you want to start?" he asked.

"Let's do it when we're fresh," she said. "How about right after breakfast tomorrow?"

"Agreed. We'll start then."

So, first thing the next day, Pharaoh and his Great Wife arrived at the Office of Foreign Correspondence, in the administrative complex behind the House of the King. The staff, having been forewarned, stood ready, with quills and papyrus for writing notes, and fresh slabs of wet clay, kept moist with damp cloths, ready to be imprinted with the thin triangular tip of a stylus in the cuneiform script that was used almost universally throughout Asia Minor. Stacked in one pile were all the clay tablets that had been received from "Great Kings" – those from important and powerful foreign nations, such as Babylon, Sumer, Mitanni, Assyria and Hatti. In another, smaller pile were those from lesser kings of allied, but more or less autonomous states, such as Byblos, and in another were missives from minor kings and chiefs of city-states and principalities that were vassals of Egypt. Once the Chief Scribe had explained to them the origin of each pile, Akhenaten was dismayed to see how high the piles had grown, especially the important one, the letters from Great Kings.

"Where shall we begin, Your Majesty?" asked the Chief Scribe.

"Let us start with the most important," said the King. "Which of them are from the most powerful kings?"

"Well, Your Majesty," ventured the scribe, glancing nervously at the Queen, "there are several from the King of Karaduniyas – that's Babylon, to us – about his daughter, whom he has promised to send you as a bride."

"Ah, yes. I do recall having agreed to something of the sort. Just what I need: another foreign princess," commented the King.

Nefertiti turned aside and hid a small smile at this remark.

"So," he continued, "refresh my memory. What is the status of arrangements for this marriage? And which king is this? I can never keep them straight."

"Kadashman-Enlil, Sire," the scribe informed him.

"Ah, yes, of course," said the King. "I must remember that: Kadashman-Enlil. They all have such strange names, these foreigners."

"Well, my dear," observed Nefertiti, "I'm sure our names seem just as strange to them."

"I guess they must, given the way they mangle them in their salutations," he agreed. "So, what does he say? I seem to recall that the daughter in question was still a child."

"Ummm..." the scribe hesitated, looking a bit embarrassed. "It's been rather a while, Sire. I think she's...matured."

"How long a while?" the King asked.

"Ah...I think...about six years, Sire," the scribe replied.

"Six years?! Surely not that long," the King exclaimed.

"I'm afraid it has been," said the scribe. "The negotiations were started not long after Your Majesty came to the throne, while your illustrious father – may he be justified! – was still alive."

"Hmmm," said the King, "I think you're right. I seem to remember that."

"And if there is any doubt," commented the scribe, "the Babylonian king mentions it in his letter."

"All right, all right," said the King. "You might as well read it to me. I assume you have already made a translation."

"Of course, my Lord King," the scribe assured him, picking up a papyrus scroll. "I have it right here."

"Read it, then," the King ordered, seating himself in a comfortable chair. Beside him, the Queen was already seated.

The scribe read from the scroll:

Say to Nimu'wareya, the king of Egypt, my brother: Thus, Kadashman-Enlil, the king Karaduniyas, your brother. For me, all indeed goes well. For you, your household, your wives, and for your sons, your country, your chariots, your horses, your courtiers, may all go very well.

With regard to the girl, my daughter, about whom you wrote to me in view of marriage, she has become a woman; she is nubile. Just send a delegation to fetch her. Previously, my father would send a messenger to you, and you would not detain him for long. You quickly sent him off, and you would also send here to my father a beautiful greeting-gift.

But now, when I sent a messenger to you, you have detained him six years, and you have sent me as my greeting-gift, the only thing in six years, 30 minas of gold that looked like silver. That gold was melted down in the presence of Kasi, your messenger, and he was a witness, When you celebrated a great festival, you did not send your messenger to me, saying, "Come to eat and drink." Nor did you send me my greeting-gift in connection with the festival. It was just 30 minas of gold that you sent me. My gift does not amount to what I have given you every year.

I have built a new house. In my house, I have built a large audience chamber. Your messengers have seen the house and the audience chamber and are pleased. Now I am going to have a house-opening. Come yourself to eat and drink with me. I shall not act as you yourself did. Twenty-five men and twenty-five women, altogether 50 servants, I send to you in honor of the house-opening.

Ten wooden chariots and 10 teams of horses I send to you as your greeting-gift.

"That is all, Your Majesty," said the scribe, lowering the scroll.

"Complain, complain!" fumed the King. "Why is it I never get a letter from a foreign king that doesn't complain about something?"

"Well, look at it this way, dear," commented Nefertiti, "for once, he didn't ask for gold!"

"No, he just complained that I only sent him 30 minas of it, and that it looked like silver! Pinhasy," he said to the scribe, "do you have a record of what I sent to him?"

"Yes, my Lord King," said the scribe, reaching for another scroll. "I have it right here." He quickly scanned the scroll, then looked back up at the king. "According to our records, Your Majesty sent him numerous beautiful bowls, flagons, bottles of fragrant oils, weapons decorated in silver, necklaces and bracelets, and statues of gold and electrum. All in all, there were 50 minas of gold, silver and electrum, all of it in jewelry and beautiful objects of art."

"And he destroyed them and melted it all down!" commented the King. "He is a barbarian with no taste, who does not value fine art! And of course some of it looked like silver – some of it was silver! And some of it was electrum!"[2]

"I believe, Your Majesty," ventured the scribe, "that most other nations do not value silver or electrum as highly as we do. They would deem either one as inferior to gold, hence, not as valuable."

"That just confirms my opinion that they lack taste," commented the King, sourly. "Well, back to the matter of the marriage – I suppose we must send for the girl. Arrange a proper escort for her."

"Yes, Your Majesty," agreed the scribe, jotting notes on a fresh scroll.

"And I am obviously not going to his house-warming party, but I shall send him gifts for his new house. Speak to Master Thutmose and tell him I said to prepare appropriate furnishings for the King of Babylon's new house, beds and chairs and the like. And tell him to make sure they are decorated with plenty of gold. That's all they think of, these foreign kings!"

"Yes, Your Majesty," said Pinhasy, noting it all down.

The king started to rise.

"Ah, there is one other matter, Your Majesty, that was raised by the King of Babylon..." the scribe interjected.

The king sat back down.

"Yes, what is it?"

"Your Majesty may, perhaps, remember that the King of Babylon had asked, some time ago, for a daughter of Pharaoh to become his wife?" asked the scribe.

Akhenaten frowned. "Yes, I remember that he had the effrontery to do so. And I also remember that I replied to him that, from time immemorial, no daughter of a king of Egypt is given to anyone!"

"Exactly so, Your Majesty," confirmed the scribe.

"Well? That should be the end of the matter! Does he persist in his request?" asked the King, exasperated.

---

[2] Electrum: an amalgam of silver and gold, highly prized by the Egyptians as the "sun" metal.

"Not exactly, Your Majesty. He, uh, suggests that you send him a substitute – a counterfeit, if you will."

"A what?"

"He says – after the usual greeting, well-wishing, etcetera – he says, 'You are a king; you do as you please. Were you to give a daughter, who would say anything? Since I was told of this message, I wrote as follows to my brother, saying, "Someone's grown daughters, beautiful women, must be available. Send me a beautiful woman as if she were your daughter. Who is going to say, 'She is no daughter of the king!?' But holding to your decision, you have not sent me anyone. Did not you yourself seek brotherhood and amity, and so wrote me about marriage that we might come closer to each other, and did not I, for my part, write you about marriage for this very same reason, that is, brotherhood and amity, that we might come closer to each other? Why, then, did my brother not send me just one woman?'"

"So," said the King, "he is asking me to lie and send him some other woman--"

"Beautiful woman," interjected the Queen.

"Some beautiful woman, claiming she is my daughter?"

"Apparently so, Your Majesty," agreed the scribe.

"Is that it? He didn't ask for gold this time?" asked the King.

"Oh, no, Your Majesty. He did." Pinhasy glanced back down at the scroll, then checked it against the original clay tablet. "He says he's engaged in some kind of work – he doesn't say what – which he's trying to finish this summer, so he asks you to send him gold – 'whatever is on hand', he says – by Tammuz or Ab[3], so he can finish the work. If you send it, then he says he will send his daughter to you. But he urges haste, and says that if you don't send it in time, it won't do him any good. He adds, 'Then you could send me 3,000 talents of gold, and I would not accept it. I would send it back to you, and I would not give my daughter in marriage.'"

"Hah!" exclaimed the king. "If I had 3,000 talents[4] of gold lying around - 'on hand', as he puts it - I would almost be tempted to send it to him, in the fall, just so that he would have to send it back to me, or be branded a liar! Three thousand talents, indeed! Does he really think his daughter is worth three thousand talents of gold? No woman is worth that much!" Then, remembering the Queen, he turned to her and said, "Except you, of course, my dear. You are worth ten thousand

---

[3] July or August.
[4] A huge amount, roughly 100 tons.

talents of gold; twenty thousand; a hundred thousand! You are a jewel beyond price."

Nefertiti laughed. "And you are a liar, my dear, but a charming liar! And since you are already a liar, I suppose we might as well send the King of Babylon some suitably beautiful, non-royal woman. If we outfit her like a princess and send enough gold with her, Kadashman-Enlil won't care if she is the offspring of a sheepherder and a she-camel!"

"Right you are, my love!" agreed the King. Turning to the scribe, he ordered, "Let it be done."

"Aye, my Lord King," agreed the scribe, bowing low.

Nefertiti turned to her husband and said, "I have one real problem with all this foreign correspondence."

"What is that, my love?" he asked.

"I don't have a clear grasp of where all these countries are – how far away they are, how they relate to each other and how they relate to us and our borders," she replied. "I wish I had a clearer picture of them in my head."

"Hmmm. Good point," he said thoughtfully. "Let us call in General Ramose to lay it all out for us. He has campaigned in all these lands. If anyone can explain it, he can."

He turned to the Steward and said, "Steward – inform the Vizier of the South that his presence will required at our afternoon meeting."

The Steward bowed and left, then sent a messenger off to find General Ramose, the Vizier of Upper Egypt.

The royal couple adjourned to their quarters for lunch and the traditional afternoon siesta, a necessity in a climate as hot as Egypt's.

They re-adjourned late in the day, when the sun was beginning to decline in the western sky and an afternoon breeze was blowing off the Nile. General Ramose, having been alerted to the planned subject of discussion, had come equipped with his own scribe bearing large sheets of papyrus, brushes, cakes of ink and small pots of water. The scribe had spread these out on a large table positioned in front of the King and Queen.

"So, General," said the King, "we would like you to give us an overview of all the nations on our borders, show us where they are in relation to the Two Lands and give us an idea of their importance to us. I know it's a tall order, but I trust your ability to enlighten us, since you have more experience of these lands than any man I know."

The grizzled old general acknowledged the request with a brief bow, then, taking a wet brush, he rolled it across the cake of ink until it was well-loaded, then drew a long, line snaking vertically over the lower third of the papyrus.

"This, Your Majesties, is the River Nile, whose flow runs from the bottom of the sheet, here, through the heart of the Two Lands. At the bottom is the Fourth Cataract, our most usual southern border. Below that is the land of Nubia; below that, not shown here, would the fabled land of Punt, to which your famous ancestress Hatshepsut sent her notable expedition," he explained.

"Ahh," the King and Queen acknowledged.

The general marked a black dot next to the line of the river a short distance from the bottom edge of the papyrus.

"This is Aswan," he commented. Marking another dot near the bottom of a large loop in the line of the river, he added, "and here is Thebes. Up here is Memphis," he commented, marking another dot just below the point where the line of the river branched, "just south of the head of the Delta. Midway between them is Akhetaten."

He drew several wiggly lines branching from a point on the river near Memphis , fanning out into a wide triangle. "This is the Nile Delta. At the time of the First Dynasty, the river had seven branches, but now there are only five – or five and a half, depending on how you look at it. The westernmost branch has dried up and disappeared. The easternmost, or Bubastite branch, still flows to the northernmost of the Bitter Lakes, but is very shallow. Another branch used to flow through the Wadi Tumilat, here," he said, indicating a point on the right-hand side, halfway between the head of the Delta and the line he had now drawn across its top, "running east and emptying into Lake Timsah. Now it carries only the overflow from the Inundation."

He drew a dotted line running to the right, ending at an irregular circle representing a lake.

"On either side of the Nile, of course, there is desert, except in the Delta, where the many branches of the river run through fertile fields and marsh land. To the east, there are hills, rising toward the south. In the north, they divide the Delta from what are called the Bitter Lakes, a string of lakes running from the Green Sea[5] in the north to the Red Sea in the south. A series of canals connects these lakes together, fed by the overflow through Wadi Tumilat and the Bubastite branch. There are forts at strategic points all along the lakes and canals, which are infested with crocodiles. Together, they form the Wall of the

---

[5] The Mediterraean

Princes, our eastern line of defense. There are very few crossing points, all of which are defended by forts.

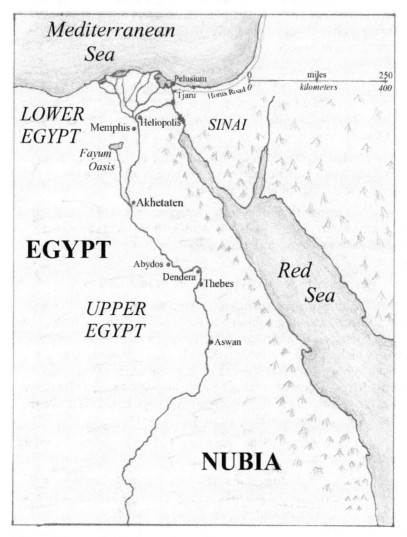

Figure 1: Egypt & Nubia, c. 1350 BC

The most important of these is the North Sinai Road, also called the Horus Road, up here in the north," he said, drawing a dotted line not far below the line of the sea shore, at the upper right edge of the Delta. The line ran from a dot marking the location of Tanis, near the site of the former Hyksos capital of Avaris, to the right, then swung vertically, heading north.

"The point where the road crosses the canal is the location of the strongest fort, at Tjaru. This is the main point where invaders have traditionally entered Egypt, so this fort is very large and well-manned, and spans both sides of the canal. From this point, the road runs north into Canaan."

He added onto the line representing the sea coast, so that it now showed the whole eastern coast of the Green Sea, running a long way north to where it curved back to the west.

"All along this eastern coast are the city-states of Canaan, all of which are vassals of the Two Lands. Most of them were conquered a hundred years ago by your illustrious ancestor, Thutmosis III, the great Warrior King."

He marked several of the most significant vassal cities.

"Most of them are distributed along the narrow coastal plain," he explained, "including Ashkelon, Ashdod and Yafo in the south, and Byblos, Sidon, and Tyre in the north. Another important southern city is Jebus[6], which is located inland, in the hill country of south central Canaan. Further north is Damascus, then, in the valley of the upper Orontes River, which parallels the sea, the important city of Qadesh, a part of the vassal state of Amurru. There is a large island off the coast, opposite Ugarit, which is called Alashiya."

He drew a large island with a finger of land pointing toward the mainland.

"Here," he continued, indicating an area east of the pointing finger of Alashiya, "is the land of our important ally, Mittani, which is bordered by Hatti in the northwest and Assyria to the east. A hundred years ago, Mittani was a major enemy, until it, too, was conquered by Thutmosis III. Since then, it has been our ally, with several generations of Kings of Mitanni sending their daughters to marry your ancestors, Your Majesty, and now yourself," he said.

Nefertiti frowned briefly at this reference to her arch-rival, Kiya.

---

[6] Later renamed Jerusalem.

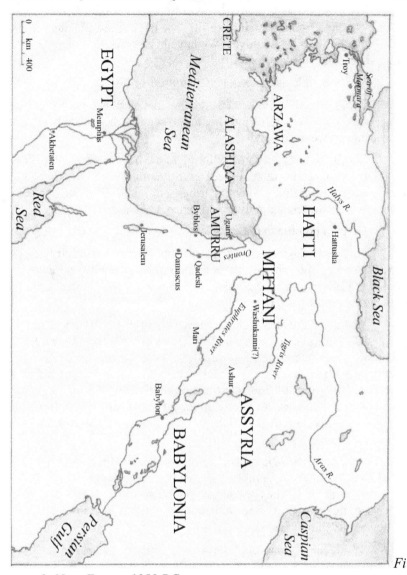

gure 2: Near East, c. 1350 BC

"At that time," the general continued, "Assyria was a small vassal state of Mitanni, and Hatti was still a new, small power. More recently, however, both states have been growing in power and eating away at Mitanni, which, as you can see, is squeezed between them. Both have now become major powers that pose potential threats to the security of the Two Lands."

"To the south-east of Mitanni, between the two great rivers Euphrates and Tigris, lies the oldest of the Great Powers, Babylonia, which claims to be even older than the Two Lands itself, although it has risen and fallen numerous times. Its own people call it Karaduniyas."

"Ah, yes," commented Nefertiti, "we have received letters from Kadashman-Enlil of Karaduniyas. We have just agreed to send a 'pretend princess' for him to marry."

She and Akhenaten exchanged amused smiles.

"So, General," commented Akhenaten, "now that you have shown us where all of these lands lie, tell us what is their military significance to the Two Lands."

"Well," said the general, pointing to the bottom of the map, "as you know, Nubia is a perennial problem. Sometimes it is quiet for years, but you never know when the tribes will rebel, so we have to keep a constant watch and military presence in the area."

He then pointed to the open area to the left of the Nile valley.

"Libya, to the west, is usually not a problem. The desert in that area is so severe, it discourages invasion – but occasionally, there are problems. The east is well-defended, by the Wall of the Princes in the north and by the sea and mountains in the south."

He tapped the area to the northeast of Egypt on the map. "It is here in this strip called Ghazzru that we are most vulnerable by land, and at the several mouths of the river along the sea coast, which are potentially vulnerable to an invasion by sea. Our sailing ships travel these waters in great numbers, alerting and protecting us from invasion by sea. We retain a loose hold over all the city-states of Canaan as a buffer against invasion by any of the Great Powers to their north and east."

"General," said Nefertiti, "we receive many letters from the vassal kings of that area, complaining that their rival kings are conspiring with the Hittites or the Assyrians against us. They are forever urging us to send troops to help them fend off some threat to our hegemony in the area. How real are these threats?"

"Your Majesty has put your finger on one of the thorniest problems our military faces," he replied, "knowing when and where troops are truly required in the buffer states."

"On the one hand," he continued, "we don't want to let them fall to any of our enemies – most notably, Hatti or Assyria – which would erode that protective zone and allow an enemy to come right to our doorstep. The great Thutmosis extended the empire's borders all the way to the Euphrates precisely so that no enemy could ever again do what the Hyksos had done: invade Egypt, itself."

"However," he observed, "having such extensive frontiers poses another problem: how can we possibly defend such enormous borders? Realistically, if we emptied all of Egypt's garrisons and stationed all our troops along the northern frontier, we could never hope to defend its whole length. Our troops would be spread impossibly thin. Worse yet," he added, "it would leave our southern and western borders entirely undefended, at the mercy of the Nubians and the Libyans.

"So you see," he said to the Queen, "it is not possible for His Majesty to send troops to every vassal king who asks for them. We have to rely on them to carry out most of the defense of our northern borders, with only occasional reinforcement by Egyptian troops."

"Ah," Nefertiti commented, "now I begin to understand why the vassal kings constantly importune us for troops and why His Majesty," she said, nodding at her husband, "so seldom sends them."

"That's right, my dear," Akhenaten agreed. "I'm glad you see my dilemma. Even though we are still the dominant power in the region, there are not enough troops in all the Two Lands to directly defend these borders. We have to rely on diplomacy to maintain this buffer zone between us and the other Great Powers of the region. This I do by playing these vassal kings off against one another, counting on them to inform me if any of their rivals appears to be colluding with the Hittites or Assyrians, or consolidating too large an area under one minor king."

"Lately, for instance," he continued, "Rib-Hadda of Byblos and several of his neighbors have complained that King Abdi-Ashirta of Amurru has been consorting with the Hittites. When I reprimanded him, he swore he was still loyal to me, but several of his rivals told me otherwise, as did my commissioners in the area. Most damning of all, I have a spy in his court who told me that Abdi-Ashirta 'sat down to eat and drink' with Hittite envoys, a strong sign of collusion. So I have ordered him to come here to see me in person, an order I am about to back up with troops. Once he arrives, I will hear testimony for and against him. If he is convicted of treason, I will execute him."

"I see," the Queen observed thoughtfully. "It is a delicate game of force, influence, persuasion and perhaps occasional...guile?" she asked, glancing at her husband.

"It is, indeed," he agreed.

"Well," she said, "this has been most instructive. Thank you, General Ramose, for this military and political education."

With that, the Vizier of Upper Egypt was dismissed and bowed out. At Nefertiti's request, the map he had sketched was mounted on linen fabric and fastened to one wall so they could refer back to it in the future.

Akhenaten was pleased with the session, commenting to his wife, "These are things you must know to rule this country wisely. You must be prepared for this, in the event that I die before my son is old enough to rule. In that case, you must be fully prepared to step into my shoes."

"Don't talk like that! You are not going to die before me! I insist that you live for at least another hundred years!" she protested.

But Nefertiti knew in her heart that her husband's fears were well-founded. His health, never the best, continued to deteriorate. Akhetaten, still a raw, new land undergoing massive construction, was subject to heavy dust storms every time the wind blew, which it often did. Every dust-laden wind started Akhenaten wheezing. She insisted he carry a square of linen with him at all times, which he could tie over his nose and mouth to filter the dust from the air. It helped, but not enough. And lately, his doctors had raised a new fear: whenever he started wheezing, his heart would beat erratically. The doctors feared that someday, one of his attacks of breathlessness would be too much for his heart and send it into a fatal attack of arrhythmia.

For this reason, she agreed to work hard at learning how to perform the duties of a king. At the very least, she could lift some of the burden from his shoulders. And if the worst happened, she would be prepared to take over and rule while her stepson was still a child.

She was also determined to begin developing her own network of spies, people who could blend in unnoticed among the common folk, especially women. She felt women would make excellent spies, as they are so often ignored and underestimated by men. She knew that Pharaoh and his generals and advisors completely discounted the common people, regarding them as docile and insignificant. But Nefertiti, always more practical than her husband, recognized that there were vastly more commoners than there were either nobles or generals. She realized that there was a great deal of untapped power in the common people. Granted, it might be difficult to get them moving in a given direction, but if some leader did manage to move them, they would be very difficult to stop. After all, she reasoned, it was the common people, not Pharaoh Khufu, who built the Great Pyramid!

Chapter 28: Foreign Relations and Machinations

Soon, it was time for Sitamun to return to her estate in the Delta. Nefertiti, who was now pregnant with her sixth child, particularly hated to see her sister-in-law leave. For the first time in her life, she had had a real friend, a confidante other than her husband, whom she could trust with her innermost secrets. In childhood, when they had both lived in the palace, the several years' difference in their ages had been enough to separate them into different cohorts, with different experiences. Now that they were both mature women, that difference was no longer significant; rather, the difference between them, as royal women, and the rest of the world was much more meaningful. And now, of course, Sitamun was the only person in the world who knew the deepest secret of Nefertiti's heart, the one she had not previously admitted even to herself: her feelings for the artist, Thutmose. But with Sitamun gone, Nefertiti had to face that feeling head on and struggle with it by herself.

So, after bidding a tearful farewell to Sitamun, she did the only thing she could to distract herself: she threw herself into helping Akhenaten with the work of running the empire. Fortunately for her sanity, there was a great deal to be done.

Having cleared the backlog of foreign correspondence in preparation for his mother's visit, Akhenaten had discovered a new interest in foreign affairs. As a young man, he had resisted it, believing Egypt to be the center of the world and the only country that mattered. Then he had become engrossed in puzzling out the nature of God, and then, in promulgating his new religion throughout his kingdom. That had been followed by his anger at the shock of near-assassination and the frantic need to build a new city in which he would be safe from such hazards. Now, for the first time in his life, Akhenaten had the time and the security to turn his attention outward, beyond the borders of the Two Lands. And doing so, he realized at last how deeply his life and his country's were intertwined with events in other nations.

So now, instead of relegating foreign correspondence to a back room, he had messengers from both foreign rulers and his own army, clay tablets in foreign tongues and papyri written in hieratic, brought to the small chamber he used as an office. He had recently instituted a regular meeting with his principal ministers each morning at which they dealt with pressing concerns, both foreign and domestic. Nefertiti had begun joining him at these staff meetings and Akhenaten had welcomed her, valuing her insights and her sage advice, as well as grooming her to be co-regent.

This morning, several days after the departure of Sitamun, Akhenaten was meeting with Grand Vizier Aye, the mayor of the new capital, Akhetaten, the Head Administrator in Charge of the Royal

Granaries and Captain Paramessu of the Royal Guard. Nefertiti sat beside her husband.

Akhenaten decided to deal with local affairs first. Turning to the Administrator of Royal Granaries, he said,

"Administrator Nakht, I have reviewed your report on the most recent grain harvest. I see that, while grain harvests throughout the Two Lands are down slightly from last year, those from the lands about Akhetaten are down substantially. This is in sharp contrast to the preceding three years, during which they rose consistently. How do you explain this sudden decline in yield?"

Faced with such negative royal scrutiny, Administrator Nakht nervously cleared his throat. Gathering his courage, he replied to Pharaoh.

"Your Majesty is very astute in observing these changes. As Your Majesty has stated, grain yields have fallen slightly throughout the Two Lands. This is a result of a somewhat lower-than-normal Inundation last year."

He glanced up at the King to gauge his response to this explanation. Since the King was traditionally regarded as the divine representative of the land itself and identified with *ma'at*, he was also mystically responsible for maintaining the proper order of nature. Hence, pointing out that the Inundation had been low was tantamount to laying the blame for low crop yields directly at the King's own feet, something no bureaucrat was anxious to do.

Akhenaten, however, seemed willing to accept this. Nodding his head, he said, "Yes, Administrator, I assumed that the general decline was due to the low Inundation. But why has the local crop yield fallen so much more than the average? The level of the Inundation here was much the same as elsewhere."

"That is true, Your Majesty. And as you observed, local harvests had been increasing for several years, as new land was brought under cultivation. Most of the arable land around the city, primarily on the West Bank, has now been irrigated and cultivated – as far as we can tell, for the first time ever. Our five years of rising harvests reflected the new areas being brought under cultivation each year. However, we have now developed almost all the available land in the immediate area of the city, so we can anticipate little new cultivation in the years to come," Nakht stated.

"That explains why the harvest did not increase," observed the King, "but not why it should have *decreased*."

"I believe that the cause of the decrease in crop yield, Your Majesty," replied Nakht, "is due to an increase in the population of Nile rats. Farmers have reported to me that the number of rats has grown right along with the area cultivated for crops."

"And why is that?" the King asked.

"Well, you see, Your Majesty, since this area was not previously irrigated or cultivated, it supported only the sparse native vegetation, with a bit of marshy growth along the river bank. Since the rats are dependent on the vegetation, and there wasn't much of that, there were very few rats. It seems likely that there was a stable, small population of rats in the area for a very long time. Then, we came along and began irrigating and plowing and planting the fields, and all of a sudden, there was much more food for the rats. It didn't take them long to discover this new, more abundant food supply, and as a result, the number of rats in the area has exploded. Now, the amount of grain being produced has leveled out, but the number of rats has continued to grow – and they are eating the grain, both before and after it is harvested. Local farmers have been fighting a losing battle against them."

"Ah, I see," said the King. "And what is being done to combat this plague of rats? Have they tried bringing in cats?"

"Yes, Your Majesty," replied Nakht, "but there are not enough cats available in the area."

"Well, then," commanded the King, "send to the Temple of Bastet in Bubastis, and say that the King orders them to send as many cats as they can to the farmers of Akhetaten. And if they complain that the cats are meant for sacrifice and mummification, for the benefit of pilgrims, point out that I have thus far allowed them to keep their temple open and to continue the practice of cat sacrifice unmolested – but if they deny my request, their temple will suffer the same fate as those of Amun: I will shut them down. Thus saith Pharaoh."

"Yes, Your Majesty," said Nakht, making a low obeisance. "It shall be done."

"You may go," said Pharaoh, dismissing him.

The Administrator of Granaries headed for the door. The mayor of Akhetaten rose and started to follow him.

"Not you, Mayor," said the King. "We have further business with you."

"Yes, Your Majesty," agreed the Mayor, resuming his seat.

"Now," said the King, "let us hear Captain Paramessu's report on the security of the city."

Captain Paramessu stood and approached the King, offering a military salute followed by a low bow.

"Your Majesty," he said, "the perimeter of the city is secure. As Your Majesty knows well, the site itself provides limited access from outside. In addition to the river, there are only three main access points through the surrounding cliffs: the entry and exit of the main road along the shoreline to north and south, and through the Royal Wadi to the east. All three of these access points are well-guarded, with patrols both day and night. The patrols are well-armed and well-trained, and are changed twice at night and twice during the day."

"And the river bank?" asked the King.

"The number of landing sites along the river bank has been reduced to only six areas, Your Majesty, as a result of construction along the riverfront. As Your Majesty knows, there are three main wharves: the Royal Wharf, the Temple Wharf, and the Traders Wharf, where boats of any substantial draft can land. In addition, there is the small Fishermen's Wharf to the south, and two shallow areas where small boats can come ashore. All of these areas now funnel into streets running between buildings, like wadis of brick and stone. As a result, all access by water is restricted to these six points. All of them are patrolled day and night, just like the landward perimeter. In addition, I have stationed watchmen on the cliffs above the northern, southern and eastern approaches, with orders to watch both the land and river traffic. If any noteworthy force approaches, they are to light signal fires. A central watch force stationed on the roof of the Great Palace will alert us, should any of the watch fires be lit."

"Very good, Captain," said the King approvingly. "And within the city?"

"We have now built up the local guard to full strength, Your Majesty, as you desired. The men have been drawn from all over the Empire, including Nubia in the south, Libya in the west, and Habiru and other Asiatics from the north and east," replied Captain Paramessu. "They have undergone extensive training in the use of standard Egyptian weapons, especially the spear and the bow, in addition to whatever native weapons they brought with them. They run several miles daily, so that they may keep pace with Your Majesties' chariots when you ride out."

"Thank you, Captain. You have done an excellent job," said the King.

Captain Paramessu took this approbation as a sign that this might be his best moment to speak out.

"If I may, Your Majesty?" he began.

"Yes?" asked Akhenaten.

"Now that the city is well-guarded, and the Guard fully manned and well-trained, I would like to respectfully submit my request to be returned to duty with the army in the field."

"I recognize that you would like to return to service with your commander, General Horemheb, Captain," commented the King. "But if you were to leave us, who would insure the continued protection of our person and the capital city?"

"If it please Your Majesty, I have a candidate in mind to take over my post," replied Paramessu. "I also recommend that the Guard be re-structured into two units, one with the specific duty of guarding the King and Royal Family, the other with the duty of guarding the city and perimeter."

"And who is this candidate you offer?"

"He is Sergeant Mahu, Your Majesty, a 12-year veteran of campaigns in Nubia and Naharin[7]. He has been largely responsible for recruiting and training the new men for our local force here. I recommend that he be made the new Chief of Police."

"I will consider your request and recommendations, Captain Paramessu. Mayor, what do you think of this proposal?"

"I am well-acquainted with Sergeant Mahu, Your Majesty. He has done an excellent job recruiting and training men. He has been very responsive to all of my requests, is a staunch disciplinarian and deeply loyal to Your Majesty. I heartily approve of Captain Paramessu's recommendations," commented the Mayor.

"Thank you, Mayor. I will take the plan under advisement. Captain Paramessu, you may expect an answer within the week."

"Thank you, Your Majesty," replied Paramessu, bowing low. "Is that all?"

"Stay, Captain. I believe you will be interested in the next item of business," said the King. "Steward, please send in the messenger from General Horemheb."

The Steward opened the door, rapped his staff on the floor and called out, "The messenger from General Horemheb may now enter!"

A travel-stained soldier stood up from where he had been resting on the floor, his back against the wall. He saluted and gave his name and rank to the Steward, who turned toward the King and announced:

"Lieutenant Abana of the Horus regiment, messenger from General Horemheb!"

---

[7] Naharin – the Egyptian name for areas to the north and east of Egypt.

Leaving his weapons with the Steward, the young soldier advanced and knelt before the King.

"You may rise, Lieutenant," said the King. When the young man was on his feet again, the King asked, "What news from the frontier?"

The young man pulled out a papyrus scroll, which he handed to the scribe seated near him.

"General Horemheb told me, 'Say to the King my Lord, Neferkheperrure-Waenre: May all be well with you! May all be well with Your Majesty, your Great Wife, your lesser wives, your children, your courtiers, and all of the Two Lands!'

"'All is well with me, and with the army of the north. We have put down several minor skirmishes among the vassal rulers of the cities of Gaza and the coast. The vassal kings continue to quarrel among themselves, as ever. Some, however, are beginning to ally themselves with the new ruler of Hatti, King Suppiluliumas, or with the Assyrians. It has come to my ears that Abdi-Ashirta of Amurru has gone over to the Hittites. Of itself, this is no great cause for concern, but it would go ill if others were to follow his lead. I am pursuing him and will return him to the Two Lands.'"

"Excellent," commented the King. "He has anticipated our wishes."

"'There is movement along the eastern and southern borders of Mitanni,'" continued the messenger. "'The Hittites have made several raids into King Tushratta's territory and have taken several cities. The Assyrians, who were formerly vassals of Mitanni, have declared their independence and have pushed in from the east. Assyria and Hatti are like the pincers of a great crab. Between them, they have squeezed much territory from Mitanni, although they have failed to take the key cities of Nuhashshe and Washukanni. We also hear that there was an attempt on the life of King Tushratta, backed by the Hittites, who attempted to put one of Tushratta's brothers on the throne. The attempt failed and Tushratta remains in control. However, the pretender, who calls himself King of the Hurrians, remains at large and is reported to be in the company of one of the Hittite princes.'

"'There is also news out of Babylon. King Kadashman-Enlil has died. There was a struggle for the succession among his sons and kinsmen, after which his son Burra-Burriash succeeded to the throne. Despite this internal conflict, Babylonia remains a strong power in the region.'"

"Well, well, well," mused the King. "It looks as though Kadashman-Enlil was more right than he knew, when he said my gold would be of no use to him after the month of Ab!"

"I wonder how this will affect your proposed marriage to the Babylonian princess?" asked Nefertiti.

"A good question," commented the King. "We shall have to write to the new king – what was his name?"

"Burra-Burriash, my Lord," said the lieutenant.

"Burra-Burriash. See that you remember that," the King said to the Chief Scribe, who bowed his head in acknowledgement. "Begin drafting a letter of greeting to the new king. Send our condolences on his father's death. Tell him how much we loved his father and his father loved us, etcetera, etcetera. Congratulate him on his accession. Tell him we are sending an escort for the princess. And send a message to General Horemheb directing him to dispatch an escort to Babylon immediately to fetch her."

"Yes, Your Majesty," agreed the scribe, taking furious notes.

Akhenaten turned back to the young soldier.

"Is there anything more, lieutenant?"

"Yes, Your Majesty," replied the soldier, hesitantly, "there is a bit more."

"Proceed," said the King.

"General Horemheb told me to say that his troops are becoming weary, being away from home for so long in the King's service, and much of the equipment is becoming worn with age and use. He begs that Your Majesty will send him fresh troops and replacement chariots and weapons. He closes by saying that he remains Your Majesty's faithful servant. That is all," ended the soldier, standing at attention.

"Thank you, lieutenant," said the King, starting to dismiss him.

Nefertiti intervened. "Wait, my Lord. Lieutenant, what is your own impression of the condition of the men and equipment of the northern army?"

The lieutenant bowed deeply to the Queen and replied, "It is just as General Horemheb says, Your Majesty. The men have been fighting back and forth through Canaan and along the northern frontier for years now, with no relief and no reinforcements. They are loyal, battle-hardened troops, but they are weary and long to see their families and their homeland again. Their weapons and their chariots are worn and much-mended. Most are in need of repair; many should be replaced."

"Thank you, lieutenant," Nefertiti said, then turned to her husband. "I fear it is true, my Lord Husband. We have taken these troops for granted for years and have neglected them. We have relied on them to keep us safe from foreign invaders, but we have done nothing to help them or insure their welfare. We should do something about this."

"All right, my dear, we shall," he agreed. "Captain Paramessu!"

"Yes, my King?" replied the guard captain, springing to attention.

"You shall have your transfer to the field, and a promotion. I hereby promote you to Battalion Commander, of a new unit, to be called the Aten Battalion. You are to begin recruiting and assembling five thousand men, together with three hundred chariots and three hundred teams of horses, and all necessary weapons and support equipment. You will meet with my scribes to draw up a full list of all that will be needed. You may requisition as much gold and grain as is needed to pay for them. You have two months to assemble your force and train them well enough to march north. They can undergo additional training on the way to the frontier. You will locate General Horemheb's army and rendezvous with him. Inform him that your battalion is to provide him with relief troops. I leave it to his judgment to determine how many men to send home, versus how many to keep."

"Aye, aye, Your Majesty!" said Paramessu with a smart salute.

"You may go, Commander," said the King. "You have a big task ahead of you."

The newly-promoted commander saluted again, bowed deeply and turned to leave, followed by the lieutenant. Before they reached the door, the King said,

"Steward – see to it that the messenger is well-fed, well-housed and well-rewarded. He has made a long, hard journey on our behalf. Show him our royal gratitude."

The Steward bowed and replied, "It shall be done." He ushered the two soldiers into the hall and issued orders to his underlings, then returned to the room.

Clearing his throat, he said, "Your Majesty – there is a trader here who wishes permission to present his wares to the ladies of the harem."

Akhenaten looked inquiringly at Nefertiti, one eyebrow raised.

She looked back at him, then turned to the Steward and said, "Let us meet this trader. Show him in."

The Steward stepped into the hall, then returned, followed by a man in long robes and a headcloth, accompanied by a boy of about ten years. Unlike most Egyptians, the man wore a long beard, and his robe was woven in many bright, colorful patterns.

The Steward announced him: "The trader, Kohath, and his son."

The trader stepped up before the King, followed by his son. Both dropped to their knees and made a deep obeisance to the King and Queen.

The royal couple studied them for a moment, then the King said, "You may rise, trader."

The Queen commented, "From your colorful robe and long beard, I perceive that you are a Habiru."

"That is correct, Your Majesty," the man replied.

"Are you one of our Egyptian Habiru from the Delta, or one of the 'wild Habiru' of the desert?" the Queen asked him. She made a face and waved her hand as she said 'wild Habiru', to make it clear she was joking.

"Not too wild, Your Majesty," said the trader, with a smile. "My folk are some of the 'domesticated Habiru' of the Delta."

"Ah, then we are distantly related," said the King. "That is, if your folk are members of the Tribe of Yacub."

"We are, Your Majesty," the trader replied. "Though I would never have presumed to claim a relationship."

"Yet we are related, since my grandfather, Yuya, was a son of your patriarch, Yacub."

"My father was Yuya's elder brother, Levi," replied the trader.

"His elder brother!" exclaimed the King. "Your family must be very long-lived folk!"

"They are, Your Majesty. While we don't know exactly how old my father was when he died, we believe him to have been well over one hundred years old. And I was a child of his old age, so I only knew him as an old, old man," said the trader.

"My word! And I thought Yuya was old when he died, but I believe he had not yet reached seventy," observed the King. "And this is your son?"

"Yes, Your Majesty," replied Kohath, putting his arm around the boy's shoulders and pulling him forward. "This is my son, Amram. He travels with me, learning the business. He is a great help to me. He has a fine ear for languages, and he knows how to write several of them, in both cuneiform and hieratic."

"Well, well," said the King, "a very sharp lad, indeed."

"Husband," interjected Nefertiti, "I have an idea."

She leaned over and whispered in his ear. When she finished, he nodded his head thoughtfully and turned back to the trader.

"What lands do you travel through, trader?" he asked.

Kohath replied, "It varies, Your Majesty, depending upon which lands are peaceful and secure enough for traveling, and whether there is a military escort available. As Your Majesty knows, the regions beyond the Two Lands' borders are in a constant state of ferment. One can never count upon being able to follow the same route twice. So I go wherever I can safely travel: the cities along the coast – Ashkelon, Ashdod, Tyre, Sidon, Akka, Byblos – if the sea is calm, or further inland, if the weather is too stormy for sea travel. On various trips, I have gone as far as Nineveh in Mitanni, to Hattusas in the Land of Hatti, and whenever possible, all the way to Babylon. We made it there on this last trip, but barely made it through the border lands on our way back, what with Hittite and Assyrian raiding parties, and renegade Apiru chieftains capturing caravans and robbing them. Thankfully, we ran across your northern army and were able to take shelter with them as they patrolled some of the most perilous territory."

"**Apiru** raiders?" asked the Queen. "But isn't 'Apiru' just another version of 'Habiru'? Like you, yourself?"

"Well, yes and no, Your Majesty," the trader explained. "True, it's pretty much the same word; but Egyptians and Canaanites use the term differently."

"How so?" asked the Queen.

"Egyptians use the term rather loosely, to mean most any nomadic tribe in the lands east and north of the Nile Valley. Canaanites use the term to indicate nomadic tribes in their area that are not pledged to any of the kings of the settled city-states. Such unaffiliated bands roam the hills and frequently raid caravans passing through their territory. When the vassal kings are getting along well with each other – which is almost never – they patrol the hill country and minimize raiding. But when they are busy fighting each other, the bandits are emboldened and get out of control, making passage through the hills very dangerous."

"I see," said the Queen.

"I have a proposition for you, trader," said the King. "If you are willing to accept it, I will buy your entire load of trade goods and supply you with new ones. And if you serve me well, you will be richly rewarded."

The trader bowed low. "I am Your Majesty's devoted servant. You have only to ask, and whatever it is, I shall gladly do it. I shall undertake any task, no matter how difficult, or guarantee to fetch whatever you ask, even from the ends of the earth!"

"Good, good!" said the King, smiling. "Although it should actually not be all that difficult. I simply want you to send me information about the lands that you travel through. Travel whatever routes you normally would. Go to any of the capitals of great nations that you can: Hatti, Mitanni, Assyria, Babylonia. Observe everything that you can, and send me word about conditions there: not only the king and his court, but how fares the economy and how it affects the people. Have there been fires, floods, earthquakes or other natural catastrophes? How are the crops? Has there been drought or famine? Is there pestilence? Are wild tribes raiding the Great Kings' far borders? Are the people content, or is there unrest in the streets? Observe all these things, and send word to me and to General Horemheb whenever you can."

"I see," said Kohath thoughtfully. "Observing will be easy. The hard part will be getting word back to Your Majesty, or even to General Horemheb in the field."

"Perhaps your son can write it all down," commented Nefertiti.

Kohath glanced at the boy. "I am sure he could, Your Majesty," he told the Queen. "The danger would be if the message were to be intercepted on its way to you, which it could easily be in these uncertain times. If it were to fall into enemy hands, it would be much to the benefit of Egypt's enemies, and much to Egypt's detriment. That is the danger of committing the information to writing."

At this point, the boy tugged at his father's sleeve.

"Father! I could write it in code! Then no one else could read it!" he said.

"Code?" asked Pharaoh. "What is this 'code'?"

"It is a system of writing where other signs are substituted for those normally used, Your Majesty," the trader replied.

"But – if other signs are substituted, is the message not reduced to a meaningless jumble?" asked Pharaoh, puzzled.

"That's the beauty of it," said the boy excitedly. "To anyone who doesn't know the system, it **is** a meaningless jumble. But if you have the key, and know which signs substitute for which others, then you can unlock the message! Here, I will show you."

He turned to the scribe sitting nearby and asked him for a sheet of papyrus and a quill and ink. The scribe handed him all of these objects and a palette to put them on. Sitting on the floor, the boy drew a line across the center of the paper. Above the line, he wrote a series of hieratic signs. Below the line, he inked in a row of strange symbols, lined up with the hieratic. Then he held the papyrus up for the King and Queen to see.

"You see here, Your Majesties, above the line it says in hieratic, 'There are a thousand soldiers camped before Nineveh.' Below, I have written the same thing, but substituting signs I made up. If I give your scribe a list of my signs, each with its matching hieratic letter, he can then translate the message. But to anyone who does not know the sign-substitution, it will appear to be gibberish."

"What if the messenger is captured and tortured?" asked the King. "Will he not tell his captors what is in the message?"

"Not if he doesn't know what is in it," said the boy. "That is the beauty of it: the messenger doesn't need to know the content of the message he carries. And if he appears to be some common, ordinary person, no one will be aware that he carries anything of importance."

"A most excellent idea, boy! I like it," said the King. "Let us do it! Today, trader, you and the boy will show your wares to the ladies of the harem. Anything they do not buy from you, I will take. Tomorrow, the boy will meet with my scribes – my Steward will tell you where to go. He will teach them his system – this 'code', as you call it. Two scribes knowledgeable in this system will travel with Commander Paramessu and his troops when they leave two months from now. They will rendezvous with General Horemheb in the field and will teach this system to a small number of additional scribes. They are to commit it to memory – I don't want any written copies of the key to leave this palace. But every separate unit in the field is to have at least one scribe with them who is capable of translating one of these coded messages. This way, we will be able to send secure messages between commanders in the field. And you, trader Kohath, and your son, will be your Pharaoh's eyes and ears in distant lands! If you send us valuable information, I will make you rich beyond your wildest dreams!"

Kohath stole a quick look at his son, then they both dropped to the floor and bowed low before the King.

"We are your most obedient servants, Your Majesty!" said Kohath. "Your wish is our command!"

"And not a word of it is to pass beyond this room," warned the King, "except to my designated scribes and officers."

"Yes, Your Majesty!" agreed Kohath and Amram, bowing low again.

"You may go," said the King. "Steward – direct the trader, with his wares, to the large courtyard in the Ladies' Wing of the palace. Then inform the ladies of the harem that he is displaying his wares there."

"Yes, Your Majesty," said the Steward, with a brief bow. He led the trader and his son out into the corridor.

"Well, my dear," said Akhenaten to Nefertiti, with a smile, "it has been a most productive morning's work. That was an excellent idea you had, to use the trader as a spy. Now, let us have some luncheon to fortify us for this afternoon's audience – and plenty of beer. It's thirsty work, all these foreign relations!"

Nefertiti was pleased, too, since she had now begun the extension of her planned use of common people as agents far afield, even to the heart of foreign lands.

Chapter 29: Queen Tiye's Visit

At last, just before the Inundation, Queen Tiye arrived for her long-awaited visit. All six princesses were very excited. They hadn't seen their grandmother in several years – the youngest two had never seen her at all.

A messenger in a small, swift sailing vessel had arrived the day before to announce her imminent arrival. Pharaoh Akhenaten had set a watchman on the palace roof to alert him when her barge was spotted. Once the watchman notified him, the King and Queen and their three oldest daughters proceeded grandly to the Royal Wharf in their chariots, with a spare chariot for the Dowager Queen.

Soon, the royal barge "Radiance of Aten" appeared, its gilded fittings glittering in the sun, its brightly colored sails and pennons flying in the breeze. Behind it rode a whole flotilla of smaller boats, like a flock of wooden goslings following a golden mother goose. Before long, the sleek ship warped smartly in beside the pier, servants on shore scurrying to catch the lines cast ashore by the sailors and making them fast to cleats on the pier. A sturdy gangplank was extended from the ship and the captain ceremoniously escorted the Queen Mother to the dock, where she was joyously greeted by the waiting Royal Family.

The Lord Chamberlain, who had accompanied the royal party from the palace, attempted to maintain a certain amount of decorum, formally announcing the Queen Mother's arrival – but in typical Akhenaten fashion, the Pharaoh abandoned formal protocol, clasping his mother in an affectionate hug. After a brief, startled moment, she shrugged and cheerfully hugged him back. Akhenaten passed her on to Nefertiti, who hugged her mother-in-law and kissed her on both cheeks, then passed her on to the three princesses, who each hugged her in turn.

"Well!" laughed the Dowager Queen, "I guess I don't need to ask if you're glad to see me!"

"We're always happy to see you, Mother," replied Akhenaten. "It's been far too long! I'm simply dying to show you my new capital city."

"Well, darling, I'm anxious to see it," she replied, "but I think I need to freshen up and rest a bit, first."

"Of course, of course!" he agreed. "We've brought a chariot for you."

"I think I'd prefer my own litter, if you don't mind. My old bones are getting a bit stiff for bouncing around in a chariot," she replied.

"Whatever you prefer, mother," he said. "Although I think you'll find the ride is very smooth on my new, stone-paved streets. They were designed for chariot wheels. Nefertiti and I drive ours everywhere."

"You drive your own chariots? No charioteer?" she asked, a bit taken aback.

"Oh, yes," he answered. "We enjoy the speed and the freedom of galloping our horses flat-out."

"We? Nefertiti, too?" she asked.

"Oh, yes," he said. "She's gotten to be quite the charioteer – handles her horses like she was born to it," he said, looking proudly over at his wife.

"Doesn't it scare you," she asked Nefertiti, "handling those big, powerful beasts?"

"Oh, no," laughed Nefertiti. "I adore it. It's very exhilarating. It makes me feel like **I'm** fast and powerful!"

"Well, you youngsters may think me an old fogey, but I'll stick with my litter for now," the Dowager Queen replied.

By now, her litter bearers had brought the gilded conveyance from the ship and set it down beside her. Without further ado, she took her steward's hand and he handed her into the litter. The Pharaoh and Nefertiti headed out at a sedate pace, followed by the Dowager Queen's litter. The three princesses in their chariots fell in behind. Twenty guards trotted along on either side to protect the royal party.

After a short journey over a smooth, stone-paved road, they arrived at the Great Palace. Attendants helped the King, Queen and Princesses out of their chariots, while grooms led the horses away. The Lord Chamberlain helped Queen Tiye out of her litter and escorted her into the elegant vestibule of the palace, which was cooled by air channels that funneled the prevailing breeze over a glittering reflecting pool in which colored fish darted through pink and yellow floating lotuses.

The royal party was met by the assembled household staff, and the mayor of the city made a brief speech welcoming the Dowager Queen to the new capital city.

After this, the Steward led the Queen Mother to her apartment, a spacious, elegant set of rooms with its own pool-lined courtyard and a fine view of the river. She agreed to meet the family for dinner later, after she had rested and bathed.

The Steward called on her later in the day, to conduct her to the private apartments of the King and Queen, where she rejoined the

monarchs and their daughters for an intimate family dinner. She greeted
the three oldest girls again, and was introduced to the younger three.
She had seen the oldest of these, Neferneferuaten-Tasherit, as a baby –
but of course, the child didn't remember her. She had asked to see the
young crown prince, so Akhenaten had invited the child and his mother
to dinner, as well (much to Nefertiti's annoyance). Kiya arrived soon
after the Queen Mother, with the little prince – now a toddler – in tow,
accompanied by his nurse.

Once everyone was seated, servants began arriving with platters
laden with fruits, freshly-baked bread, savory roasted water fowl and
racks of lamb and beef. Each diner was surrounded by several small
tables laden with platters of food and fine goblets of gold or faience,
into which servants poured filtered beer or honeyed wine, at the diner's
choice.

At one end of the room, a group of musicians played. One
plucked a curved harp as tall as she was, while another played a flute
and a third played a three-stringed instrument with a bow, while a
fourth kept the beat on a small drum.

After the main courses were finished, a dessert course
consisting of fruit, small pastries stuffed with nuts and sweetened with
honey was served, all washed down by a fermented honey drink. Just as
the adults were relaxing, enjoying the music and effects of a fine meal,
the pleasant mood was broken by the raised voices of the two eldest
princesses, bickering over something.

Nefertiti turned to them with a frown. "Girls! Lower your
voices and quit that bickering!"

The noise level dropped off and both girls muttered, "Yes,
mother."

"That's better," said Nefertiti. "Now, tell me – quietly, calmly!
– what this is all about."

Both of them tried to speak at once, until Nefertiti shushed
them once again.

"Enough! Meritaten – what are you girls quibbling about?"

"She started it," Meritaten complained. "She says it isn't fair
that I get to drive my own horses and she doesn't. I told her that's
because I'm a grown woman, and she isn't."

"Meket?" queried the Queen, turning to Meketaten, the second-
oldest princess.

"It still isn't fair!" protested Meketaten. "I'm a grown woman,
too, now that my courses have started! I should be able to drive my own
horses, too!"

"And I told her she is still too small," commented Meritaten. "She's too little to handle two big horses by herself."

"Well," said the Queen, considering, "I can see there's a certain amount of truth on both sides. Technically, Meket is a woman now, since her courses have begun. On the other hand, Meket, you still have some growing left to do. Merit is probably right in thinking you may be a bit small to handle two big horses. And the chariot you've been using may also be a bit large and heavy for you."

"But, Mother!" Meket started to protest.

Nefertiti cut her off. "Hear me out, Meket. I will speak to the head groom about finding you a smaller pair of horses and having a smaller chariot built for you. Then he can begin teaching you how to handle them."

"But that will take forever!" lamented Meketaten.

"No, it won't," Nefertiti told her. "It's just that you're so young and impatient, everything seems like forever! It only seems that way, though."

"Oh, all right," the princess grumbled, "I guess I can wait a little while. But I still think it isn't fair!"

"You'll live," her mother assured her. "Now, I don't want to hear any more bickering. You two should be setting an example for your younger sisters. Let's show your grandmother what well-bred young ladies you are!"

"Yes, mother," both girls replied politely.

Kiya, seated off to one side near the nurse who was feeding her son, listened to this interchange with great interest.

"Aha," she thought to herself, "so there is a chink in their apparent family solidarity! Everything is not as lovey-dovey as Pharaoh would have us believe. I must find a way to drive a wedge into this chink."

By this time, the young prince was becoming tired and fussy, so Kiya made a great show of retiring gracefully to put him to bed. She picked him up, despite his squirming, and carried him over to the Queen Mother for a good night kiss. Unaccustomed to being carried by his mother, the child was tense and crabby and not inclined to tolerate being kissed by a stranger.

Queen Tiye, who had raised half a dozen children of her own and knew how to make her wishes obeyed, said,

"Here – hand him to me."

Kiya reluctantly obeyed.

The old queen bounced him up and down on her knee, an entertainment universally understood and enjoyed by babies, and to his mother's amazement, he quieted down. Tiye gradually slowed the rate of bouncing, and by the time her knee stopped moving, the child was asleep, his little head resting on her chest. Queen Tiye kissed him on the top of his head, then gently handed him back to his mother.

Kiya gingerly picked up her son, careful not to wake him. She forced a smile and whispered softly to her mother-in-law,

"Thank you – and good night."

The Favorite and her son left the room, followed by her attendants and the child's nurse – to whom his mother promptly returned him the minute they were out of the room.

Once Kiya was gone, Nefertiti began to relax – but then she became aware that someone else was missing. Looking around, she counted noses: all six princesses, present and accounted for. Then she realized who was absent: her half-sister, Mutnodjmet.

Ever since Akhenaten had proclaimed his new religion, Mutnodjmet had distanced herself from the rest of the royal family. She attended official events, but reluctantly. At royal audiences, she sat at the very back of the dais. At celebrations, she was at the back or far side of the royal family group. She often joined Nefertiti and the princesses in the family's private apartments, but by and large, she sat apart, with her own ladies and her dwarves as companions. For the child who had stridently declared her desire to be queen, she had put a surprising distance between herself and her sister and brother-in-law.

Nefertiti decided she could not allow this absence to pass. Calling her steward over, she said,

"Go to my sister, Lady Mutnodjmet, and tell her that her presence is required at this family dinner in honor of the Queen Mother. Tell her I will brook no excuses."

"Yes, Your Majesty," agreed the Steward, bowing low. He turned and quickly left through a side door.

A short time later, the Steward returned, followed by a clearly disgruntled Lady Mutnodjmet, accompanied by her dwarf attendants, Mutefpre and Hemetnisu-weterneheh. The lady made the minimum required obeisance to the King, Queen and Queen Mother, then plopped herself down in a chair at the far fringes of the family group. Servants scurried to bring her small tables and load them with food and drink. Mutnodjmet ate and drank in sullen silence.

"Whatever is the matter with her?" asked the Queen Mother.

"She's just being her usual charming self," commented Akhenaten.

"I think she resents us for proclaiming a new religion and thereby making ourselves unpopular with the people," observed Nefertiti shrewdly. "She wants to be adored and admired. To her way of thinking, we have willfully abandoned that, and she doesn't want to be tarred with the brush of our unpopularity."

An uncomfortable silence followed this painfully accurate analysis, finally broken by the Queen Mother.

"I think it's high time we find her a husband," she said firmly. "She's certainly old enough and very eligible. While my side of the family may not be 'old nobility', she is part of the royal family, by marriage, yet not close enough to the throne that we need to worry about her children becoming rival claimants. She's certainly not contributing anything positive here."

"That is all too true, Mother," Akhenaten agreed. "She is ill-tempered and arrogant, putting on airs and screaming at the servants. And she doesn't really participate in the rituals of Aten worship – she just stands off to one side. I have only tolerated her for Nefertiti's sake."

"For my sake?" asked Nefertiti, surprised. "She's always been a thorn in my side. I've done my best to care for her and watch out for her interests over the years, for the sake of my father and her mother. But I confess, I would be relieved to see her go. By all means, Mother Tiye, let us find her a husband!"

"I will begin looking about for a suitable match," the Queen Mother replied, then continued, "Well, my dears, it has been a joy to see you all again, but I'm afraid I'm still worn out from travel. I feel a need to seek my couch early tonight."

With that, she rose and took her leave, and the rest soon followed her example.

The next day, the King and Queen took the Queen Mother on a tour of their splendid new capital city. Queen Tiye was duly impressed.

"It is magnificent, my son, truly magnificent," she told Akhenaten. "It is remarkable, what you have been able to achieve in such a short time. And you say the site was entirely vacant when you started?"

"Yes, Mother," he replied. "It was a virgin site, completely undeveloped, and thus, never dedicated to any other god. That is part of why I chose it."

"Of course," Nefertiti added, "that's not all. The reasons are far more complex – and arcane."

"Arcane?" Queen Tiye questioned.

"Well," said Pharaoh, "for one thing, this site is in the exact center of the country. My surveyors have measured it – and that is the more remarkable because it was not known to me at the time I chose it. As you will recall, I dreamt of the site before I ever saw it."

"And you remember the boundary stelae we pointed out?" asked Nefertiti.

"Yes," replied the Queen Mother.

"Well, if you draw lines from the royal tomb to each of the boundary stelae, they form a series of rays, like the rays of the sunrise seen through the notch in the cliffs, and each ray passes through a major structure, such as the Great Aten Temple and the Great Palace."

"But no one could ever see that," objected Queen Tiye.

"No one but God," replied her son. "I believe the divine eyes of Aten see the mystical architecture of His city as He sails across the sky each day."

"Ahh! I see," she acknowledged. "A secret, mystical tribute seen only by God. Very poetic!"

The next morning, when the Queen Mother went in search of her son, the Steward directed her to the King's office. To her great surprise, she found Akhenaten and Nefertiti pouring over the latest correspondence from abroad. She stood quietly inside the door, listening as a scribe read the latest letter from Akizzi, the vassal King of Qatna[8], pleading with Pharaoh to send troops to defend his land from the incursion of the Hittites and their treacherous ally, King Aitukama.

"'And now, the King of Hatti has sent Aitukama out against me, and he seeks my life,'" read the scribe.

"'And now Aitukama has written me and said, "Come with me to the King of Hatti." I said, "How could I go to the King of Hatti? I am a servant of the king, my lord, the King of Egypt." I wrote and replied thus to the King of Hatti.'

"He goes on like this for several lines," said the scribe, "complaining of the treachery of Aitukama and begging Your Majesty to send troops to defend him. He goes on to tell of the sack of much of the land of Upu:

"'Aitukama came and he sent Upu, the land of my lord, up in flames. He took the ruler's house and sacked it, and he took 200 disks of bronze, and he took 3 disks of gold and he took 1 disk of silver from the house of Birwaza.'

---

[8] A city in modern Syria.

"He goes on in the same vein," continued the scribe, "complaining that 'Teuwatti of Lapana and Arawuya of Ruhizzi place themselves at the disposition of Aitukama, and he sends Upu, the land of my lord, up in flames.' He adds that the kings of Nuhashshe, Nii, Zinzar and Tunanab – all of whom are Your Majesty's vassals – are saying that Your Majesty will not send troops. He goes on to plead with Your Majesty to send archers to his country. He says that so far, he has received only messengers from Your Majesty. He warns that, if troops do not come, Upu will no longer belong to Your Majesty – but if your troops do come, they will be welcomed in Qatna. That is all," said the scribe, rolling up his papyrus translation.

"Well," said Nefertiti, "it looks as though we need to send troops into Upu to put down this desertion of our allies to the Hittites!"

"Unfortunately," said Akhenaten, "by the time we could get troops there, we are likely to have lost more territory. Indeed, it may already have happened, in the time since Akizzi sent this letter. I will instruct Commander Paramessu to notify General Horemheb of the situation in Upu, if he is not already aware of it, and let him know that he will need to stiffen the spines of our allies in the area. Scribe: draw up a message to General Horemheb, notifying him to send troops to Qatna."

"Yes, Your Majesty," acknowledged the scribe.

Queen Tiye chose this moment to make her presence known. Stepping forward, she said,

"Well, my son, I see that you have taken up the reins of foreign correspondence! Well done!"

"Mother!" he replied. "Come join us."

A servant quickly brought a chair for the Queen Mother.

"I believe you are just in time to hear the latest letter from an old acquaintance of yours," Akhenaten commented. "I had the scribe hold back the letter from King Tushratta 'til last. I gather it is rather lengthy – several clay tablets' worth."

"Ah, yes – an old acquaintance, indeed," Queen Tiye agreed.

"Read us King Tushratta's letter," he directed the scribe.

The scribe picked a particularly thick scroll out of the pile of translated correspondence. He unrolled it, cleared his throat and began.

"'Say to Naphureya, the king of Egypt, my brother, my son-in-law, whom I love and who loves me: Message of Tushratta, Great King, King of Mitanni', etcetera. 'For me all goes well. For you may all go well. For Teye, may all go well.'"

"Ah – I see he has not forgotten me," Tiye commented.

The scribe glanced at her, then continued. "'For Tadukhipa, my daughter, may all go well. For the rest of your wives, may all go well.'"

Nefertiti frowned at hearing this greeting to her arch rival, while she, herself, was apparently regarded as only part of "the rest of your wives."

"'For your sons, for your magnates, for your chariots, for your horses, for your troops, for your country, and for whatever else belongs to you, may all go very, very well,'" read the scribe.

"Well, that's courteous of him!" commented Nefertiti. "He greets your mother, his daughter, and all of your horses, but neglects to mention your Queen!" she said, obviously annoyed. "It's a trait that appears to run in that family!"

"Remember, my dear, all these foreigners have less regard for women than we Egyptians do," Akhenaten said, in an attempt to mollify her. Turning back to the scribe, he said, "Go on – tell us what else he has to say."

"He goes on to speak of the correspondence between your father and himself, and how your father wrote to him about peace. He notes that 'Teye, the principal and favorite wife of Nimmureya, your father, knows all the words that...he would write to me over and over. It is Teye, your mother, whom you must ask about all of them', etcetera, etcetera," the scribe continued. "Do you want to hear all of it, Your Majesty? It's very long."

"Perhaps, for now, you could just give us a summary," said the King, who had been listening to letters from his fellow kings for several hours already.

"Yes, My Lord," said the scribe. "Uhh, he goes on to remind you of the love between himself and your father...that your father would never do anything to cause him distress, and vice versa, etcetera. He mentions three generations of royal daughters who have been given in marriage to your ancestors and yourself...and the sacks of gold and the jewelry sent to him by your father...and of all the gold that was sent to him after the arrival of Tadukhipa, and that was given to his messengers, etcetera, etcetera. But then he goes on to say, 'Because he sent him' – the messenger, that is – 'because he sent him posthaste, he did not have the statues brought to me, but everything else, whatever he did have brought, was limitless.'"

"Oh, no," protested the King, "not those statues again!"

"I'm afraid so, My Lord," the scribe acknowledged. "He goes on to mention again that your mother knows about this, and he says that, not only did your father agree to send statues of solid gold, he said,

'Don't talk of just gold ones! I will make ones with genuine lapis lazuli, too, and send them to you.'"

"Somehow, that's not quite how I remember it," commented Tiye.

"He goes on to talk about how he lamented your father's death," said the scribe, "and took neither food nor water, then goes on to say, 'Nimmureya, my brother, is not dead. Naphureya, his oldest son, now exercises the kingship in his place. Nothing whatsoever is going to be changed from the way it was before.'"

"I see," said the King. "So, in other words, my father was incredibly generous with him, so I should be, too."

"I believe that is the gist of it, My Lord," agreed the scribe. "He goes on to reiterate your father's love for him – and then he complains – again! – that the statues you sent him were merely wood, covered with gold."

"Not those statues again! I am really tired of hearing about those statues!" exclaimed Pharaoh.

"I'm afraid so, My Lord. King Tushratta seems to be absolutely obsessed with those gold statues. He goes on to remind you that your messenger, Mane – that would be Lord Menes, of course – your messenger was aware of your father's promise, and rejoiced with him. He goes on to say you should inquire of your mother about the words that she spoke to Keliya, his messenger...that he asked for statues of solid, chased gold, but you have not sent him what your father promised...and you haven't sent back his messengers since four years ago..."

"Well, that we can certainly do," commented the King. "Steward: locate King Tushratta's messengers and send them back to him."

"Yes, my King," acknowledged the Steward. The second scribe, whose job it was to record Pharaoh's orders, made a note of it.

The Chief Scribe continued, "He goes on in the same vein for several clay tablets." He glanced over the papyrus scroll, running it through his hands. "Then he goes on to request yet again that you give him the statues of chased gold, and that you further provide him with 'much gold that has not been worked' for his mausoleum. May you not cause him distress by withholding this, because, as they inevitably say, 'in my brother's country, gold is as plentiful as dirt.'"

"I'm really getting tired of that phrase," commented Akhenaten. "Even if it were true, I'm getting tired of hearing it!"

"He goes on to say that, if you grant his request, he will send a large delegation to you," continued the scribe. "He also says that he imprisoned the criminals you wrote to him about, Artashuba and Asali. He put them in chains and fetters and transported them to another town. But now he would like to know what their crime was, and what you would like him to do with them."

"Tell him they are traitors and he should send them to me," the King instructed. The recording scribe made a note of it.

"He goes on to describe his greeting gift to you," continued the scribe, indicating a pile of gifts on a nearby table, "and also the gold jewelry and two garments he sends as a greeting gift to your mother. And of course, there are also greeting gifts for Tadukhipa, his daughter."

Akhenaten waited to see if there was anything further. When it was apparent there was not, he glanced over at Nefertiti, whose jaw tightened at this repeated slight. She was becoming less of a fan of Tushratta by the minute.

"Is that it?" asked Pharaoh.

"Yes, my King," said the scribe.

"Finally!" said the King. "Send him his messengers back, and the usual sort of greeting gift, and the instructions about the criminals – and that's all. I am not sending him any gold statues. You can send him a few *minas* of unworked gold for his tomb, but nothing more. He needs to learn that no amount of nagging, or trying to make me feel cheap compared to my father, is going to get him his solid gold statues. Besides, the way his defense of his country is going, if I sent him the statues, the Hittites would have them inside a year. Either that, or he will need that tomb sooner than planned. I will hear no more of solid gold statues!"

So saying, the King rose and swept out of the room, followed by his Great Wife and his mother.

Chapter 30: Unexpected Envoys

An unexpected messenger arrived with Queen Tiye's party, one of Mariamne's household servants, carrying a letter from her to Thutmose. Thutmose ordered one of his servants to provide refreshments for the messenger, then carried the letter into his office. Seating himself at a large table he used as a desk, he broke the wax seal on the papyrus scroll.

"Greetings to my husband, Thutmose," he read, "from Mariamne, your wife. May all be well with you. All is well by me, and by our son, and by my son, and our servants and our horses and all our household.

"I am writing to you by the hand of the scribe Ahmose."

"Ah, so that's it," thought Thutmose. "Must be one of those wandering scribes that sell their services around the country."

"All is well with our son, Senmut. He grows like a river weed. I think he wants to follow in his father's trade. He painted a picture on the wall, which he says is Pharaoh and the Queen driving their chariots, drawn by teams of white horses. Or so he says. To my eyes, it more nearly resembled a herd of white hippos rising out of the river. If he has inherited any of his father's talent, perhaps it will bloom later. And alas! since he chose to paint this masterpiece on the gathering-room wall, I had the servants remove it, so you will have no opportunity to judge its artistic merit for yourself."

Thutmose laughed heartily at this image of his son. His laughter startled the serving girl who had just entered with a tray of thick beer and steaming bread fresh from the nearby communal bake oven. She set the tray down apologetically on the table and beat an obsequious retreat.

All of the servants were in awe of Thutmose, who not only regularly consorted with the King and Queen, divinities in their own right, but who also could create the most astonishingly lifelike images from the simple clay of the earth. This skill seemed more like magic than art to them and they superstitiously regarded him as some kind of wizard.

Given the magnitude of the task of building an entire city, Thutmose had been under a great deal of strain for several years now. Even though he bore it remarkably well, the strain was taking its toll. Fine lines were beginning to find their way across his handsome face. Each morning, it took him a little bit longer to limber up his fingers and work the kinks out of his back and shoulders. The serving girl was both surprised and glad to hear him laughing. She privately thought that her master needed to laugh a lot more.

Tearing off a hunk of bread, he continued to read.

"My son Shemu-el is rapidly becoming a man. This coming Inundation will be his thirteenth. He is beginning to sprout a few hairs on his chin, of which he is inordinately proud. A few days ago, he stopped at the stall of a barber in the marketplace and asked, 'Can a man get a shave here?' With all solemnity, the barber seated him in a chair, sharpened his razor on a strop, and then said, 'You point 'em out and I'll cut 'em off.' The entire marketplace thought it was very funny."

Thutmose thought it was pretty funny, too, and laughed so loudly, the servants down the hall looked at each other and smiled.

Thutmose shook his head at the mental image of the silly boy and thought back nostalgically to when he, himself, just teetered on the brink of manhood.

"Ah, was I ever that young?" he wondered, then returned to the letter.

"I have sent the lad to my father, who will continue training him in the management of the farm, which he will inherit when he comes of age. Although he is at the age of circumcision, that, of course, does not apply to him, as a member of the tribe of Yacub."

It was usual for Egyptian boys to be circumcised at puberty. This constituted a major rite of passage, one of which most boys were very proud. Thutmose had seen wall paintings more than a thousand years old celebrating this rite. Shemu-el, however, was a descendant of Yuya's father, Yacub (who was also called "Isra-el", to signify that he had been chosen by his god, El), and members of that tribe were circumcised soon after birth, so he would not be going through the rite with other boys his age. Sending him to his grandfather at this time had the added benefit of not drawing attention to how he differed from his friends. Thutmose thought that was very tactful of the boy's mother.

After some debate, he had yielded to his wife's insistence that their own son, Senmut, also be circumcised soon after birth, according to her tribe's custom. Although Thutmose himself, the boy's father, was thoroughly Egyptian, making the boy only half-Habiru, Mariamne had pointed out that, among the Israelites, it was the mother's tribal affiliation that determined the child's. So, according to their tradition, the boy was considered Habiru. Since the end result – removal of the foreskin - was much the same, but for minor differences in procedure and extent, and was regarded by both groups as a necessary form of ritual purity, Thutmose didn't feel that it mattered all that much whether the rite was performed in infancy or at puberty.

He read on: "My father has sent a large shipment of processed flax, which my women and I are busy spinning into thread and weaving into cloth. I have established a regular trade with merchants who travel the Middle East trading in dyestuffs. I now have reliable sources of dyes for all four colors. My people and I are very busy turning out our many-colored cloth, which is much in demand here in Thebes."

Mariamne's farm in the delta grew both grapes and flax. The farm she had inherited from her previous husband adjoined that of her father, who managed both, until her son should come of age. There was an area on the farm devoted to the preparation of linen fiber from the harvested flax, a very messy, smelly operation that entailed keeping the flax wet for several weeks in a shallow pond, allowing its outer husk to rot. This "retted" flax was then dried and beaten with flails to break up and remove the stiff outer husk, which was allowed to blow away in the wind, leaving behind the long "line" fibers, which could be spun into thread. The thread could be left its natural off-white or dyed any of the four available colors: blue, green, red or yellow, plus the mixture, brown. The Habiru weavers were noted for their vibrant geometrical patterns worked in many colors, so Mariamne's weavers required a plentiful supply of dyes.

Mariamne had begun by having a loom erected in an unused bedroom, on which she wove cloth for the family. Her brightly colored fabrics were much admired around Thebes and she soon received requests from fashionable women who wanted to buy them to use as wall hangings, rugs and cushion covers. In time, she had more weaving rooms added onto the back of the house, which grew into a substantial factory. She asked her father to devote more of her land to flax production, so he was able to keep her factory well supplied with linen fiber, which she and her women spun into fine linen thread on hand spindles. For some time, however, the principal limitation on her weavers' production had been a shortage of dyestuffs. Green and yellow were easy enough, and in ample supply, since many plants provided these colors. Blue and red were harder to come by – as Thutmose had learned in childhood, when he looked for red dye to color the sash for Nefertiti's doll. And now, of course, as an artist, he knew how difficult it could be to obtain pure, bright pigments for painting, even with the powerful assistance of Pharaoh's patronage. For Mariamne to have established reliable sources of red and blue dyes was a major commercial coup. He had to admire his wife's gift for commerce. He would have to remember to commend her for it in his reply. Mariamne went on to say:

"Have you built us a house yet in Pharaoh's new city? I am very anxious to join you there. The house here is very nice, but it is not home without you. If you do not hurry up and build us a house, I will come anyway, even if I have to sleep in a tent."

"Uh-oh," he thought. "I had better get to work on that, or she'll show up here unbidden, like she did before!"

He unrolled some more of the scroll and was surprised to see that the writing suddenly changed, from a polished hand to a much less certain one.

"I, Mariamne, write this," he read. "The scribe and his assistant teach me to write. I feed them and let them sleep on roof of house and they teach me. I think it smart for business woman to read and write."

Thutmose thought it was pretty smart, too. Once again, he had to admire Mariamne's enterprise.

"I also write to warn you," the letter continued. "I think these scribes former priests. I hear them talking and tell my servants to watch them and listen them. They talk of old gods and priests when they think they alone. I hear name of old First Prophet, Ptahmose, and quarry at Aswan, where I know him sent. These scribes speak of him with love. They plan some mischief for King and Queen. I try, but cannot hear what. Please warn Pharaoh. These men speak of others – I think there be many of them. They dangerous. Please be careful. Tell Pharaoh be careful.

"May all be well with you. I wish to see you soon. Mariamne."

I read Mariamne's letter with surprise and a certain admiration, as well as a great deal of concern. Not only was she a very determined and enterprising woman who was now adding reading and writing to her repertoire, she had also uncovered what could be a dangerous plot by the former priesthood of Amun. I determined to do as she had recommended and pass her warning on to Pharaoh, and to Mahu, the new Chief of Police.

Thutmose decided Mariamne's warning was urgent and must be passed on immediately. He rose and went straight to the new police headquarters, which was not far from his workshop. There, he sought out Mahu, the new Chief of Police, and read him the relevant parts of Mariamne's letter.

At first, the Chief was not inclined to take seriously a warning sent by a mere woman, until Thutmose filled him in on the whole story behind the Amun priesthood's attempt to assassinate the King and Queen back in Thebes. Once Mahu learned the depth of the involvement of Thutmose and his pupils in ferreting out and thwarting that attempt on the lives of the royal couple, he had more reason to believe that a member of the artist's family would be in a position to recognize evidence of a further plot against Pharaoh. By the time Thutmose left, the Chief was convinced of the seriousness of the warning. He agreed to Thutmose's suggestion that he send out agents to find and spy on former members of the Amun priesthood, in hopes of averting any further plots against the royal family.

Thutmose also took the warning straight to the King, as Mariamne had requested. Since Akhenaten was only too well aware of how close he had come to being killed that day in Thebes, and how much he owed to Thutmose and his protégé, he listened very attentively to Mariamne's warning. He was glad to hear that his new Chief of Police had been informed of the threat and was already acting on the tip. He called the Chief in to a meeting to discuss his planned recruitment of agents to spy on the former priesthood, and allocated additional funds to pay for the program. In an appropriate twist of irony, Pharaoh used gold taken from melting down statues of Amun confiscated from his temples.

Thutmose was gratified that the warning was taken seriously. He sent a short message back to Mariamne, thanking her for the warning. He put it in cautiously obscure terms, just in case it should fall into the wrong hands.

"To my esteemed wife, Mariamne, from her husband, Thutmose the artist. All is well with me. May all be well with you, and with our son, and with your son, and with all the household.

"My Lord – may he be well! – thanks you for the message about your visitors. Your message to him was well received. He is doing as you suggested. Indeed, he is watching and listening throughout the land. You may be visited by his servants from time to time. They will watch over you. My Lord is grateful to you and sends his greetings.

"As for the house, I have begun to build it. All should be complete and ready to receive you before the Indundation. It will be a fine house, spacious and pleasant. I believe you will be pleased. I look forward to seeing you. Your husband, Thutmose."

Mariamne's was not the only surprising letter received in Akhetaten at that time. As Pharaoh and his Great Wife were going over foreign correspondence with their scribes, they received word that a delegation had just arrived from Assyria, carrying a letter from their king. Pharaoh instructed his Steward to show the messenger into his office and to provide refreshments in the waiting room for the envoy's men. (The envoy himself, of course, had already been shown to a room where he could bathe and change into fresh clothing, since no one could be allowed to enter Pharaoh's presence unclean. Egyptian supplicants would be expected to shave, as well, but allowances were made for foreign visitors, most of whom wore long curly locks and luxuriant beards. They were, after all, merely uncouth foreigners, not civilized Egyptians.)

The Steward rapped on the floor with his staff, opened the door and announced, "The envoy from His Majesty Asshur-Uballit, King of Assyria."

The envoy entered and dropped to one knee before Pharaoh, his right fist over his heart in a salute of greeting. He was a short, stocky man with swarthy skin and a powerful build. His oily black hair was worn in long ringlets, topped by a tall felt cap. His long beard was styled in matching ringlets, and gold rings dangled at his ears. Black fringe spiraled down the length of his long woolen robe, which was topped with a multi-colored cloak thrown back over one shoulder. Several gold rings featuring carnelian and lapis lazuli adorned his thick fingers. He exuded an ominous power that spoke volumes of things to come. His confident swagger shouted that his people were on the rise.

Pharaoh bade the Assyrian to rise and signaled that he should hand his cuneiform tablets to the scribe. The envoy handed them to the scribe and asked permission to deliver his king's message to Pharaoh. Like all good messengers, he had committed it to memory. Pharaoh nodded his permission.

In a stentorian voice that could be heard all the way to the market square, the messenger recited:

"My master says: 'Say to the king of Egypt: Thus Asshur-uballit, the King of Assyria. For you, your household, for your country, for your chariots and your troops, may all go well. I send my messenger to you to visit you and to visit your country. Up to now, my predecessors have not written; today I write to you. I send you a beautiful chariot, two horses and one date-shaped stone of genuine lapis lazuli, as your greeting gift. Do not delay the messenger whom I send to you for a visit. He should visit and then leave for here. He should see what you are like and what your country is like, and then leave for here.' Thus saith my master," stated the messenger, ending with another fist-to-chest salute.

The King and Queen waited politely for a moment to see if more would follow, but it appeared that that terse message was all there was. Akhenaten looked at Nefertiti and raised an eyebrow. She looked back and shrugged. Akhenaten turned back to the messenger, who still stood at attention.

He replied courteously, "We welcome the envoy from the King of Assyria. Enjoy your stay with us while we assemble a suitable greeting gift for your master and compose a reply. When those are ready, we will be happy to send you back to your master, our brother, King Asshur-Uballit of Assyria," said Pharaoh to the messenger. He turned then to the Chief of Police.

"Chief Mahu, see to the *security* of our Assyrian visitors," he said with careful emphasis.

The cautious Chief of Police got the message. "Aye, Your Majesty. I will see to it that our visitors are *kept safe*," he replied, meaning that he would not let them out of his sight while they were in the Two Lands.

Pharaoh knew he could count on his new Chief of Police to insure that the Assyrians saw only what he wanted them to see, and nothing else. They would see endless numbers of Egyptian troops, well-supplied with weapons; and well-fortified border towns. On their way home, they would see the crocodile-filled canal and string of well-garrisoned forts forming the Wall of the Princes. The message would be clear: we are willing to open a dialogue with you, Assyria, but don't even think about marching on the fully-manned, well-equipped, well-guarded borders of Egypt.

Chapter 31: Houses Mortal and Eternal

At last, the work on Kiya's Northern Palace was nearing completion. It now needed only a modicum of supervision as the artists and artisans completed the mosaic tiled floors, the wall paintings and the final trim work. The wooden interior doors with bronze fittings were in the process of being installed. The casting of the large bronze front doors was complete; once final cleanup of the bronze was completed, the doors would be installed. After that and a final cleaning, the furniture could be moved in, and her Royal Highness, the Favorite, could move in. Thutmose would be only too glad to be done with her and her palace.

In the mean time, the load had slackened sufficiently that he was able to turn his attention to the design and building of his own house. The design was now complete and Thutmose had placed an order for materials. Mud brick, of course, was made on the spot, from Nile mud, with straw from nearby fields brought in to use as a binder. Wood, however, was not available nearby and had to be imported, the majority of it from Lebanon. Wood was costly and usually used only for structural supports and roof beams, but since Thutmose enjoyed the King's favor, he also had fine imported cedar planks from which doors would be constructed.

The house would adjoin his existing workshop. Up to now, he had usually slept on the roof of the workshop, or in an alcove in the room he used as a studio. Now, he would have a fine master bedroom in the new house. At the back of the new house would be the kitchen area, with all the latest conveniences. The house would boast its own beehive-shaped bake oven in a small courtyard off the kitchen, with servants' quarters and storerooms behind it. He gave a lot of thought to designing a sophisticated system for bringing in and distributing drinking and bathing water.

Mindful of what Mariamne had written to him about her weaving business, Thutmose had designed an additional building behind the main house which would serve as the weaving factory. It would house several weaving rooms, rooms for storing supplies and equipment, and a courtyard for dyeing yarn and fabric. In front of the courtyard, facing the street, was a large room that could be used as a showroom and shop.

The plans for the house and weaving factory were completed by the time Kiya moved into the Northern Palace. Rows of mud bricks sat baking in the sun, while the pile of completed bricks grew higher and wider.

While Kiya made plans for a grand party to celebrate the completion of her new palace, Thutmose and his workmen began erecting the timber framework for his new house and factory. Kiya condescended to invite him, a mere artist, to her party, but he politely declined, citing the need to work on his own house, now that he had completed hers.

Since his house, unlike Kiya's palace, was basically a simple structure, albeit a roomy one, work progressed quickly. He was soon able to write to Mariamne, telling her to begin preparing for the move, and letting her know that she should transport all of her spinning, dyeing and weaving equipment, as well.

In the midst of all this construction, he still had to find time to create additional statues of the royal family. While the faces and bodies of the King and Queen had matured, so had the depth of Thutmose's work. He had recently begun work on new busts of both Akhenaten and Nefertiti which he felt would be his finest work to date.

Until Akhenaten's reign, art in Egypt had served not so much an "artistic" or decorative function, as a formal, ritual function, almost magical or religious in nature. Many images, especially those in tombs and temples, served to document the lives, titles and ritual functions of important individuals. A secondary purpose was to serve as substitute vessels for the soul, should the mummy of the individual be damaged and, hence, uninhabitable in the afterlife. It was partly for this reason that people were traditionally portrayed in the characteristic strange, rigid stance, with the feet and legs shown from the side, the shoulders turned widthwise toward the viewer, and the face portrayed in profile. In this traditional pose, all body parts were shown and accounted for, to insure that the subject had access to them all in the afterlife.

Both Bek and Thutmose had broken with this tradition, with Akhenaten's backing. First had come Bek's distorted, attenuated style, which was almost a caricature of the features typical of the royal family. It was radically different from the traditional poses of the past, but was even further from an accurate representation of reality. Thutmose had broken away from both tradition and Bek's style, seeking to reproduce a faithful three-dimensional reality in his sculpture. In recent years, he had striven to go beyond the surface reality of his subjects, in an attempt to portray something of their inner being. This was particularly true of his principal subjects, Akhenaten and Nefertiti.

He had recently completed a very fine bust of the Queen Mother, as well, which had been commissioned for a shrine in her honor at Gurob, in the Sinai. It was small, but very powerful, portraying Queen Tiye's forceful character in gilded wood, wearing the tall, two-feathered Hathor crown. He felt it was his best work to date.

Now, he had recently started work on a new bust of Nefertiti, which he felt would be even finer than the bust of Queen Tiye. Today, the Queen had graciously consented to sit for this work at Thutmose's studio, rather than having him come to the palace. Nefertiti knew that he was busy overseeing the work of at last building his own house, as well as continuing to create statues of the royal family, so she had agreed to pose in the studio, where he could keep an eye on the construction work next door.

Thutmose had first made numerous drawings as studies for the new bust. Having settled on a very simple, straightforward pose, he had then made a model in clay. Finally, he had begun work on the block of fine limestone which would become the finished piece. He glanced back and forth from the living model to the drawings, to the clay model, to the block of limestone, from which the Queen's face and tall crown were beginning to emerge.

Most of the statues of the King and Queen were made in separate pieces, with the face and neck modeled from one block of stone and the back and top of the head and the crown made from another block. The two pieces would then be joined together with internal fittings of bronze, and the completed piece painted to resemble life.

This bust, however, would be made in one piece, except for the lenses of the eyes, which would be ground from rock crystal. Once these rock crystal lenses were installed, the eyes would look startlingly lifelike. In some cases, eyebrows would also be made of glass paste, shaped to fit into grooves in the stone, fired and then attached; but for this bust, the eyebrows would be painted on.

After working without pause for an hour, Thutmose decided to take a break and check on the progress on his house. He sloshed his hands in a bowl of water, then wiped them on a piece of cloth.

"Excuse me, Your Majesty," he said to the Queen. "I just need to go next door and see how the workmen are doing on my house."

"Go right ahead, Thutmose," she told him. "You deserve time to complete your own house. You have been so devoted to us. I am sorry that it has taken this long for you to have been allowed enough time to work on your own house.

"You go on and check on your house. I need to stretch a bit, anyway," she said, rising.

Thutmose dashed out the door, leaving Nefertiti and her attendants behind. Nefertiti stretched, then wandered over to the sculptor's table, where she inspected the drawings, the model and the work in progress. It looked to her as though her own face was emerging blindly from the stone block. It was a bit eerie to see her own features, known from her silver hand mirror, appearing out of the stone like that, as though some strange alter ego were trapped inside the block, trying to get out. In a way, it was uncannily close to how she sometimes felt, trapped in a role she had never chosen, one she had simply been born into. She had striven all her life to accept and fulfill that role with grace, yet sometimes she longed to be free of her golden chains, free to follow her own heart. Perhaps, she thought, the artist should just leave the work like this, to portray how trapped she felt.

But then, as she looked at her own face straining to get out of the stone, she felt a moment of panic, as though she were suffocating. Suddenly, she wanted the sculptor to return and wield his chisel, to finish freeing her from her prison of stone, to let her breathe.

At that moment, thankfully, Thutmose returned.

Nefertiti drew a deep breath as she returned to her seated pose.

"How's the house coming?" she asked.

"Good. Good," he replied. "It's almost done. I should be able to move in in about another week."

"Congratulations," she said. "I'm sure your wife will be thrilled."

"Yes," he agreed, carefully chipping away flakes of stone from the bust. "I've already written to her, telling her to pack up and begin the move."

They went on chatting as he slowly freed more of Nefertiti's face from the stone.

After another hour, he realized the sun was riding low in the sky, the light striking long through the grillwork of the small west-facing windows. He put down his tools and wiped his hands on a cloth, then brushed the loose stone dust from the bust, now almost entirely free from the block.

Nefertiti rose and stretched, then stepped over to inspect the bust. It was still rough, but already showed an uncanny likeness to her own face, even to a haunting trace of sadness in the blank eyes. Nefertiti caught her breath.

"Oh, Thutmose, it's amazing. I've seen your work over the years, but you never cease to astound me. Even rough like this, I feel as though you've looked inside me and captured...my very soul," she said, reverently.

She walked around the table, looking at the work from every angle.

"I don't know how you do it," she said. "I'm glad I know you and trust you, because, seeing this, I feel utterly *exposed*. We both know that, as Queen, I wear a public face, always calm and in control, a mask that hides what I really feel, what I can never allow the world to see. But you! You see through that, to the heart and soul beneath. It's a little bit frightening, having someone see through me like that," she said, looking into his eyes. "It gives you a sort of power over me, and that's a bit scary – as though you could steal my soul, if you wanted to."

Thutmose fell to one knee before her. He clasped her outstretched hand and pressed his forehead to it.

"My Queen!" he exclaimed. "I am your most devoted and adoring subject! I would never let any harm befall you! You can trust me."

"I know I can," she replied, feeling a wave of warmth move from the hand he held to course through her entire body. "I think...there is no one I trust as deeply as I trust you. I already owe you my life three times over. But dare I trust you with...my heart as well?" she said, her voice dropping to a whisper inaudible to her attendants, who sat at a small game table across the room, playing Hounds and Jackals.

She turned to one side, her back between her attendants and the artist. She squeezed his hand with the one he held and held his gaze with her own.

"I envy you the ability to express yourself in your art," she said. "I do not have such a skill, and there is much I cannot say, that I must keep hidden behind my royal mask. I can only hope that you can truly see what is in my heart — see it, and keep silent about what must never be spoken."

He raised his head and looked into her eyes, and she looked back into his for a long moment. Hidden from view of her attendants, he raised her hand and reverently pressed his lips to her hand, holding it there a long moment.

He looked up at her. Softly, so her attendants couldn't hear, he said, "My heart has always belonged to you, my Queen, since the day I first saw you."

She squeezed his hand with the one he still held.

Releasing her hand, he got to his feet, bowed slightly and said loudly, "I see, and I obey, my Queen. As always, your wish is my command."

In a louder voice, she said, "Very good, Master of Works. The work progresses well. I shall come again soon."

"I look forward to it, Your Majesty," he said, bowing.

With that, she turned and swept regally out of the room. Her attendants jumped up, hastily gathering the game pieces into the compartment in the game table, which folded into a carrying case. They quickly followed her out to the street, where chariots awaited the party.

Thutmose heard the horses' hooves clatter away on the stone pavement outside. He stood for a while without moving, staring blindly at the half-completed bust as the late sunlight reddened and grew dim. At last, he covered the bust with a cloth and put it away on a shelf. He felt that his heart was ready to burst within him.

Master Auta decided that it was time he paid a visit to the workshop of his friend and former pupil, Thutmose. He was embarrassed to realize he had been in town this long without visiting his protégé's workshop, so he headed out of the palace and walked briskly to the south.

Thutmose was hard at work putting a smooth finish on the bust of Nefertiti when one of his apprentices told him he had a visitor.

"Tell him I'll be there in just a minute," he said over his shoulder, involved in the delicate job of polishing the queen's fine limestone features.

Auta, who had followed the boy, put his finger to his lips to enjoin the lad to silence, then stood quietly just inside the doorway, watching Thutmose at work. Several minutes later, the sculptor reached a stopping point, put down his polishing cloth and brushed away the haze of limestone dust and polishing compound from the sculpture. Wiping his hands on another cloth, he turned toward the doorway, then stopped when he noticed his visitor.

"Auta!" he cried. "I didn't hear you come in."

He stepped over to the old man and clasped him in a bear hug. The two men pummeled each other's backs in happy greeting.

"It's so good to see you!" Thutmose exclaimed, stepping back to arm's length and surveying his old master. "How are you? When did you get here?"

"I'm fine, lad, just fine. Older, stiffer, but otherwise all in working order," the old man assured him. "I arrived with the Queen Mother. I'm sorry I didn't get over here to see you sooner, but my queen has been keeping me busy. I see yours has been keeping you busy, too," he added, stepping over to the table to inspect the limestone bust of Nefertiti. "A beautiful piece of work, my boy! Your talent just continues to grow. What a gift you have!"

The old man bent down and peered closely at the sculpture, inspecting it minutely.

"It's remarkable, how you've captured her expression, even in the unpainted stone. I can't wait to see it when it's painted and the lenses installed in the eyes," he said. "It looks like you should finish it soon."

"Yes," Thutmose agreed, somewhat reluctantly. "I'll paint it over the next few days. While the paint dries, I plan to work on grinding the lenses. I've obtained a splendid piece of dark rock crystal that should do very nicely. I managed to strike a couple of large flakes off, so I'm almost ready to begin grinding them into shape. As you know, that's a pretty laborious process."

"Why don't you have your apprentices work on that?" the old man asked.

Thutmose hesitated, looking almost embarrassed. "If the subject were anyone else, I would," he said, "but for the Queen, for this bust, I want them to be perfect. I think it's my greatest work, and I want it to be absolutely perfect."

Master Auta was a very shrewd old man who had seen a lot in his time, and he knew Thutmose well. He knew it was Nefertiti who had first spotted the sculptor's talent when he was just a boy, and that Thutmose had always been particularly devoted to her, even more devoted than he was to the King. Yet, there was something more here, some deeper feeling. He looked intently at the younger man, who dropped his eyes, then looked away, busying himself with putting things away.

"Ah," thought the old man to himself, "so that's how it is. I can hardly blame him, but I pray to all the old gods and the new one that his heart doesn't lead him to do anything foolish. There is nothing but pain in this for him."

Aloud, he said, "I understand, my son. I have some inkling of how you feel."

Alarmed, Thutmose asked, "Is it that obvious?"

"No," Auta replied, "only to someone who knows you as well as I do. And of course, I would never speak of it to anyone."

"Thank the Aten for that!" Thutmose exclaimed.

After a moment of awkward silence, Auta asked, "Does the Queen know?"

Thutmose thought about it a moment, then answered slowly, "I believe she does. She has not said so in as many words, of course, not with her attendants always about, but I believe she knows. And I think...she feels something for me, as well."

The old man closed his eyes and shook his head from side to side.

"Oh, my boy," he said. "This is not good. This can lead to nothing but trouble."

"I know, I know!" Thutmose agreed. He checked quickly outside the door, to see if anyone was within earshot. Thankfully, no one was, and the loud sounds of chisel on stone, adze on wood, the grinding of pigments and rhythmic scrape of handsaws rising from the sculpture and furniture workshops on either side reassured him that no one could overhear. "Do you not think that I have tried to free my heart of this hopeless passion? I have tried, but I have failed utterly. I have prayed to gods both old and new to take this from me, but all have turned a deaf ear. I have no power over my own heart."

"My poor boy," said the old man. "I pity you this. The heart is like a wild horse, untamed, powerful and uncontrollable. It can take you on a wild ride – take care it does not kill you," he said, shaking his head. "Well, I trust that, if you cannot deny your emotions, you are at least well skilled in concealing them. If you cannot control your heart, at least control your actions."

"I believe I do," Thutmose assured him. "You said, yourself, that you know me far better than most, having known me since I was a boy. You know me better than my own father. I believe I can hide my true feelings from others, though not from you."

"I hope so, my son," he said. "I hope so. I know you are suffering – but this is something you must simply endure, something you must suffer in silence."

"I know," Thutmose agreed.

"What are the plans for this bust?" asked Auta, turning back to the sculpture. "Has the King seen it?"

"No," said Thutmose. "He hasn't seen it, and there are no plans for it."

Auta turned and scrutinized his former apprentice.

"The King doesn't know it exists, does he?" he asked.

Thutmose hesitated, then admitted, "No. He doesn't."

"And you don't plan to show it to him, do you?" Auta asked shrewdly.

Thutmose looked back at him in silence. Finally, he said, "No. I don't."

"You're going to keep it for yourself," Auta stated. It was not a question.

"You're right. I am," Thutmose agreed.

"Your wife's not going to like it when she gets here," the old man observed.

"I'm sure that's true," Thutmose conceded. He thought about it, then said, "I'll have to keep it hidden in here, where she won't see it."

"Hah!" snorted the old man derisively. "Good luck with that!"

They were both awkwardly silent for a minute. At last, Auta broke the silence, asking Thutmose to show him around the rest of the workshop. Relieved, Thutmose led him around to the other rooms, introducing him to the newer apprentices he didn't already know. Many of the older ones had been his pupils in previous years and were happy to see him again.

After the old man had greeted all and sundry and inspected the work in progress, he and Thutmose had lunch at a nearby tavern, washed down with plenty of thick, yeasty beer. But no amount of beer was sufficient to wash away the sense of foreboding Auta felt when he thought about what he had learned this afternoon. Thutmose was like a son to him; he wanted to see the younger man happy in his life. But no matter how he looked at what he had learned today, he could see nothing but grief ahead for his former student.

Chapter 32: Plans & Preparations

Not long after the Dowager Queen arrived, she and Nefertiti decided that it was time to celebrate the new regime with an appropriate festival.

Akhenaten's agents had fanned out all over Egypt, observing the mood of the people. The King's officials made sure that members of the nobility adhered to the new religion, even entering and inspecting their city homes and country villas and smashing or confiscating shrines and statues of the old gods wherever they found them. Offending nobles were admonished to turn their eyes to the Aten, the One True God, and were even given small images of the royal couple worshipping the Aten, cast in bronze or gold, as suitable to the recipient's rank. While no severe punishment was meted out, unless they were suspected of plotting against the King, the offenders were turned out of any public offices they held. Any gold, silver or bronze idols were confiscated, melted down and added to the coffers of the King.

Common people were not deemed significant enough to merit such direct royal attention. They were pretty much left to worship their traditional household gods as they chose. Most of these were minor deities held to have an influence over common daily activities, such as childbirth, sickness and health.

What did impact the common people, however, was the loss of their traditional festivals, associated with significant events of their lives, the solar year or important astronomical events. For most of them, these were almost the only real celebrations in their lives, high points of merrymaking, singing, dancing and feasting. For most people, these festivals were the only times they got to eat meat. The loss of all the traditional religious festivals made their lives dreary, cheerless rounds of thankless toil. They didn't miss the temples all that much, since they were not generally welcome in them, but they did miss the festivals and resented the authority that had arbitrarily deprived them of one of the few sources of merriment in their lives. The King's spies had carried news of this widespread disaffection back to Akhetaten.

Nefertiti and Tiye felt that a new celebration was needed to replace the old festivals and give the people something new to rejoice about. So, they decided to throw a huge reception, a Great Durbar, at Akhetaten. It would be celebrated throughout the land, and all the Great Kings and vassal kings would be invited. There would be pomp and circumstance for the nobility, and music, dancing and feasting for all. The Royal Treasury would provide funds for entertainment, food and drink, not only for Akhetaten, but for all the major cities in the land.

When the two queens proposed the celebration to Pharaoh, he was enthusiastic about the idea. He felt it was high time to celebrate both his new religion and his new capital city. He heartily approved the planned events, decorations, menus and entertainment. However, he felt there was one more element needed.

"It is high time to announce your Co-Regency, my dear," he said to Nefertiti. "I have been grooming you for some time now, training you to carry out all the offices of Pharaoh. It is time to make it official. At the culmination of the Great Durbar, I will crown you as my Co-Pharaoh."

"Are you sure that is wise?" Nefertiti asked. "I'm not sure the people will accept a woman Pharaoh, and the nobles certainly won't. After all, look what happened to Hatshepsut. Her successor wiped her out of history. I don't want to suffer her fate."

"That was at least partly because her father had not publicly designated her as his heir," Akhenaten pointed out. "She insisted that he had named her his heir, after the fact, but there was no public record to support her claim. She couldn't take the throne until after her brother-husband, Thutmosis II, died, and she had the excuse of acting as regent for his son. And she kept the son, the legal heir, in submission until she was too old and ill to go on. So, there were real legal grounds to dispute the legitimacy of her claim to the throne. I can understand why Thutmosis felt it necessary to insure his son's succession by wiping out Hatshepsut's claim – and her memory, along with it, terrible though that fate was for her. That's one more reason why I want to publicly crown you Pharaoh, with the whole world watching. Then no one can question your legitimacy as Pharaoh after I die."

Nefertiti did not like this talk of dying, nor did Tiye. Nevertheless, Akhenaten was adamant. Nefertiti would be crowned as Co-Pharaoh at the Great Durbar. As a first step, she would change her name. Effective immediately, she now became known as Neferneferuaten-Nefertiti.

They set a time for the festive event, the following spring, far enough in the future to allow invitations to reach even the furthest of the Great Kings, a thousand miles away in Babylonia and Hatti, and allowed enough additional time for the recipients to assemble appropriate envoys and gifts to send. Invitations were immediately sent out to the Great Kings, and soon after that, to the vassal kings of the city-states in the regions of Canaan and Naharin.

The two queens were kept busy planning the great event. An army of weavers and seamstresses were employed to turn out additional kilts, gowns and robes for the royal family, and the royal corps of artists were even busier, creating additional crowns, scepters, collars, bracelets and other jewelry for the royal party and "Gold of Honor" *shebu* necklaces to be given out by the pair of Pharaohs as rewards for their most loyal followers.

Their messengers traveled to the furthest reaches of the Middle East, carrying the invitations to the Great Durbar to all the great and petty kings of the known world. While few kings would travel to the event, themselves, none could afford to offend the most powerful king in the world by failing to send a delegation and lavish greeting gifts.

Soon, the envoys began to arrive. Accommodations had to be arranged for all of them in Akhetaten. The population of the city had already grown to nearly 50,000 regular, full-time inhabitants. The Great Durbar was expected to add another ten to twenty thousand. Every family would be expected to play host to visiting dignitaries. Assigning visitors to appropriate hosts, according to rank, was a major organizational headache for the Royal Steward, assisted by a small army of scribes. Additional Akhetaten residents would be pressed into service to act as guides for visitors as they arrived.

It was chaos, but remarkably cheerful chaos, as most people were happy to finally have the chance to celebrate *something*. By now, they were so starved for fun, they were willing to celebrate just about anything.

Of course, since travel was slow and distances to foreign kingdoms very large, it often took messengers two or more months to travel from Egypt to foreign kings, and vice versa. It was not uncommon for these messengers to pass each other on the way, sometimes meeting their countrymen coming or going, and sometimes crossing unawares as their parties followed different routes. This lag often caused confusion, making it difficult to determine to what prior message a current message was replying. Often, circumstances had changed between the time a message was sent and the time its reply was received. It was also not uncommon for several envoys from one king to arrive in series. They would all remain as guests of the crown until Pharaoh saw fit to send them home.

One morning as Pharaoh was holding audience, a delegation from Hatti arrived.

Following several local and regional petitioners, there was a stir at the door. The Lord Chamberlain rapped his staff on the floor and announced:

"A delegation from the Land of Hatti, with a letter for His Majesty from the King of Hatti!"

There was a stir among the courtiers, all of whom were surprised to find a party of Hittites in their midst. It had been a long time since the king of that notoriously warlike nation had sent an envoy to the Egyptian court. In the years since the previous Hittite king had last corresponded with Akhenaten's father, the Hittites had expanded their territory considerably, engulfing several small kingdoms that had formerly been vassals of Egypt, as well as a large part of Mitanni. What did this embassage mean? Was it to be a resumption of diplomatic relations, of peaceful co-existence? Or was it the prelude to a declaration of war? Everyone was whispering to his neighbor.

The party of Hittites – minus their weapons, of course – proceeded toward the dais, where Pharaoh sat with his entourage. Queen Tiye sat on his left, Nefertiti on his right. Kiya sat behind Akhenaten, to his left, while other lesser wives clustered around the back of the dais, or below the steps on either side. Several huge black Nubian guards armed with spears and swords stood around the back and sides of the dais.

The Hittite and his entourage stopped before the dais and fell to one knee, right fist to heart in a salute similar to the Assyrians'.

"O Great King," announced the Hittite ambassador in a ringing voice, "I bring you greetings from His Majesty Suppiluliumash, King of Hatti."

Pharaoh signaled that the envoy might rise. He did so, followed by the rest of his party, about a dozen in all. Their dress was similar to that of the Assyrians: long woolen robes in various colors, trimmed with spiral fringe and topped with a patterned, multicolored stole, also trimmed with fringe. As befitting his rank, the ambassador's robe was dyed a rich, deep red and his fringes were of gold. He wore a tall round cap edged with gold. A servant hovered beside him, carrying a clay tablet on a red cushion, edged with still more gold fringe.

Akhenaten's Chief Scribe stepped forward. The Hittite ambassador indicated that his servant should present the clay tablet to the scribe, who took it, bowed to the ambassador and retired to his post at one side of the dais. The ambassador's servant melted back into the group.

Like the Assyrian envoy, this one had committed his king's message to memory. He recited it in a stentorian voice clearly heard by all:

"'Thus the Sun'" – meaning the Hittite king – "'Suppiluliumash, Great King, King of Hatti. Say to Huriya, the King of Egypt, my brother:'

"'For me all goes well. For you may all go well. For your wives, your sons, your household, your troops, your chariots and in your country, may all go very well.'

"'Neither my messengers, whom I sent to your father, nor the request that your father made, saying 'Let us establish only the most friendly relations between us,' did I indeed refuse. Whatsoever your father said to me, I indeed did absolutely everything he asked. And my own request, indeed, that I made to your father, he never refused; he gave me absolutely everything.'

"Why, my brother, have you held back the presents that your father made to me when he was alive?"

Akhenaten raised his hand to his mouth and murmured beneath it to Nefertiti, "Here it comes. Here's what he's asking for."

The ambassador continued his memorized missive:

"'Now, my brother, you have ascended the throne of your father, and just as your father and I were desirous of peace between us, so now too should you and I be friendly with one another. The request that I expressed to your father I shall express to my brother, too. Let us be helpful to each other.'"

The ambassador took a breath and continued his sovereign's message:

"'My brother, do not hold back anything that I asked of your father. As to the two statues of gold, one should be standing, one should be seated. And, my brother, send me the two silver statues of women, and a large piece of lapis lazuli, and a large stand for...'"

Pharaoh's attention wandered off the ambassador's speech, then back again.

The ambassador went on with his king's message:

"'...If my brother wants to give them. But if my brother does not want to give them, when my chariots have been readied for sending to him, along with many linen garments, I will send them to my brother. Whatever you desire, my brother, write to me so I can send it to you.'"

"'I herewith send you as your greeting-gift:'" continued the envoy, signaling several gift-bearers to come forward, "one silver rhyton, with the head of a stag, three minas its weight; two silver disks, ten minas their weight, depicting two large *nikiptu* trees."

The bearers paraded the Hittite king's greeting gifts before him as the ambassador described them.

He smiled at the ambassador and inclined his head to signify that the gifts had been acknowledged and accepted.

After an exchange of polite diplomatic pleasantries, the Hittite delegation was dismissed and led off by the Steward, to settle in to their designated quarters in the palace. There would be a state banquet later, in their honor, at which the Hittites and Egyptians could become better acquainted. Over the next several weeks, there would be formal reviews of troops, visits to the Great Aten Temple, numerous hunts for water fowl or, for the boldest among them, wild lions.

And so on it went, as delegation after delegation arrived from all over the known world, until it seemed that Akhetaten must burst at the seams. To make life even more difficult for the overworked steward, multiple messengers and delegations arrived from several foreign kingdoms. Some of these represented opposing factions within their own country and were not always friendly to one another. The most difficult of these were the Hittites.

In addition to the first delegation, which appeared to have left Hatti long before the invitation to the Durbar arrived, there was another one from King Suppililiuma, responding to the invitation with a lavish display of greeting gifts. In addition, there were two separate delegations from sons of the Great King, Zita and Arnuwanda, each apparently currying favor with the King of Egypt. The messengers from Prince Zita, who also appeared to be unaware of the planned Durbar, arrived last, after the delegation from Prince Arnuwanda.

As with the previous groups, they arrived during one of Pharaoh's public audiences and were announced by the Lord Chamberlain.

"A delegation from Prince Zita, son of the King of Hatti," he announced loudly, striking the floor with his staff.

As before, Pharaoh was flanked by the two queens, his mother on the left and his Great Wife on the right, with Favorite Kiya behind and to his left and other, lesser wives arrayed behind her.

Prince Zita's envoy marched up the aisle and dropped to one knee before Pharaoh. He bowed his head and saluted the Egyptian king with an outstretched right arm, then brought his fist to his chest. It made a loud smack as it connected with his bronze-studded leather breastplate. This envoy was clearly a military man.

The sound got Kiya's attention away from the gossip going on in the ranks of women behind her. Curious, she peered around Pharaoh's left shoulder to see this visiting warrior. She always found martial accomplishments very attractive in a man.

At first, all she could see was the top of the man's head as he knelt before Pharaoh. After a moment, Pharaoh signaled that the man might rise. When he did, Kiya was able to get a better look at him.

As she had hoped, he was tall and well-built, with a very martial air about him. He was dressed simply, in the usual spiral-fringed robe, topped with the bronze-studded leather cuirass, and like the rest of the party, he wore his hair and beard in ringlets. Although he was not gold-decked like the previous ambassador, something about this man said that he was accustomed to giving orders and being obeyed.

Kiya frowned, trying to place him. She studied him from behind her fan. (She was always hot in this accursed desert country, and made a habit of carrying a fan, since the ministrations of the fan-wielding servants were never sufficient.)

Beside the senior envoy stood a youth, his still-sparse beard styled in an unsuccessful attempt at the ringlet style of his elders. From the similarity of his features to the tall man's, she guessed he must be the latter's son. There was something very familiar about them both.

Pharaoh indicated that the envoy might deliver his message.

Handing his clay tablet to the Chief Scribe, the envoy announced in a deep bass voice:

"My lord, Prince Zita, told me, 'Say to the lord, the king of Egypt, my father: Thus Zita, the king's son, your son.'

"'May all go well with the lord, my Father. On any earlier embassies of any of your messengers, they came to Hatti, and when they went back to you, then it was I that sent greetings to you and had a present brought to you.'"

"So," whispered Akhenaten to his mother, "are we to give this prince all the credit for his father's letter's and gifts to us?"

The warrior envoy continued, "'Here I send on to you your own messengers returning from Hatti, and I also send to you, My Father, my own messengers along with yours, and I send as your greeting gift a present of sixteen men.'"

Here the envoy turned and stepped to the side, indicating a platoon of sixteen soldiers standing at attention behind him, all dressed in matching bronze-studded leather armor. They all saluted Pharaoh smartly with outstretched right arms. At a command from their sergeant, they all dropped to one knee, head bowed, and made the fist-to-chest salute.

Pharaoh indicated they might rise. At another verbal command, they rose in unison and stood at attention.

Kiya studied the envoy and his son throughout this display. Who did they remind her of? She fanned herself impatiently, thinking.

Suddenly, it came to her. The tall man resembled her own father – with some differences, of course, but the resemblance was definitely there! She peered cautiously over her fan again, trying to appear casual.

Could it be - ? It must be – her uncle, Artatama, her father's brother! And the boy – he had to be her cousin, Shuttarna! But what the devil were they doing here, as a delegation representing a Hittite prince?

The envoy continued the message from his prince, "My lord says further: 'I, myself, am desirous of gold. My Father, send me gold. Whatever you, the lord, My Father, are desirous of, write to me so I can send it to you.'"

Kiya had not seen her uncle or cousin in many years. She had been a little girl when she last saw them. She could not figure out what they were doing now, or why they would come as a Hittite delegation, but she suspected that their motivation, whatever it was, boded ill for her father and his country. She decided to watch them closely and try to ferret out their purpose in coming here – preferably without revealing her own identity. She also felt she ought to warn Pharaoh. She leaned forward and tapped him on the shoulder.

Pharaoh glanced back over his shoulder to see what The Favorite wanted.

She whispered to him, "I know these two men! The older one is my father's half-brother, my uncle Artatama; and the younger one is his son, my cousin Shuttarna. I do not trust them! Do not mention my name – I want to find out what they are up to, without them knowing me!"

Pharaoh nodded slightly to indicate that he had heard. He smiled at the envoy and inclined his head to signify that the gift of soldiers had been acknowledged and accepted.

After an exchange of polite diplomatic pleasantries, this latest Hittite delegation was dismissed and led off by the Steward, to settle in to their designated quarters in the city. He had decided to place them separately from the other two delegations from the Hittite king, which were quartered together in the palace, and from the delegation from Prince Mursili, since he suspected the two princes' parties might be opponents in a long-term struggle for the throne. He wanted to safeguard the peace of Egypt, not allow it to become embroiled in other nations' politics.

Finding space for the newcomers wasn't easy, as the main event was now not far off, and there were already visitors quartered in almost every palace, house, stable and shop in the city. He finally found a merchant with a house in the eastern part of the city who was able to accommodate them in a pair of rooms he normally used to store merchandise.

The merchant apologized for housing them in such a shabby space, but Artatama dismissed the apology and thanked him for putting them up at this late date.

"No need to apologize to us," the envoy commented. "We are soldiers, used to sleeping on the bare ground out under the stars. This is luxury to us."

"My Lord is too kind," said the merchant, indicating that they should stow their gear, then join his family and other guests for dinner.

The Steward was relieved to have found them acceptable accommodation.

After the audience was over, Kiya sought out the King. Acknowledging her with a brief nod, he sent Nefertiti and his mother off to the family's private quarters, saying he would join them shortly. He indicated that Kiya should follow him to his private office. Dismissing all other attendants except the guard outside the door, he took a seat and indicated that Kiya should sit near him. She sat briefly, but then jumped to her feet again, tapping her fan nervously on the chair back.

"Now," said the King, "what is all this about the delegate of this Hittite prince being your uncle?"

"It's him, Artatama. I'm sure it is. He's one of my father's half-brothers. I don't know what he's up to, or why he's here, but I'm sure it isn't good. He's tried to take my father's throne before. I doubt that he knows I know it. And I don't think he recognized me," she rambled on, pacing nervously back and forth. "The last time he saw me, I was just a child – and a girl child, at that, beneath his notice, so I doubt that he paid any attention to me. The boy is his son, Shuttarna. He's quite a bit younger than me. I never knew him very well. Just enough to know that he was always a troublemaker."

"And you don't have any idea why they would come here now?" Pharaoh asked. "Or why they would be presenting themselves as Hittites?"

"No, unless it's to spy on you – us," she replied. "And it certainly suggests that he's in league with the Hittites, who have definitely not been friends to my father. My father always believed they were behind the assassination of his father and his elder brother, Artashumara."

"I had heard it was one of his nobles – Udo or Udi, or some such," commented Akhenaten.

"Uthi," Kiya corrected. "Yes, he arranged the assassination of my grandfather, King Shuttarna, but I believe he had the backing of the Hittites. He first put one of my father's older brothers, Artashumara, on the throne, but he couldn't control him, so he murdered him, as well, and put my father on the throne. My father was still very young, and Uthi thought that he could control him. But my father was clever. He bided his time and strengthened his position, then, when he was secure on the throne, he had Uthi arrested and executed. But I'm sure Uthi wasn't the only one who was secretly in collusion with the Hittites."

"So you think this uncle, Artatama, is also backed by the Hittites?" Akhenaten asked.

"His presence here representing a Hittite prince, bringing soldiers with him, would certainly suggest as much," Kiya replied.

"True," Akhenaten agreed. "What do you want to do about it? While it is certainly interesting, they've committed no crime by being here, no matter who they came with or on behalf of. Thus far, they are our honored guests."

"Oh, I understand that. I don't suggest that you do anything about it," she replied. "However, I would like to do a little investigating, myself, to find out what they are up to. What I would ask of you, my Lord Husband, is simply that you don't let them know who I am. If it comes up, tell them my name is Kiya, and don't mention anything further. Just treat me like one of your lesser wives."

Pharaoh laughed. "Well, that's a switch. You usually want special treatment!"

Kiya stopped her pacing and acknowledged the jab with a wry smile.

"I know," she admitted. "But for once, I want to be *incognito* – unknown. One more courtier. One more concubine. Someone who belongs here, but nobody special. Definitely not the daughter of the King of Mitanni. But, of course, I want to attend any state events the Hittite envoys attend."

"Of course. All right, my dear, you have my agreement to your little game," he said. "I expect you to report back to me on whatever you find out, though."

"Naturally," she agreed, coyly, batting her eyelashes.

With that, he dismissed her. She blithely kissed his cheek and left.

Later, as he was eating dinner with his principal wife and his mother, he told them about Kiya's recognition of her uncle and cousin, and her plan to spy on them, and warned them to play along with the game.

Nefertiti couldn't entirely suppress a surge of pleasure at the idea.

"Act like she's nobody special?" she said, casting a quick glance at her mother-in-law. "I think I can manage that."

Queen Tiye concurred, with a little smile back at her chief daughter-in-law.

Chapter 33: Leading to Temptation

Several days later, there was a state dinner in honor of the various delegations of kings, both greater and lesser. Scores of chairs and hundreds of small tables were arranged around the great audience chamber. Musicians played while dancers and acrobats performed, as a parade of servants brought a constant stream of food and drink for Pharaoh, his family and his guests. The three eldest princesses were present, as were Nefertiti, Queen Tiye, and all the lesser wives and concubines. At Akhenaten's command, the lesser wives and concubines were scattered around the room, with orders to be charming to the guests.

As planned, Kiya was positioned behind her uncle and cousin, dressed in Egyptian garb undistinguishable from that of the other Egyptian ladies. She hoped that the passage of years, together with her finely pleated linen gown, gold collar of moderate dimensions, beaded Nubian wig and kohl-lined eyes would be sufficient to insure against their recognizing her. As added insurance, she had worn her sheerest linen gown, knowing that the eyes of the northern men, accustomed to heavier, more concealing clothing, would be irresistibly drawn to her barely-concealed body beneath it, and away from her face. To reinforce the distracting effect, she had carefully rouged her nipples with henna to make them stand out beneath the sheer fabric. As the evening progressed, she was amused to witness the efficacy of her ruse, as not a single delegate looked her in the face. They might have been able to recognize her chest, should they see it again, but certainly not her face!

Over the course of the evening, she made polite conversation with the Mitannian pair, as well as with a couple of the nearby Hittites, all of whom spoke rather halting Egyptian. By now, her Egyptian was quite fluent; although an Egyptian might have detected her accent, it was not at all evident to these foreigners. She never gave any indication that she was following every word of her uncle and cousin's conversation in Hurrian, which was, of course, her native language. She also spoke a bit of Hittite, enough to get the gist of her uncle's conversation with the other members of the Hittite party.

Kiya was very pleased to find that her two relatives showed no signs of recognizing her, and that they talked quite freely in front of her. It soon became apparent that they were currying favor with their Hittite allies, who had agreed to back them in yet another try for the throne of Mitanni. While they were visiting with Prince Zita, he had expressed the intention of sending an emissary to Egypt. Artatama had leapt at the chance to visit Egypt and sound out the strength of the Egyptian/Mitanni alliance, which had endured for several generations now. Rumor suggested that this Pharaoh was not very militant in character and might not be very aggressive about defending his own borders, let alone helping his allies to defend theirs. If the rumor was true, it meant Tushratta would be on his own, without the might of the Egyptian empire to back him up. That would mean that their bid for the throne, with Hittite backing, would stand a good chance of succeeding.

As the plot to assassinate and replace her father on the throne was revealed, it made Kiya so angry, she had to fight to school her face to remain pleasant and unperturbed.

By the time the dessert of fruit and honeyed pastries was served, the guests had imbibed a great deal of wine or the thick Egyptian beer, which was sipped through straws that allowed the liquid to pass while filtering out the yeasty mash. A drink of fermented honey, a type of mead, was served with dessert. With the aid of all this alcohol, inhibitions were lowered, and the men spoke more freely still. Kiya took the opportunity to befriend young Shuttarna, although it was a challenge to maintain a friendly conversation while managing to evade his groping hands.

It became very clear to her that both father and son felt they had been unjustly passed over for the succession, of which they felt they were imminently more deserving than Tushratta, whose mother was of less elevated status than Artatama's. She felt they both had very inflated opinions of themselves – the boy in particular, since he was as yet totally unproven in battle or any other form of leadership. The father, at least, had some accomplishments as a warrior, although he had not shown any great administrative ability in his own province, nor had he been able to attract a strong following. Kiya felt she could see why: they were both whiny braggarts, more talk than ability, who were too stupid to realize that their allies, the Hittites, would simply use them to gain entrée to Mitanni, then would cast them aside and take control of the country themselves.

It was also clear that they both fancied themselves irresistible to women. Although both were good looking, in what an Egyptian would deem an "Asiatic" sort of way, they seemed uncouth and unrefined to her now, after her years in the elegant, well-mannered Egyptian court, with its exquisite art and music. She plied young Shuttarna with plenty of mead and used her most seductive feminine wiles to excite him, yet keep him at arm's length. She suggested to him that the ultimate coup for a young man who wanted to ascend to a throne would be to marry an Egyptian princess. With the Pharaoh of Egypt as a father-in-law, she whispered, he would have a very powerful ally.

"But, but," he stammered, "I thought Egyptian princesses were never allowed to marry foreign kings! I heard that this Pharaoh flatly refused any of his daughters to the King of Babylonia!"

"Well, yes, that's generally true," Kiya conceded. "But then, of course, the King of Babylonia wasn't here to woo any of the daughters of Pharaoh."

"To woo...to do...what?" Shuttarna asked blankly, his eyes a bit unfocussed from the alcohol.

"To woo a daughter of Pharaoh, to win her over," observed Kiya. "I mean, surely you must have noticed that women have much more freedom here in Egypt."

"Yesh," agreed Shuttarna, slurring his words slightly, "yes, I had noticed that. I see 'em everywhere – in the market, on the roads and the river, out workin' in the fields alongside the men. And half-naked! It's enough to drive a man crazy, all these half-naked women everywhere you turn!"

With this, he made a grab for Kiya's breast, hovering so tantalizingly near. She, however, had anticipated this and moved effortlessly away, leaving him grasping at thin air. As he sat there frowning at his empty hand, she adroitly poured more mead into his cup.

"Yes," she said softly. "I've heard how hot-blooded you northern men are. All the Egyptian girls have been warned about you. These Egyptian men are so well-mannered and polite, not the kind to sweep a girl off her feet--"

"Weak, wimpy creatures, all of them!" blustered Shuttarna.

"Not at all like you manly, hot-blooded northern men," Kiya purred, looking sidelong at him. "And a handsome, virile fellow like you - why, you could just sweep one of these pampered Egyptian princesses right off her dainty little feet! Show her what a real man is like!"

"That's right!" said Shuttarna, clearly turned on by the idea. He wasn't quite sure, though, that it was the thing to do. "Do you really think so?" he asked.

"Oh, I'm sure of it," Kiya assured him. "If you picked the right princess, that is. If you pick the wrong one, she might just look down her ancient, royal nose at you. You wouldn't want that!"

"No, no," he mumbled. "Course not. Don't want 'ny royal snobs."

"That's right. You want a princess who will appreciate you, see you for the handsome, sexy, macho man you are," she told him.

"Darn right!" he agreed. Clearly, this image of himself as the virile ladykiller appealed to him. "Gotta find the right princess. How 'bout you?" he asked, making another grab.

She evaded him as gracefully as before. "Not me, silly! I'm not Pharaoh's daughter – I'm his wife, and liberal as he might be, his generosity does not extend to sharing his wives. You need to make him your ally, not your enemy!"

Now he was confused. "So, how c'n I figur' out which princess is the right princess? I don' know one from t'other."

"I'll help you," she said in a conspiratorial whisper. "You see those women sitting around Pharaoh?"

He nodded and squinted, trying to focus his bleary eyes on the group.

"The older woman is his mother. The younger one with the tall headdress is his principal wife, Nefertiti. The young girl next to Pharaoh, with the side lock and shaved head, is his third daughter, Ankhsenpaaten."

"Her? She's still a child," he muttered.

"Yes, of course," said Kiya. "I'm just telling you who they all are. Now, the one right next to Nefertiti is the oldest daughter, Meritaten."

Shuttarna sat up a little straighter. This princess had some possibilities.

"Is that the one?" he asked. "She's not too bad – downright pretty, in fact. I could go for her."

"No, no, that's not the one you want. She's the snobby kind. She's the oldest royal child – very full of herself. She probably wouldn't give you the time of day.

"No, no – the one you should focus on is the second daughter, Meketaten. She's the one with the blue-beaded wig right behind the old queen," Kiya whispered.

"I don't know," Shuttarna muttered. "She looks kind of young. Is she even a woman yet?"

"Just. She just came of age a few months ago," Kiya told him. "That's the beauty of it. She's just old enough to be eligible, and young enough to be susceptible. She's eying all the boys a couple of years older, and she's desperate to prove how grown up she is. She wants to prove she's more grown up than her older sister. And there's another thing I bet you've got in common with her."

"What's that?" Shuttarna asked.

"Horses. She's crazy about horses. She's nagging her parents to allow her to drive her own chariot."

"I'm great with horses," declared Shuttarna.

"See! I knew it," exclaimed Kiya. "I was sure you would be." Her people's skill with horses was legendary.

"I could offer to teach her how to drive them!" he said.

"Well, yes," agreed Kiya, "but you have to meet her first."

His shoulders sagged. "How'm I going to do that?"

"Well, you have your team of horses here, don't you? And your own chariot?" she asked.

"Of course," he replied.

"And they have to be exercised daily, don't they?"

"Yes," he agreed.

"Well, then: you exercise them on the parade ground, where she can see you," she said.

"Yes!" he agreed, but then asked, "But how would I know when she'd be watching?"

"I happen to know that her groom is teaching her to drive every morning while it's still cool," she said. "If you get out there bright and early, you can be driving your chariot around by the time she gets there. If you put on a good show, she'll be sure to watch."

"That's a great idea!" he exclaimed. "She can see what a fine figure I cut!"

"That's the spirit!" she said, urging him on. "And maybe you can show off some of your martial skills. How are you with a bow and arrow?"

"I'm a crack shot," he assured her. "I can hit a target with six arrows in a row while galloping at full tilt."

"Excellent!" said Kiya. "There's a row of targets for practice on both ends of the parade ground. You can show off your skill and really impress her. She'll stop to watch you, then you can slow your horses down to cool them off, and stop right by her. It'll be the perfect chance to strike up a conversation. Then, after two or three days, you can ask her if she'd like to ride a couple of laps with you. After another day or so, you can offer to teach her to drive. Point out how safe it is, right there on the palace grounds, with her groom watching."

"Could be a little limiting," he muttered.

"That's all right," she assured him. "Remember, this is for the long run, not some one-night fling. You're trying to woo Pharaoh's daughter so she'll nag him to let her marry you. Then you'll have the ally you need to gain the throne."

"Yeah," he said, "tha's right. I wanna woo Pharaoh's daughter."

Kiya had a sneaking hunch that *wooing* was an alien concept to him. He was going to need a lot of coaching.

"But I still can't do much *wooing* on the parade ground," he protested.

"No, maybe not," she agreed. "But once everybody's used to you driving her around the parade ground, then you can invite her to ride out into the countryside."

"That sounds good," he said. "But won't she have her guards and her nanny or whoever along?"

"Oh, undoubtedly," said Kiya. "But it still gives you a chance to talk to her, to charm her."

"Charm her?" he asked blankly. Clearly another alien concept.

Kiya could see that she would have her work cut out for her, teaching this insensitive clod how to make a young girl fall in love with him. Fortunately, the girl in question was very young and foolish, and ready to rebel. The odds were, with the slightest bit of help, she would convince herself she was in love with him.

"Don't worry about it," she said. "I'll help you. I'll teach you just what you need to do to get her to fall in love with you."

"Then what?" he asked.

"Why, then comes the fun part," she said, with a sly little smile. "You persuade her to meet you privately, for a secret tryst. Then, you seduce her."

Shuttarna lit up at this prospect. This was clearly more to his liking.

"You're going to have to take it slow, though," she cautioned him. "Remember, this is Pharaoh's daughter we're talking about. If you rape her, she'll run crying to papa, and he'll have your head for it."

Shuttarna looked a bit nervous. By now, he was just sober enough that the enormity of what was being discussed was beginning to penetrate his alcohol-sodden brain.

Kiya continued. "Take it slower than you would with anybody else. Treat her like a nervous filly. Go real easy with her. Then, when you've got her all hot and bothered, you can take her. Remember, she's got to want more. You want her to be crazy about you. Do you think you can do that?"

"Of course!" he exclaimed.

Now it was Kiya's turn to be doubtful.

"I don't know," she said. "Do you have the self-discipline to do this? If you go charging in like a bull after a cow in heat, you'll just scare her away."

"Of course I have the self-discipline!" he exclaimed indignantly. "What do you take me for? I'm a prince, not a barbarian!"

"Well, actually," Kiya thought to herself, "a barbarian is exactly what you are." But outwardly, she smiled approvingly and patted him on the arm.

"Of course!" she assured him. "If I didn't know you were a worthy prince, would I be fool enough to suggest that you pursue a Pharaoh's daughter?"

"No, no, of course not," he agreed. But then a thought occurred to him. "But why should Pharaoh agree to let his daughter marry me, when he turned down the King of Babylonia?"

"Two reasons," she said. "One: she will beg him to let her marry you. As you have seen, women have a great deal of freedom in this country, and a lot of influence. Most Egyptian women can decide for themselves who they will marry. Of course, a princess is not an ordinary woman. She would need to have her father's permission. But unlike how it is in your country – that is, how I have heard it is – she can make her wishes known.

"And second," she continued, "if you get her pregnant, her father will need to marry her off so that she doesn't bring shame on the royal family."

What Shuttarna didn't know was that this latter assertion was entirely untrue in Egypt. It would certainly have been the case in Mitanni, or Hatti, or Babylonia, but not in Egypt. She was counting on his lack of understanding of this foreign culture to lead him into her trap.

"Ah, I see," he said, falling right into it. "If she's pregnant, he'll have to let her marry me – and he'll probably send her right out of the country with me."

"You've got it," she said. "That's it, exactly. And that's something the King of Babylonia just didn't have going for him. There are some things you just can't do long distance!"

"Yes, indeed," he said with a salacious grin.

"Oh, brother," she thought to herself, "this silly boy really thinks he's the gods' gift to women! What a conceited idiot! He deserves what he's going to get."

"But remember," she whispered, "this is our secret. You can't tell anyone I told you all this. I could get in a lot of trouble." She batted her eyelashes at him and put on her best innocent-damsel-in-danger look.

"No, no, of course not," he assured her. "It's our secret. I'm won't breathe a word of it!"

"Thank you!" she said, with an apparent sigh of relief. "You're a real prince!"

By then, the hour had grown late. Many of the guests had already left, and others were being gathered up by their servants. Several of the Hittites were snoring among the floor cushions nearby, the result of overindulgence in food and drink.

"I better go," she told him. "And you should get to bed. Remember, you need to be out riding first thing in the morning!"

"That's right!" he said, stumbling to his feet. He looked around for his father and found him snoring among the Hittites on the floor nearby. "Well, thank you for your advice. Where can I find you, if I need to talk to you some more?"

"Oh, don't worry," she replied. "I'll find you. I'll check in on you every so often, to see how it's coming."

"Good night, then," he said with what almost passed for a courtly bow, but for a slight inebriated wobble.

She swept off, collecting up her servants as she went, while Shuttarna shook his father's shoulder to wake him up. She was very pleased with her night's work.

Chapter 34: Danger Approaches

Much of Queen Tiye's staff had accompanied her to Akhetaten, including her Steward, her Chamberlain and her Master of Works, Auta. Auta was in the process of catching up on his visual record of the six princesses, whom he had not seen for several years. A couple of days after the banquet welcoming the foreign envoys, he accompanied Princess Meketaten on her morning chariot-driving lesson. Her parents had given her a new, smaller chariot, specially made for her. Auta thought that the princess would want to commemorate the process of learning to drive her own chariot. When he presented the idea to her, she was enthusiastic about it.

So, here he was, an hour after dawn, trotting his old bones along beside the chariot, his palette and bag of materials in hand, as the head charioteer drove the princess to the parade ground. Once they arrived on the field, Auta settled on the ground at one side and took a few minutes to catch his breath before setting out his sketching materials. The charioteer pulled the chariot to a stop nearby and began instructing the princess in the handling of the horses, praising her for her progress of the day before and pointing out what she needed to improve on.

Suddenly, Auta heard the pounding of several sets of hooves going at high speed, coming his direction. He looked up and saw a chariot drawn by four white horses, all galloping from the left end of the field in his general direction. A moment later, the chariot tore past in front of him in a cloud of dust and continued to the other end of the field, where its driver, a young man in the beard, ringlets and spiral fringes of a Hittite, cast a spear into a straw-backed target, hitting the mark dead center. Sweeping around the end of the field, he wheeled his chariot about and charged back toward the other end, where his next spear found the center of another target. He continued this until he had used up his six spears, at which point he pulled out a bow. Wrapping the reins around his waist, he fired four arrows in succession into the targets at one end of the field, all but one finding its mark. He wheeled about, charged the other end of the field and repeated the performance there, all four arrows finding their marks this time.

Auta quickly sketched the young Hittite's performance, then glanced over to where Princess Meketaten stood in her chariot with her charioteer. They had paused in their lesson to watch the wild antics of the Hittite youth and pulled over to the side to avoid being run over by him. The old artist saw that the princess watched the young man raptly, her eyes shining with excitement and admiration.

Having expended all his arrows, the young Hittite slowed his horses down and trotted them to the other end of the field, then slowed them to a walk and let them circle the field while they cooled off and his servants collected his missiles from their targets. The princess couldn't take her eyes off him.

As the chariot approached, the ever-observant artist noticed that its design was different from that of Egyptian chariots. He sketched it, noting that it was built more heavily than the light, openwork chariots of Egypt (hence the need for twice as many horses), with the driver positioned directly over the wheels, rather than forward as in the Egyptian version, and the wheels were thicker, with four spokes rather than six. The cab was also heavier, with more solid sides, and judging from the equipment quivers on the sides, was principally designed for spear-throwing rather than archery, despite the young man's proficiency in the latter.

As the Hittite approached the princess's chariot a final time, he slowed his team and drew to a halt beside her. From their exchange of greetings, Auta gathered that this was not the first time they had met. He sketched the two young people in their respective chariots.

As he sketched, they continued their conversation; then there was a spirited exchange with the princess's charioteer. Finally, it appeared that the charioteer reluctantly conceded something – he had apparently agreed to let the princess ride in the young man's chariot, as the latter helped her out of her own chariot and into his. With her chariot trailing along behind, the princess and the young Hittite walked the horses sedately around the field several times. Before long, she had the reins in her hands, and the young man stood behind her, with his arms reaching around her and his hands on hers to guide her on the reins. Glancing at the royal charioteer riding several lengths behind them, Auta saw the man frown anxiously at this presumption. The princess, on the other hand, appeared to be thoroughly enjoying it, her face aglow with pleasure.

After walking the horses around the field several times, the princess appeared to ask her companion something. He, it seemed, agreed. With his hands on hers holding the reins, he signaled the horses, which obediently shifted up to a trot. They trotted several more times around the field, then the princess requested something again. This time, however, the young man shook his head, slowing the horses to a walk again. The Egyptian charioteer behind them followed suit, looking relieved to see that he wasn't going to have to chase them at full gallop.

At last, the Hittite chariot drew to a halt not far from where Master Auta was seated on the ground. The royal charioteer pulled to a stop behind them, then leaped down and ran to help his mistress down, but the Hittite youth was there before him. Jumping down, he turned and placed his hands on the princess's waist and lifted her lightly to the ground. Her charioteer, arriving too late, frowned again at the young man's familiarity with Pharaoh's Number Two Daughter. But the princess, far from being offended, was thrilled by the young man's masculine strength and the excitement of his touch, experiences hitherto unknown to her.

After a further brief exchange, the young man bowed over her hand, touching it to his forehead. She bade him farewell, adding,

"Until tomorrow, then!"

The young man returned to his chariot and drove it off the field. Meketaten's eyes followed him all the way.

As they returned to the stable, Auta once again trotting along in their wake, he worried over what he should do about the scene he'd just witnessed. It seemed to him that the young foreigner was getting far too familiar with a daughter of the Pharaoh of Egypt. On the other hand, he had been polite and well-mannered, and he was an honored guest, part of an official delegation from a powerful king whose goodwill Pharaoh wished to retain. Auta didn't want to cause an international incident. And the princess had been under the watchful eye of her charioteer the entire time. The charioteer was a good man and Auta didn't want to make trouble for him.

So, in the end, he decided to keep his counsel, but vowed that he would check back from time to time to make sure the princess wasn't getting into trouble.

There was another, secret witness to the performance: Kiya watched from a canopied perch on the palace roof. While she couldn't make out details from this distance, she could see the Hittite's whirlwind display of horsemanship, followed by the transfer of the small, feminine figure to his chariot, then the boy's taller figure merging with the smaller one. She had seen enough to confirm that her strategy was working. The game was afoot. As long as no one interfered, she was certain it would proceed to its logical culmination.

Smiling slyly to herself, she descended the stairs and returned to her own splendid new palace. She was already planning the next item on her agenda: getting Pharaoh back in her bed so she could conceive another son. A second, back-up heir would surely cement her position, possibly even raise it to most important Queen.

Meanwhile, preparations for the Durbar proceeded at a furious pace and visitors continued to pour into the city.

Among the new arrivals was Mariamne, with her household staff. Although Thutmose had written to her only a few days previously to tell her that the new house was ready, she had already packed up her most essential possessions in anticipation of receiving word, so she was able to leave the day after the messenger arrived. Thutmose was astonished at her appearance on his doorstep less than ten days after he had written to her. Fortunately, his crew was just putting the finishing touches on the house and most of the furnishings sat completed in his workshop, ready to move next door as soon as the paint was dry on the walls.

Mariamne dropped her bags on the doorstep and threw her arms around Thutmose. After only the slightest hesitation, he embraced her back and planted a welcoming kiss on her lips. Several neighbors and passersby chuckled in approval.

"Oh, and there's someone else who is anxious to see you," she said. She turned and gestured to someone who was peeking around the corner.

A lanky boy of about seven stepped out from behind the wall.

"Senmut!" cried Thutmose, stretching out his arms to the boy, who ran into them. "My son! I'm so happy to see you."

Thutmose called a servant to carry Mariamne's bags inside, then led her through the workshop to a side door. Before opening it, he insisted that she close her eyes, then led her through into the entry courtyard of their new house. Senmut tagged along behind them.

"You can open your eyes now," he said, grinning from ear to ear.

Mariamne opened her eyes and took in the lovely entry garden and courtyard. It ran between the outer wall and an inner wall that led to a fountain and small shrine where the wall jogged abruptly to the right. She glanced back at Thutmose, her eyes shining, and ran down the path to the fountain. There, she could see that the shrine held an image of the Pharaoh and Nefertiti worshipping the sun disk of the Aten, whose rays ended in tiny hands holding the *ankh*, the symbol of life, before their noses. Young Senmut splashed his hands in the fountain.

After a glance at the shrine, she turned the corner into the main entry to the house. Thutmose followed close behind, not wanting to miss her reaction. He stepped past her and opened the massive front door, which was carved from thick planks of costly Lebanese cedar. Mariamne stepped through it into the main courtyard of the house. This central court was open to the sky, but had movable awnings of coarse linen running on lines stretched overhead. They could be pulled open or closed by ropes attached to their leading edges, so the courtyard could have shade or sun to suit the weather. There was a beautiful reflecting pool in the center, with water flowing in through a fountain in the image of the Nile god, Hapy. The water poured down from his open mouth into the pool, which was filled with pink, white and yellow lotuses and colored fish. Thutmose explained that all the water in pools throughout the house came from a cistern on the roof, which was kept filled by a donkey-driven *shadouf* that lifted buckets of water from the river and dumped them into a raised trough leading to the roof cistern.

Around the sides of the courtyard ran a covered arcade, leading on one side to a large gathering-room, at the back, to the kitchen, and on the other side, to the private master bedroom and several other bedrooms. The walls of all the public and family rooms were covered with frescoes of Egyptian life: marshes with wildlife, fields with grapes and barley, a town market scene, and views of the palace and Great Aten Temple. The floors were tiled with bright-colored decorative tiles.

The kitchen section contained several masonry counters with built-in, plaster-lined storage areas for dry foods, all with heavy, tight-fitting lids to keep out mice and bugs; and several additional open bins fitted with removable ceramic pots in which wet or dry ingredients could be mixed. Two of these were broad, shallow basins, with corks fitted in an opening in the bottom. Thutmose demonstrated how rain water caught in another cistern on the roof was led down the wall through a series of reed tubes which could be opened or shut by a small door operated by a hand lever. When it was opened, fresh water flowed into one of the basins. It could be drained by removing the cork, which allowed the water to flow down into a slanted trough which exited through a wall into the garden, watering the flowers planted there. Mariamne oohed and aahed over this ingenious arrangement.

In a separate small courtyard at the back was the *piece de resistance*, a beehive-shaped oven, built of adobe bricks and plastered inside and out. It was a great luxury for a villa to have its own bake oven, which meant that the women didn't have to make the trek to the nearest communal oven to cook their bread and other foods. Attached to the oven was a raised open hearth for cooking other foods, with a built-up portion from which hung a series a hooks suspended from bronze chains, from which the cook could hang cooking pots over the open flame. Off of the back and sides of the kitchen courtyard opened doors to the servants' quarters. It was, in short, an ultra-modern kitchen with every traditional convenience and several new and innovative ones, as well. Mariamne was thrilled.

Next, Thutmose showed her through the bedroom wing. He showed Senmut his very own bedroom, with pictures of wildlife painted on the walls and birds flying across the ceiling. The boy was enthralled by all the lifelike animals. There were several other bedrooms, including one for Mariamne's older son, and several spare rooms.

They continued on to the spacious master suite, which was furnished with matching carved sleeping couches topped with thickly padded mattresses and fashionable curved headrests, plus several beautiful carved and painted chairs, and several painted chests for clothes, as well as tables for cosmetics. Thutmose opened a door at one side, showing her a spacious room with a bathing pool in the floor, another built-in basin with piped-in water, beside which lay Thutmose's bronze razor and a polished silver mirror with an ivory handle carved in the shape of a swimming woman. There was a bronze ring attached to the wall through which the handle of the mirror could be inserted, to hold it while Thutmose shaved or Mariamne applied kohl to line her eyes.

At one side was a half-wall. On the other side, Thutmose showed her, was a built-in masonry seat with a hole in it. Another of the reed pipes ran down the wall behind it, with a lever to open the valve and let water wash away wastes from beneath the seat, carrying it to a drain pit near the river. Mariamne had never seen such a technological marvel. Imagine never having to empty the night soil from a chamber pot ever again!

"Oh, Thutmose, what a marvelous house! I love it!" she exclaimed, twirling around like a child.

"Ah, just wait," he replied, taking her arm. "We're not through."

"Not through?!" she exclaimed. "I don't know what more you could add!"

He led her through a door at the back of the kitchen courtyard, through a passageway into yet another courtyard. This yard had a series of raised adobe platforms, each with several large earthenware pots set into its top, with an open fire pit below. Another series of reed pipes fed water into troughs along the sides of each platform. Around the sides of the courtyard were a series of posts joined together into head-high rectangles. Long, round poles ran in ranks between these.

"A dye workshop!" exclaimed Mariamne, examining the pots set into the platforms. "With more running water and built-in hearths! How marvelous!"

"Yes," said Thutmose. Then he pointed to the tall rectangles. "And drying racks for the dyed yarn."

"Wonderful!" she said.

He pointed at rooms at the back and sides of the courtyard. "And here are rooms for looms and other equipment, and at the back, rooms for the storage of raw materials and finished goods. Up front," he said, opening a door for her, "is the shop, which fronts on the street behind the house."

They entered the shop. It had shelves built in along three sides, on which woven goods could be placed. Along the front wall were multiple large folding doors (made of more Lebanese cedar) which could be opened all the way up to display goods on portable racks. Scattered around the room were a number of comfortable chairs and small tables, so that Mariamne and her staff could relax or entertain their high-class clientele.

There was also a large, bronze-plated box attached to the back wall. It had several compartments in its interior, and its lid could be fastened shut by a heavy bronze device Thutmose described as a "lock". He demonstrated how this device could be sealed shut by the use of a long bronze rod with a flat round plate on one end and a couple of short, projecting rods on the other end. He had her attempt to pull it open, and when she couldn't, he showed her how to unseal it again with the rod, which he called a "key".

"What is the box for?" she asked.

"You can store the silver, gold or whatever else you exchange for your weaving, in the box. It can be securely fastened so that thieves can't take the contents while you are busy with customers. But secure as it is, we should probably take any valuables into my workshop at night," he added. "I have a strongroom at the back of the shop where I store the silver, gold and stones I use in my work, with two watchmen always on duty."

"I'm sure that would be wise," she agreed.

They returned to the courtyard and she looked into each of the weaving rooms. They had windows which looked onto the courtyard and could be closed by shutters (more valuable cedar!), and they also had rows of small clerestory windows at the top of the walls to let in light and air. Those on the outside walls had bronze bars set into the wall and ceiling, to keep out intruders. The storage rooms, on the other hand, had only tiny vent openings covered with linen on the inside, to allow a minimum of air while keeping out bugs.

"Thutmose, this is amazing," Mariamne said when they were again in the dye yard. "It's the perfect weaving factory – and dye factory – and shop! I never dreamed you would do all this! This is...beyond wonderful. I don't know how to thank you," throwing her arms around him.

After a barely perceptible hesitation, he hugged her back.

"I'm glad you like it, my dear," he said. "You are such a remarkably enterprising woman, with your dyeing and your weaving and your reading and writing – I felt you deserved a place that would support you in doing all those things."

"Oh, it certainly does!" she replied. "I can't wait to bring all my equipment here, once this Durbar is over."

"I have to admit, I was a bit surprised that you got here so fast," he said, "especially when every boat on the river must be tied up transporting visitors coming here for the celebration."

"Well," she said, "I had a boat already paid for, knowing you'd be finishing the house sometime soon. And I came on ahead as soon as I got your message – I didn't want to miss the big celebration!"

"Ah, of course," he said. "I'm so used to it, I don't even give it a second thought – but, of course, it's of much more interest to everyone else who is not used to it! Well, I guess my timing was good, then, to have the house finished just in time for the Great Durbar."

"We can even put up some of the overflow crowd in the weaving factory and make a nice profit on it," she observed.

"Ah, ever the business woman!" he commented, with a laugh. "I suspect the Royal Steward will be very happy to have some more rooms to allocate to important guests. If his head weren't already shaved, it would be bald from tearing his hair out by now! The poor man has been going mad, trying to find places for guests, all the while keeping mortal enemies apart so they don't spoil the festivities by killing each off while they're here!"

And, indeed, Thutmose was entirely right. The poor Steward was on the verge of a total breakdown, even though Pharaoh had by now assigned a small army of scribes and servants to assist him. But it seemed that, no matter how many spaces he assigned to guests, new visitors just kept on arriving.

A delegation arrived from the temple of Bastet in Bubastis, bringing dozens of wicker cages full of cats. These they presented at the daily audience. Pharaoh instructed them to see the Minister of Agriculture, who would distribute them among the farmers battling the rat problem.

Nefertiti leaned over and whispered in Akhenaten's ear.

"Ah," he said, turning back to the Priest of Bastet. "The Great Wife requests that you bring a litter of kittens to the family quarters, so that my daughters may choose among them."

The priest acknowledged the request and was led away by the Chamberlain, who directed a servant to show him the way.

During the last week before the Durbar, a doctor arrived from one of the nomes upriver. He hurried to the palace and informed the Chamberlain that he had an urgent message for the King. The Chamberlain at first told him that was impossible, until the man whispered the news into his ear. The Chamberlain blanched, then arranged for the visitor to be admitted to see Pharaoh, who was informed that there was an urgent message he should hear in private. The other petitioners were told to return the next day, then the physician was admitted by himself. The Chamberlain had already notified the court physicians, two of whom were now present.

Pharaoh indicated that he should approach. After the appropriate obeisance had been made, he signaled the man to rise.

"I understand that you have an urgent message for me and my physicians," said Pharaoh. "What is this emergency?"

"Your Majesty," said the man, "I am a physician. I have been making the rounds of villages upriver, between Thebes and Aswan. I fear I must report that there is plague raging in a number of these villages, and it is spreading."

"Plague?" asked Pharaoh. "What manner of plague?"

"A pestilence characterized by high fever, large swellings of the neck, armpits and groin, and sometimes by vesicles under the skin which make it appear black. A very high number of those affected do not recover," replied the doctor.

"What proportion of them?" asked Pentu, the senior court physician.

"About half of them die," replied the doctor. "And the disease appears to be making its way downriver. With all the visitors coming to Akhetaten, it could arrive here at any minute. Your Majesty, you must cancel this Durbar!"

The two court physicians conferred with each other. Finally, one of them turned to the King.

"We concur, Your Majesty. We are familiar with this disease. It is very, very dangerous," the Chief Physician said.

Pharaoh looked distraught, but shook his head.

"I can't call it off," he said. "It's too late! All these people are already here, and more are on their way. It would take us days just to inform the people here, and there's no way to get a message to those already on their way. The festivities start in eight days. We'll just have to hurry through them and hope the pestilence doesn't arrive before we're through!"

Chapter 35: The Great Durbar

For the next several days, Master Auta continued to accompany Princess Meketaten to her daily chariot-driving lessons, but there was little he could do to discourage her acquaintance with the young Hittite delegate. He learned that the young man's name was Shuttarna, the son of envoy Artatama. The names puzzled Auta, who was old enough to remember that these two names had belonged to an earlier pair of Kings of Mittani – not Hittite kings. He spoke with the Chief Archivist, the keeper of official court documents, who confirmed that his memory was correct. He was already uneasy about the young man's relationship with Pharaoh's daughter; learning that the boy and his father bore Hurrian names, yet were part of a Hittite delegation made him even more uneasy. Something was not right.

It wasn't long before Meketaten was quite competently driving either the young man's chariot or the new, lighter Egyptian model her parents had had made for her. Auta accompanied the princess to her lessons, still suspicious of Shuttarna's motives. However, their activities on the parade ground seemed innocent enough, if a bit overly familiar.

Auta had confided his suspicions to his queen, and she had passed them on to her daughter-in-law. Both queens kept a watchful eye on the girl, but the princess and her young swain were meticulously well-behaved.

What neither the queens nor Master Auta knew, however, was that Shuttarna had managed to persuade the impressionable princess to meet him secretly on the palace roof at night. After her maid and governess were sound asleep, she was able to sneak away from her room to a rendezvous in a private corner of the roof. This enabled her amorous suitor to steal a few kisses, then progress to more intimate touching. The pair met several nights over the next week, the young man taking more liberties each time.

Kiya managed to meet with her young protégé every two or three days, as well, to check his progress with Pharaoh's daughter and coach him on how to seduce the girl. Privately, she likened him to an ill-trained stallion, wanting to charge in wildly. She had to almost forcibly restrain him to keep him from simply raping the girl. Finesse was simply not in the lad's vocabulary!

Kiya persevered, however, and eventually both she and the boy succeeded. He managed to seduce the foolish girl, apparently satisfactorily, as he was able to repeat the performance on at least two subsequent occasions. The inevitable result ensued: although she didn't know it yet, by the time the Durbar opened, the princess was pregnant.

During the same period, Kiya had been meeting with Pharaoh regularly to report on the results of her spying on Artatama and son. Of course, she only informed him of what she learned of their Mittanian origins, their alliance with the Hittites and their plans to assassinate her father. She had to dribble information to him to explain her continued contacts with the boy, who, she told Akhenaten, was much easier to pump for information than the father.

As a side benefit of these meetings with Akhenaten, Kiya was able to lure him into her bed again during the weeks prior to and following the Durbar. She was convinced that, if she became pregnant again, the child would be another boy, and that having provided not just one, but two royal heirs would elevate her status still further.

Royal envoys and common people continued to stream into Akhetaten in droves, arriving even during the night. The vast majority arrived by boat, mostly small river craft, but also a few large, sea-going vessels from all up and down the eastern Mediterranean, and as far away as the Sea of Marmara north of the Hittite capital, Hattusas. The wharves were so crowded, Chief Mahu had platoons of police directing ships where to dock long enough to offload their passengers, then special pilots would take the craft to designated mooring places up and down the river. Inevitably, along with the passengers and supplies, a few more covert, less welcome guests debarked: Asian brown rats. And occasionally, some of the local Nile rats snuck aboard the moored vessels. Sometimes, the local and visiting species met up and squabbled over food supplies, sometimes mated and in the process, exchanged fleas.

Some visitors also arrived by land. The enclosing cliffs approached the river bank both north and south of the town, funneling all traffic in and out of the city along the King's Way. In the north, the administrative checkpoint was housed in a building that actually straddled the roadway, resembling a large, ornamental gateway. This allowed the police to keep an eye on people coming or going, and made it easy for them to collect customs duties.

At last, the great day approached.

The King and Queen were up before dawn to prepare to greet the rising of the Aten in the Great Temple. They spent several hours being ceremonially prepared within their royal robing rooms. They were bathed, anointed and dressed identically in fine linen robes tied with long red sashes, sandals whose soles depicted prostrate enemies of Egypt, great golden collars studded with turquoise, lapis and carnelian stones, and matching tall double crowns, the low Red Crown of Lower Egypt over the tall White Crown of Upper Egypt. Once attired, they stepped into the great Palanquin of State, a huge golden carrying chair adorned with protective figures of lions, cobras and sphinxes. The chair was so heavy, it required fifteen men to lift it.

Led by a priest burning incense, and accompanied by ten fan-bearers, they were followed by their two eldest daughters, Meritaten and Meketaten, along with their nurses and ladies-in-waiting. Alongside trotted the full complement of royal bodyguards, wearing feathers in their hair to mark the occasion. They proceeded first to the Great Aten Temple to offer a sacrifice and greet the dawn appearance of their god.

After greeting the sun god and making their offerings, they changed into matching blue *khepresh* war crowns, then resumed their seats in the Palanquin of State and re-emerged onto the Royal Road, turning north toward the parade ground and ceremonial enclosure at the northern edge of the city where it encroached on the open desert. Crowds lined the streets the entire way, gaily dressed visitors from Upper and Lower Egypt and all over the known world, cheering and shouting in dozens of tongues. As the golden procession approached the great ceremonial enclosure, the cheers became deafening. At last, the great gilded chair was lowered to the ground before the columned and canopied dais. The royal couple stepped out of the palanquin and ascended the ramp to the dais, where they greeted the cheering crowd before taking their places on matching golden thrones. All six princesses were now present, ranged behind their parents on the dais, two of them trailed by their pet gazelles on leashes.

Now, rank after rank of envoys from all over Africa and the Middle East moved forward in ordered lines to present their gifts. Chief Mahu and Lord Chamberlain Tutu had labored long and hard to assign each group their place and keep them in order, waiting their turn to pay homage, all arrayed in their distinctive national dress. There were Syrians with curled beards and multi-layered robes, Hittites with their swept-back hairstyles, long-haired Keftiu from Crete, and Libyans with their distinctive side-lock and feathers. There were scores of dark-skinned Nubians, not only men, but also women carrying babies in slings on their backs. Court officials at the head of each line signaled each delegation when it was their turn to step forward and approach the double thrones, prostrate themselves on the ground and present their tribute.

As twin rulers of the largest empire on earth at the time, Akhenaten and Nefertiti received huge quantities of rich, lavish and exotic gifts. There were chariots – often gilded - and horses, richly caparisoned; bows, throwing sticks, bronze and occasional iron swords; shields and slaves. (Iron was still quite rare, especially in Egypt, which lacked deposits of its own, and was therefore considered a precious metal.) There were animal skins, ostrich feathers and living animals; and litter-loads of spices piled high into elaborate pyramid and obelisk shapes. There were huge gold rings, disks and ingots, as well as rings of silver and bronze. There were countless beautiful dishes, vases, cups and ewers crafted of colored glass – the latest thing! - or precious metals, many studded with gems. There was even a novelty gold palm tree, typical of the exquisite but utterly useless gifts so often given to royalty. (What do you give the Pharaoh who has everything? Why, a golden palm tree, of course!) After being presented and acknowledged, the gifts were displayed on tables and stands for all to see.

The monarchs also received enough living animals to stock a sizable zoo: hounds, leopards, antelopes, gazelles, monkeys, and even a lion. These would, indeed, eventually populate a zoo at the Northern Palace.

In addition to all the envoys of kings and princes, the promised Babylonian princess had also arrived, escorted by General Horemheb and his furloughed soldiers after her father had complained that the original five-chariot escort was woefully inadequate. Commander Paramessu had reached the General with his fresh troops and announcement of the Durbar in time for Horemheb to make a side trip to meet the Babylonian princess and escort her to Egypt. Horemheb's weary troops were happy to spend time at home and to be able to attend the international social event of the decade, marching along in the procession after their monarchs.

After the receipt of tribute, Pharaoh announced the official co-regency of his Great Royal Wife, now named Neferneferuaten-Smenkare. While the cheering was still dutifully loud, there was also a great deal of muttering and quiet discussion, out of earshot of the numerous police and soldiers present.

Next, Akhenaten announced that Nefertiti's half-sister, Mutnodjmet, was soon to be married to Prince Senusert, nomarch of the Oryx. The Prince stepped forward from one side of the dais as this announcement was made and took the hand of Lady Mutnodjmet as she stepped forward. They raised their joined hands as the throng cheered, the Prince smiling broadly, his bride with a strained smile. Mutnodjmet had conceded the brilliance of the match made by her parents and Queen Tiye, but was not enthusiastic about her promised husband, who was many years her senior and not an outstanding physical specimen.

This was followed by awards given by the joint Pharaohs to their faithful followers: golden *shebu* collars and arm bracelets, bottles of costly perfumes, rare glass vessels and colorful beads.

After this, General Horemheb and a contingent of his soldiers led in the vassal king Abdi-Ashirta of Amurru, in chains. They had chased him down in northern Canaan and brought him back to Egypt, where he had been tried for treason before the King. With the written testimony of several fellow kings and the eyewitness testimony of the Egyptian Commissioner to Amurru, Pharaoh Akhenaten had found him guilty of conspiring with the Hittites and had condemned him to death. That sentence was now to be carried out.

Since the condemned man was a king, albeit a minor one, he was accorded the honor of a clean death. A gilded basket was brought out and set before the prisoner. A soldier lifted off the lid and stepped back quickly as a cobra, symbol of Egyptian royalty, raised its head from the basket, hood regally spread. Abdi-Ashirta struggled to pull away from the soldiers holding his bonds, away from the hooded death awaiting him. The crowd booed. The soldiers hauled on the chains on either side, pulling him forward toward the basket. Finally, recognizing the inevitability of his fate, he raised his voice and asked Pharaoh to let him go forward on his own. Pharaoh granted his request. The soldiers allowed his chains to go slack.

Abdi-Ashirta pulled himself together, took a deep breath and stepped up to the gilded basket. The cobra reared up, hissed and whipped forward, striking his bare chest, right over his heart. Appeased, the snake subsided back into its basket. The lid was clapped on and the basket carried away.

Within seconds, Abdi-Ashirta began to sway and stagger. He fell to his knees, then collapsed face-first in the sand. His body convulsed briefly, then lay still. At General Horemheb's signal, the soldiers carried his body away. While it would not be beautified, it would be sealed in a double coffin, *cartonnage*[9] instead of wood, and returned to his son Akizzi for burial.

The message was plain to all, including the envoys of foreign kings, both great and small: Pharaoh may be tolerant, but he has eyes everywhere, his reach is long, and his justice is sure. He rewards those who serve him well and punishes those who betray him.

This sobering reminder was followed by more light-hearted entertainments: an endless series of jugglers, dancers, musicians, snake charmers and displays of athletic ability, from footraces, to spear casting, to archery contests, with archers shooting from on foot and from galloping chariots. The excited crowd roared their approval and carried the victors on their shoulders to the royal pavilion, where the twin Pharaohs awarded them the Gold of Honor.

Finally, the royal couple offered the Aten's blessing to the crowd, then climbed into their own chariots for a speedier trip back to the palace. They were followed by both Meritaten and Meketaten driving their own chariots, then the younger four princesses with their charioteers, followed by their own entourage, and all flanked by

---

[9] Cartonnage – layers of linen stiffened with plaster

running bodyguards. They were all quite exhausted and only too happy to retire for a nap before resuming festivities with a royal banquet that night.

Meanwhile, the town exploded with celebration. Flowers decked all the public buildings and garlands stretched across the streets. The smell of incense burning in braziers wafted throughout the city, mixed with the mouth-watering odors of roasting meat: oxen, oryx, gazelle, ibex, duck and other wildfowl. Festivals were the only times most of the common folk got to eat meat, and they were determined to make the most of it. Beer flowed as freely as the Nile flood, with wine as plentiful as the Red Sea. Drunkenness ran happily rampant, and joyful young men embraced lovely laughing girls. Every secluded corner was filled with amorous couples. There was rejoicing everywhere and festivity in every quarter.

The feasting at the Great Palace was even more lavish, with the highest ranking envoys dining in the Great Hall with the twin Pharaohs, and their lesser colleagues in smaller halls throughout the palace. Kiya was once again seated near the Hittite Prince Zita's delegation, behind her uncle and cousin. She was able to confer with a cheerfully inebriated Shuttarna to confirm his successful conquest of Princess Meketaten, and to egg him on to one more tryst with her this most festive – and least sober – of nights.

By now, Shuttarna had developed his own contacts in the royal household and was able to bribe a servant to take a message to the princess and bring back her reply. As Kiya suspected, the girls' entourage were also celebrating this night and she was easily able to slip away to their meeting place on the roof. Indeed, this night, their biggest problem was finding a corner that was not already occupied by an amorous couple. They succeeded, nonetheless, and Shuttarna proceeded to seal his conquest of Egypt – three times, no less! Meketaten returned to her bed, and he to his, very late that night.

It took several days for the merrymakers to sober up and more still to clean up the streets and restore some semblance of order to the town. The thousands of visitors began to flow away, even more quickly than they had arrived, by boat or ship, by chariot or donkey, or more rarely, by camel, or most often, on foot.

The various royal envoys, on the other hand, were much slower to leave, since they could not go until Pharaoh dismissed them. Like most of them, Prince Zita's delegation were still there several weeks past the winter solstice.

By this time, another visitor had begun to make its presence known: plague began to stalk the streets of Akhetaten. As the doctor had warned, the dread pestilence had arrived on their doorstep.

The first people affected were those in most frequent contact with rats and their fleas: farmers, sailors, anyone who sold or stored food, the poor who slept in the streets. These were comfortably distant from Pharaoh and his family. They were a matter of great concern to everyone else, however. The remaining foreign envoys began to nervously petition Pharaoh to let them leave, which he was quick to do.

Many of those who left by boat or ship unknowingly took rats with them, along with their tiny disease-bearing companions, the flea *Xenopsylla cheopis*. Their ships returned to ports all over the Middle East, taking the plague with them. Soon, reports of outbreaks began to filter back to Egypt from port cities all around the eastern Mediterranean: Ashkelon, Tyre, Sidon, Byblos and many others. Some of the foreign kings even asked for Egyptian doctors to help them deal with the epidemic.

But Egyptian doctors had their hands full at home.

Chapter 36: Death Stalks the Land

For a time, the importation of cats had helped to curb the population of Nile rats. However, the Durbar had produced an influx of people, food and rats of the both the Nile and Asian brown species. Rats from villages that harbored pockets of plague sailed downriver in the grand barges of nobles and the humble fishing craft of commoners. The doctor's fears had been well-founded.

And once plague-bearing fleas had arrived, they not only took up long-term residence on any rats they encountered, they were happy to take the occasional blood meal from any other warm bodies that happened by, especially once their rodent hosts died. And unlike hot-climate Egyptians, with their scanty, airy linen clothing and frequent immersion in the waters of the Nile, the many northern visitors often wore many layers of woolen clothing and rarely bathed, a set of circumstances supporting large populations of human body fleas. So the returning northerners carried infected fleas on their bodies, as well as on the rats in their ships. And unfortunately, while the local cats helped to reduce the rat population, they were often bitten by fleas in the process, so they, too, carried the plague.

Before the Durbar, one of the priests of Bastet had offered the choice of a litter of kittens to the daughters of Pharaoh. Nefertiti had allowed them to choose one. They had picked a lovely beige-colored female with black-tufted ears, nose and tail. They agreed to name it "Ta-Miu" (meaning "Lady Cat"), like the cat once owned by their father's deceased elder brother, Prince Thutmosis. They all adored her and loved to dangle ribbons for her to chase, while baby Setepenre crawled along behind on her pudgy little hands and knees.

The cat had the free run of the palace, and when she wasn't playing with Pharaoh's daughters, she was fond of visiting the kitchens, where the staff petted her and gave her lots of tasty tidbits. She had won the favor of even the large and formidable head cook by killing a number of mice in the royal pantry, and recently, even a large and unpleasant rat. Unfortunately, as she shook the dead rat, a number of its fleas jumped onto her.

A few days later, the cat became ill, much to the girls' distress. It crawled off into a quiet corner behind a decorative chest, as cats are wont to do when they are sick. It stopped eating, and drank only a little. The girls' nurses told them to leave it alone.

Three days later, Princess Ankhsenpaaten noticed the baby down on the floor, poking her hand into the corner where the cat had holed up, saying repeatedly, "Miu! Miu! G'up! Miu, g'up!"

Ankhsen ran over and pulled her away, saying, "Penya! Stay away from there!"

She peered in from several feet away and could see the cat, not moving. She hauled the baby over to her nurse and told the woman that the cat had died and she should have someone come and remove it. The nurse pulled out the chest the cat had crawled behind, saw the furry little body, threw a cloth over it and called a servant to take it away.

Setepenre clearly didn't understand what had happened and why Ta-Miu wouldn't come out and play with her. She cried and carried on until she finally fell asleep.

The next day, she awakened fussy and feverish. The nurse became alarmed when her fever continued to rise. By evening, she was burning up and Nefertiti called for the physician, Pentu.

The physician arrived and examined the child, then delivered the news her parents dreaded to hear.

"She has the plague," the doctor told them. "See, she is developing the characteristic swellings in her groin and armpits. I am afraid there is nothing we can do for her but pray. Perhaps Aten will hear your prayers and heal her. I can do nothing."

Nefertiti collapsed in Akhenaten's arms, sobbing. He turned to the physician.

"Is it contagious, doctor? Are the other girls at risk?"

"We don't really know, Your Majesty," he replied. "It doesn't usually seem to spread from person to person, except when the swellings rupture and people come in contact with the evil effusion that comes forth. There seem to be occasional exceptions, however, when it does seem to pass from one person to another, so to be safe, Your Majesties and the other children should stay away from her."

He turned to the child's nurse and instructed her, "About the only thing you can do, nurse, is to keep her cool. Sponge her down with wet cloths. Get her to drink water, if you can. Throw away any cloth that has touched her, and burn them. If her swellings burst open, avoid coming in contact with the fluid. Mop it up with a cloth, burn the cloth, and wash your hands with clean water. Then dispose of the water. If she dies, which she almost certainly will, wrap the body carefully, then wash yourself and get rid of your clothing."

He turned to Pharaoh. "I am very sorry to have to say this, but the bodies of plague victims must not go to the *wab* priests to be beautified, lest they spread the infection."

"But, doctor," protested Nefertiti, "how can she live on in the afterlife if her body decays? How can we condemn our child to a final, irrevocable death?"

"I know it is a terrible thing," he said sympathetically, " but, if it is any comfort to you, the sands of the desert naturally dry out and preserve the body, without any other treatment. Even Pharaohs were once buried directly in the sand. It is only since we began to bury people in stone or brick tombs that their bodies have needed artificial purification. I believe that, if we bury our plague dead out in the desert, in direct contact with the sand, the earth of the Two Lands itself will preserve them for the afterlife. I think we must trust them to the bosom of the earth, itself."

Nefertiti sobbed, but nodded her agreement. Akhenaten nodded, as well, saying, "I will give the order, doctor, that all who die of the plague are to be wrapped up and taken to the desert for burial. I will have soldiers find a suitable burial ground and dig deep pits to receive the dead. They will also stand guard to protect the dead from the attentions of lions, jackals or hyenas."

"That is good, Your Majesty," the doctor agreed. "It is precisely what I was about to recommend. It should help diminish the spread of this disease."

They kept watch over their youngest child all through the night and the next day. Despite the ministration of the nurse, who kept her bathed with cool water, the child's temperature continued to rise, and by sunset of the next day, she passed away.

Nefertiti was beside herself with grief, but she knew that the mortality rate among even royal children was very high. They were lucky to have been spared this long.

Pharaoh issued an edict requiring all plague victims to be buried at a special site out in the desert, and set the example by interring his youngest child there, entrusting preservation of her tiny body to the desiccating desert sands. The common people, who had never been able to afford mummification or elaborate tombs, willingly followed suit. The wealthier nobility at first protested, but eventually had to agree to follow Pharaoh's example. The wabet centers of beautification were ordered not to accept the bodies of plague victims. The Chief Wab Priest, who never actually touched the dead, himself, was furious at the loss of income, but the common priests and assistants who actually prepared the dead were happy to escape exposure to the mysterious and terrifying disease.

All available physicians made the rounds of the city, instructing people in the care of the sick and, most importantly, in the proper hygiene to prevent spread of the disease. This was a population in which plague had been endemic for a long time, with outbreaks occurring in small pockets every few years, so it was a population with a modicum of natural resistance to the disease. With good hygiene and proper supportive care, about four out of every ten infected adults survived. The mortality rate was much higher in children, who had had less chance to develop immunity.

Pharaoh asked his physicians to confer among themselves and devise a plan to limit the spread and mitigate the effects of the plague. Pentu and the other royal physicians met in a small audience chamber, together with the physician Hapuseneb, who had brought the warning of the epidemic, and a few of the other senior physicians from the city.

Pentu called the meeting to order, then explained Pharaoh's order to his medical colleagues.

"So our duty is to come up with a plan to limit the spread of this disease and anything we can suggest to mitigate its effects," he told them. "Does anyone have any suggestions?"

"It would help," said one of the city doctors, "if we had any idea of how this disease spreads. It doesn't usually seem to go from person to person, as long as contamination with pestilent bodily fluids is avoided."

"That is correct," agreed Pentu. "Hapuseneb, you were the first to warn us. Have you formed any opinion of how the epidemic started, or how it spreads?"

"Well," he said thoughtfully, "as I told you when I arrived, the disease seems to live on between outbreaks in small pockets in villages or around farms. Every few years, it flares up and there's a small local outbreak. Sometimes, these spread and we get a major epidemic, such as we are facing now. I don't know what causes these sudden flare-ups, but it seems to happen most often after one or more years of drought."

The other physicians present discussed their experience with the disease throughout various districts of Egypt and concluded that their combined experience supported Hapuseneb's theory: the disease did seem more likely to flare up after a drought, although not every drought led to an outbreak.

"All right, gentlemen," said Pentu, "we seem to agree on one predisposing factor – but we have no idea why a drought should lead to an outbreak of plague. Has anyone observed anything else that seems to coincide with an outbreak?"

"Well, if it follows drought," said one older physician, "it's not likely to be caused by a miasma in the air, since that more often happens when conditions are wet."

"I have noticed one thing," ventured one of the younger physicians. "As our visitor mentioned, this outbreak seems to have started around farms, and when it moved to the city, there were more cases around food storage areas. I also noticed that there seemed to be a lot of small animals dying before people got the disease."

"Small animals?" asked Pentu. "Like what?"

"Well," the younger man replied, "I saw a lot of dead rats and mice in the countryside and around granaries and taverns in the city. There were also quite a few dead cats and a few dogs. Since there were more dead mice and rats, and they showed up earliest, I'm inclined to think that they might be the original source of the disease, with the dogs and cats catching it from them."

"Come to think of it," said Hapuseneb, "I did notice a lot of dead rodents in the villages and farms that were first infected. I think you may be onto something."

"But why should an outbreak follow a drought?" asked one of the city physicians. "What's the connection to rats?"

"Well," said Hapuseneb, "in a normal year, with a good Inundation, most fields all along the Nile are flooded, and that drowns many of the Nile rats that live in the fields. They can't survive very far from the fields, because then they're in the desert and there isn't much for them to eat. But in a drought year, the water doesn't come up very high, so it doesn't kill as many rats. When there isn't enough for them to eat in the fields, they start invading people's homes and migrating into the cities, where there is stored food. Dogs and cats and people come into contact with them there."

"I must say, that makes a lot of sense to me," said one grizzled old medical veteran.

"All right," said Pentu, "if this theory is correct, how can we use it to stop the spread of this disease?"

"Well, for starters," said the old veteran, "we tell people to avoid contact with rats, living or dead, or any other dead animals. They should use a cloth or other covering to dispose of them. Since we don't know how the disease moves from dead animals to people, everyone should avoid contact with them."

"That makes good sense," said Pentu. "I can tell you that Pharaoh's youngest daughter, who died recently of the plague, had been in contact with her dead cat, which was known to have killed a rat in the kitchen – which suggests that the disease somehow moved from the rat to the cat to the child."

"Ahh!" said several others at this confirmation of the theory.

"They should also make sure to clean up any food scraps and securely store any grain or other foodstuffs rodents might go after," suggested the young physician.

"Good idea," said Pentu, making sure his scribe was getting all of this down. "Has anyone found anything that helps to lessen or cure the disease?"

A few offered suggestions, but the only measure they agreed on was that good supportive care seemed to offer the best hope of enhanced survival. The young physician mentioned that he had seen a few victims improve after consuming moldy bread, which was known to help wounds heal, but admitted that it was difficult for patients to choke it down, especially if they had swellings of the nodes at the side of the neck. Another physician suggested that moldy bread could be soaked in wine, beer or milk to make it easier to swallow and to mask the taste. So, in their report to Pharaoh, these were the only palliatives they could suggest.

Pharaoh had scribes copy the report and sent the copies to the mayors of every major city, up and down the river. He also ordered stringent efforts to clean up rats in Akhetaten. These measures helped and the rate of infection began to drop, but it came too late to prevent many deaths.

Akhenaten and Nefertiti were devastated at the loss of their youngest daughter. It was a heavy blow for such a close-knit royal family to lose a child. But their tribulations were only beginning.

Chapter 37: Birth and Death

Despite the appearance of plague in Akhetaten and the mass exodus of most foreign envoys, Shuttarna managed to persuade his father to stay on. He pointed out that the plague had already spread ahead of them, anyway, so they would not escape it by leaving – and that, in fact, Pharaoh's physicians seemed to be winning the battle against further spread here in the Egyptian capital city. Egyptian physicians were renowned for their skill throughout the world. Shuttarna made a convincing case that the safest place to be might be right where they were.

Of course, he didn't tell his father that his real reason for wanting to stay had anything to do with seducing Pharaoh's daughter.

He continued to meet Meketaten on the roof, but had to admit to himself that his encounters with the naïve child were beginning to bore him. Nevertheless, he had to cement her attachment to him to be sure that she would advocate their marriage to her father.

As plague raged outside her palace walls, Kiya was also glad to be in this city with the best physicians in the world. One advantage of the newness of her palace was that it was still quite clean and uninfested with rats. She made sure her staff kept it that way and implemented all the measures suggested by Pharaoh's physicians. So far, it seemed to be working. None of her people had gotten sick.

Since Nefertiti, in her grief over the death of of her youngest child, had lost interest in the pleasures of the bed chamber, Kiya seized the opportunity to distract Akhenaten from his sorrows. And indeed, before long, she succeeded in becoming pregnant again. Sure that this child would be another son, yet another heir to insure the strength of her position, she played her advantage to the hilt. If she had been arrogant and annoying before, she now became insufferable. But Pharaoh, who could forget his grief in her arms, refused to hear any complaints against her.

It soon became apparent to the two queens that something was wrong with Meketaten, although, thankfully, it did not appear to be the plague. At first, the girl was very tired and listless. She was less active than usual and she slept a lot. Soon, she began to complain that food tasted strange, then she began throwing up. Nefertiti was puzzled and concerned about her daughter.

"If I didn't know better," she commented to Queen Tiye, "I'd think she was pregnant. But she's too young and too well-guarded for that, Aten be thanked."

Queen Tiye looked thoughtful. "Actually," she said, "she's not too young. After all, she did start her courses almost a year ago. She made a point of announcing it to me when I arrived. And with all the strangers in town for the Durbar and all the confusion and excitement, she's been less well-guarded than usual."

"That's true," Nefertiti agreed. She turned to Meketaten's maid and called, "Hebnut! Come over here."

The maid hurried over and made her obeisance to the Queen.

"Yes, Your Majesty?"

"You're responsible for your mistress's laundry, are you not?" the Queen asked.

"Yes, ma'am," the woman replied.

"Well, then, judging from her clothing and bed linens," the Queen asked, "when was Princess Meketaten's last course?"

"Well, let me think, Your Majesty..." The maid frowned and counted on her fingers. She frowned harder and scratched her head. Finally, she said hesitantly, "I think...I think it was at least two full moons ago, Your Majesty. Since just before the Durbar. Maybe more."

"Thank you, Hebnut. That will be all," said Nefertiti, dismissing her. She turned to her mother-in-law. "It looks as if...but surely, it can't be! How could such a thing happen?"

"I don't know," said the elder queen grimly. "But I think we better find out."

"Yes," agreed Nefertiti, "we should." Raising her voice slightly, she called across the room. "Lady Mutreshti! Come here, please."

The princesses' governess hurried over to the Queen and made her obeisance.

"Your Majesty?"

"Lady Mutreshti, you sleep in the same room as my two eldest daughters, do you not?"

"Yes, madam, I do," the lady agreed.

"Is there any way Princess Meketaten could have gotten out of the room at night without your knowing?" the Queen asked.

Lady Mutreshti looked thoughtful. "I don't *think* so, Your Majesty. I admit, though, that I do sleep pretty soundly, and I'm told I snore quite loudly. I suppose it's conceivable that the princess could get by me without awakening me, if she were very quiet."

"*Conceivable* may be exactly what it is," muttered Queen Tiye so that only Nefertiti could hear her.

"Thank you, Mutreshti," Nefertiti told her. "You may go."

The lady bowed and left.

The eldest princess, Meritaten, was called and questioned next. She did her utmost to avoid answering the question head on, since she had been aware of a number of her sister's absences, but did not want to be the one to tattle on her. Nefertiti was persistent, however, and Meritaten was eventually forced to reveal that her sister had, indeed, been sneaking out at night for quite some time. Nefertiti assured her that, despite her loyalty to her sister, it was right to confess that the girl had been engaging in behavior that was not only forbidden, but that might also expose her to harm.

Finally, it was time to confront her wayward number two daughter. Nefertiti instructed Lady Mutreshti to find Princess Meketaten and have her brought to the Queen's small audience chamber.

When the princess arrived, she was confronted by her mother behind closed doors. Nefertiti came straight to the point.

"Meketaten: have you been sneaking out of your room at night?" she asked.

Meketaten knew she was caught, but she didn't know how much her mother knew.

"W-well, sometimes when it's hot and I can't sleep, I like to go up on the roof," she said. "It's cooler up there."

"And who's the boy you've been meeting on the roof?" her mother asked.

Dumbfounded that her mother somehow knew, Meketaten felt her heart sink to the very bottom of her queasy stomach.

"W-what makes you think I've been meeting a boy?" she stammered, still trying to avoid making a full confession.

"Because that's how one usually gets pregnant," her mother answered, pulling no punches.

"**What?!**" Meketaten gasped. "I'm not...no, I can't be!"

She knew she hadn't been feeling well, but her knowledge of reproduction was scanty, so the notion of pregnancy had not even crossed her mind. In earlier times, the traditional religion's many forms of fertility rites might have provided her with a clue as to the relationship between sexual activity and reproduction, but in this new monotheistic era, simple offerings of food and flowers to an abstract deity had replaced the more explicit rites of Bes or Isis and Osiris or the Apis bull. And in the royal household, she was seldom exposed to the full range of activities of domestic animals, so she had missed out on the barnyard education any peasant child might have had. It had genuinely never occurred to her that her midnight trysts might result in pregnancy.

"I'm afraid so, my child," her mother said, realizing that her daughter's naïveté, which was at least partly her fault, may have allowed the girl to unwittingly get into serious trouble. "When did you last have your courses?"

Meketaten thought about this. Frowning, she said slowly, "I think...two or three moons ago."

"And you've been feeling queasy and food tastes strange?" her mother asked.

The girl nodded.

"And are your breasts swollen and tender?"

The girl nodded again. The daunting realization showed in her eyes.

"Well, I hate to have to say it, child, but you're pregnant. The next question is: who's the father?" Nefertiti asked her.

Meketaten shook her head numbly, but said nothing.

"You might as well tell me now," Nefertiti told her. "I will get it out of you, sooner or later." None of her children was able to successfully lie to her for long. "Who is it, Meket?"

With tears now streaming down her face, Meket finally admitted, "It was Shuttarna, the son of one of the Hittite delegates. Except that they aren't really Hittites, they're from Mitanni, and his father's the rightful king, not Tushratta, Kiya's father!" she blurted out in a rush.

"Shuttarna? Artatama's son?" asked Nefertiti, who had a very sharp memory for names and faces.

The girl nodded.

"But how could this have happened? You girls are guarded all the time. How did you meet this boy?" Nefertiti asked.

Meketaten explained how Shuttarna had been exercising his horses on the parade ground when she, herself, was taking chariot driving lessons. She went on to unburden herself of the whole story of how the relationship had progressed, a little at a time, until the impressionable girl had been totally bedazzled by the older boy and overcome by powerful feelings she did not know how to handle.

As she listened to this tale of the seduction of an innocent, Nefertiti cursed herself for not having been more aware of what her child was up to. She also began to form a suspicion that there was more here than met the eye. Why would a visitor to the court of the world's

most powerful king risk offending his host in such a drastic way? It was
not likely to be because he was dazzled by the child's beauty and
couldn't resist her charms – the girl was pleasing to the eye, but in no
way extraordinary, certainly no *femme fatale* irresistible to men. No,
there had to be something more to it. This had all the earmarks of a
conscious campaign, a planned seduction. But why? What could the
young man hope to gain? Didn't he realize that a hasty execution would
be his most likely reward?

But then, again, maybe he didn't. But maybe someone else did,
someone who wouldn't mind seeing him executed... And she could
think of only one person at court who would benefit – or whose family
would benefit – from that: Kiya. Kiya, whose relatives these were (for
Akhenaten had confided to her what Kiya had told him). Kiya, whose
father Artatama had already tried to assassinate at least once, and failed.
Kiya, who hated Nefertiti and, by extension, all of her children.
Nefertiti had a strong hunch that she could see Kiya's deceitful hand in
this. But she doubted she could ever convince Akhenaten of the
woman's duplicity. All of her efforts to enlighten him had so far met
with disbelief, even anger.

But in the mean time, what were they to do about Meketaten
and her baby? While she knew that there were plants that could bring
about abortions, Meket's child would be a royal child. Such an artificial
termination would be unthinkable. On the other hand, any child of a
Pharaoh's daughter could potentially be a claimant to the throne. And
with only one prince currently in the line of succession, if Meket's child
were a son, he could be next in the line of inheritance. Clearly, this was
a problem she would have to take to Akhenaten.

Unnoticed by Nefertiti or Meketaten, one of the maids had been
listening outside the door, with the pretense of dusting the furniture.
When the royal ladies stopped talking, she crept away. Once out of the
palace, she trotted as quickly as she could along the Processional Way,
to the Northern Palace. There, she informed The Favorite of what she
had heard. She was well rewarded for the information.

After the informant left, Kiya smiled to herself, like a cat well
fed with cream. This information was worth a cat's weight in gold –
well, a small cat, anyway! So far, her plan was working flawlessly.

Meanwhile, Artatama was also receiving a spy's report. He had
been paying one of his servants to follow his son ever since they had
arrived at the Egyptian court, and another to find out more about Lady
Kiya. He had already learned that his son had been meeting with the
lady several times a week, but apparently just to talk. His spy, however,
was not able to get close enough to overhear them, as they usually met
out in the open, in places like the palace gardens – a precaution

instigated by Kiya, who was wise in the ways of spies. Earlier today, he had heard back from this spy, and been disturbed by the woman's message. She had asked around among the palace staff and learned that Kiya was, in fact, none other than Princess Tadukhipa of Mitanni, Artatama's own niece, the daughter of his brother and rival, Tushratta. This was troublesome news. But there was worse to come.

Artatama had been mildly surprised when Shuttarna began rising at the crack of dawn to exercise his horses and he was puzzled to hear that his son was teaching one of the royal daughters to drive a chariot. He had also been aware that the young man had later switched to sneaking out at night, but he had assumed the boy was meeting some servant or lesser lady of the court. It never occurred to him that Shuttarna would be foolish enough to seduce a daughter of Pharaoh, and the manservant assigned to trail him had been unable to follow him through the palace until recently to confirm the lady's identity. Last night, however, he had succeeded, and had been able to overhear the young man's conversation with the princess.

"I follered him up onta th' roof of the Grand Palace," the servant told his master. "I was able t'hide behind the parapet around an adjoinin' section of roof. I could hear your son and the princess, but they couldn't see me."

"One of Pharaoh's daughters, you say?" asked Artatama. "Was it the same one he was driving in his chariot in the mornings?"

"I believe it was, m'lord, although I can't be abs'lutely sure. T'was very dark, so I couldn't see her clearly," the servant replied. "At any rate, they was a'kissing and a'carryin' on, so's it was very clear they'd been a'meetin' for some time. And what the girl told him then, sir, well, it knocked me right flat!"

"And what was that?" Artatama asked.

"Well, sir, she told 'im she were pregnant."

"Pregnant?!" Artatama roared. "The idiot boy's gotten Pharaoh's daughter pregnant?"

"Yes, m'lord. That's what she said. And what's more, it was 'er mother and th' old queen what figgered it out! That's what she told 'im," the servant concluded triumphantly, holding a grubby palm out for his payment.

"By Ishtar and all the gods!" exclaimed Artatama. "We're in deep trouble now! Pharaoh will have us executed, for sure!"

He reluctantly dropped a thin gold ring into the informant's outstretched hand, then paced furiously back and forth for several minutes, thinking. Finally, he stopped and turned back to the servant.

"We've got to leave Egypt!" he said. "Tonight! Go find my son and tell him to get back here immediately!"

"Yes, m'lord!" said the servant, bobbing a bow. He turned and ran out of the room.

Artatama called his other servants and told them to pack all of his belongings, and his son's. He sent one of them to the stables to tell his groom to begin preparing their chariots for a departure once it got dark.

After a while, the first servant arrived back with his son in tow, both of them out of breath.

"What is it, Father? Why did you want to see me in such haste?" the young man asked.

Mindful of the servants, Artatama pulled him into the next room and shut the door. His voice, however, was so loud, he might as well not have bothered. The horrified servants heard everything he had to say to his son, although the boy's voice didn't carry so well.

"I have just learned that you have gotten one of Pharaoh's daughters pregnant!" Artatama roared. "How could you do such a thing!"

"It was intentional, Father," the young man said proudly. "That was my plan!"

"Plan?!?" yelled his father. "What kind of idiotic plan is this?"

"A plan to marry Pharaoh's daughter. This way," explained the son, "Pharaoh will have to let me marry his daughter. And with an alliance cemented in such a way, we will have Pharaoh's backing – or at least his permission – in our bid for the throne."

"Oh, by Ba'al, how could you be so stupid?" lamented Artatama, tearing at his long, curly hair.

"Stupid?" bridled his son. "How can you call it stupid, when I've found a way to make us an alliance with Egypt?"

"You haven't made us an alliance," replied his father. "You've made us an enemy! You've dug our grave! Haven't you heard? Pharaoh doesn't allow his daughters to marry foreigners, not ever! He wouldn't even give one of them to the King of Babylonia! What makes you think he would give one of them to *you*?"

"Because she's pregnant, that's why! Burra-Burriash wasn't here and he didn't get Pharaoh's daughter pregnant, so Pharaoh could easily deny him one of his daughters. But he'll have to let the girl marry me, to avoid bringing shame on his house!" Shuttarna replied smugly.

"You young fool!" his father yelled. "Pharaoh won't let you marry the girl! That would give you a legitimate claim on his throne, something he would **never** do! He'll expunge the shame, all right – he'll expunge it by expunging **us**! You've signed our death warrant."

"W-what?" the young man stammered. "No! It can't be! That's not what I was told..."

"Told?" his father asked, whirling to face him. "Told by whom?"

"Why, by Lady Kiya!" the son replied.

"Lady Kiya? Oh, by all the gods, I should have known it!" Artatama exclaimed, smacking his forehead with his palm.

"What do you mean?" asked his son.

"I just found out who this 'Lady Kiya' really is," replied Artatama. "She's Tushratta's daughter, your cousin Tadukhipa!"

"My cousin!" the boy exclaimed.

"Yes," his father replied. "your devious cousin, Tadukhipa. This was clearly a plot of hers, to get us disgraced and discredited, and probably executed, as well."

"Oh, no," the boy groaned, his face in his hands. "How could I be so stupid? I fell right into her trap! I let her use me!"

"Yes, well, the harm's done now," Artatama replied. "We need to get out of here as fast as we can. I've got the servants packing everything, and the groom is preparing our chariots. I mean to be out of here as soon as it gets dark."

"But what about the guards on all the roads?" Shuttarna asked.

"We'll just have to brazen it out and hope they won't stop an official Hittite delegate."

When they returned to the other room, the frightened servants had finished packing.

Taking only what would fit in their chariots, including whatever gold they had, the two men and their grooms quietly left the stables soon after dark. Their remaining servants would either have to find a way home with the rest of the Hittite delegation, or stay behind in Egypt.

Arriving at the northern pass out of the city, Artatama was able to persuade the guard that they had received an urgent summons from the King of Hatti and must return immediately to Hattusas. Downriver, at Hermopolis, they were able to find a ship to take them to the Delta, and from Tanis, a larger ship that could carry them up the

Mediterranean coast to Ugarit, where they could reassemble their chariots and strike out overland for a safe haven.

At the same time Artatama was grilling his son, Nefertiti was informing Akhenaten of the Hurrians' perfidy and Meketaten's condition.

"By the Aten!" Pharaoh exclaimed. "My daughter, pregnant by some foreigner! I'll have his head, and his father's, too!"

"Be careful, my dear," Nefertiti cautioned him. "Remember, they're official members of the Hittite delegation. If there's one foreign power we don't want a war with right now, it's the Hittites."

"That's true enough," Akhenaten acknowledged. "But it's also true that these two aren't actually Hittites. I wouldn't be surprised to learn that the King of Hatti isn't even aware of their presence among his envoys. I doubt that he would consider the loss of a couple of Hurrian pretenders worth going to war for!"

"You may be right," the Queen agreed.

"But what I want to know," Akhenaten continued, "is how this could happen? I thought my daughters were well-watched."

"I thought so, too. When Lady Mutreshti realized what had happened, she was horrified, and accepted all the blame. But when I questioned Meket further, I learned that she had put a sleeping draft in the lady's evening cup of mead."

"And where did Meket get a sleeping draft?"

"Where else? From the boy," Nefertiti answered. "Where he got it, I have no idea."

"No?" Pharaoh said speculatively. "Hmmm. I think I might."

Nefertiti wondered if the light was beginning to dawn on Akhenaten, as it had on her.

"Not..." she started to say.

"Who else? Kiya," he replied. "She's been spying on them, with my permission. She's been meeting with the boy. She claimed it was because he was easier to pump for information."

"And he was easier to manipulate!" she exclaimed. "The poor fool would have been wet clay in her devious hands!"

Pharaoh made a wry face. "I'm afraid he was not the only one," he said. "I know you've tried to warn me before about Kiya's machinations, but I always thought you were just jealous and trying to turn me against her. Now, I'm beginning to see that you may have been right all along. I'm afraid I owe you an apology, my dear."

"Ah, well," she said with a sad smile, "at least that's one good thing that's come out of this mess."

"Yes," Pharaoh agreed. "But I can't very well punish Kiya while she's pregnant with my child. I will keep her under house arrest until after the child is born, though. Then, we'll see."

"But in the mean time," said Nefertiti, "what are we going to do about Meket's pregnancy? We can't let the world find out that some foreigner has gotten Pharaoh's daughter pregnant. We'd be a laughing stock among the Great Kings of the world!"

"No," answered Pharaoh, "we certainly can't let that happen. We'll have to revert to tradition: let the world believe it's my child."

"Your child?" exclaimed Nefertiti. "But you've spoken out against the practice of father-daughter marriage in the royal family! It would make you look like a hypocrite!"

"Perhaps. Better a hypocrite than a laughing stock. But there is precedent for it, and no one would dare criticize me," he replied. "Besides, if it's a son, an additional prince would help insure the line of succession. He would have our blood, at least on the mother's side, and that would be enough to give him a legitimate claim to the throne. And if it's a daughter, she can be raised with the other princesses."

So it was agreed that everyone would be allowed to believe that the child was Akhenaten's, although no official announcement was ever made. There were some whispers around court, but as Akhenaten had predicted, no one dared criticize Pharaoh.

However, when Akhenaten sent men to arrest the two Hurrians, they found their quarters empty. He was furious when he learned that Artatama and his devious son had escaped during the night. He sent troops downriver after them, but the errant pair eluded them. Akhenaten didn't want to make too much of a fuss about their hasty departure, lest it draw too much attention to Meketaten's condition. So, the Hurrian pretender and his son were able to make good their escape.

Several months later, Meketaten's time came to be delivered. Akhenaten's own physician had examined the girl and watched over her pregnancy. The doctor was very concerned about her chances for a safe delivery.

"She's very young," he told the King. "Technically, she's mature enough to have a child – obviously, since she's pregnant. But the reality is, her body was still growing. She's very small, and her pelvis is very narrow. The prognosis for a safe delivery is not good."

The King called in the best midwives for his daughter, and her mother was in attendance at her lying in. As the doctor feared, the birth was very difficult, the birth canal too narrow for the baby's head to pass through. After a long-drawn-out labor, the skilled chief midwife was able to extricate the baby, but the process was too much for the immature mother. Meketaten hemorrhaged, and the doctor and the midwives were unable to stop the bleeding. Despite their best efforts, the girl died.

Weeping over her daughter's blood-soaked, pale body, Nefertiti cried out, "O mighty Aten, Creator and Father of all, bring justice for Thy daughter, Meketaten! My curse upon the foreign woman, Tadukhipa, whose conniving led to the seduction, pregnancy and death of my child! May she suffer what she has inflicted on my child and know the bitterness of betrayal ere she dies!"

The doctor and the midwife exchanged knowing looks on hearing this.

Nefertiti and Akhenaten were beside themselves with grief. Theirs had been a very close and affectionate family, extraordinary in the history of Egyptian Pharaohs. They both deeply loved their daughters, and now, a second daughter had been taken from them. Their family circle was broken, two of their six daughters dead within a year. It would never be whole again.

To add insult to injury, Meketaten's daughter resembled her northern-born father, with fair skin, curly black hair and grey-green eyes. Every time the King and Queen looked at her, they were reminded of her parentage and the death of their daughter. Finally, Nefertiti persuaded Akhenaten that they should send the girl to his sister Sitamun, to be raised as her adoptive daughter. Nefertiti assured her husband that this would be a good solution, as the child would still be raised by a Pharaoh's Daughter, as a royal child should be; and she would be loved by the childless Sitamun – more than she could be loved by her grandparents, to whom she was a source of grief. So, as soon as the child was strong enough, she and her wet nurse were sent north to the estate of Princess Sitamun. As predicted, Sitamun welcomed the girl and took her to her heart. She was named Neferuaten, "Aten's Beauty," in keeping with her grandfather's religion.

Not long after Meketaten's death, while her body was undergoing its seventy-day preparation for burial, Kiya's time also came due. Her hopes for a second son were dashed, as the child was a girl. Despite her greater maturity, her labor, like Meketaten's, was also long and difficult. Never one to suffer stoically, she screamed and moaned and pleaded with the physician to give her poppy juice to relieve the pain. But the physician had watched poor little Meketaten's struggle to give birth and been unable to prevent her death. He had no sympathy for the woman he knew had connived at the girl's seduction and too-early pregnancy. He denied her the poppy juice, saying, truthfully enough, that it was not good for the baby and would only slow down the delivery.

After a long and unrelieved labor, Kiya's daughter was born. And like Meketaten, she, too, began to hemorrhage. This time, however, the doctor and the midwife made no attempt to stop the bleeding. Kiya was conscious just long enough to realize with horror that no one was lifting a finger to help her. In the doctor's personal opinion, her death was far too kind. When Nefertiti was informed of the manner of her rival's death, she had to agree.

A wet nurse was provided for the child, but the little girl never thrived. She outlived her mother by only a few days, then quietly stopped breathing.

While Kiya's body was being prepared for the grave, Meketaten was buried in a side chamber of her father's tomb in the Royal Wadi behind Akhetaten. Her parents followed the funeral sledge to the tomb, their faces smeared with ashes, tearing their garments and weeping profusely. They were followed by a cortege of mourners lamenting loudly. The entire city was in mourning for the young princess.

A few weeks later, Kiya was also buried in another side chamber of Akhenaten's tomb. While Akhenaten and Nefertiti went through all the appropriate motions, accompanied by a cortege of official mourners, few real tears were shed for the arrogant foreign princess who had made so many lives miserable. Once she was interred, the chamber was sealed and everyone went home with dry faces. The only real mourners were some of Kiya's own ladies, many of whom packed up and headed back to Mitanni, with Pharaoh's blessing.

Thus ended the reign of "The Favorite". Bek decorated both her tomb and Meketaten's. Meritaten, the eldest princess, moved into the Northern Palace I had built for Kiya. I redecorated it for her, replacing Kiya's name in the inscriptions with Meritaten's and adding more frescoes of wildlife for the princess, who adored animals. I even converted several of the rooms to house a menagerie of wild animals, to the princess's delight. I took far more pleasure decorating it for her than for its previous occupant.

Meritaten also took over Kiya's sunshade temple in the southern part of the city, not too far from my house and workshop. There, too, I struck out the Favorite's name and replaced it with Meritaten's. Soon, few signs of the foreign princess were left in Akhetaten.

Chapter 38: Curses at Aswan

Mariamne had returned to Thebes after the Durbar, with the intention of moving her looms and equipment to her new weaving factory in Akhetaten. But when she got there, she decided it would be foolish to give up such a thriving enterprise to move it all to a new location. It would make better sense to keep the business going in the old location, while expanding into the new one. So she left half her looms and equipment in place and appointed her best assistant as manager of the Theban factory and shop. She brought the other half of the equipment and supplies to Akhetaten, to set up her new factory there, bringing half her staff along with her. She also set about recruiting and training new spinners, weavers and dyers to fill out the staff in both locations. She soon had enough finished goods on hand to open the shop in the new location. With my assistance and the Queen's influence, the new shop soon enjoyed the patronage of a large and distinguished clientele.

She had already established a business relationship with the trader Kohath, who was one of her maternal uncles, as well as with a number of others who regularly traded up and down the river. Kohath was one of her most reliable sources of dyestuffs from abroad, even bringing periodic shipments of a prized blue dye called "indigo" from the distant land of Mohenjo-Daro, far to the east of Babylonia, near the fabled Indus River.

I was proud of my enterprising wife and felt that her skills in the textile arts were a fitting complement to my own artistic skills, and I greatly admired her business acumen.

While she did not inspire in me the passion I felt for the Queen, Mariamne was a good wife and I felt great affection for her. This affection soon produced another child, a daughter this time. We named her Meryre – Mery for short. It gave me great pleasure to see Mariamne so happy.

Shortly after the deaths of Meketaten and Kiya, Pharaoh Akhenaten ordered Thutmose to go to the quarries at Aswan to check on the progress of stone ordered for temples at Thebes and elsewhere in Egypt. Nefertiti called him aside into a small antechamber that was empty for the moment and asked him to keep his eyes and ears open on his journey, to assess the mood of the people and see whether they supported Akhenaten's new religion, or not.

"Please be careful, Thutmose. Reports of active pockets of plague are still coming in, although much less than a few months ago," she told him. "And my informants tell me there is widespread unrest and lawlessness, so be careful on the streets at night. I have already lost too many of the people I love – I don't want to lose you, as well."

He was aware that she had been developing her own intelligence network among the common people, heretofore overlooked by Akhenaten. She had always been a more practical person than her husband, whose head was always in the clouds. And since the deaths of their daughters, he seemed to be growing weaker and even more remote than before. While Thutmose wasn't sure yet, he suspected the king's health was declining. Every day, it seemed Nefertiti was shouldering more of the load of governing.

Thutmose promised her that he would be careful.

"I have too much to come back for to allow myself to grow careless," he assured her. Looking around to be sure they were still alone, he bowed over her hand and kissed it. She squeezed his fingers in acknowledgement before he left.

Thutmose returned home to prepare for his journey south. Before taking ship for the first leg of his voyage upriver, he carefully wrapped up the almost-finished bust of Nefertiti and put it on a shelf at the back of a cupboard in his workshop.

Normally, he would have pushed the sailors to make the best time possible; however, given Nefertiti's request, he made the journey more slowly, stopping each night at a town or village along the way, strolling through the market, staying in caravanserais and eating in taverns, rather than on the ship. This gave him ample opportunity to listen to what people were saying and observe what they were doing. He also made a point of visiting the temples in each town.

He found that, although the doors of the temples were closed, people were leaving offerings of food and flowers outside the closed gates. And while the priests were officially dispersed, he learned that there were small groups of former priests living together in little enclaves all over the country. He also discovered that, while these were not formal temples of Amun or the other proscribed gods, renegade priests were conducting secret rites in their homes, honoring their old gods.

There was widespread disaffection among the people, as well, with frequent muttering against the king who had caused so much upheaval. Egypt was a country where tradition was ancient and sacrosanct and change was suspect. This Pharaoh had brought nothing but change. Akhenaten was being spoken of as a breaker, not an upholder, of *ma'at*. It was said that this had brought, first, a series of low Inundations, and now, this plague. The arrival of the epidemic right on the heels of Pharaoh's Durbar and his announcement of Nefertiti as co-regent was taken as a sure sign that the old gods were angry. The deaths of two of the king's daughters was seen as proof of the old gods' wrath.

He also heard rumors that there were plots afoot to overthrow
the king and restore the old religion – but no one he spoke to seemed to
know any specifics. Or they wouldn't tell him. He suspected the latter.
The more he learned, the more uneasy he became.

He continued his voyage south, with fair winds helping his ship
beat its way upstream. At last, he reached Aswan, where he was
quartered with the quarry foreman and his family of four boisterous
sons and two daughters. After all he had seen and heard on his journey,
it was a relief to be among others who were devoted to his king and his
beloved queen.

He spent the next several days examining the stones that had
been quarried and were being loaded on barges for their journey down
the river, then those that were in the process of being cut. He took the
opportunity to speak with the skilled stone masons and the less-skilled
quarry workers who assisted the masons and hauled the cut stone down
to the river. Some of the latter were free men, farmers and other
peasants paying their taxes to Pharaoh by working as *corvée* labor on
public works several months a year. Others were prisoners, sentenced to
hard labor for their crimes. One of these was Ptahmose, the former high
priest of Amun, sentenced to work here for his role in the attempt on
Pharaoh's life. It was a mark of Akhenaten's extraordinary leniency that
the man was still alive.

Thutmose almost didn't recognize the former First Prophet as
he strolled through the quarry, chatting with laborers as he went. The
man looked ancient, although he was only in his mid-forties (though
even that was beyond the average Egyptian life-span of thirty-five).
When Thutmose had last seen him in Thebes at the time of his
sentencing, Ptahmose had been well-padded, as became a well-fed man
of high rank. Now, he was gaunt, with ropes of stringy muscle beneath
his desiccated, sun-scorched skin. What caught Thutmose's attention
was the visible hatred burning in the man's intense black eyes. That
look of murderous loathing for the man who had foiled his plot chilled
Thutmose to the bone, despite the sun's searing heat.

"So, Evil One," Thutmose said to the old man, "I see you still
live."

"Aye, servant of the Heretic King, so I do," the priest replied in
a ringing voice. "And I shall carry on, until I see Amun arise
triumphant, restored to his rightful place throughout the Two Lands,
and this upstart god and his king thrown down!"

"That will never happen," answered Thutmose.

"Little do you know, fool," hissed the old man. "Amun is
powerful. The day is coming when he will humble your king and then
destroy him."

He raised his voice so that all around might hear him. "I am First Prophet of Amun! Hear me! I say unto you, when this Heretic King thought himself most secure in his power, when he paraded it proudly before the kings of foreign lands, his ruin had already begun! Already Amun destroys his family, one by one! Pestilence stalks the land. People curse his name. His days are numbered; the days of his house shall be few. He will bequeath his throne to a false Pharaoh, one not born a man, who will die a violent death! Their names will be erased. His son's reign will not be long. He will restore the old gods, but too late. He will die in youth, thrown down by his own pride, but because he restored them, the gods will allow his name to live. No child of his house will live to inherit the throne! The house of the Heretic will vanish forever and his name will be wiped out of history!"

The quarry superintendent stepped forward, his face thunderous, and brought his whip down across the old priest's abdomen.

"Silence, you evil-tongued son of Set!" he cried.

The priest doubled over and staggered backward. Then he caught himself and drew himself painfully upright so that all could see the defiant sneer on his face. All around the quarry, work had stopped, the workers frozen in horror at this *lesez majesté*.

The superintendent raised his arm to strike again, but Thutmose stopped him. He spoke to the old priest.

"Just because your vile tongue speaks a curse does not make it so, old man," he said coolly. "Amun is dead. Your curses have no power in the Two Lands now!"

Thutmose spoke boldly, defying the old man's power. He may or may not have convinced the quarry workers, but he felt as though his own heart had stopped within his chest at the priest's evil words against the rightful king, the embodiment of *ma'at* whose well-being was one with that of Egypt. To curse the king was to lay a curse on the land itself. Thutmose felt a darkness gathering, blotting out the blistering heat of the African sun.

"It is you who will die," Thutmose continued, pointing a finger at the old man. "You will never leave this rocky place. And when you die, your body will be destroyed. None shall beautify it. None shall bury it. The children of Nekhbet, the vulture goddess, protector of Upper Egypt, shall eat your flesh! Jackals, children of Anubis, will scatter and break your bones so they can never be reunited. Your heart shall be devoured by Ammit, the Eater of Souls. You will be utterly wiped out from both this world and the next, unrecognizable by the gods you serve!"

Thutmose wasn't sure where the words came from. They seemed to well up from within him, from some hidden reservoir of angry power. Whatever their source, his words formed a powerful curse, denying the priest eternal life in the blessed fields of the *Duat*, the Egyptian afterlife.

The priest cowered momentarily, horrified at the counter-curse, but then he pulled himself together and opened his mouth to speak.

The foreman put a stop to that. His powerful fist smashed into the old priest's mouth, knocking several teeth out in a gush of blood, effectively silencing him.

"Silence, evil dog!" the foreman yelled, brandishing his whip. "Everyone get back to work!"

The masons returned to cutting channels in the rock and hammering wedges into them to split the blocks free, and the other workers resumed hauling the cut stones down to the river.

It seemed an ill omen, indeed, for Thutmose to end his visit on such a note, but he had seen all he needed to see. The next day, he set out down river, traveling faster this time, with minimal layovers.

Thutmose's curse and the foreman's fist had had a greater effect on the former High Priest than either man realized. Or perhaps it was the effect of whatever life force his own curse took out of him. Either way, the old man's remaining strength declined rapidly after that. He soon became too feeble to haul stones any longer.

The foreman reduced his load to carrying buckets of water to the other workers. Soon, even that was too much for him, and he collapsed. The workers dumped him in camp and left him there, presumably to die.

That was where the scribe Ani found him. The High Priest's former recruit had been making a living as an itinerant scribe, working his way upriver, going from village to village. He would set up his writing materials in the market square in each town he came to, and there he would write letters and draw up documents for townsfolk in exchange for food and lodging. It had taken a long time, but he had at last made his way all the way up to Aswan.

He came in the devout hope of finding his old mentor still alive – and indeed, he did find him. Ani had followed the sound of mallets ringing on stone to the quarry, where he inquired after the former High Priest, claiming to be the old man's nephew. One of the workers, a secret adherent of Amun, told him he would find the old priest in the worker's camp and pointed him in the right direction. By the time he found him, the old man was in bad shape, his mouth swollen and bloodied, a deep whip wound across his belly.

Ani wasn't sure what to do, but since no one was around, he simply heaved the gaunt old man up on his back and carried him out of the camp. No one saw them go.

He had already located the villa housing a small group of dedicated followers of Amun in the nearby town of Aswan, so he carried the old man there. It was risky – if the King's officers realized the attempted assassin of the King was missing, the first place they would look would be among known followers of the old gods. But under the circumstances, it was the only place Ani could think of where he might hide the old man.

Fortunately for him, the renegade priests were prepared for this and had long prayed that their former master might somehow be released to them. They cleaned the old man up and dressed his wounds, carefully spooning water and soup into his battered mouth. Under their attentive care, he recovered some of his strength. Nevertheless, it was clear he would not last much longer.

Back at the workers' camp, the foreman noticed that an important prisoner was missing. He asked around, to see if anyone had seen him go. The general opinion was that the old man was too weak to walk. It was generally agreed that he had probably died. Maybe his body had been dragged off by jackals or hyenas from the nearby desert.

Finally, one man, the same man who had directed Ani to the camp, spoke up. "When I left camp this morning, the old man was clearly dying, nearly dead. A young man came seeking him. He said he was the old man's nephew. I told him where he could find the old man. I thought it likely he would find only a dead body."

The foreman was more annoyed than angry, since he, too, thought it likely the old priest was already dead. If so, he felt it would be good riddance, as the old bastard was nothing but trouble. Nevertheless, the prisoner was his responsibility and must be accounted for.

The foreman enlisted the aid of the local constabulary to search for the missing prisoner. Since night had already fallen, the search would not begin until the next morning.

In the former priests' secret enclave, Ani lovingly tended his old master. He felt he owed everything to the old man. He had been an unwanted orphan living on the streets until the old man had come along and rescued him. His time among the acolytes of Amun had been the best time in his life. And even though he had been denied the opportunity to continue living the easy life of a priest, he had been among them long enough and had worked hard enough that he was able to acquire sufficient skill at reading and writing to provide him with a continued means of livelihood. He loved the man who had rescued him and hated the king who had destroyed his happiness and his greatest chance at living a good life.

Once the old priest had been given food and water and had his wounds tended, he recovered his senses and recognized his rescuer.

"Ani?" he croaked, peering at the young man. "Is that young Ani?"

"Yes, Master," answered Ani eagerly. "I am, indeed, Ani, who you took in off the streets."

"Ah, you're a good lad," the priest said. He looked around him. "Where am I?"

"You're in the house of some loyal followers of Amun," replied one of their hosts. "Young Ani, here, rescued you from the workers' camp and brought you here to us. You didn't know it, but we have tried for years to find a way to rescue you, without success. And then, one day, this young man shows up on our doorstep, with you on his back! Amun has, indeed, worked a miracle!"

"Amun be praised," rasped the High Priest. "He has, indeed, worked a miracle, to have freed me and brought me among friends before I die!"

"You mustn't die, Master!" cried Ani, clutching the old man's hand. "We need you! We need your wisdom and your guidance and your leadership."

"I'm afraid it's too late for that," the old man wheezed. "I will go soon to face the Forty-two Assessors. May my soul balance against the Feather of Ma'at!"

"May you be justified!" chanted several of the other priests present.

"No!" cried Ani. "Don't go!"

"I'm afraid I have no choice in the matter," rasped the old man. "But you and the other brethren must carry on the work. You must see Amun and the other gods restored."

The gathered priests murmured agreement.

The old man raised himself up on one elbow. "And you, my son, Ani – you must seek out this Heretic King and his Heretic Wife and find a way to kill them. Free the Two Lands from this destroyer of Ma'at and defiler of temples! Promise me you will!" he cried out, then collapsed breathlessly back on the bed.

"I promise, my Master! I will find a way," Ani cried, "no matter how long it takes me, or how difficult or fraught with peril it may be! I swear it!"

"Good, good! May Amun bless you, my son," he whispered, placing one withered hand on the young man's head. Then his hand fell away, his eyes closed and his breathing became shallower and shallower.

The gathered priests knelt by their leader's bedside and began chanting an invocation for the dying. Ani held the old man's limp hand and wept into the bedclothes.

After a while, the High Priest's chest ceased to move. One of the priests held a polished bronze mirror before his nose. It remained clear.

"Our Father is gone," he said and pulled the sheet up over the old man's face.

The group began praying, ritual mourning prayers for the dead. The leaders of the group quietly debated how they might have the old man's body properly embalmed without the authorities finding out.

However, their plans came to naught, as they were soon interrupted by loud pounding on the door. The local police had arrived, seeking the escaped prisoner. Despite the priests' best efforts to prevent it, the police insisted on searching the house, and quickly found what they were after: the body of the dead High Priest. They hauled the body away, despite the wails of protest from the former priests.

Ani was beside himself, screaming curses after the policemen carrying off the body. Finally, the other priests restrained him, fearing reprisals. They reminded him that he had made a deathbed promise to the late First Prophet, and that, to keep it, he would have to remain alive and free – and that meant not provoking the police, who would be within their rights to punish him for having helped a prisoner escape.

Ani agreed that he would restrain his grief for now and channel all his hatred into finding a way to carry out his promise to his dead master.

The leader of the group pointed out that the authorities might well come looking for Ani, so it would be wisest for him to hide out somewhere else for a while. They sent him out to a secret stronghold in the hills of the eastern desert. There, he joined a group of the most hardened and determined fanatics, plotting the overthrow of the King and Queen. He trained as an assassin, mastering the use of ritual dagger and sword, learning techniques of stealth and the art of disguise, preparing to take the vengeance he had sworn.

Back at Aswan, the superintendent of the quarry recalled what Thutmose had said about the High Priest's fate and decided the prophecy must be fulfilled. Therefore, he had his men carry the unembalmed body of the late First Prophet out into the desert, where they left it in an area known to be frequented by lions, jackals and hyenas. As they left, the circling vultures settled to the ground and began tearing at the body. When the Constable's men checked back a few days later, there was nothing left but shattered bones, cracked open by sharp beaks and teeth for their marrow.

Thus ended First Prophet Ptahmose, as Thutmose had foretold, unbeautified, unburied, his bones gnawed and scattered by wild animals. Unfortunately, his hatred of the King and Queen lived on in his followers, who continued to plot against them.

Chapter 39: Pharaoh Smenkare

As Thutmose journeyed back down the river, he heard more and more stories about the mysterious new co-regent, Pharaoh Smenkare. He made a point of taking at least one meal ashore every day, usually in the most popular tavern he could find, so he could listen in on what people were saying.

Some were saying the new co-pharaoh was a younger brother of Akhenaten's by a lesser wife, previously kept out of the public eye by the Queen Mother. (Speculation about the reasons for such a deception ran rampant.) Still others were saying he was a homosexual lover of the king, a shameful secret paramour now gaining scandalous power. A few whispered that the new Pharaoh was not a man, at all, having breasts, but no beard. In spite of Nefertiti's public presentation as co-pharaoh at the Great Durbar, it was surprising how few people actually realized that **she** was Pharaoh Smenkare, also known by her new throne name, or prenomen, of Ankhkheperrure. Public opinion about the new co-regent seemed to be divided between approval and disapproval, with most people taking a wait-and-see attitude. Some even went so far as to intimate that anything would be better than the Heretic Pharaoh.

Word of the death of the old High Priest was traveling down the river even more rapidly than Thutmose himself. Stories about the brutality of Akhenaten's vengeance on the old man grew steadily at each port, generating an increasing level of outrage with each re-telling. Before long, there were tales that Pharaoh had personally tortured the old man to death, despite the patent impossibility of such an occurrence, given that Akhenaten was known to be residing in his new capital, while the former First Prophet had been imprisoned at Aswan for years. Thutmose took people's willingness to believe such arrant nonsense as a very bad sign of their dislike for Pharaoh Akhenaten.

On his return to Akhetaten, Thutmose presented himself at court to report on his findings: to Akhenaten, about the readiness of the stone; to Nefertiti, about the discontent of the people; and to both of them about the rumors of plotting on the part of the old priesthood, and about his clash with the former First Prophet and the old man's subsequent death.

Akhenaten was inclined to discount the threats, saying, "Surely they cannot harm us now. The Amun priesthood has been disbanded and stripped of its temples and its wealth. As you have seen, these priests are gathered only in small groups, receiving offerings of flowers and fruit. I doubt that they can fund much of a resistance effort with that! Besides, we are safe now, here in Akhetaten, where my troops control all traffic in or out of the city."

"I wouldn't be so sure you are safe, Your Majesty," Thutmose respectfully replied. "With the level of dissatisfaction I have seen among the people, these murderous priests may find a lot of popular support. That makes them very dangerous, even without the use of their temple treasure."

"Pah! Common people!" Akhenaten replied. "Do you honestly think some farmer is going to come into the Aten temple and skewer me with his wooden pitchfork? That's absurd!"

"Perhaps not, Your Majesty – but you should know that I had a run-in with the former First Prophet of Amun while I was visiting the quarry at Aswan. We exchanged curses and dire prophecies. When he attempted to curse me further, the quarry foreman whipped him – "

"As well he should!" exclaimed the king. "I was far too lenient with that old viper!"

"Well, he won't trouble us any more, sire. After the foreman whipped him, he became ill," Thutmose told him. "He was left in the workers' camp in the morning, but was gone when the crews returned at night."

"What! He escaped?"

"Not exactly. It seems that a former acolyte, one of those boys he took in off the street and trained as an assassin, showed up and carried him off to a house in the town where some former priests were living," Thutmose explained. "By the time the police got there, the old man was dead. Despite the priests' protests, the police seized the body and fed it to the carrion eaters."

"A fitting end for the evil-doer!" exclaimed Pharaoh, gratified to know he would not need to worry about encountering the old man in the next world.

"However," continued Thutmose, "the police never found the young man who carried him away. The former priests denied any knowledge of where he had gone, but the police chief believes there are groups of fanatical adherents of the old religion in secret hideouts in the desert, plotting their revenge. So I do not feel entirely certain that you or your wife are safe, even here in Akhetaten, although it probably is still the safest place in the country."

"Well, we have done all we can to make it safe," Akhenaten said. "Beyond that, we can only pray to Aten to safeguard us."

Nefertiti was more inclined to take his warning seriously, when they met in private, as they began to do more frequently. They often met together with Nefertiti's father, Aye, the Grand Vizier, and sometimes with the Viziers of North or South, depending on whether they were in the city or not. Sometimes they even managed to snatch a few minutes alone together.

However, even then, they maintained a decorous distance, by unspoken agreement. They both knew that, if they once broke down and came together, their ability to resist the temptation to do more would be shattered – and that would be very, very dangerous, especially while Akhenaten still lived. Thutmose was also still very aware of the great social gulf between them; and they both felt a deep loyalty to Akhenaten as husband and suzerain. They both loved him deeply, each in their own way.

To Nefertiti, Akhenaten was the good, kind, loving husband who had given her so much, the loving father of her children, the source of her regency. To Thutmose, he was the beneficent patron and childhood friend, the brilliant intellectual and admired visionary who had challenged a stagnant culture, liberated art and seen that all the many gods were really one. Neither of them could bear to betray his love and trust.

By now, they both realized that Akhenaten's religious revolution had failed. His vision was too far ahead of its time. People weren't ready to accept such a radical re-definition of divinity. Thutmose, having spent time among the people, was also aware of certain shortcomings in the doctrines of Atenism, itself. Still, neither he nor Nefertiti could bear to let the ailing Akhenaten see how disastrously his spiritual experiment was turning out. So they discussed it between themselves and with Aye, Ramose and Aper-El, but kept it from the king.

Nefertiti feared that they might not need to keep the secret of the religious restoration much longer. Akhenaten's doctors had examined him and reported to her that his heart was beating very erratically. Since childhood, he had always had recurrent attacks of inability to breathe, with a persistent wheeze and a rattle in his lungs the doctors called "rales". Now, the attacks were more frequent and severe and threatened to overwhelm his weakened heart.

The trader Kohath had brought Akhenaten a medicinal plant called "ma huang" that came from a country far to the east of Babylonia, beyond a vast range of mountains known as the Roof of the World. He had shown the court physicians how a tea made from the dried stems of the plant could help relieve the king's breathing symptoms. He had been fortunate enough to procure some of the seed-bearing cones, as well as the medicinal stems of the plant, so the court gardener was able to grow it. The result was a tough, brownish-green shrub about a cubit tall, with tiny leaves that soon withered, leaving the long stems with their multiple leaf-nodes. Fortunately, the plant appeared to thrive in the desert climate. The stems could be cut and dried in the sun for a couple of weeks, then broken to remove any bark. The medicinal tea could then be brewed from the remaining part of the stems.

This tea helped alleviate Pharaoh's wheezing and shortness of breath, but Kohath had warned the doctors that too much could interfere with his sleep and overstimulate his heart. They wrestled with a precarious balancing act, knowing that too low a dosage could allow an increased difficulty in breathing that could bring on a fatal irregularity of the heart, while too high a dose might, itself, cause Pharaoh's heart to fail.

Nefertiti was grateful to the trader for bringing this sovereign remedy, along with inside information about what was happening in the world outside the Nile valley.

Knowing that Akhenaten might not survive much longer, Thutmose began to sculpt a new bust of the king in fine yellow limestone. So many of the adult images of him were in Bek's distorted caricature style; no realistic sculptures of Akhenaten as a mature man existed. Thutmose hated to think that posterity would remember this brilliant, fascinating man only by those bizarre, misshapen images. He strove instead to show him as the wise, mature, thoughtful king he had become, a statesman as well as a religious and social reformer. He was sure that this bust, too, would be one of his greatest works.

Meanwhile, the rate of infection with plague continued to decline, but never wholly went away. News from the outside world suggested that it was much worse in other countries which had not implemented the measures promulgated by Pharaoh and his physicians in Egypt. Reports of outbreaks continued to come in from countries around the Middle East.

And of course, plague was not the only disease afflicting the area. During the winter of the year after the Durbar, the royal couple's two remaining younger daughters both fell ill with a high fever and severe cough. Although the doctors did their best to save them, both girls died within a few days of each other. It was yet another burden for Nefertiti and another blow to Akhenaten's health.

To make it even worse, Queen Tiye, who had always been such a tower of strength, now began to weaken. She had already suffered from stiffness and pain in her lower back, hips and knees for several years, making it increasingly difficult for her to stand or walk. The pain was making it hard for her to sleep at night, and lack of sleep was wearing her away, making her more susceptible to other diseases that came along. She resisted drinking poppy juice during the day, having long ago learned of its tendency to produce dependency and knowing that it made her too groggy to function. Nevertheless, her health and strength continued to decline, and in the spring of Akhenaten's 13th regnal year, she succumbed to a fever and died.

The loss of his mother, the rock upon whom he had always been able to rely, was a severe shock to Akhenaten. It seemed to sap what little strength remained to him. He took to his bed and seldom rose from it. The doctors warned Nefertiti that any additional shock might kill him.

After the deaths of her younger daughters, Nefertiti could not shake off a dark conviction that the people were right: the old gods *were* punishing her and Akhenaten for banishing them. This conviction and the continued news of unrest from around the country at last convinced her that she would have to bring the old religion back in order to restore peace and order to Egypt.

Reluctantly, she met with her closest advisors and announced her intention to them. They all agreed that it was the wisest course of action.

Each of the regional viziers was sent out to his area with orders to announce the re-opening of the temples and put out the word that their priests might now return. She sent her father out to try to locate the former Second Prophet, who would now be the highest-ranking surviving official of the Amun clergy. The Vizier was to inform him that he might now return to his chief temple at Karnak, the original home of Amun, and begin restoring the worship of his god. He would presumably advance to become the new First Prophet, Amun willing.

At first the priests were wary, wondering if this new policy was a trick to draw them out into the open. But when the first few returned to their temples and were able to practice their rites unmolested, they gained confidence that the restoration was real. Soon, priests began surfacing from their secret enclaves and re-opening temples all over the Two Lands.

However, far from being grateful to Pharaoh Smenkare for lifting the ban, they now spoke out more openly against the two pharaohs. They clearly resented their years in hiding and their continued poverty, since Pharaoh had not seen fit to restore their tribute nor replenish their plundered temple treasures. The most fanatical groups continued secretly training assassins in their desert hideaways.

Back in Akhetaten, Nefertiti kept this change of policy secret from her ailing husband. She felt that knowledge of her defection and the complete failure of his religious reforms would kill him, and the doctors agreed. All palace staff were warned not to breathe a word of it to him.

So Akhenaten hung on, blessedly unaware that the old religion was making a quiet comeback. He continued to send Thutmose out to oversee the construction of new or expanded Aten temples all around the country.

After one of these journeys, Thutmose returned home just after dark. Entering the workshop, he saw a light shining out the doorway of his studio. Frowning, he went to check who was in his studio at this hour. He looked in the open doorway and saw Mariamne standing in front of his worktable, studying the bust of Nefertiti. She looked up and saw him in the doorway.

"You're home," she said in a flat voice.

"Yes," he replied. "What are you doing in here?"

"I was curious," she said. "I've seen you come in here so often, late at night. When I've asked your apprentices what you were doing, they've always just said 'working'. When I've asked the servants, several of them said you were just staring at some statue – always the same one, they said, a statue of the queen. So I was curious to see what you were staring at. I came looking and found this," she gestured, "in the cupboard, behind some plaster body parts, all wrapped up."

"Well, so now you've seen it," he said, with studied calm. "If you're satisfied, let's put it back and go in the house. I'm tired and hungry – I've had a long trip."

"Am I satisfied?" she asked. "I don't know. Now I know what you were looking at all this time – but what I don't know is *why*. Why do you spend so much time looking at this statue of the Queen, Thutmose? Does it have some special meaning for you?"

"I think it's my best work, is all," he said. "But you know how I am: I'm never satisfied. No piece is ever perfect – there's always some way to improve it."

"Except for this piece, Thutmose. The only way to improve this piece would be to replace it with the original," she said, attempting to catch his eye.

"What? I don't know what you're talking about," he replied.

"Yes, you do," she said. "You're in love with her, aren't you?"

"That's crazy!" he protested. "She's the Queen, and I'm just a lowly potter's son! Loving her would be like falling in love with the sun: unreachable and pointless!"

"Not to mention hot and deadly," Mariamne retorted.

"This is a ridiculous argument," he said.

She looked at him sadly and shook her head. "I've always known I didn't have your heart," she said. "A part of you was always distant, even when you were in my arms. I've loved you all my life, and

I knew you didn't really love me back. But I figured having part of you was better than having nothing at all. At least I've had you as a husband and provider, and sometimes in my bed. I never knew where that other part of you went. I knew you weren't fooling around with other women – but little did I know who owned your heart. Tell me the truth – are you in love with her?"

She stared at him until he was forced to meet her gaze.

"Yes," he said very softly. "I can't help it. I've loved her since we were children. But it doesn't matter – there's no way anything can ever come of it. Whatever my wayward heart has done, my actions have always been faithful to you."

"It does matter," she said, tears sliding silently down her cheeks. "To me, it matters. What you feel matters."

"I'm sorry, Mariamne, I really am," he said sadly. "You're a good woman and a good wife, and you deserve my whole heart – but I can't give it to you, because it isn't mine to give. It hasn't been since I was a little boy."

They stood there silently for a while, neither one wanting to do or say anything rash that might shatter their family forever. Thutmose wanted to put his arms around her and comfort her, but feared that the gesture would be unwelcome under the circumstances, so he did nothing. Mariamne just stood there with her eyes closed, tears streaming from beneath them. Finally, Thutmose pulled off his headcloth and handed it to her.

"So, now what do we do?" he asked as she wiped her eyes. He left it up to her to decide, as the wronged party.

"I don't know," she said. "I thought it was enough for me, being married to you, sharing your house, your bed, your children. I thought I could settle for that, even if I didn't have your heart. But that was all speculation, since I only guessed at the truth. Now that I know the truth, I'm not so sure I can live with it. I guess I'll have to think about it for a while."

"If it's any consolation," he said, "all the rest of me belongs to you. Since we have been married, I have never lain with any other woman."

She gave a short laugh, then sighed and said, "Well, I guess that's some consolation. At least I have your body, if not your heart. Well, I guess that'll have to do for now."

With that, she turned and headed back to the main house, with Thutmose following behind.

Chapter 40: The Death of Akhenaten

Thutmose had continued to work on the limestone bust of Akhenaten, which was now nearly finished. Where Bek had chosen to exaggerate the king's broad cheekbones and elongate his somewhat pointed chin until it formed a long diamond shape with the chin hooked under, Thutmose faithfully portrayed it as a strong face with full, determined lips and pensive, deep-set eyes. Above the brow band, the king wore the blue leather war crown, the khepresh, its two rounded tortoise-shell halves joined at a flange running from ear to ear across the top of the head. He modeled the texture of the myriad small rings of bronze attached all over the helmet to armor it. Although this king had never actually gone to war, it was appropriate headgear to convey the sense of strong character the artist sought to portray. This was a thoughtful and determined man, not a weak, indecisive dreamer.

Although Thutmose had not yet set in the rock crystal eyes or painted the stone in lifelike colors, the king had seen the work and was very pleased with it. Thutmose felt it was his second best piece, after the bust of Nefertiti – of which, of course, Akhenaten knew nothing.

One afternoon in late winter, five years after the famous Durbar, Akhenaten called Thutmose in to his sickroom to find out how work on his latest Aten temple was going. Thutmose had recently returned from working on a new temple in the complex at Karnak, whose talatat blocks were in the process of being painted with hundreds of colorful scenes of the royal family, most of them drawn from happier days when the whole family had still been intact. Painting those scenes had been a painfully nostalgic experience for Thutmose, who knew those days were gone and would never come again. Nevertheless, when Akhenaten asked him about his progress, he focused on the status of the work and reported that all went well.

The king also asked him whether people were coming to his temples, not just at Karnak, but all over the country. Were they bringing offerings, he wanted to know, and did they seem to be glad that they were welcome in the house of this god?

Nefertiti, who sat on the other side of Akhenaten's bed, glanced anxiously at Thutmose, worried that he might reveal the true extent of the new religion's unpopularity.

Thutmose hesitated.

But now, at last, Akhenaten was beginning to have his own doubts about that. He looked at Thutmose long and keenly, and finally said,

"It's time to let me know the truth, old friend."

Nefertiti looked in alarm from one man to the other. Looking at Thutmose, she gave a surreptitious shake of her head — but Akhenaten saw it.

"It's all right, my dear," he said to her. "I have known for some time now that my new faith has not really caught on." He looked over at Thutmose. "You might as well tell me all of it. You're not a very successful liar, you know. I know you too well. You have too honest a face."

Thutmose knew the king was right. He took a deep breath, considering where to begin and how much to tell.

"You are right, my king. I am not a very good liar," he agreed, "and your religion has not really won over the people. Oh, it has a small following, mostly among the people you have promoted to positions of power and among a certain class of intellectuals. But the old nobles, the ones you threw out of office, resent you and pay only lip service to Aten. The old priesthood continue to plot against you, and the common people simply don't understand your new religion."

Thutmose paused, considering the issue of the common people.

"I think your concept of One God is just too advanced for them," he said. "They can't seem to wrap their minds around it. I can understand that. Since I grew up with the old gods, too, it was hard enough for me to grasp such a radical idea – and I was there with you while you were developing it. You talked to me about it while you were reasoning it out, so I heard it develop, little by little – although I think maybe you were not really talking to **me**, but just thinking out loud. Maybe, if the people could all hear you speak, in person, if they could hear your passion, they would catch that fire from you, as I have. But there's no way for that to happen – there's only one of you: you could never get to them all, even if you wanted to – even if your health would support traveling around the country."

"No, that will never happen now," Akhenaten conceded. "And even though you haven't said it, you are right about something else, Thutmose: I haven't tried to reach out to the common people," he acknowledged. "I think now that that was a mistake. I disregarded the common people, thinking them unimportant. You tried to tell me, my dear," he said to Nefertiti, "but I didn't listen to you. I thought that I was king, and they were my subjects, and they would have to obey me. I failed to recognize that you can't command people to believe as you would have them believe. You can't reach men's souls by royal decree."

"I'm afraid that's true," agreed Thutmose. "I think you have to appeal to their hearts, persuade them to believe as you do."

Nefertiti pulled her stool closer to her husband's bed and grasped his hand.

"You persuaded those of us who know you and are close to you," she assured him. "Thutmose is right: you were on fire with your vision of God, and you set us on fire, too."

"Well, I wanted a great bonfire, the whole country on fire with this new vision," he said, "but all I seem to have managed is a feeble, flickering little lamp."

"Still, coming up with something that new, that revolutionary is extraordinary in this land that never changes," said Nefertiti. "No one else has done that."

"Pah!" said Pharaoh. "Other people have come up with new gods, lots of them!"

"Yes, but that's just the point," said Thutmose, "they came up with lots of them. They added gods. No one else ever saw the deeper truth: that all those apparently different gods were really just one Being, one source of power that created everything. You are the only one who saw that the many were really One. That is unique and new – and very, very powerful."

"Thank you, Thutmose," Akhenaten said with surprising humility, coming from a man officially revered as semi-divine. "It makes me feel better, knowing that someone understands."

He reached out with his free hand. Surprised, Thutmose stepped closer to the bed and, after a moment's hesitation, grasped the offered hand. It was a gesture that was almost unthinkable, from Pharaoh to a commoner. Pharaoh held his hand a moment, then squeezed it briefly and released it.

"Sit, my friend," he said to Thutmose.

The artist pulled up a low, cushioned stool and sat by the bedside.

"I pray that you are right," Akhenaten said, "and that the idea of the One is powerful enough to live on in at least a few men's hearts after I am gone, that the light of the Aten will not go out in the land when I leave it. I think that will not be much longer. I feel my end approaching."

"No, my husband!" cried Nefertiti. "You must not think like that!"

"No, my dear," he said to her. "It is time for us both to face the truth. I can feel my life slipping away. My heart jumps erratically and I feel the wings of my ba[10] beating against my chest, trying to get out. And that makes me painfully aware of one very serious flaw, something very important that I overlooked when I formulated this new religion."

"What is that?" she asked.

"The Afterlife. I left out any concept of an Afterlife," he said. "How could I have done that, here in this land that is obsessed with life after death, this land where we spend our entire lives preparing for the Afterlife? How could I have overlooked something so important? And now, here I am, knocking at Death's door, not knowing what I'll find on the other side – or if there will even be an Other Side."

"Of course there will!" said Nefertiti. "You will go to join your Father, the Aten, and become one with him!"

"But then, what happens to all those common folks I brushed aside?" he asked. "Do they all simply vanish when they die? Or do they, too, become One with the Aten, and therefore, One with me, as well? I do not know," he lamented, shaking his head. "This is a vision I have not seen. And now I am facing that black abyss."

"If the common people vanish from existence after death," he continued, "then I have cheated them of whatever hope of an Afterlife they had before. Instead of enriching their spiritual lives, I will have robbed them of all hope for eternal life. And if, instead, they, too, become One with the Aten, and with me, then we are no different. Then the common folk are no less divine than I, and I am no more divine than they are. What a conundrum! What do you think, Thutmose?"

"I don't know, my lord. I am not a mystic, as you are. I am an ordinary man – I hardly dare aspire to Oneness, either with God or with a great man such as yourself," Thutmose replied.

"Somehow, Thutmose, I don't think posterity will call you an ordinary man, not when they see the miraculous work of your hands. If Aten created man, then surely you share some part of His creative power, to bring forth such statues as you do, so lifelike that they seem about to speak," the king commented, shaking his head in wonder. "Since I have failed to see whether there is an afterlife for me, I must rely on your magic to insure that my face, at least, lives on. So many of my images have been Bek's, symbolic rather than lifelike. Promise me that you will portray me as I truly am in the new wall paintings and statues, neither idealized nor distorted. Will you do that for me?"

"Of course, my king!" Thutmose assured him. "This new bust will be a good beginning. It is almost done."

---

[10] The portion of the soul that leaves the body at death.

"Thank you, my friend," said Akhenaten, smiling weakly. "I know I can count on you."

"Absolutely," said Thutmose, falling to his knees beside the bed. "I will do everything in my power to preserve and safeguard your image and your message, my king."

"Look after Nefertiti, as well," the king admonished him. "I know you are devoted to her, and she can rely on you."

"Always!" Thutmose replied.

"And you, Nefertiti, my dearest wife..."

"Yes, my husband?"

"Promise me that you will keep my faith alive. Keep the light of Aten shining in the Two Lands, and try to set the people alight with it."

"I will do my best, my dear," she promised.

Akhenaten's eyelids closed and his voice trailed off. It was clear the king was slipping away. His physicians were called, as were the three viziers and his son, Tutankhaten, and his two remaining daughters. The High Priest of Aten, Meryre, arrived with his acolytes. They began burning incense and reciting prayers.

The king recovered consciousness long enough to bless his children and make his farewells to his remaining family and closest followers. He beckoned for Tutankhaten and Ankhsenpaaten to come close and for Aye to help him sit partially up. He placed a hand on the head of either child and blessed them, joining them in marriage while he still lived. After that, Aye lowered him to his cushioned headrest and he closed his eyes.

He continued to breathe for a few hours more without regaining consciousness. But as his god, the Aten, slipped below the horizon in the West, Akhenaten ceased to breathe and joined him in the Afterlife, sped on his way by the tearful prayers of his family and loyal followers.

The word went out across the Two Lands: "Akhenaten, the servant of Aten is dead – May he be justified! Long live King Tutankhaten and King Smenkare!"

Young Tutankhaten looked frightened and clung to his new bride, Ankhsenpaaten. Nefertiti leaned her arms on the bed, put her head down on them and wept.

Thutmose ached to put his arms around her and comfort her, but dared not. How strange it all was, he thought. Akhenaten had never been a strong man, and there were many who accused him of being a weak king – and yet, he had been such a strong presence in their lives for so many years. He had drastically altered the very fabric of Egyptian society. And now, he was gone. Which way should they turn now? What was Nefertiti to do, he wondered, trapped between the need to restore order in the land and her deathbed vow to Akhenaten?

Since Tutankhaten was only eight years old, and Ankhsenpaaten just a couple of years older, the whole burden of ruling the country now fell on the slender shoulders of Nefertiti. She had never wanted the job, but accepted it as her responsibility. She faced it bravely, one woman alone, trying to manage a vast country in internal chaos, battered by drought and plague, besieged by a hostile priesthood within and warlike nations without. I resolved to do everything within my power to help her, but feared it could never be enough.

Chapter 41: Plots and Counter-Plots

The word of Akhenaten's death traveled up and down the Nile, throughout the Two Lands. It traveled by boat and caravan and camel train throughout Canaan and Naharin, where it reached the plaintive Rib-Hadda of Byblos, now besieged behind his city walls by the man whose treachery he had complained of, Akizzi of Amurru, son of the vassal king Abdi-Ashirta who had been executed at the Durbar five years before. It reached King Suppililiuma of Hatti, who was busy waging war against Mitanni. It reached Artatama, who now styled himself "King of the Hurrians." Although the Hittites had backed the plot which had succeeded in assassinating King Tushratta, they had simply seized more of the dwindling land of Mittani for themselves and let a son of Tushratta succeed, rather than helping Artatama to take the throne. The news also reached King Burra-Burriash in Babylonia and King Asshur-Uballit of Assyria.

They all heard that Pharaoh Neferkheperure-Waenre (Akhenaten) was dead, and that Pharaoh Ankhkheperure- Merwaenre now ruled Egypt. Nothing in diplomatic communications told them that their "brother", Ankhkheperure, was a woman – and Nefertiti preferred to keep it that way as long as possible, knowing that they would inevitably believe a woman to be a weaker "king" than a man. Any such perception of weakness on Egypt's part would be an open invitation to other nations to begin raiding Egypt's borders.

But no such deception was possible where Egypt's official representatives abroad were concerned. Egypt's commissioners to various vassal regions and her envoys to the courts of Great Kings had to be privately notified. And, of course, her commanders in the field must be informed. This included, most particularly, General Horemheb, who was presently in northern Canaan, trying to keep order among the vassal states and make enough of a show of force to discourage the Hittites and Assyrians from moving south into Egypt's buffer zone.

When the hot, tired, travel-stained courier arrived, Horemheb returned his salute, received the papyrus scroll from him and sent him off to the mess tent for food and drink. He called his scribe into the tent and had him read the urgent dispatch to him.

"So," he commented softly when the scribe finished reading, "the Great Wife now rules Egypt."

"Surely, only as regent for her stepson, Tutankhaten, my lord," observed the scribe. "After all, he's only a little boy."

"Maybe – and maybe not," Horemheb replied. "She's been growing in power for years. Remember, Akhenaten himself crowned her as co-pharaoh at the Great Durbar. She's been going by the throne name 'Smenkare' for several years now. And she's been wearing all the traditional pharaonic crowns and even dressing as a man, in a kilt, rather than a gown. I have seen that with my own eyes. I have heard that the only item of masculine attire she hasn't worn has been the pharaonic beard."

For centuries, perhaps even millennia, pharaohs had been clean-shaven, but had worn an artificial, braided beard, held on by a strap over the head. A hundred and fifty years earlier, when Queen Hatshepsut had styled herself pharaoh, she had even resorted to wearing the artificial beard. But apparently Nefertiti had stopped short of that artifice.

Unbeknownst to Nefertiti and her advisors, a second, more secretive delegation to Horemheb followed not long after the military courier, one sent by the new First Prophet of Amun. It included his official spokesman and a few of his more radical supporters, together with several prominent members of the old aristocracy who had been displaced by Akhenaten and a few merchants whose trade had suffered during his regime. It was, in short, a cross-section of the dissatisfied and malcontent factions in Egypt.

When his lieutenant announced that a delegation of priests and their allies was waiting to see him, he replied, "Admit them, but stay close. I don't trust these priests. I don't trust any priests."

The priesthood and the military were long-standing rivals for power in the Two Lands. For priests to seek out a commanding general was extraordinary, to say the least. They had to be up to something.

The lieutenant ushered them into the tent and sent an ensign to fetch a number of campstools for them.

The priest who was evidently the head of the delegation introduced them all.

"My Lord General," he said, "I am Userhat, *sed* priest of Amun. This is Prince Kerasher, Nomarch of the Prospering Scepter, with its seat at Heliopolis, and these are his lieutenant, Sneferu, his scribe and his bodyguards. And these two gentlemen are merchants: Hapu, a trader whose ships sail the Nile and the Green Sea, and Hunefer, a wine merchant from the Nome of the Ibis."

Horemheb was more than a little surprised to find this group of men doing anything together, since they included members of several factions that had long been at odds with each other. This lot made very odd bedfellows, indeed.

The nomarchs of Egypt were divided in their support of or opposition to Akhenaten and his successor. Many of the nomarchs of Upper Egypt, especially those of Nomes 4 through 18, which bracketed

Akhenaten's two capitals of Thebes and Akhetaten, tended to support his policies and religion; while many of the nomarchs of the Delta, in Lower Egypt, tended to oppose him.

The forty-two nomes (or as they are called in old Egyptian, *sepats*) were the pre-dynastic city-states of the Nile valley, which dated back thousands of years. They were all originally small, independent kingdoms, each with its own gods, culture and ruler. They had gradually joined forces, eventually becoming the two kingdoms of Upper and Lower Egypt, which were finally united under the legendary first Pharaoh, King Menes, nearly two thousand years before Akhenaten's time.[11] Their degree of independent power waxed and waned, complementing the degree of centralized power in the Two Lands: when the Pharaoh and his central government were strong, the nomarchs' power waned; when the central government weakened, the nomarchs gained power.

The nomarchs, as a group, were not happy with the ascendancy of the family of Yuya, since, during the seven years of famine early in the reign of Amenhotep III, they had been forced to sell all of their land to Pharaoh in order to buy grain. This had marked a new high in the centralization of power in Egypt; hence, a low in the power of the nomarchs. In addition, Yuya had brought his entire tribe into Lower Egypt, where they occupied some of the choicest land in the eastern part of the Delta, in the region known as Goshen, which included most of Nomes 13 through 20. This constituted a sizable portion of the area dominated by the Hyksos less than 200 years before, so it particularly galled the nomarchs of the area to once again have a large – and rapidly growing – group of sheep-herders invading their jurisdiction. Kerasher, ruler of the Thirteenth Nome, called the Prospering Scepter, represented this group.

When they were all seated and had been served with beer and bread, the general asked them, "So what brings you gentlemen here to Canaan, so far from home?"

The representative of First Prophet spoke first.

"I am here on behalf of Merenptah, who is now First Prophet of Amun in Thebes."

"Ah, yes," said Horemheb, "I had heard that the old First Prophet had died, and that the priests had been allowed to return to their temples. So Merenptah has taken Ptahmose's place, has he?"

"Aye, General, he has," agreed Userhat. "And he has set about putting all the temples of Amun to rights. His aim is to restore them to

---

[11] Around 3100 BCE.

their former glory and eventually, to reclaim all of the lands and tribute formerly belonging to Amun."

"Has the new pharaoh agreed to that?" asked Horemheb slyly.

"Not exactly," Userhat conceded reluctantly. "That's part of the problem: Nefertiti – pardon me, Pharaoh Smenkare - has allowed us to re-open the temples and resume our rituals, but without restoring the income needed to do so."

"I see," said Horemheb. "So, you can't really complain of oppression any longer, if you are now allowed to practice your religion freely. If I understand aright, then, your actual complaint is one of poverty."

"In part, my lord," conceded the priest. "But more than that," he added pompously, "it is one of continued heresy and impropriety on the part of this ruler."

"Heresy?" Horemheb asked.

"Certainly. The woman still continues to support the worship of the Aten, even in the sacred precincts of Karnak," replied the priest indignantly.

"And impropriety?"

"Why, for a woman to rule Egypt as Pharaoh, pretending to be a man, is certainly improper!" huffed the priest. "She even dresses as a man!"

"So you object to her clothing?" asked Horemheb, feigning naïveté.

"Yes, when it supports the pretense that she's a man!" said the priest. "Surely you, as a military man, can appreciate the danger to Egypt of having a weak king or, worse yet, a *woman* on the throne!"

Horemheb was taking a certain pleasure in playing devil's advocate and upsetting the pompous priest. He was also skilled enough in diplomacy, as well as military tactics, to know that keeping his opponent off balance gave him a tactical advantage.

"And what is it you want from me?" he asked. "I have no influence over what Pharaoh wears or whether she restores your temple treasure to you."

"We want your support in our efforts to restore the old order – or at least your agreement not to interfere," the priest replied.

"I don't see why you would need my agreement to that," Horemheb said. "I wouldn't normally be called upon to interfere unless you were trying to restore the old order by violently overthrowing the present regime. I could never support that. I am a faithful son of Egypt, loyal to my Pharaoh."

"Of course, General, of course! I would never ask you to be disloyal to Egypt!" the priest hastened to assure him. "I only ask you to consider the greater good of your country."

"Aha – here it comes," thought Horemheb. Aloud, he asked, "And what might that be?"

"For over two thousand years," said Userhat, "Egypt has remained stable under strong kings who have honored the ancient gods. When weak kings have been on the throne, or worse, when there was no mature male heir and a woman has sat on the throne, Egypt has slid into chaos and outsiders like the Hyksos have been able to take power."

Still taking the opposite side of the debate, Horemheb replied, "Yet, Queen Ahmose helped defeat the Hyksos, and when Hatshepsut was Pharaoh, she ruled for over twenty years without any outside power seizing Egypt."

"Yes, but Ahmose turned the throne over to her son as soon as he was ready, and even Hatshepsut eventually yielded her throne to her nephew Thutmosis III, the rightful, *male* heir, who turned out to be Egypt's greatest warrior king," Userhat pointed out. "In each case, it was the proper male king who drove out invaders and expanded our borders. And Thutmosis ultimately acknowledged that by striking out the images and inscriptions of Hatshepsut as Pharaoh. But even Hatshepsut honored the ancient gods, particularly Amun. *This* heretical woman still worships the Aten above Amun, the very god to whom her family owes its ascendancy. This cannot be allowed to continue! *She* cannot be allowed to continue! She must be stopped!"

By now, the priest was red in the face and quivering with outrage.

"And how do you propose to do that?" asked Horemheb ingenuously.

"By...whatever means necessary," sputtered the priest.

"As I said, I can't condone violence," Horemheb reiterated.

Prince Kerasher spoke up, saying, "We're not asking you to condone it."

Horemheb gave him a long, hard look. "What are you asking me to do?"

The priest and Prince Kerasher exchanged glances. The Nomarch replied, "Nothing. All we're asking you to do is to stay here and continue to guard Egypt's borders. Stay out of the country until we tell you otherwise."

"And what's in it for me?" the general asked shrewdly.

"When we send word, we want you to come back to Thebes and be the chief advisor to the rightful king, young Tutankhaten. You'd be in position to be the most powerful man in the country – and who knows where that might lead?" suggested Kerasher.

"What about Aye?" the general asked. "He's Grand Vizier, and he's the boy's grandfather."

"He's an old man," replied the Nomarch. "He's over fifty. He can't last all that long – whereas you're still young. What are you, thirty?"

"Thirty-one," replied Horemheb.

"There you have it. The boy king is very young, not yet ten, and we all know how fragile children's lives are, how few of them live to see adulthood. If he is to survive as king, he will need strong advisors – and who better than yourself?"

"And you would back me in this?" Horemheb asked.

"Absolutely," replied the Nomarch.

"Definitely," said the priest.

"And even if the boy survives to adulthood, who knows whether he will succeed in producing an heir? " said Kerasher. "The Heretic fathered many daughters, but only managed to produce one son by his whole harem. And if the boy should die without an heir, who would be available to succeed him? There are no more male members of this dynasty."

"It has happened before," the priest pointed out, "and in this dynasty. Thutmosis I was a soldier who was appointed to succeed to the throne when there were no male heirs available."

"Yes, but he married a royal daughter who was a legitimate Heiress," objected Horemheb. "That made his reign legitimate."

"Yes, and there are two or three royal daughters presently available," replied the Nomarch. "There is Meritaten, the Heretic's eldest daughter, who is presently acting as Queen to her mother's Pharaoh."

What was left unspoken was that Meritaten would not be free to marry as long as her mother and pharaonic alter ego, Nefertiti, still lived and ruled as pharaoh.

"There is also Tutankhaten's queen, Ankhsenpaaten. If young Tutankhaten were to die without issue, she would be left a widow. And who better to console the grieving widow than yourself?"

"True enough," Horemheb replied thoughtfully. The idea was beginning to appeal to him.

"In a pinch, there's also Princess Sitamun, who is now head of the Godswives of Amun," the priest added. "Throughout this dynasty, it has been common for the chief Godswife to be a royal daughter, and also for her to lay down the office in order to marry the next Pharaoh and become Great Wife."

"She's a lot older than the other two, older than I am," Horemheb pointed out. "She might be past her childbearing years by the time the throne...became available."

"True enough," agreed the priest, "but she does have the great advantage of being the daughter of Amenhotep III and thus relatively untainted by her brother's heresy. You could always have an heir by some other wife."

"True, true," conceded Horemheb. "But you know, I already have a wife, Amenia."

"Yes, we know," said the Nomarch. "And we also know that she has not given you any children. You could either divorce her, or she could simply remain as a lesser wife."

"I don't want to divorce her," Horemheb objected. "I love her. But she might object strenuously to becoming a lesser wife after having been my only wife for so many years."

"Well, that problem remains well in the future," said the priest. "You can deal with it when the time comes. After all, none of us knows how long he – or she – may live. It may not be an issue when, and if, the time comes."

"Yes," agreed Horemheb, "that's true enough."

"Meanwhile," said Kerasher, "the important thing in the near future is that you stay here, on the frontier, and don't return to Egypt until we send word."

"And what of Nefertiti – Pharaoh Smenkare?" Horemheb asked.

"That is not your concern," the priest told him.

"I won't betray my country," he warned.

"We're not asking you to," Kerasher assured him. "We're asking you to act for the greater good of your country. First, stay here and defend its borders from the Hittites and the Assyrians. Then, return home and advise and protect the young king. And third, if he fails to produce an heir, be prepared to step in and assume the throne."

"The throne..." mused Horemheb softly.

The Nomarch and the priest exchanged knowing glances. They knew they had him.

Meanwhile, in a camp hidden in the eastern hills in the southern part of the Two Lands, Ani now lived among a group of fanatical devotees of the god Amun. The zealous priests were joined by a few old soldiers who also wanted to see a return of the old ways, which they saw as supporting Egypt's strength in the face of its enemies.

The young fanatics were trained by the old soldiers in all the arts of war. They learned the use of the bow and arrow, the dominant weapons of Egypt's army, as well as the throwing axe, the spear, the dagger, the curved scimitar called the *khopesh* and the newer, straight sword adopted from the Syrians during the campaigns of Thutmosis III. Metals were expensive and metal weapons were hard to come by, but the zealots were well supplied with weapons paid for out of the carefully hoarded remnants of the temple treasure preserved by the priests.

The zealots trained hard, building endurance by running and doing exercises in the heat of the day; and practicing stealth by night. They learned how to approach a guard post silently in the dark and slit the guard's throat before he could make a sound. They learned how to scale walls and climb palm trees. They learned wrestling throws and holds and other forms of unarmed combat, including how to strangle someone with their bare hands or break his neck with a single twist.

They also learned the art of disguise and how to move unnoticed through a crowd. At this, Ani excelled. Both his childhood on the streets and his years as an itinerant scribe had given him a solid grounding in this art. As a child, he had made his living by petty theft, and he had seen and observed all kinds of people in his travels. He had a natural gift of mimicry and could flawlessly impersonate people of any craft or station in life. It wasn't long before he was teaching his fellow zealots these skills.

Ani's hatred of Akhenaten, his family and his religion had never faded. Since the Heretic King was dead, the focus now shifted to his wife, the so-called "Pharaoh" Smenkare, and her daughter, the "Great Wife", Meritaten. With his fellow fanatics, he was determined they should die. The son and his wife they would allow to live, since the boy was the legitimate king and they were young enough to be re-educated in the old religion and the proper maintenance of *ma'at*.

The day was coming. The warriors of Amun were ready. Ani was ready. He was determined to be among the chosen ones. It would not be long now.

Chapter 42: Return to Thebes

Less than six months after Akhenaten had been interred in his tomb in the Royal Wadi, Nefertiti decided to move the court back to the traditional southern capital, Thebes. She held Akhetaten in reserve, as a third capital lying midway between Thebes and the northern capital, Memphis, which was located near the point where the Nile split to form the Delta. While administrative functions now shifted to the traditional capitals, copies of all the archives were maintained in readiness at Akhetaten, as well.

The bulk of the royal household goods were moved to Thebes, and many of the nobles and some of the merchants followed suit. A deep quiet, almost of shock, fell on those remaining in Akhetaten. The city had risen so abruptly from the desert, to become a bustling, busy city of fifty thousand, swelling with visitors 'til it nearly burst its seams during the Great Durbar. Now it was half deserted, emptied even more quickly than it had filled.

As Chief of Works, Thutmose would, of course, have to move with the court. He announced his planned departure to Mariamne, but left it up to her to determine what she wanted to do with her thriving newest weaving establishment at Akhetaten. Meanwhile, he and his assistants began packing up their equipment, supplies and works-in-progress. The old queen's Chief of Works, Auta, arrived to help with the move.

Under their joint supervision, the apprentices carefully wrapped finished pieces and works-in-progress in linen padded with straw, then crated them up for transport up river on boats. They left Thutmose's studio until last, as he wanted to take charge of that, himself.

Thutmose and Auta carefully packed several small pieces, including a bust of the young junior Queen, Ankhsenpaaten, and a small full-body statue of Nefertiti as Pharaoh Smenkare. This last piece was Thutmose's latest work, showing Nefertiti in the cap crown and kilt of a Pharaoh. Her lovely face and body showed the beginning signs of age: the suggestion of lines between mouth and nose, a bit of a rounded belly, and while the breasts were still well-rounded, they were a bit lower than before. While these changes were hardly unexpected in a woman who had given birth to six children before the age of thirty, there was also a tension in her posture and expression that had not been there before. Looking at the statue before he wrapped it up, Auta definitely got a sense of the strain the new Pharaoh was under.

Thutmose came back into the studio just as Auta finished wrapping the statue. He called two of his assistants in to crate the wrapped statue up, while he packed up his sculpting tools. After the boxes and crated statuary were carted out, Auta turned to him expectantly.

"Well," the old man asked, "what about the bust? I know you still have it here."

"What about it?" asked Thutmose.

"Aren't you going to pack it up?"

"No."

Auta was surprised. "Surely you aren't going to leave it here!"

"As a matter of fact, I am," Thutmose replied.

"Why?" asked Auta.

"It's hard to explain," Thutmose said. "It's just a feeling I have – call it a hunch. I think it's meant to stay here. Strange as it may seem, I think it's actually *safer* here."

"Safer?" asked Auta, puzzled. "How can it be safer here, in a workshop you're about to abandon?"

"I have this terrible sense of foreboding," Thutmose said, "a sense that a dark time is coming and terrible things are about to happen. I fear that all that Pharaoh Akhenaten wrought is about to come unraveled, that everything he created here may soon perish. Everywhere I go, I hear people murmuring, whispering against the Pharaoh. It's like a gigantic wave, building, building, building in the depths of the sea. Sooner or later, it's bound to break over us. And when it does, its focus will be the Royal Family. I fear for them, the few who are left. They could all be wiped out.

"And if that happens," he continued, "all my work could be wiped out, too. The mob might even come after me, if I'm with them. Who knows? But if this place is empty, but for the trash – a few plaster body parts, some stone fragments, old rags and empty paint pots – it might escape their notice."

"An ominous vision, indeed, my boy," the old man said. "I hope you're wrong."

"So do I," Thutmose agreed.

"I have to admit, though," Auta continued, "your visionary flashes have an annoying habit of being right. I do hope you'll be careful, if that mob shows up. You're like a son to me. I'd hate to see anything happen to you."

"Don't worry – I'll be careful," Thutmose assured him.

"Good. Meanwhile, let me see that bust one last time, before we go."

"All right," agreed Thutmose. "I admit, I want to see it again, too."

He turned to the closed cupboard and pulled the door open. Squatting down, he pulled out a motley collection of plaster body parts from the bottom shelf, then carefully lifted out the bust, which was draped in a linen towel.

He set the bust carefully on the table, then reverently removed the towel. The reddish rays of the late afternoon sun shown through the clerestory windows and were reflected off the white plaster walls, bathing the magnificent bust in warm, rosy light. Once again, the Queen seemed almost alive as the two men regarded her in silence.

Auta was the first to speak. "You never put the crystal lens in her left eye," he said. "Why not?"

"I left it that way on purpose," Thutmose replied.

"Why?" Auta persisted.

"Several reasons," Thutmose said. "One, if I had ever finished it, I would have been honor bound to tell the king about it, and then it would have been taken away from me. Two, call it a silly superstition, but I had the feeling that, if it was too perfect, the god or gods might strike me down for my presumption, for overreaching my bounds as a mere mortal. And three, I wanted to leave an open doorway, in case Nefertiti's *ba* should ever need to take refuge there. It's all probably very foolish on my part, but that's the way I feel. And there you have it."

"I understand," said Auta. "I hope you're wrong, but I understand. So be it."

They admired the bust a few minutes more, then Thutmose carefully rewrapped it in the towel, slid it to the back of the shelf, then stacked a random mixture of plaster body parts in front of it. He closed the cupboard door and latched, but did not lock it.

The two men left the studio and closed the door behind them just as the sun set behind the hills on the far side of the river.

They visited the ship onto which the cargo from the workshop had been loaded, made sure everything was properly stowed, then returned to Thutmose's house for dinner.

After dinner, Thutmose and Auta sat on the roof and talked for a while, then the old man headed to bed in one of the spare bedrooms. Before Thutmose could descend to the master bedroom, Mariamne appeared at the head of the stairs.

"I need to talk to you," she said.

"By all means," he said, strolling over to the parapet.

Mariamne joined him there, looking out over the river.

"I've made my decision," she said. "I'm not returning to Thebes with you."

"As you wish," he said, keeping his voice even. "Are you going to stay here, then?"

"No," she said. "I'm going to return to my farm in the Delta."

"What about your shops, in Thebes and here?" he asked.

"I'll make regular visits, and I'm thinking about opening another one in Memphis or Heliopolis, or maybe both. They'll be a lot closer to my source of supplies," she said. She kept her voice calm, but it quavered a bit near the end.

"All right," he said, "if that's what you want."

"No," she snapped, "that's not what I *want*! What I want is you, your whole heart, but I haven't got that! I've never had that. And now that Akhenaten is dead, I'm the only thing left standing between you and the woman you really love! I can't compete with her, and I know it. So I will withdraw gracefully from the field of battle, retire to my farm and lick my wounds!"

"Mariamne, I-" he started to say.

She held up one hand. "Don't say anything," she said. "I don't want to hear it."

She turned and headed for the staircase.

"Wait!" he said. "I just wanted to say: you don't have to do that. You can have the house in Thebes. I'll move back into the artists' quarters in the palace. It's where I've spent much of my life, anyway. I don't need much: my studio, and a pallet in a cell at night. You're welcome to everything else."

"I'll keep that in mind," she replied. "I will need to visit the business from time to time. A place to sleep could come in handy."

"What about the children?" he asked.

"They'll come with me, of course, although Senmut will soon be old enough to join you as an apprentice, if he so chooses," she said.

Although Thutmose worked long hours and didn't get to spend as much time with his children as he, or they, would have liked, he enjoyed having them around. He knew that he would miss them sorely.

"And Mery?" he asked.

"You can come and visit her from time to time, and I might bring her some of the times when I come to check on the business."

"That's good," he replied. "I'll miss them – and you. I'll miss you, too, Mariamne, although I know your leaving me is no more than I deserve."

He reached out for her. She put her hands out in front of her, palms out, and said, "Don't! Just stay away. I can't bear any fond farewells."

He dropped his arms by his sides.

"All right. I will respect your wishes. Good night, my dear," he said.

In the end, he dragged a pallet up onto the roof and slept there. Not for long, however: Nefertiti had given him one more assignment.

At about midnight, he rose from his pallet and made his way quietly to his empty studio. A few minutes later, Ipy and two trusted assistants joined him. They picked up two sacks of tools he had stashed behind a fountain in the entryway, and the two of them slipped silently through the sleeping town to where the road to the Royal Wadi passed through the east gate. Police Chief Mahu and five of his most trusted men joined them there. At a sign from the Chief, the guard on duty opened the gate and they slipped quietly out. Only after passing a sharp bend in the wadi did they light their oil lamps. They pulled a pair of sledges and a pile of tools from a hollow behind the rocks on one side of the canyon and loaded the tools on the sledges.

The men worked their way up the wadi to the Royal Tomb, dragging the sledges behind them. Chief Mahu signaled the guard in front of the tomb with his lantern. The guard signaled back, then unbarred the gate to the tomb.

Thutmose and Mahu and their men entered the tomb and carefully lowered the sledges down the entryway ramp. One man stayed outside to guard the gate, while the other went ahead and lit torches in holders on the walls as the men moved into the tomb. Thutmose and Ipy and their assistants went ahead of the sledges to two side chambers, where they pried the lids off the stone sarcophagi inside. One of the sledges was pulled into each side chamber. In the first chamber, the gilded mummiform coffin of Princess Meketaten was carefully levered up from the bottom of the stone sarcophagus. Ropes were passed beneath it in three places. The men then raised it level with the lip of the sarcophagus and carefully slid it down a wooden ramp brought along for the purpose, onto one of the sledges. It was hauled to the base of the entry ramp.

In the second chamber, the coffin of Kiya was removed in the same manner and slid onto a second sledge, which was then hauled into the main burial chamber and moved into position near the sarcophagus of the late Pharaoh Akhenaten. The lid of Kiya's coffin was removed. Her mummy was carefully lifted out and placed on the floor at one side of the room.

It took six men to lift off the grey granite lid of Akhenaten's sarcophagus. They laid it on the floor near Kiya's mummy, then returned to carefully pry off the lid of his outermost coffin. They laid it aside and pried off the lids of the second and third gilded coffins, laying them aside also. Finally, they reverently removed the mummy of Akhenaten and transferred it to Kiya's coffin. Kiya's mummy was placed in Akhenaten's inner coffin and each of the coffin lids replaced and sealed.

Since Thutmose's workshop had made the seals used by the High Priest of Aten to seal the Royal Tomb and its coffins, it had been easy for him to make duplicates. He now used these to re-seal Akhenaten's and Kiya's coffins and the granite sarcophagus. He also re-sealed the coffins, sarcophagi and doors of each of the side chambers. Now, if the tomb should be broken into, it would look as though it had not been disturbed.

Thutmose and Ipy wrapped the gilded wooden coffins of Akhenaten and Meketaten in linen, then boxed them in boards, just the way the statues from his workshop had been boxed. They were positioned on the sledges and carefully tied down.

Torches were doused behind the men as they pulled the two sledges, now bearing the mummies of the late king and his second daughter, up the entryway ramp, through the gate of the tomb, then down into the wadi. They strained to move as fast as possible, knowing dawn was not far off. Mahu gave the signal at the eastern gate and they were quietly admitted. They hauled the sledges through town at a near run, hoping to be out of sight before any curious townsfolk awakened by the noise could peer out of their houses. They reached Thutmose's workshop and pulled their burdens inside just as the edge of the sun peeked through the gap in the cliffs made by the Royal Wadi. Inside, they all collapsed on benches and the floor, breathing hard and dripping sweat.

Once he had caught his breath, Thutmose called on his servants to prepare breakfast for ten. After they had caught their breath and eaten, Mahu and his men slipped out, one and two at a time. A short time later, several more of Thutmose's assistants showed up to move the two crates onto a waiting ship, where they were positioned between other large crates containing statuary. Not long after that, Thutmose and Ipy came aboard, carrying their personal belongings.

Thutmose checked that all the crates and boxes had been stowed and secured to his satisfaction. Once he was sure everything was secure, he gave the word and the captain cast off. The sails were raised and caught the southbound wind. They headed upriver to Thebes with their artistic cargo and its precious, secret additions, bound for secret re-burial in the Valley of the Kings.

Chapter 43: Consummation

After their ship docked in Thebes, Thutmose oversaw the unloading of the cargo onto several large sledges. The boxes with the two coffins, which looked just like any of the others, were transported with the rest to the Artists' Workshop at Malkata Palace. There, Thutmose would re-work the portrait and inscriptions on Kiya's coffin to better suit its new occupant before it was interred in its new resting place.

While Ipy accompanied the shipment to the palace, Thutmose stayed behind to supervise the unloading of a second, smaller ship carrying tools and smaller items. By the time this shipment had been unloaded, Ipy had returned with the sledges. Once everything had been loaded up, Thutmose assigned one of his assistants to accompany this load to the palace, while he and Ipy headed for a local tavern to have dinner.

The proprietor recognized them from previous years.

"Thutmose! Ipy! My favorite artists! I haven't seen you two in years," he cried. "Come in, come in! I can give you a nice private table in the back room - "

"No, no, no," said Thutmose, "we'd prefer to sit out here with everybody else. It's friendlier that way – gives us a chance to get reacquainted with our neighbors."

"Whatever you say," the proprietor agreed, finding them a space in the common room. "What'll you have?"

"We'll start with a nice big pitcher of your best beer," Thutmose told him, "and two big platters of whatever you're serving today. We're hungry men – we've been moving heavy statuary. Moving stone is hard work."

"Coming right up!" the proprietor acknowledged.

He was back in short order with two large ceramic cups, a large pitcher of thick, foamy beer, and a pair of straws cut from Nile reeds. The bundles of narrow passageways through the interior of the reeds made these straws natural filters that kept the residue of the barley mash from reaching the drinker's mouth, while allowing the liquid to pass.

Ipy said in a low voice, "I assume you had some reason for dining here, and not at the palace."

"You're quite right. I did," Thutmose replied quietly. "I wanted to listen to people talk, to get a sense of how the common folk feel about Pharaoh, the new religion and the old, and so on."

"I see," said Ipy. "You wanted to take the pulse of the people, as it were."

"Exactly," agreed Thutmose. "So let us be jovial and friendly and engage our neighbors in conversation. I know you are very good at that."

Indeed, from his days on the streets, Ipy was very adept at making conversation with just about anybody. It wasn't long before the two artists were drinking toasts and becoming bosom buddies with half the people in the common room.

By the time they left, they had learned that there was great unease and dissatisfaction in the old capital. Ipy had spotted two men at a table in the back that he recognized as part of the old priesthood, from his stint as an acolyte at the temple of Amun. It was soon clear to the artists that these two were initiating or provoking much of the negative commentary about Pharaoh or the new religion. It was clear that most of the crowd were glad that the old temples had reopened and that they regarded this as an indication of the restoration of *ma'at*; but Thutmose was glad to hear that most of them stopped short of wishing Pharaoh ill, let alone advocating any action to remove her. Several people observed that the legitimate heir, Tutankhaten, was too young to rule and that Nefertiti – that is, Smenkare – seemed to be doing an adequate job as regent.

The two undercover priests, acting as *agents provocateurs*, grumbled loudly about the impropriety of a woman acting as Pharaoh. There were some who agreed with this sentiment, but also several who did not.

Thutmose got the distinct impression that most people would not go along with any violent overthrow of Nefertiti's regime, but they also would do nothing to oppose it. Just before they left, Ipy nudged him and gestured with his head toward two men who had just entered. They joined the undercover priests, and the four men soon had their heads together. It gave Thutmose a very uneasy feeling.

After Thutmose paid the proprietor with a carved scarab amulet, he and Ipy left and strolled through the marketplace, chatting with stall-keepers as they went. Not far from the palace, they stopped at the local police station. Thutmose greeted the chief, Nebamun, who he had known years ago, before the court moved to Akhetaten. Ipy hung back behind his mentor, hoping to remain unnoticed – but to no avail. The chief recognized him from his days as a juvenile delinquent.

"No use hanging back there, Ipy, you young miscreant! You may be all grown up and respectable now, but I'd know that face anywhere," Nebamun said, stepping past Thutmose.

He scowled at Ipy for a minute, then burst out laughing. "Hah! Had you worried there, didn't I, lad?"

He stuck out a hand, and after a moment's hesitation, Ipy shook it. The chief slapped him jovially on the back.

"It's all right, m'boy! I know you're all reformed and you've come up in the world. I only wish more of our young troublemakers could turn out so well," he added. Then, turning to Thutmose, he asked, "So what brings you gents here?"

"We just spent some time in a tavern and strolled through the market on the way here," Thutmose told him, "and I'm very concerned by what I'm hearing."

"And what is that?" asked the chief.

"Nothing terribly specific," Thutmose said. "Just a lot of general grumbling and dissatisfaction – and a lot of it seems to be originating with people we recognize as being associated with the old religion, particularly the temple of Amun. I'm afraid the old priesthood are brewing up some kind of trouble, especially the more fanatical followers of the old First Prophet. I was there in Aswan when he died, you know."

"Were you now?" the chief asked speculatively. "I heard he made some rather ominous pronouncements before he died."

"He did," Thutmose confirmed. "I heard him. However, I also made some pretty ominous pronouncements about his fate – and if I do say so myself, they came true."

"My, my, my," said the chief, "taken up the prophecy business, have you?"

"In my own small way," Thutmose replied.

"Whatever did you tell him?" asked the chief.

"I told him he would die unburied and unbeautified, and the vultures and jackals would pick his bones – and they did."

"Served the old bastard right," said the chief.

"But that was only after the local police got his body back from some of his followers, who had spirited the old man out of the quarry workers' camp," Thutmose told him. "When they went back, looking for the young man who had carried him away, they couldn't find him. Rumor has it that he and a number of the old man's more fanatical followers joined a group somewhere out in the eastern hills. I think they're up to no good – and I'm worried about Her Majesty's safety."

"I'll have my men keep a watch out for these trouble-making priests," the chief replied. "We've already tripled the watch, and we're working with the Royal Guard to insure Her Majesty's safety. I don't think there's anything more we can do, other than to be constantly alert to any danger. But thanks for letting me know about these priests."

"I'm glad to know you'll be on the lookout for them," Thutmose said. "Thanks, Chief."

The two artists shook the chief's hand, then left the station and headed on to the palace.

It was growing dark by the time they arrived at the palace. The guard at the postern gate nearest the artists' workshop recognized them and admitted them promptly. After the two shipments had arrived earlier, the guards had been expecting the Chief of Works and his chief assistant to follow them.

The two artists went first to the workshop, to check on the condition of the shipments. All appeared to be in order, so they each headed for their quarters, a small sleeping cell for each, with a simple pallet on the floor, a small table and a shelf for a few personal items. It was much the same type of monastic cell that Ipy had experienced during his stint as an acolyte of Amun, except that here, as senior staff members, he and Thutmose both rated a private room, rather than one shared with half a dozen others.

Thutmose had just washed off the dirt of travel and was preparing to go to bed when a messenger arrived from Pharaoh, requesting his presence in her private audience chamber. He hastily donned a clean kilt and his collar of office and ran a carved wooden comb through his still-damp hair, then followed the messenger through the labyrinthine corridors of the palace.

The messenger brought him to the door to Nefertiti's private apartments, where he handed him off to the door guard. One of the guardsmen opened the door and informed the steward of the artist's arrival, then ushered Thutmose inside.

The steward stepped over to an open door and announced his arrival, "The Chief of Works is here, Your Majesty."

"Show him into my study, Tutu," she called from the next room. "Then you may go. This will be my last meeting of the evening. Inform the guards that I am not to be disturbed for anything else, unless the palace is burning down! I am exhausted."

"Yes, Your Majesty," the steward acknowledged, bowing in the doorway. He gestured for Thutmose to enter the study, then left through the main door.

"Thutmose," called Nefertiti, as he bowed in the doorway. "Come in, come in! I'm so glad you are here. I trust you had a good trip?"

"Very good, Your Majesty. Everything went exactly as planned – no problems," he replied.

"Excellent!" she said, smiling. "And you were able to fetch that other, special cargo we agreed upon?"

"Yes, Your Majesty. The remains of His Majesty and your daughter are in my studio here in the palace, boxed up just like all the statues I brought. Only Ipy and two of my most trusted assistants, and Chief Mahu and several of his men, are any the wiser – and Mahu and his men only know that they were removed to my workshop in Akhetaten."

"Very good," she said. "I am relieved to know that they are here, where no one can attack them like thieves in the night. I have scarcely been able to sleep since we left Akhetaten, fearing that someone would damage the remains of my loved ones and cut them off from the Afterlife. I shall sleep much easier now. Once again, dear Thutmose, you have served me in a way I could trust to no other."

Thutmose dropped to one knee in front of her, his hand to his heart, and bowed his head.

"Your Majesty, I live to serve you. I have no greater wish in life than to be your best and most devoted servant," he said.

She took his right hand and drew him to his feet. "Get up, get up, Thutmose! You are my dearest and most trusted friend. You do not need to bow to me when we are in private."

Since she still held his hand clutched in both of hers, he had to stand close to her. This was the closest he had come to her since the incident with the crocodile, those many years before. He could smell the scent of her skin through the remnant of costly frankincense perfume. His heart beat so hard he thought it would deafen him.

Thutmose was an unusually tall man, nearly four cubits[12], and Nefertiti was quite petite, so he towered more than a half cubit over her. It made him aware of how small and fragile she was, how very vulnerable. More than ever, he wanted to protect her.

Holding his hand and looking up at him, Nefertiti was aware of how big and strong and solid he was, one person she knew she could rely on completely. It was immensely comforting to have him standing there next to her, warm and alive and devoted. She suddenly became aware of the weight of the burden she had been carrying, with the responsibility for the whole empire on her back. She realized abruptly how much she wanted to put it down.

It was all so overwhelming: the economy was in chaos, the old priesthood threatening rebellion, the Hittites and Assyrians threatening

---

[12] 6 feet.

her borders, the vassal kings betraying her, her children dying. It was just too much to bear all by herself.

She swayed on her feet and started to fall – but his strong arms caught her. He swept her up in his arms and carried her into her bedroom.

"Your Majesty!" he said, worried. "Let me call your maid. You should rest."

"No!" she said, as he bent to put her down on the bed. "No, please. I'm all right. Just tired, is all. Please – do me a favor."

"Anything," he said, still holding her like a small child. "Anything at all."

"I know this will sound silly, but, please, just sit down and hold me for a while," she said.

He looked around for a chair, then finally sat down on the bed, holding her on his lap as though she were one of his children. After a moment's hesitation, he closed his arms around her and held her tightly, her head tucked beneath his chin. Her arms circled his neck and held him tightly.

"Oh, Thutmose," she sobbed against his chest, "you don't know what it's been like! I've been so alone! I feel like the sacrificial calf in a den of hyenas and wolves! There's almost no one I can trust – everyone wants my throne, or my head, or my god, or some favor – I don't know where to turn. There are enemies all around me. The only people I can count on are my father and you!"

He rocked her back and forth and stroked her back to calm her down.

"It's all right," he said. "I'm here now. I won't let anyone hurt you. You can relax now."

"Thank you, Thutmose. Just hold me. It feels so good to let it all go for a while," she murmured. "It feels so good...to have your strong arms around me."

She felt the weight of an empire melting off her shoulders, her tense muscles letting go as salty tears streamed silently down her face and trickled onto his chest. The hard, knotted muscles beneath the smooth skin of his chest and arms were strong and reassuring. She could smell the warm scent of his freshly-washed skin.

He glanced down at her tear-stained face and looked around for something to wipe it with. He grabbed a corner of the sheet and pulled it up to wipe the tears from her face. He blotted the moisture away with the sheet, then stroked the soft, smooth skin of her face, his sculptor's fingers feeling the living flesh he had so often modeled in clay and stone. He marveled at its fine shape and living warmth, yielding flesh over delicate bones, so warm and alive, not cold like stone. He felt an answering warmth in his own flesh. An involuntary moan escaped his lips.

Suddenly, he felt a flash of horror, realizing that this was his sovereign – and she must feel his aroused manhood against her body. He released his grip on her and tried to move his upper body away – but she wound her arms about his chest and held him tightly. He felt the fire in his loins blaze like a torch and feared it must scorch them both.

"Your Majesty," he stammered, "forgive me – I..."

"Shhh, Thutmose," she said, "hold me. Please hold me. I need to feel your arms around me."

He groaned, but slid his arms around her, clasping her tightly. Her hands slid over his muscular back, exploring its taut form, then around to his chest. She leaned her head back and looked up at him, her hands sliding over his chest and down his lean abdomen.

He bent his head and put his lips to hers, expecting to be struck by divine lightning at any moment – but he didn't care, he couldn't help himself. Giving up all hope of restraint, he reveled in the sensual softness of her lips, the taste of her mouth, the feel of her soft, full breasts moving against his chest.

He pulled at the sheer linen of her gown, so fine it was almost transparent. It fell away from her shoulders and slid down her torso, revealing her warm, glowing skin and softly rounded, feminine curves. He slid his hands down her back and around the front of her body, cupping her generously rounded breasts in his hands, stroking the dark brown-red nipples with his thumbs. He felt them swell and harden beneath his touch.

Nefertiti groaned softly and whispered, "Oh, yes! Touch me, Thutmose – sculpt me like clay beneath your fingers! Make me your own!"

He fumbled at the fine linen of her gown, then ripped it away, revealing her body in all its female glory. Her fingers worked at the fabric of his kilt, finding and freeing the knot that held it. She pushed the fabric away and slid her hand down over his hard, throbbing penis, down and around to cup his testes, then sliding back up to grasp his member firmly, stroking it against her warm, wet labia.

He slid his lips down her long, graceful neck, to her nipples, sucking and licking first one, then the other. She gasped.

"Thutmose, take me! Come into me, now! I want you so," she moaned.

He raised his lips back to hers and murmured, "Are you certain, my Queen?"

"Oh, yes," she cried. "I want to feel you in me! I have wanted you for years."

"And I have wanted you, my Queen, my love, wanted you and dared not touch you!"

"Touch me now, Thutmose, my darling, my love! Come into me!"

He lifted her hips and rearranged her so that she was facing him. She put her knees on either side of him and moved her body closer to his, weaving back and forth like a dancer as he stroked and licked her breasts, and she stroked the head of his engorged member against her warm wetness. Finally, when he could bear it no more, he pulled her hips toward him and entered her. She gasped and arched her back, thrusting against him.

Fearing he would be overcome by this mad desire, and come too soon, he held her tight against him and murmured, "Wait, my love. Let us hold still for just a bit and savor this moment. We have waited so long – let us make the moment last!"

She held still a moment, feeling him throbbing within her, filling the emptiness inside her, as she had never felt before. She could feel every tingling bit of skin touching skin, almost unbearably aware of it all. Finally, he began to move again, slowly, sensually.

"I have waited so long for this," he whispered. "I want to feel all of you, to know all of you, inside and out!"

"Oh, yes, yes!" she murmured. "I want to hold you within me, become one with you for all time."

They moved together like two dancers weaving an intricate pattern to the same music of love, two hearts beating as one, two parts of the same whole. Their passion mounted, a joined fire burning brighter, brighter, until it exploded over them, in a single timeless moment that went on and on, then slowly subsided like a wave upon the sand.

They lay tangled together, spent, in a warm, wet afterglow. After a while, she opened her eyes, to find him looking back at her in the flickering light of the oil lamp.

"By the Aten!" she exclaimed. "I never knew it could be like that! I'm an experienced woman – as the wife of a king, I was trained in the ways of pleasing a man, and after all, I've had six children – but I have never known anything like that!"

"Neither have I," he agreed. "I have dreamed about it – dreamed about you – but the dreams are dim beside the reality."

"I have watched you and wanted you for so long – at least since that incident with the crocodile – but I didn't dare acknowledge it, even to myself. I had to school myself to deny my feelings for you, lest I get us both killed," she said, looking into his eyes.

"I did, too," he said. "I have loved you since I first saw you, when you were just a little girl. My heart has been yours alone, since that first moment. I was deathly afraid it would show. The only thing I could do was to pour all my love for you into my work, into every painting I painted, every statue of you I sculpted. Even portraits of your family – they were all for you."

"I think I knew," she said. "Your work is so extraordinary, so alive. It's unlike anyone else's. But every time I sat for you, and watched your hands molding and shaping the clay, I yearned to feel those hands on me, stroking *my* flesh, molding me to your will, making me yours..."

As she spoke, his hands began caressing her, stroking her smooth, silky skin, gliding over her shoulders, back, hips, sliding up over her breasts. He gathered her breasts up in his hands, then bent his lips to suck and lick first one, and then the other. His hands roamed down over her slender waist, then down, down to the warm cleft between her legs. He explored her warm softness, found her clitoris and squeezed it firmly, stroking it slowly as his fingers probed deeper. Slipping a finger inside, he moved with sensual slowness, noting her response. Finding the spot that made her gasp and quiver with delight, he stroked her there, until at last she pleaded,

"Come into me, Thutmose, come into me now!"

He entered her and shifted their bodies about until they lay on their sides, their legs entwined like scissors, where they both could move, yet clasp each other tightly. This time, less desperate to be sated, they could each take their time to savor the other fully, allowing their passion to wax and wane, and rise again, until it overcame them at last, exploding over them in a volcanic eruption of pleasure.

They collapsed together, blissfully exhausted, and slept for several hours.

About an hour before dawn, Thutmose awoke and gradually became aware of his surroundings. Once he realized where he was, he was suddenly fully awake. He knew that the palace would soon start coming to life, and he had better get out of Pharaoh's private chamber before that. Moving slowly and quietly to avoid awakening Nefertiti, he extricated his arms and legs and sat up on the edge of the bed – but before he could stand up, her hand reached out and grasped his wrist.

"Don't go yet, Thutmose," she said.

"I must, Your Majesty, else the servants will know," he replied. "It will be dawn soon, and they'll all be up and about."

She sighed deeply and rolled over on her back.

"I know," she said. "How I wish I could say, 'let them know, and be damned!' But I know I can't. I'm a prisoner, as surely as any thief in my jails."

"No, you can't," he said, turning to her. "If you wish to continue ruling this land, your reputation must remain pristine. I can only appear as your most devoted servant."

She sat up and looked into his eyes.

"Will you then be Senmut to my Hatshepsut?" she asked.

He looked back into her eyes, long and hard. "Is that what you want?" he asked. "It didn't work out all that well for them in the long run."

"I don't see what other choice we have," she replied.

He reached over and took her hand. "Well," he said, "there are other choices. It's just that none of them is very good."

"What other choices?" she asked.

"First," he said, "we can continue as we have started, with me sneaking into your room at night, bribing the night guards to silence. But the story will inevitably get out, and will add fuel to the rumors the old priesthood are putting out against you."

"What rumors?" she exclaimed.

"That's part of what I wanted to warn you about today: the priests of Amun are feeding the people's discontent and unease, and laying all the blame at your door."

"At my door? But I reopened their temples! I let them resume their worship! They owe me better thanks than that!"

He shook his head with a wry smile. "They do owe you more, but that's not the way they see it. To them, it's too little, too late – and you're indelibly tarred with the brush of Akhenaten's religion. They'll never forgive you. Now that he's gone, you're the focus of all their hatred. I wanted to warn you to be extra wary of them. Triple, quadruple the guard around you."

"I've already increased it as much as I can. I can hardly move without tripping over soldiers, as it is," she replied. "But you said there were other choices."

"Bad ones," he answered.

"Let me hear them, anyway."

"We could pretend that last night never happened, and go back to being the way we were before," he said.

"Not acceptable," she replied. "I can't live that way again. I need you too much. I cannot forswear you."

"Nor I, you," he agreed, kissing her deeply. Then, tearing himself away, he pulled back. "So that brings us to the other two choices."

"Only two?" she asked.

"That's all I can think of. Perhaps you can come up with more."

"What are these two?"

"First, most final and least attractive, we could choose to die together," he said. "But even then, we wouldn't be buried together, and your father would probably see to it that my body was destroyed, so we wouldn't be together in the Afterlife."

"You're right – that's not an attractive alternative. What's your last choice?"

He looked at her long and hard.

"We could run away together. You give up your crown and throne and we become two ordinary people somewhere. Maybe have a small farm, or be traders with a ship and sail around the Green Sea," he said.

"You *are* a dreamer," she said, with a short laugh. "As if we could get away with it! I'm afraid you've already made that impossible, my love: thanks to you, my face is much too well known. No, I'm afraid it wouldn't work."

"I don't know," he said. "In ordinary clothes and no jewelry, with a plain cloth on your head, and if we smear a little dirt on you, you might pass as a country woman."

"Right," she said. "And what about you? Your face may not be as famous as mine, but you are known up and down this land. It might be harder to disguise you."

"I could put on colorful robes and grow a beard and pass myself off as a Habiru," he said. "We could hide among your Habiru kinsmen in the eastern Delta. Or I could curl my beard and pass myself off as a Hittite and we could flee to one of the city-states of Canaan."

"Give it up, my love. It would never work. They'd find us before the first day was out."

"You're probably right," he said with a sigh.

"Besides, I couldn't simply run away," she said.

"Would you miss all this that much?" he asked, gesturing around him.

"Not at all," she said. "I'd give up the throne and crown and palace in an instant, to be with you – but I have a responsibility I cannot shirk. I made a deathbed promise to Akhenaten – and so did you," she reminded him, "and that is binding on us both. I promised to continue to rule this country and keep it on an even keel until young Tutankhaten is old enough to rule it on his own. And we both promised to watch over him and Ankhsenpaaten and keep them true to the faith of the Aten until they're grown."

"Your father, Aye, will be here to watch over them," he said.

She shook her head. "That still doesn't absolve us of our duty. I was raised with that sense of duty foremost, as an Heiress and future sovereign of the Two Lands. The first words I heard were 'Duty and Honor'. I can't run away from that – it's a part of me. To betray my duty to my country would be to betray myself, to become less than what I am. Would you have me do that?"

"No," he said, reaching out to touch her face. "I could never ask you to betray yourself. That is part of what I love so much about you: that you are a good and honorable woman, to the very core. I honor and respect that. I would rather die than see that damaged in any way. So, I will defend you and your honor with everything in me, for as long as I shall live."

"Thank you," she said. "I can ask no more than that. So you see," she continued, "that brings us back where we began. Out of all your four choices, the only one we can live with, however poor it may be, is the first one: to go on as we have begun, loving each other as discreetly as we can, for as long as we can. I cannot live without you. I denied my love for you for years, as long as Akhenaten was alive. I had a duty to both my husband and my country. Now, only my country remains as a partial obstacle between us. I love you, Thutmose, and I need you close to me."

"I love you, too, my beloved Queen. I cannot leave you. Whatever you desire of me, I will do. I am yours till I die – and, Aten willing, beyond the grave, through all eternity," he pledged.

She threw her arms around his neck and kissed him.

After several minutes, they drew back and he caught his breath. Opening his eyes, he saw with alarm that the sky was beginning to pale in the east.

"I must go, my love," he said, rising. "Your servants will be here any minute."

"Go, then, my darling," she said. "I will see you later today."

He picked up his kilt from where it had fallen on the floor and fastened it around his hips. He blew Nefertiti a kiss, then turned and strode quickly from the room. He slipped quietly out the main door to her suite. The guards outside the door made no sign of anything out of the ordinary as he slipped by them, but when he was gone, they glanced at each other with raised brows. As Thutmose had warned, their relationship could not stay secret for long in a place as gossip-ridden as a palace.

Back in the artists' workshop, Ipy noted the quiet reappearance of his mentor with a pang of anxiety. He had heard the Queen's messenger arrive the night before and seen Thutmose follow him out. Knowing where his master had gone, Ipy feared that this overnight absence did not bode well.

Chapter 44: Death of a Dream

In the months that followed, Nefertiti continued to permit the restoration of the old religion. She allowed the gradual resumption of tribute to the temples of Amun and other gods, and the refurbishing of their temples. However, she also maintained the Aten temples and continued to support the proselytizing efforts of the Aten priesthood. She felt that it had been a mistake to deny the people the right to worship as they saw fit, and an even greater mistake to try to force them to believe something else. She had become convinced that people needed to be *persuaded* into a new belief, not coerced into it. To this end, she met with groups of Aten priests to review ideas for how this might be done. She felt encouraged by these meetings, which seemed to produce many good ideas for reaching the hearts and minds of the people with the concept of One God.

At the same time, however, she was still faced with a theological, political and economic crisis within Egypt. She felt it was essential to get the economy back on track in order to establish a secure foundation on which to build a stable regime. The occurrence of several moderate drought years during Akhenaten's reign had not helped matters. This had led to poor crop yields and widespread hunger. With the advice of her agricultural advisors, she instituted a program of canal building to help bring more water to parched fields. She also had her water supply experts surveying possible sites along the river where dams might be built to store water for use in dry years. And she ordered repairs of all the granaries built at the command of her grandfather Yuya, which had helped stave off starvation during the infamous seven-year drought early in the reign of Amenhotep III.

Another continuing source of resistance to her reign was the old nobility, many of whom had been displaced from their traditional offices by her late husband. Many of these old noble families had been in power for over a thousand years. They were not simply going to slink peacefully away because one pharaoh told them to. Their power was based in their own home regions, the nomes and city-states originally established in pre-dynastic times, over two thousand years earlier. Although these regions had gradually coalesced into the two major Kingdoms of Upper and Lower Egypt, and then been united into one by the legendary Menes, this union had also fallen apart at times in the past, particularly during two previous "intermediate periods". The most recent of these, ending only two hundred years previously, had allowed the influx of the foreigners called the Hyksos, until they had been driven out by Theban rulers, Nefertiti's own ancestors who founded the present, 18th Dynasty. If the conflict between regional nobles and pharaoh grew too great, there was a real danger that such disintegration of the kingdom could happen again, and Egypt could once more fall into chaos. Ambitious neighbors like the Hittites and Assyrians would be only too happy to take advantage of an Egypt weakened by internal dissension.

This posed a quandary. The new officials promoted and ennobled by her late husband constituted Nefertiti's staunchest supporters, and she certainly didn't want to alienate them. On the other hand, she needed to appease the traditional nobles and win back their support. For the present, she took the cautious course of replacing officials who died or retired with members of the old nobility, as well as going out of her way to invite them to court social functions and adding senior nomarchs to her advisory councils.

It was starting to work, but slowly. Thutmose worried a great deal about Nefertiti's safety, despite the constant presence of a heavy guard around her.

Despite her cooperation with the priesthood of Amun, their hostility towards her remained almost palpable. Finally, she decided to borrow a page from her predecessor Hatshepsut, who had used the worship of Amun to reinforce the concept of her divine conception. While Nefertiti was not willing to retreat from the Aten religion to the extent of claiming divine conception by Amun, she was willing to make some concessions. She decided to reinstate the Opet Festival, the principal celebration of Amun in Thebes, the god's own home town.

Until it was suspended by Akhenaten, the Beautiful Feast of the Opet had been the city's biggest celebration, occurring at the beginning of the Inundation, shortly after the start of the New Year. The festival had grown over the years, until it had stretched for nearly three weeks during Amenhotep III's reign. It was a celebration the citizens eagerly looked forward to and it also drew a great many visitors into the city. This influx of religious celebrants, visiting priests, singers, dancers, actors, food vendors, sellers of charms and amulets, itinerant scribes and hordes of others, was a major boost to the local economy. In addition, Pharaoh traditionally supplied free food for much of the festival, amounting to many thousands of loaves of bread, meat, fowl and hundreds of jars of beer. It was a huge party, and everybody wanted to get in on it. For many less affluent citizens, it was the only time in the year they got to eat meat.

There was widespread rejoicing in Thebes when the reinstatement of the festival was announced. Thutmose worried about Pharaoh's safety during such a crowded, chaotic event, but Chief Nebamun felt he had security under control. Many additional army troops had been pulled in from other areas to reinforce local security during the festival, and they all had orders to be on watch for the more fanatical elements of the priesthood of Amun. Ipy had provided a sketch of Ani, both shaven-headed and with hair, and Thutmose's other assistants had made dozens of copies (with varying degrees of accuracy) on sheets of papyrus. These had been given to the Chief of Police and circulated among his troops, in the hope that somebody would recognize the suspect if he showed up.

Thutmose still could not shake the feeling of foreboding that hung over him, but Nefertiti and her eldest daughter, Meritaten, who had to act the role of Queen to her mother's "Pharaoh Smenkare", continued to prepare to play their parts in the ritual.

Thutmose and Nefertiti had continued to meet in secret, and had seldom spent a night apart since that fateful night when they had confessed their love for one another. No matter how discreet they were, their love showed. People around them could not help noticing that both of them glowed with a new radiance. And of course, their trysts could not be hidden from Nefertiti's ladies or her guards, nor from Thutmose's assistants. And while all of them were loyal and remarkably close-mouthed, inevitably, the story began to trickle out. It was too juicy a piece of gossip to remain secret.

At least, their public behavior could not be faulted. In public, Thutmose continued to act as Chief of Works and as one of the ruler's closest advisors, but no more so than several others. He never presumed on his relationship with Pharaoh, neither taking liberties in his public dealings with her, nor lording it over other members of the inner circle. And for her part, Nefertiti showed him no excessive favoritism, treating him just as she had always done.

Nevertheless, once the stories did begin to circulate, disgruntled nobles and priests were quick to fan the flames. And the stories, of course, grew wilder with every re-telling.

Preparations for the festival proceeded apace. Boatloads of grain had been arriving for weeks and workers were kept busy grinding it into flour to make bread and fermenting it into beer. As the old year waned and the new year approached, people began to pour into the city from all over Egypt, as well as some from abroad.

At last, the baking, dry heat of early summer gave way to gathering clouds in the south. There, rain in the highlands of Abyssinia began to swell the headwaters of the Nile, which poured down the mountains carrying fresh soil, headed down the gorges of the White and Blue Nile Rivers toward the Two Lands. And finally, the rising of the star Sothis[13] after 70 days of invisibility signaled the New Year and the approach of the Inundation.

The waters began to rise, first at the upper Cataracts, flowing past the string of massive forts erected by earlier Pharaohs throughout

---

[13] Sirius.

the frequently embattled land of Nubia, then surging past Aswan and down through Upper Egypt. Measurements of the depth of the water at the Nilometer carved into the banks at Edfu showed a height of 24 cubits, a very good year. Less than 20 indicated a drought, while 27 or more was a disastrous flood.

At last, the water began to rise at Thebes, then flowed on downstream to Akhetaten and on to Memphis and Heliopolis. It then spread out over the Delta, through the many channels, canals and marshes, covering the fields and depositing its load of fresh, fertile soil, the annual tribute of the mountains of Ethiopia to the Nile god, Hapy; and his gift, in turn, to the Two Lands.

Because of the flooding, people could not work in the fields at this time, making it the perfect time for a festival. As the water rose, the crowds of Thebes poured into the streets like a human Inundation, as the citizens of Thebes and their guests from afar celebrated the fruitful link between their Pharaoh and the mighty god, Amun. During the ritual, the might and power of Amun were ritually bequeathed to his living son (or, in this case, daughter), the king. As the repository of divine power, Pharaoh was deeply involved in this ritual. Now, Nefertiti was taking part as Pharaoh for the first time in twelve years, since Akhenaten had closed all the Amun temples and moved the capital to Akhetaten.

Nefertiti had painfully mixed feelings about her participation in this ritual. On the one hand, she was convinced it was the right thing to do, for the sake of the people and the country. She believed she was restoring *ma'at*. On the other hand, she knew she was undoing much of what her husband, Akhenaten, had labored so long and hard to create: the religion of the Aten, the belief that there was only One God, not this overpopulated, bewildering pantheon of deities. At times, she thought she could feel Akhenaten's spirit crying out to her in protest.

As though to further emphasize the dichotomy, the birthday celebration of the Aten occurred a couple of days into the period of the Opet Festival. Nefertiti spent dawn and several hours thereafter worshipping at the Aten temple at Karnak, then went home and changed her clothing and returned to Karnak to continue the Opet rituals honoring Amun.

Among the people pouring into the city were hundreds of the reinstated priests of Amun, including several dozen of the fanatics who styled themselves the Holy Warriors of Amun. Among these were Ani and his brethren, come from their secret enclave in the southeastern hills. Knowing there would be beefed-up security and that the police and soldiers would be on the watch for them, they came disguised as a group of Habiru, wearing colorful woven robes hitched over one shoulder and sporting long hair and beards. To complete the disguise, several of them carried a lamb over one shoulder, to be given as a sacrifice at the temple of Amun. It was unfortunate that Ipy's foresight in drawing Ani with long hair had not extended to envisioning him with a beard. So, as it was, the soldiers who had been supplied with sketches of Ani with and without hair were unable to match these images to the face of the bearded Habiru shepherd. So it was that Ani and his cohorts were able to slip in among the crowds unnoticed by the police and soldiers.

At Karnak, the gathered throngs of people watched the priests disappear into the temple precincts. Only Pharaoh and the priests were allowed beyond the forecourt of the temple. Inside, the priests bathed the statue of the god, arrayed it in colorful linen and adorned it with jewelry from the temple treasury, including magnificent necklaces, bracelets, scepters, amulets and trinkets of gold or silver encrusted with lapis lazuli, enamel, glass and semi-precious gems. The priests then enclosed the god in a shrine and placed the shrine on top of a ceremonial barque or boat, supported by poles for carrying.

The priests emerged from the inner sanctum carrying the barque on their shoulders. They carried it through the throngs in the forecourt and on through the pillared halls of Karnak, then out into the crowded streets, where people elbowed each other to catch a glimpse of the god in his shrine. Parents hoisted small children onto their shoulders to give them a glimpse of the deity in all his finery.

Pharaoh herself was there to greet the god as he emerged from his sanctuary, together with the "Great Wife", Meritaten, together with her Co-Pharaoh, the boy king, Tutankhaten, and his Great Wife, Ankhsenpaaten. They led the way down the great Avenue of Sphinxes, all the way to the Temple of Amun at Luxor, in Thebes proper, over a mile and a half away. Ani and his men were unable to get close to the royal party, surrounded as they were by soldiers, but they kept pace with the procession along the outskirts of the crowd, looking for their chance to close in, like wolves slipping through a forest to surround their prey.

Thutmose tried to stay as close to Nefertiti and Meritaten as he could, but as a non-royal member of their entourage, he was forced to stay several paces behind them, and was not allowed into the sanctuary itself. He watched from the doorway as the two Pharaohs and their Great Wives made their sacrifices to the statue of the god and received his blessings in return, and the ritual conveyance of divine power. Once this divine gift had been received, Nefertiti and Meritaten, Tutankhaten and Ankhsenpaaten turned and proceeded regally through the center of the colonnaded hall toward the crowded forecourt.

It was there that Ani and his co-conspirators made their move. As former priests, they were well acquainted with all the passages and byways of the Amun temples, both at Karnak and here at Luxor. They were able to slip away from the crowd when the royal party entered the inner hall, to a small cell in the priests' living quarters, where they shaved their beards and hair and completed the rest of their ritual purification while the two Pharaohs and their Great Wives were making their offerings in the inner court. Newly dressed in the white robes of priests, the assassins slipped in amongst the columns supporting the stone roof of the great hall, and waited.

As Nefertiti and Meritaten approached the exit from the great hall to the forecourt, the assassins struck. They moved in quickly, two men behind each of the women. They ignored the boy king and his wife. One man grabbed Meritaten from behind, while a second man stabbed her in the chest.

Ani's partner stepped up to Nefertiti's left side and, reaching over her shoulder, slashed her face with his short sword. She cried out and raised her arms to shield her face. As her left arm came up, Ani stepped in and thrust his short sword into her side, between the ribs just below her heart. She gasped and looked at him in horror, her left hand to her bleeding cheek, her right reaching for the sword protruding from between her ribs.

Thutmose, waiting in the doorway, had started to move the instant Ani and his henchmen stepped from behind the pillars, as had Chief Nebamun and his men. But they were too far away, and not fast enough. It took only seconds for both women to be fatally wounded. While the soldiers brought down the assassins, Thutmose caught Nefertiti as she swayed and started to fall. As the soldiers tackled Ani, his hold on the sword yanked it out of her side, to be followed by a gush of bright red blood. Thutmose dropped to his knees and lowered her gently to the floor. Snatching off his headcloth, he attempted to stanch the bleeding of the wound in her side.

"Get a doctor!" he yelled. The Chief sent one of his men running for the royal physician. Kneeling, he whipped off his own head cloth and pressed it to Nefertiti's slashed cheek, which was also bleeding profusely.

"Thutmose," gasped Nefertiti, speaking with difficulty, "my daughter, Merit, is she - ?"

He glanced over at where Meritaten lay, the knife hilt protruding from her chest, her sightless eyes staring at the ceiling far above. It was clear that she was dead.

"I'm sorry, my love," he replied. "She is dead."

"Tutankhaten and Ankhsen?" she asked.

He looked around and saw the younger couple, untouched.

"They're all right," he reassured her. "The assassins didn't touch them. But you rest easy, now. The doctor is on the way. He will save you yet."

"No, Thutmose," she whispered. "I know I am dying."

"No, no, my darling, my love – you must not die!" he cried, clasping her bleeding form to him.

"Please," she whispered, "don't let me die here, in the temple of Amun. Take me to the temple of Aten, my divine father. Let me die there, a sacrifice to the One True God."

"All right, my love," he agreed, tears pouring down his face.

He picked her up and rose to his feet, aided by Chief Nebamun, then turned and carried her to the doorway. As he reached the top of the steps carrying the bloody figure of the Pharaoh, the assembled crowd gasped in horror. He descended the steps, and the crowd opened a path for him. As he passed, the people sank to their knees and began to pray. Such a sacrilege! Pharaoh murdered, and in the Temple of Amun! It was a very bad omen, a gross violation of *ma'at*.

Thutmose carried Nefertiti out of the Temple of Amun, down the processional way, and turned in at the Temple of Aten. He carried her through the familiar doorway, into the light-filled sanctuary, up the aisle between rows of offering tables, to the large altar in front of the great golden sun-disk with its many rays ending in hands carrying the *ankh* symbols of life. He placed her gently on the altar, pressing the blood-soaked cloth against her side in the vain hope of slowing the bleeding.

Nefertiti glanced at the great golden disk on one side, then back at Thutmose on the other side. She spoke softly and with difficulty, as the cut on her face had sliced through the left side of her mouth. He bent his ear close to her lips to hear her.

"Thutmose, my dearest love," she murmured. "You have made these last months very happy for me. It grieves me to have to leave you now, when I have just found you."

He kissed her fingers, clasped in his own, as tears streamed down his cheeks.

"I will always love you," he whispered back, "even beyond the grave. I will seek you in the *Duat*," he murmured, "and I will find you. I promise you, my darling, we will spend eternity together."

"I believe you," she assured him. "I will wait for you there. But first, you must stay here and help Tutankhaten and Ankhsenpaaten. They will need your help."

"I will. I promise."

Just then, the senior royal physician arrived, together with Nefertiti's father, the Grand Vizier, Aye. The physician took the blood-soaked cloth from Thutmose and lifted it from the wound. He took one look, then looked up at the two men and shook his head.

"I can do nothing," he said. "The wound is too deep. She is losing too much blood."

He took a fresh cloth from his bag and wadded it against the wound. Holding it in place, he said, "She doesn't have much time. She's bleeding internally."

Aye took his place on Nefertiti's other side, beneath the sun disk of the Aten, and held her other hand.

"Take care of the children," she said to him. "They will need your guidance."

"I will give them all the help I can," he promised. "Know that I love you, my daughter, and I have been very proud of you."

"Thank you, Father. I love you, too," she whispered, barely audible. She turned her eyes to Thutmose. "And Thutmose – I love you..."

Her lids closed and her words faded away. They were her last words. Moments later, her breathing ceased.

The doctor bent his ear to her chest, then straightened up and shook his head.

"She's gone," he said.

In spite of the bright light and heat in the great open courtyard, it seemed to Thutmose that the sun itself had gone out. The woman he loved more than life itself was gone.

Chapter 45: To Sleep, Perchance to Dream

The light had gone out of my world. I continued to breathe, to walk about, even to eat, when I thought about it or my friends reminded me – I don't know why. There was no longer any point in it.

During the next seventy days, while Nefertiti's body was being beautified for burial, I and all my assistants worked on preparing her tomb. She had ordered work begun on a rock-cut tomb in the Valley of the Kings even before the death of Akhenaten. Although work had been done on a tomb for her at Akhetaten, she had shifted the effort to Valley of the Kings long ago, when she had begun to take over the load of ruling from an ailing husband. She had kept it from him, since he would have recognized it as an indication that she planned to return to Thebes, leaving his shiny new capital behind. And, of course, he would have been right. It would have hurt him – always the idealist – and that was something the kind-hearted Nefertiti did not want to do.

So now my crew and I labored in the sweltering, stuffy heat to finish the small tomb in time. The tomb was well away from others in the valley, in a hard-to-reach location. I thought it was a good location, perhaps less well-guarded for being off the beaten path, but also a location less apt to be guessed at by tomb robbers. However, it made for a long walk from the workmen's village, so I often just spent the night there, in the small natural cave that formed the entrance. Beyond, a passageway sloped down, but at its base was a deep vertical shaft, designed to foil tomb robbers, but also an effective way of diverting rain water from flowing into the tomb proper. The workmen had to cross this shaft on a precarious walkway of loose boards to get to the chambers beyond.

There were three of these, an antechamber, a main burial chamber and an additional room for grave goods. As the excavation crew were hammering and chipping away at the last part of the storage room, plasterers were finishing the coat of white plaster in the burial chamber, and my crew and I were painting the finished walls of the antechamber.

As in Akhenaten's tomb in the Royal Wadi at Akhetaten, we portrayed life as it had been at Akhetaten's peak, with all six of Nefertiti's daughters still alive, gathered around her. Though there were some pictures of her with Akhenaten, most were of her individual reign. And of course, unlike Akhenaten's tomb, this one was decorated in my style, which I regarded as "realistic", not Bek's.

Bek's peculiar, caricatured style had fallen out of favor late in Akhenaten's reign, though he continued to decorate tombs at Akhetaten and up north, at Saqqara. These days, he spent most of his time designing buildings and supervising their construction, up and down the Nile, from Avaris to Aswan. I seldom saw him, and missed the easy camaraderie we had shared for so long.

I thought about Bek as I worked, and realized sadly that so many of the people I loved had disappeared, one way or another. Bek was busy elsewhere; Akhenaten and five of his seven children were dead, as were old Yuya, the old king, Amenhotep, and the indomitable old Queen, Tiye; even troublemakers like Kiya; and now, my beloved Nefertiti was gone. My own parents still lived, but I very rarely saw them, or any of my brothers or sisters, who I scarcely knew, anyway. Mariamne was gone, moved back to the Delta, along with my son, Senmut, and my daughter, Meryre. Only my faithful protégé, Ipy, remained, along with my students and assistants.

Soon, the masons finished squaring out the last room and carried out the last buckets of stone chips. The plasterers finished smoothing on the last coat of plaster, and once they left and the plaster dried, my men and I moved in. I poured my heart – what was left of it – into decorating her burial chamber with scenes of everything she had loved in life. I included a scene I knew she remembered with pride: herself casting the spear that finished off the great crocodile, Set, with myself clinging desperately to its back. While Nefertiti's heroic spear cast took center stage, an attentive viewer could have just made out my arms around its neck, knife in hand, and a bit of my head peering over its shoulder.

I painted scenes of daily life in Akhetaten, with Akhenaten and Nefertiti with their children playing around them and Queen Tiye visiting. My assistants and I painted scenes from the Great Durbar, with representatives from the Great Kings and from peoples of the larger world all around the Two Lands bringing tribute and paying homage to Akhenaten and Nefertiti, newly crowned as Co-Pharaoh. And at night, when all the other men were gone, I closed the great doors to the burial chamber, and behind them, I painted myself paying homage to my Queen. These scenes were proper and respectful, yet showed her recognition of me as a special person in her life. If things went as I expected, no living soul but me would ever see these scenes, as the doors would remain open, pushed back against the inner walls, until they were pulled shut and sealed by the priests at the end of the funeral.

As the seventy days drew to a close, we raced to finish painting the tomb. We finished applying the last bits of paint just hours before the funeral procession arrived. I had rushed back to the workmen's village and bathed and put on a fresh linen kilt and my collar of office just in time to join the funeral cortege on its way to the tomb.

Before the tomb, the procession stopped and the mummy was set upright in a gilded wooden shrine. Young Tutankhaten, as the next

Pharaoh, wielded the ceremonial adze and performed the Opening of the Mouth ritual, which allows the deceased to eat, breathe and speak in the Afterlife. The mummy was then placed in its first mummiform coffin and the gold and lapis funerary mask was placed over her face. The lid was placed on top, but not sealed, and the cortege proceeded into the tomb.

The pallbearers carried the coffin and its occupant down the entry passageway and shuffled cautiously over the makeshift bridge spanning the shaft, then on into the antechamber and finally, into the burial chamber. There, it was placed into a second and third set of mummiform coffins waiting for it on a pair of stands. The lid of the first coffin was opened and mourners filed past, depositing wreaths of flowers and garlands of garlic (for protection) on top of the mummy. The Aten priests burned incense and chanted prayers for the well-being of the deceased in the Afterlife. Tutankhaten placed garlands of flowers over the mummy's neck and Ankhsenpaaten put a papyrus scroll with prayers from the Book of the Dead on her mother's chest.

When my turn came, at the end of a long line of more important mourners, I, too, placed a scroll in the coffin, near her face. But my scroll, after a few prayers for the dead, contained scenes of our time together, images clearly not intended for any other living eyes to see.

After this, the lid of the first coffin was sealed in place, then those of the second and third coffins. Finally, the trio of nested coffins was lifted by straps placed under it, running up over the upper framework of the shrine, and hoisted into the shrine and the waiting stone sarcophagus. Six men then lifted the lid of the sarcophagus into place. The priests sealed the sarcophagus lid, then the doors of the shrine were closed and sealed. Finally, after all the funeral gifts – beds, chairs, jewelry, clothes, statuary, containers of food, perfume, unguents, incense and rare oils – had all been deposited in the inner chambers, the great doors were pulled shut and sealed. Standing on either side in front of the doors were life-size guardian figures, each with a staff, finished in gold leaf and black bitumen.

After the last prayer had been chanted, the funeral party filed back over the makeshift bridge. Workmen then withdrew the boards from over the shaft and carried them out. The outer stone door to the tomb was levered into place and sealed by the priests, then a prearranged load of stones was released to cover it. Afterwards, the workmen would fill in the remainder of the entryway, disguising its very existence. There she would sleep, hopefully for eternity.

Thutmose had an uneasy feeling about it. Well-hidden though the tomb might be, too many people knew its location. In particular, its location was known to the priests. Even though it was the priests of

Aten who had presided over the ceremony, the priesthood of Amun had charge of the royal cemetery and were responsible for guarding the resting places of the Pharaohs of the Eighteenth Dynasty. And the priesthood of Amun had been involved in the assassination of Nefertiti. How could they be trusted not to defile her tomb, and even her mummy, to destroy her in the Afterlife just as they had in this one? That was the down side of the Egyptians' elaborate concept of the Afterlife: one was not safe from one's enemies, even after death.

Watching First Prophet seal the tomb, Thutmose vowed that he would set his own watch over her resting place, first while he lived, and then, through all eternity.

He returned to work at the palace long enough to see the new king, Tutankhaten, safely crowned, along with his young wife, Ankhsenpaaten. Although it grieved him, he oversaw the work of converting many of Akhenaten and Nefertiti's pieces of furniture, jewelry and wall decorations for the use of the new royal couple. Akhenaten's beautiful gilded and enameled throne was re-worked to show the young couple, instead of their parents, on front and back, while Tutankhaten's name replaced his father's in the cartouches on the side and legs, although Akhenaten's cartouches remained on the back of the throne, where no one would see them.

Thutmose was also glad to see that their grandfather, Aye, remained to serve them as Grand Vizier. He knew the old man would watch over them and provide them sound guidance.

He made a few pieces of statuary representing the young couple. Both had charming faces and strongly resembled each other, which was not surprising, given that they were half-siblings. Thutmose was particularly fond of Ankhsenpaaten. She had always been his favorite among Nefertiti's six girls, having been born in his house, almost on his very knees. She also seemed to him to be the brightest of the lot, with a stronger character than her sisters. He suspected that she would wind up largely ruling her young husband, who was a much less self-directed individual – and that that would be a good thing, since there were plenty of others at court who would be busy trying to manipulate him.

He stayed at court long enough to see the return of the foremost of these manipulators: General Horemheb. The general returned not long after the funeral of Nefertiti. Thutmose strongly suspected he had been notified of her death by the High Priest. He knew the general had not been notified by the Council, having been present at the meeting of the young king's advisors when they decided it was not necessary to recall the general at that time.

His suspicions were confirmed quite by accident one day when he came out of the Aten temple at Luxor after making an offering for

the souls of the late king and queen. As he came out of the front
entrance, he was almost mowed down by General Horemheb and three
of his aides, heading at full march down the processional way toward
the Temple of Amun. Curious, Thutmose followed them as far as the
forecourt, the furthest part of the temple open to the public. He
pretended to pray to the statue of Amun nearest the entry to the inner
court, watching Horemheb pass inside. The general was greeted by a
young priest who ushered him out of sight, while his men stood watch
at the doors.

Not wishing to arouse suspicion, Thutmose left the courtyard,
but took up his vigil behind a huge column near the entryway. From
there, after a time, he was able to see the general reappear, together with
the High Priest.

Back at the palace, he informed the Grand Vizier of what he
had seen.

"Watch out for him," he warned the Vizier. "I think he has
designs on the throne. I suspect he may have made some kind of deal
with the priesthood of Amun, that they would support him in a bid for
power if he agreed to restore their privileges."

"Yes, I already suspected as much, myself," Aye agreed. "He's
made it clear that he intends to stay here, not return to the field – and
he's got the backing of the army, so there's damn little I can do to force
him to do otherwise."

"Yes, I can see your predicament," Thutmose conceded. "If
he's got the priesthood, as well as the army, on his side, he's got you
and all the king's other advisors boxed in. The king himself is far too
young to put up any resistance – which may be just as well, for I
suspect he wouldn't live long if he did."

"Do you think Horemheb would go as far as assassination?"
Aye asked him.

"I don't know," said Thutmose, thoughtfully. "I think...he will
try to avoid it, if he can. He will try to get what he wants through less
extreme means. I believe he is an honorable man with Egypt's best
interests at heart – at least, what he believes are its best interests. But
they may not be what you believe are its best interests, or the king's.
And we have already seen that the priesthood will not hesitate to use
assassination to get what they want. Please, be careful, my Lord, and
keep a close watch on the young king."

"I agree with you, Thutmose, and I will do my best to protect
him."

"Watch your own back, too, my Lord. If anything should happen to this boy king, you would be all that stands between the general and the throne," Thutmose cautioned.

Aye looked taken aback at that. "I hadn't thought of it that way," he said.

"I would hate to see anything happen to you, my Lord. You and the young royals are all that remains of this Dynasty. And individual lives are so frighteningly fragile," Thutmose observed, shaking his head sadly.

"That is true," the old man agreed. "We must pray that my grandchildren will quickly produce an heir."

"That would help."

"And I hope that you will continue to support us, Thutmose," the old man said. "You have been a good and loyal friend, rendering service far beyond anything this family could have expected of you."

"I am sorry, my Lord, but I fear I must disappoint you. I have not the heart to remain here at court any longer. I have seen too much death. I don't think I can bear to watch what I feel is coming. It is my intention to go now and prepare my own tomb. I feel that I may need it ere long."

"Why, my son? Are you ill?" the Vizier asked.

"No, only sick at heart. I have no more tolerance for all the self-seeking, venial intrigues of court. I would prefer to return to a simpler, cleaner life, and to prepare myself for the Afterlife."

"I will be sorry to see you go," the old man said, "but I understand how you feel. There are many times I wish I could give it up, myself."

So Thutmose left the court, retiring to the village of the cemetery workers at Deir el-Medina. He was assured of earning a living, decorating the great tombs in the Valley of the Kings, including a new one recently begun for the boy king, Tutankhaten.

And unknown to anyone but Ipy, he spent many hours scouring the stony, arid peaks above the Valley, looking for a natural cave he could expand into a tomb of his own. It was necessary to stay far enough away from the Valley proper to avoid the guards maintained by the mortuary priesthood guarding the sacred burial place of Egypt's monarchs. To do what he was planning – create his own tomb above the Valley of the Kings – would be considered sacrilege of the highest order. If he was discovered, it would not only cost him his life, but his body would be destroyed, denying him any chance at an Afterlife.

Nevertheless, he secretly kept at it, and eventually found a suitable cave, high on the eastern slope of the pyramid-shaped mountain above the Valley. He preferred to think of himself not as an interloper, a violator of the Valley's sanctity, but rather, a guardian, watching over their safety through eternity. Of course, he was really only concerned with the safety of one dead Pharaoh.

To that end, he labored many long years by himself, whenever he had time, chiseling out a tunnel, then a fair-sized room behind the cave. He had to take care to scatter the tailings about the countryside so that their tell-tale presence should not reveal fresh digging and thus, the presence of his tomb behind the cave.

When he finished carving out the rock, he hauled many loads of lime powder from the village to make plaster, and many bladders filled with water to mix with it. It was very laborious, slow going, but eventually, he finished plastering the walls.

Then began the real work of love: painting scenes on the walls of the tomb. As in Nefertiti's tomb, he painted scenes from both of their lives, including especially their brief time together before her death. But he went far beyond this, painting scenes that had never happened in this life, scenes he longed for in the next. He showed them both together in a simple, peaceful domestic existence, with their wished-for children around them, and their arms about each other. And here he re-created the magnificent bust he had left behind at Akhetaten, but now on a complete body, its arms wide open to welcome him. Instead of an ineffable sadness behind her regal hauteur, this image of the queen was radiant with joy, as he had so briefly and privately seen her in the months before her death. Remarkably, the flickering lamplight in the tomb revealed eyes (both lenses completed) that sparkled with happiness. This was how he wanted to remember her.

For the first time, too, Thutmose created a life-size statue of himself to be her eternal companion. He had patiently acquired a substantial hoard of silver – a metal harder to obtain than gold in the Two Lands – which he sand-cast into a rectangular sheet. Mounted in a frame of Lebanese cedar, it made a mirror fit for a queen – or for a sculptor unused to seeing his own image.

Only Ipy grew suspicious of his mentor's nocturnal perambulations. While he continued to work at the palace, now as one of the most senior artists, Ipy often visited Thutmose at his house at the edge of the workmen's village. Several times, he had arrived to find the older man absent. A few of these times, he had spent the night at Thutmose's house and had observed his mentor's return before dawn.

Finally, one of these times, Ipy confronted him and learned he had been working on a secret tomb. At first, Thutmose was unwilling to let the younger man in on the location of the tomb, which would make him an accomplice in the eyes of the mortuary priests, if they ever learned of it. But when Ipy raised the argument that *somebody* was going to have to bury Thutmose in his tomb, and that he, himself, was the most likely candidate for the job, Thutmose conceded that he was right.

Nevertheless, when he finally saw the tomb, Ipy was stunned by both its contents and the risks his old friend was taking. While even he was a bit scandalized by the relationship depicted on the walls, as an artist, he had to admire what were clearly a collection of masterpieces on the walls of this tomb. As both an artist and a devoted friend, he prayed that the priests never discover this tomb and destroy it and its creator. And he had to admire the two greatest masterworks of all, the pair of statues of Nefertiti and Thutmose.

"Extraordinary!" he exclaimed, walking around the two statues. "What a gift the Aten has given you! I think I'm doing all right, with my little decorative paintings – and then I look at this work of yours and I realize I'm deluding myself. My work is just pretty pictures – your work is *alive*. My ears keep straining to hear them speak. What a pity the world can never be allowed to see this! The world will never know what it has missed."

"I devoutly hope so!" Thutmose commented, with a certain sense of alarm at the mere thought.

"Do you think, old friend," Ipy asked, "that the world will ever come to appreciate art for art's sake? That people will ever learn to value what the artist sees, and what he shows them through his art, and not restrict what he can portray or make it meet other, artificial requirements?"

"I don't know, my boy, I don't know. Akhenaten started down that path. He got us partway there – but nobody understood it, but just us few."

"But even he dictated what we could portray: his family, his God," Ipy pointed out.

"Well, even aside from who's got the political power," Thutmose observed, "the buyer still has the economic power to dictate the content of art. As the saying goes, 'he who pays the harpist calls the song'."

"I suppose that will always be the case," Ipy sighed. "I suppose artistic freedom is as much a dream as the happy domesticity you've painted on these walls, shared with a woman from a different world, a life that will certainly never exist in this world."

"Now you see why I have labored here so long," Thutmose said. "I have created a different world here. Now you see why I am so anxious to embrace it."

Ipy did understand, but felt a pang of premonitory grief at the thought of losing his friend and mentor, who had been the only father he had ever known. He sensed that, now that the tomb was finished, it would not have long to wait for its occupant. Thutmose's heart had already gone on to another world. Ipy knew his master's body would not linger long behind it.

Chapter 46: Resurrection of the Old Order

Thutmose still visited Thebes from time to time, whenever he needed supplies not available in the workmen's village or when he got word that his children were in town. Sometimes he made the hike down the hill and across the river to visit Ipy, or Bek, when he was in town. For the most part, though, he avoided the capital city: seeing Akhenaten's work – *his* work – undone, altered or destroyed was too depressing.

Once General Horemheb returned, the Amun priests had a powerful ally in the palace, and they made full use of him to reassert their influence. Since the general arrived with a thousand troops and had the full backing of the rest of the army, Aye and the young king had little choice but to accept him as one of the king's closest advisors.

It soon became clear that accepting Horemheb also meant accepting Amun. The priests, usually in the person of First Prophet Merenptah, became frequent visitors to the palace once again. He nagged the young king relentlessly to begin participating in the worship of Amun. Tutankhaten was very reluctant to do this, partly because he still adhered to the Aten religion he had been raised in, but even more, because he was terrified to enter the Temple of Amun after what had happened to his stepmother there. Aye was well aware of the source of the boy's horror of the temple, although the High Priest apparently remained completely oblivious to the youngster's phobia. Finally, Aye drew him aside one day and explained it to him.

"Can't you see?" he said. "The king is terrified of entering the temple, since his predecessor was killed there. He lives in fear of the same thing happening to him. He tries hard to be brave and act the king, but he's just a child, with a child's fears. And in this case, he has good reason to be afraid. There are, thankfully, damn few children who have seen their mother or stepmother murdered right in front of them. And he knows the assassins were former priests of Amun – no, don't bother to deny it. We've got all the evidence we need on that score! So, you see, his fear of the Temple of Amun is not at all irrational. If you want him there, you're going to have to find some way to deal with that."

Merenptah longed to be able to deny the accusation, but knew that he couldn't. He could honestly say that he, himself, had had nothing to do with the assassination of Nefertiti; but the evidence tying the assassins to the priesthood and the former First Prophet was incontrovertible. Merenptah knew that he and all his fellow priests were guilty by association, if nothing more. A way of atonement was needed. He thought silently about it.

"Perhaps we could have a ceremony and sacrifice to honor Pharaoh Smenkare and to atone for the spilling of her sacred royal blood," he suggested. "It would require the young Pharaoh's participation. We could sacrifice a sacred white bullock, and we could honor the late Pharaoh's death as a sacrifice for the good of the nation, for the restoration of *ma'at* – which, in many ways, it was."

"That's cutting it a bit close," commented Aye, his jaw clenched in anger at the thought of his daughter's death. "The Two Lands gave up human sacrifice over a thousand years ago – and even then, it was only meaningful if the victim gave up his, or her, life voluntarily. My daughter certainly did not volunteer to give up her life for Amun!"

Merenptah remembered belatedly that the man he was addressing was the father of the late Pharaoh.

"All the more reason we should both honor and mourn her," he said hastily, "and cleanse the temple of this sacrilege against the person of a divine Pharaoh."

Aye regarded him distrustfully from under lowered brows.

"All right," he said at last. "I'll talk to His Majesty and see if I can persuade him to participate in such a ceremony."

Horemheb, of course, was in full support of the ceremony and urged the king to agree.

So it was that the boy king was persuaded to enter the temple to honor and help atone for the death of his step-mother and co-ruler, Pharaoh Ankhkheperure-Merwaenre. And once this was done, it was easy to conquer the remainder of his phobia of the Temple of Amun. From there, it became increasingly easy, over time, to persuade the boy to participate in the worship of Amun, eventually assuming all the traditional pharaonic religious responsibilities.

This helped greatly in the priesthood's efforts to restore the old religion and to regain all their rights, privileges and temple tribute. Eventually, they were able, with Horemheb's help, to prevail on the boy to change his name and his wife's, replacing the *Aten* element with *Amun*. Tutankhaten now became Tutankhamun, and Ankhsenpa'aten became Ankhsenamun.

Once that change was made, it was clear to the entire land that Amun was back in favor and that the Aten religion, never very popular, was clearly on its way out. Under the combined pressure of Horemheb and the priesthood, most of the temple tribute was restored, as were most of the lands that had been confiscated by Akhenaten.

After that, the priests began agitating for the Aten religion to be officially suppressed, but Tutankhamun showed surprisingly firm resistance to this demand. Unlike the populace at large, he and Ankhsen had been raised in the Aten religion and their faith went deeper than anyone else realized. Sometimes they felt that they were the only two people left who truly believed in the One God. They knew that they were hopelessly outnumbered and weak, being still only children, even though they were king and queen. In private, they both expressed the hope that they would grow strong enough to be able to resist any further erosion of the faith of their father.

They both knew that one of the best ways to strengthen their position would be to secure the succession by having an heir. They were too young to be able to do this right away, although Ankhsen had begun her courses shortly before her mother's death. They both anxiously awaited the coming of Tutankhamun's manhood. Ankhsen searched his chin daily for the sprouting of hairs. When at last a few straggly beard hairs arrived, along with underarm hair and the stirring of new feelings, they were both exhilarated at these signs of physical maturity.

Others around them also duly noted the signs. The young Pharaoh was initiated into the mysteries of sex by an appropriately trained young courtesan and promptly passed along this newfound knowledge to his young bride. Everyone in the palace was delighted when the young queen announced that she was pregnant – everyone, that is, except Horemheb, who saw his chances of obtaining the throne slipping away.

But, alas, before her time was due, the young queen miscarried. The stillborn child was seen to have a severe defect of the spine, the base of the spinal column being open, with tissue protruding from it. It was clear that, if the child had survived, it would have been severely disabled. This was a very bad omen and was, of course, concealed from the public.

The doctors suggested that the queen might still be a bit young for childbearing, and expressed the opinion that things might go better when she was a little bit older.

Princess Sitamun, who, with the restoration of the old religion, had been able to resume her role as Chief Godswife of Amun, was reminded of her long-ago conversations with the old doctor and the horse-breeder, suggesting that pharaonic marriages between half or full siblings tended to produce a high incidence of birth defects. She didn't share this information with the young couple, since they were already married to the only available, appropriate partners, and there was nothing they could do about their consanguinity. There was no point in making them feel worse than they already did.

This was the state of affairs the last time Thutmose came to court. He had promised the dying Nefertiti that he would do what little he could to help her daughter and stepson, so he made a visit to the palace to pay his respects and see how they were doing.

He found the palace in mourning over the death of the baby, and was grieved to hear of it. As an old family friend and former royal advisor, he was admitted to see the young king and queen in the family's private quarters, where the queen was still recuperating.

Thutmose dropped to one knee and made a deep obeisance. "Your Majesties! I am so glad to see you – but I offer my deepest sympathies for your loss, which is all Egypt's loss."

"Thutmose! Old friend!" cried the young king, standing to welcome him. "We are so happy to see you! Please, stand up!"

Thutmose stood, somewhat stiffly. "My knees are not what they used to be, I'm afraid," he commented wryly.

Tutankhamun embraced him warmly. "You needn't kneel when we're in private," he said. "Come, sit. You're a part of our family – and Aten knows, there's little enough of it left!"

Embracing him back, Thutmose felt that the young man was almost another adoptive son, like Ipy or Mariamne's boy, Shemu-el.

"You've grown so since I last saw you!" he said, stepping back. "A couple more years of this, and you may outgrow me!"

Thutmose was unusually tall for an Egyptian, just topping four cubits[14], while the young king was barely average height for young men of his generation[15]. Even though he probably had several years of growth left, he was unlikely ever to reach Thutmose's height, but the thought was flattering. The young man expanded his chest proudly, drawing himself to his full height. Thutmose, without appearing to do so, let himself sag just a bit, to make their heights more nearly equal.

"I wish I could take after my ancestor Amenhotep II," the king said, wistfully.

His great-great-grandfather, Amenhotep II, had been a huge man, well over four cubits tall, renowned as a mighty hunter and notable warrior king.

"I've been training in all the arts of war," he continued. "I'm an excellent shot with a bow, and very good with the spear and sword. And I'm a crack charioteer. You should come and watch!"

Thutmose happened to look over at the queen as the king said this. He saw a look of concern cross her face. "Ah," he thought, "she worries about him. I wonder if he pushes himself too far, in his efforts to be grown up and a warrior on a par with his ancestors."

---

[14] Six feet.
[15] About 5'4".

"That's wonderful, my king," Thutmose said. "I'll try to get out to the parade ground while I'm in town. But remember, you've got lots of time to perfect your skills. You don't have to do it all right now. Remember what happened to your uncle Thutmosis."

Crown Prince Thutmosis, Akhenaten's elder brother, had died as a result of a chariot accident when he was about twelve years old. Just riding in a chariot was a hazardous activity, even with a professional driver handling the horses. While the parade ground was reasonably smooth and even, there were no paved roads, and the countryside where chariots were driven on campaign and on hunting trips was liable to be extremely bumpy and uneven. A chariot's occupants rode standing up, in a very lightweight conveyance with hard wooden wheels, no springs and a woven wicker floor. Simply maintaining one's balance without being bounced out was a challenge, let alone shooting arrows in rapid succession while jolting over uneven ground at full gallop. To make things worse, Pharaohs were expected to be more heroic than the average soldier. The great warrior-kings of this dynasty had established their heroic image by acting as their own charioteers, with the reigns tied around their hips, while galloping full-tilt at the enemy, shooting arrows rapid-fire as they went. Young Thutmosis had been a very competent charioteer, but while trying to master this difficult technique, he had been thrown out of the chariot and killed. Thutmose suspected that this was what the young Queen feared, and with good reason.

"Remember, Your Majesty," Thutmose added, "you're the last of your line. You must safeguard yourself, at least until you have an heir – and preferably, long after that!"

"Yes, yes," Tutankhamun replied, "I know all that. But I also know that all my advisors regard me as just a boy yet, especially Horemheb and First Prophetic Merenptah. I must prove that I am strong enough to wield the scepter on my own."

Thutmose felt a deep sense of foreboding about this. He turned to pay his respects to the queen. He started to drop to one knee, then remembered what the king had said, and settled for kissing the hand she extended to him.

"Your Majesty is well, I trust?" he asked.

"Uncle Thutmose, it's so nice to see you here again!" she said, beaming at him. To his surprise, she jumped up and threw her arms around him and kissed his cheek. "I've missed you!" she said. "*We've* missed you!"

Ever since she had been born in his house, almost on his knees, he had had a special fondness for this daughter of Nefertiti. He had played with her when she was little and made toys for her, even a doll akin to the one he had made so long ago for her mother. She had returned his affection and regarded him as a member of the family, calling him "Uncle Thutmose" whenever they were not in formal company. It warmed his heart to be called that now.

"Come, sit with us," she said, signaling to a servant to bring them refreshments.

The three of them sat and talked for hours. Thutmose knew, as they did not, that he would never see them again. He knew that this was goodbye.

Now that his tomb was complete, the time had come for him to say goodbye to those he loved. He had sent word to Mariamne, asking her to send the children to see him. He didn't tell her that it was so he could say goodbye, but it seemed that somehow she sensed it. She longed to go herself, to see him one last time. She still loved him, and she knew she always would. But she also knew that his heart would always belong to someone else, through all eternity. She had said her goodbyes to him years ago, and despite Nefertiti's death, nothing had really changed. So she resolutely resisted the urge and sent her children to Thebes without her.

What Thutmose didn't know was that Ipy had been keeping her apprised of her estranged husband's situation for years. The younger man had always hoped his former master would reconcile with his wife and regain his will to live. But nothing could make up for the loss of Nefertiti. With her death, some vital spirit had gone out of Thutmose. Ipy suspected that the only thing that had kept him alive this many years was his drive to complete his tomb, his need to safeguard Nefertiti's tomb, and the promise he had made to look after her children. Now, those children were almost grown up, well established in their reign and hopefully on the way to producing an heir. He felt he could safely relinquish that responsibility.

So he visited with his children, who were almost grown up now, themselves. His son was now sixteen, a big, strapping lad like his father, and his daughter was thirteen, an age by which many girls married and some even began childbearing. His son, Senmut, had a modest artistic talent, but nothing like the extraordinary ability of his father. He had been training with Thutmose's father, Ahmose, to be a potter. The old man was still vigorous and active, still turning out a multitude of pots, which were still in demand, but his eyesight was growing dim, so he relied on the boy to paint his wares. They made a good pair, and Thutmose was happy that the two had formed a close bond. It was good for both of them and assured that the boy would carry on the family trade, which Thutmose had long ago outgrown. It was good that his son was back in the family fold.

Mariamne had informed him some months earlier that the son of a neighbor, a prosperous Habiru farmer, was greatly taken with young Meryre and had made an offer for her hand. Mariamne had written, asking for his approval of the match. He had written back, saying that he trusted her judgment in this matter, and that any young man who met with her approval had his, also. He had, however, suggested that they wait a year or two longer before establishing their own house, to let both of the youngsters mature a bit. Mariamne agreed, despite her daughter's complaints that her parents were unreasonably holding her back, that she was all grown up. Knowing that the restriction had originated with her father, she was at first angry and resentful towards him – but having always been "daddy's little girl", she couldn't stay mad at him, and soon relented.

So the three of them had a very nice visit, went sight-seeing and fowling together, stuffed themselves on exotic foods and talked long hours into the night. Meryre went happily to bed, having obtained her father's agreement that she was old enough to marry her young suitor on her return home. Senmut, however, was old enough and shrewd enough to have guessed at something of his father's intentions. He lingered behind after his sister stumbled sleepily off to bed. He looked keenly at his father.

"You're planning on killing yourself, aren't you?" he asked point-blank. "All of this...*friendliness*... You've been saying goodbye, haven't you?"

Surprised, Thutmose didn't answer immediately, looking intently into the bottom of his wine cup. Finally, he answered softly.

"Yes."

"Why? It's because of *her*, isn't it? Nefertiti?" the boy asked resentfully.

"Yes," Thutmose whispered.

"And what about us, Mery and me, your children? You're just leaving us? But then, that's what you've always done, is turn your back on your family! You left your parents for the fame and glory of a life at court. You left our mother, your wife, for love of a queen you couldn't have, and your own children for a life on the fringes of the royal family!" Senmut hissed at him, fighting back tears.

"I know I have, my son," Thutmose agreed, allowing his own tears to flow freely. "And for that, I can only ask you to forgive me. It seems to me that I have been driven all my life by forces beyond my control, first by talent and then by love. I didn't choose either – they chose me."

"Excuses, excuses!" shouted Senmut. "You didn't have to spend all your time on the royal family, instead of your own – you *chose* to do that! You didn't have to lust after the king's wife and neglect your own! You didn't have to choose to leave your faithful, loving wife to chase after some cold, distant, arrogant royal – "

"Actually, I didn't," interjected Thutmose. "Mariamne left me."

"You drove her to it!" Senmut countered.

"Undoubtedly true," agreed Thutmose, sadly.

"You don't care about any of us!" Senmut cried. "You don't care about your own family! And now you're planning to go away again and leave us forever! It's totally selfish of you. Well, I don't care. I hate you! Go ahead and die!"

And with that, he ran out of the room. Thutmose tried to decide what to do, whether he should run after his son, or not.

Just then, Ipy spoke from the doorway.

"Let me talk to him," he said. "He won't listen to you right now. He's hurting too much."

"All right," Thutmose conceded. He slumped back into a chair and poured himself some more wine.

Ipy found Senmut on the roof, staring out at the city over the parapet.

"He really does love you, you know," he said to the boy. "It's just hard for him to tell you. He had to hide his feelings for so many years, he doesn't know how to show them."

"If he hadn't been in love with the wrong woman, he wouldn't have had to hide his feelings," snapped Senmut.

"You think he *wanted* that?" Ipy asked. "It made his life hell! As much as your mother's love for him made her life hell! Do you think we choose who we fall in love with? He prayed to Aten for years to take this painful love away from him – I heard him. But the god did not see fit to remove that curse from him. He suffered terribly for it. He's suffering still."

"Well, he deserves to suffer, for what he's done to my mother," Senmut said.

"But don't you see," said Ipy, "she's suffered from the same disease, loving someone she can't have. I think, because of that, she understands what he's going through, even though it hurts her terribly. But she couldn't stop loving him, any more than he could stop loving the queen. That's why she left: she couldn't bear being so close to him, yet unable to reach him."

"No, I have to agree with him," Ipy continued. "We don't choose who we love – love chooses us. We can't control what we feel, only what we choose to do about it. And your father chose to behave as honorably as he possibly could. He never betrayed his king or acted on his feelings for Nefertiti until after the king was dead. He did not lie to your mother about his feelings, but he always acted discreetly and treated her with the greatest of respect and consideration."

The young man thought about this in silence for a while, then he said grudgingly, "I suppose that's true. She's never said a harsh word about him. That always puzzled me, since it seemed she had good reason to hate him."

"No, your mother, bless her *ka*, was always a bigger person than that. She knows that carrying around hate only burdens the person carrying it," Ipy observed, then added, "As you may have guessed, I've always been a great admirer of your mother. She's one of the best people I know."

Senmut smiled wryly at this. "Yes, she is. I guess she's a bigger person than I am. I have more trouble forgiving him."

Ipy put an arm around the younger man's shoulders.

"I know he hasn't been a very attentive father to you and your sister," he said, "and I can understand that you're angry at him about that. But he didn't have a whole lot of choice about that, either. He was a trusted advisor to the king, from the time they were both very young – younger than you are now. The king had him doing everything, especially after he became Chief of Works. Your father was always a perfectionist: whatever was assigned to him, he wanted to do it perfectly. He worked insane hours. I know, because I worked a lot of them with him. That's why he didn't have a lot of time for you. His king, and therefore, his country, required it. What would you have had him do? Say no to the king?"

"No, I suppose he couldn't do that," muttered Senmut.

"And as to his talent – you sneer at that and act as though he somehow chose it, but I have been trying for years to choose a talent even half so great, and let me tell you, it cannot be done! A talent like your father's comes along very rarely. Once in a hundred years? No, more likely, once in a thousand years, maybe more! But talent, especially great talent, is a demanding mistress. It is a gift of the gods, and mere mortals neglect it at their peril. Great gifts, unused, don't just slink quietly away into the night. Oh, no, unused talents fester and rot and drive the bearer mad. And I have never known anyone with a talent even remotely close to your father's. He had to express it, or die. And now, with the return of the old religion and all its rigid strictures, he soon will not be allowed to create his art his own way, and that would be a terrible torment for him, a death of the spirit. So, in many ways, maybe he's right. Maybe it's better for him to die now, a free man and great artist, rather than let the old order slowly strangle him."

"But he's leaving us again!" cried the boy. "Why doesn't he love us enough to just stay with us? Why? Why aren't we enough for him?"

"I'm sorry, my boy," said Ipy, putting his arms around the boy, who sobbed uncontrollably on his shoulder. Once the sobs subsided a bit, Ipy stepped back, gripping the boy by both shoulders. "You must be brave now. Your father loves you very much, but he has carried his burdens a long time now, and you must allow him to put them down. There is no longer a place for him in this world, and he knows it. It is time for him to go. You are a man now. It is time for you to let him go and take your place as head of the family. See to it that your mother and sister are taken care of, and start a family of your own. Be thankful that you have a family and a place to go to. Your father gave me the only family I have ever had, and I shall miss him more than you'll ever know. Let us help him now and grieve him together when he's gone."

Tearfully, the young man agreed. Together, they returned downstairs, where Thutmose and his son were reconciled while he yet lived.

They all agreed that Meryre should not be subjected to her father's death, but sent back downriver to her mother and waiting fiancé. As it happened, Princess Sitamun was about to pay a visit to her estates in the Delta and invited the girl to accompany her. Thutmose was glad to entrust her to the princess's motherly care.

Thutmose had originally planned to enclose himself in his waiting tomb and trust the preservation of his body to the desiccating desert heat, trusting that his spirit could take refuge in the statues of himself prepared for it, should his body not fare well in the rock-cut tomb. But Ipy had convinced him to carry out the fatal act in his home, trusting the younger man to have his body properly mummified and interred in the tomb.

For this purpose, Ipy had procured an asp in a basket from a dealer in one of the less savory parts of town, a man who dealt in poisons and serpents and other nefarious means of disposing of unwanted rivals and supernumerary family members. After some discussion with this merchant of death, Ipy had determined that the bite of the asp was both quick and fairly painless, far less painful than any poison that could be drunk or eaten, and the snake would be less dangerous to dispose of than a cobra once its work was done.

So Thutmose bade farewell to his friends and family, and lying down in his bed, clasped the snake to his neck, where its bite would be most quickly fatal.

Ipy and Senmut saw to it that the body was delivered quickly to the mortuary priests, who began the elaborate process of preparing, drying and embalming it. Thutmose had left a stack of gold rings, plaques and the Gold of Honor *shebu* collars he had received over his many years of service to the Crown. There was more than enough to pay for the best possible level of embalming, almost as good as a king's.

When the seventy days were over, Ipy and Senmut, accompanied by Bek and his eldest son, carried Thutmose's mummy up the long, arduous trail to his secret tomb high above the Valley of the Kings. Given the nature and location of the tomb, they decided to forego having a priest accompany them. The four of them took turns reading the ritual for the dead and Senmut performed the Opening of the Mouth ceremony before they carried his father's body into the tomb. There, it was interred in a single mummiform coffin. At its feet was the life-size statue of Nefertiti, arms outstretched, where he might gaze at her for eternity; and at the coffin's head was a life-size statue of Thutmose himself, an alternate resting place for his *ka* should his body decay.

The small funeral party filed out and the four men heaved the blocking stone in place. Then Ipy pulled a cord that released a pile of rocks and debris that thundered down into the entryway, hiding it and disguising its presence. Now Thutmose could safely watch over his beloved queen's resting place throughout eternity. The four men turned and trudged back down the mountain.

A few days later, Ipy accompanied Senmut back down the river to his mother's house. They carried with them the gold left over after paying for the embalming of Thutmose, including most of the Gold of Honor. They told her they had buried his body in a secret tomb he had prepared, but told her nothing of its location or decoration. She could guess, however.

Ipy stayed several weeks as an honored guest and a restored member of their extended family. Frankly, he was reluctant to tear himself away from the bosom of the only family he had ever really been a part of – and they were equally reluctant to let him leave.

He stayed to celebrate the marriage of young Meryre to her prosperous neighbor. While the Egyptians didn't really have a marriage ceremony, as such, this wedding was formalized in the Habiru tradition. And of course, it was celebrated with a joyous feast, with plenty of food, wine, music and dancing. By the end of the evening, amorous couples were entwined in dark corners of the house and vineyard, and the celebrating went on late into the night. Somehow, Ipy found himself in one of those corners with Mariamne. One thing led to another, and they soon retired to her bedroom. The aid of honeyed wine released all her tangled, pent-up emotions, and she spent the night alternately soaring and sobbing in his arms. They finally fell into a deep and satisfied slumber a couple of hours before dawn.

As the rising sun reached probing fingers through the shuttered window, Mariamne awoke, aware of the warm, strong masculine body next to hers. She lay there for a few minutes, exploring her unaccustomed feelings, unsure what to make of the situation. Finally, she started to slip quietly out of bed, not wanting to disturb her unexpected sleeping partner. Just as she started to slide out from under the coverlet, a strong hand gripped her arm.

"Don't go," Ipy said. "Stay here with me."

"There's such a mess to clean up," she said, not looking at him. Her cheeks felt very hot.

"You have plenty of servants to do that," he said. "But there is something I need to ask you."

"What is that?" she asked.

"Will you marry me?" he asked.

At this, she turned, startled, and looked at him.

"Are you serious?" she asked, searching his face.

"Very serious," he said. "I've admired you and been fond of you for years, but I realized last night that it was more than that. This feels very right to me, and I don't ever want it to end. So, please, be my wife. I know I'm no Thutmose, but I will give you the love he wasn't able to."

"I hardly know what to say. This is so unexpected. And I'm older than you, nearly past my childbearing years. I don't know whether I could still give you any children."

"That doesn't matter," he said. "If we have children, that would be wonderful. But if we don't, well, I'll just enjoy the three you already have."

"But I'll grow old before you," she protested. "Look, there's already gray in my hair and lines on my face."

"That doesn't matter, either. In my line of work, I've seen the greatest young beauties in the land, and they were either petty, domineering and demanding, or cold and remote. I'd much rather have a real living, breathing, thinking, feeling woman, someone who knows life and love, who can be a true companion and partner, not some self-absorbed, empty-headed, cold-hearted young beauty. Besides, there's only a difference of five or six years between us. Thutmose was barely twenty when he rescued me from the streets, and you were even younger. Please say you'll be my wife!"

Her eyes overflowing with tears of joy, Mariamne said, "I would be thrilled and honored to be your wife, Ipy."

With that, he pulled her into his arms and kissed her long and passionately.

So Mariamne found the love she had always longed for and Ipy found the family he had never had.

Epilogue: The Immortal Queen
Berlin, Egyptian Museum, 2007

The museum guide led her flock of American and Japanese tourists into yet another room filled with mummies, statuary and glass cases full of strange, ancient objects.

"...And so the brilliant Eighteenth Dynasty drew to a violent and inglorious close," the guide concluded.

"So, when do we get to see the famous bust?" asked one of the older Americans.

"Coming up next," said the guide, leading the way into another room.

There, in the center, stood a glass case housing the world-famous bust of the Great Royal Wife, Neferneferuaten Nefertiti. The tourists gathered round, awestruck at her lifelike beauty, complete except for the strangely absent lens of her left eye.

"She was found in the ruins of the workshop of the sculptor Thutmose at a place now called Amarna, in December of 1912. The bust was found underneath a pile of plaster casts of body parts, which apparently were considered part of the trash, too insignificant for even the Amun priests to bother destroying. Somehow, the German archaeologist, Ludwig Borchardt, managed to get the Director of Antiquities to allow him to take the bust as part of the excavator's portion of the dig's findings for the season. Once the Egyptians became aware of it, in the 1930s, they demanded it back. But by then, it had become Adolph Hitler's favorite work of art, and he refused to part with it. The Egyptians have continued to demand it back ever since, but have so far been unsuccessful. It remains the Crown Jewel of our collection," the guide finished proudly.

The group continued to mill around the bust, mostly in silence, admiring it from all sides.

"Ironic, isn't it," said the boyfriend of an American girl, "that this statue only survived because it was buried under trash?"

"But don't you see," said the girl, "the real reason _she_ survived was because an amazingly gifted artist preserved her image. It was his devotion, and his talent, that saved her. Thanks to him, her face is known to millions – she's become immortal."

CPSIA information can be obtained
at www.ICGtesting.com
Printed in the USA
LVHW022351030121
675628LV00014B/965